Murder Most Deserving

Lacetown Murder Mysteries, Volume 2

Deanna Wadsworth and Hank Edwards

Published by Edwards ~ Wadsworth, 2022.

MURDER MOST DESERVING

First edition. June 13, 2022.

Copyright © 2022 Deanna Wadsworth and Hank Edwards.

ISBN: 979-8201672157

Written by Deanna Wadsworth and Hank Edwards.

To our husbands,

who overheard all our conversations about sex and murder, and they
didn't worry... too much.

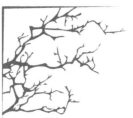

CHAPTER ONE

"I know this is the worst thing in the entire world for us, but I love the burgers here." Jazz Dilworth opened the diner door and waved for his boyfriend, Michael Fleishman, to enter Gruff's Grub ahead of him.

"I'm just glad you called." Michael gifted him with that shy smile Jazz had grown to adore. "I usually don't get to see you on Thursdays."

"Lucky for me I had a no-show." Being one of Lacetown's most popular hairstylists, Jazz was slammed on Thursday nights at Misty's Makeover Palace.

"Indeed."

When his elderly client Ruth Blankenship didn't show up for her perm appointment, the salon receptionist, Lisa Ann, had called her. Poor Ruth had been so frazzled, Jazz wondered if dementia was setting in. So with a big gap in his schedule, he'd texted Michael about grabbing a quick bite before he went back to work.

Adjusting his glasses, Michael looked around the diner's dim interior. "The smell alone could coat your arteries," he said, but with a smile that let Jazz know he was kidding.

Well, kidding with a side of serious. Gruff's Grub gave new meaning to greasy spoon. Tucked away down a short side street off Coastline Road, it wasn't one of the more popular restaurants in Lacetown, Michigan.

"I know, I know, but I don't eat here that often," Jazz said, studying his boyfriend's face and enjoying the way Michael's warm brown eyes took in the details of the room from behind tortoise-shell glasses, his straight dark hair combed perfectly in place. "You've really never eaten here?"

Michael shook his head. "Don't think I've ever really heard of this place."

"And you've lived here all your life." Jazz smirked. "I've been introducing you to all the hot spots in Lacetown. First Heavy Petting Point and now Gruff's." The mere mention of the scenic overlook and somewhat secret

1

make-out point known by locals as HPP conjured images of Jazz riding Michael hard and fast in the front seat of his car.

We need to take another drive out there soon....

"HPP and Gruff's are the hot spots?" Michael said with a serious expression. "I suppose my funeral home is considered a cold spot?"

Jazz laughed and had to resist leaning in to kiss Michael. "There's that dry sense of humor I adore. You'll like this place, trust me. The food is far from healthy and so good. And besides, Gruff is a sweet old bear."

As if on cue, a tall, wide man with a long beard bumped open the swinging kitchen doors. He wore a white apron and carried two plates of food. His eyes narrowed in what looked to be perpetual annoyance, but when he caught sight of Jazz, he flashed a big bright smile and gave a shout of happiness that startled the customers sitting closest to him.

"Jazz Dilworth, as I live and breathe!" Gruff's voice rumbled like an earthquake. "It's been weeks since you darkened my door."

"Oh, Gruff, you old sweet-talker," Jazz said. "Got an open table for us before the health department shuts you down?"

Gruff gave a hearty laugh and waved toward a booth by the windows. "Take a seat over there. I'll be over in a minute."

Grabbing Michael's hand, Jazz led him on a winding path through the tables scattered about the long narrow space and past a middle-aged couple who looked sad. A young, rather androgynous person with a stern expression, short dark hair slicked back like a 1950s greaser, and fingers clutching a thick hamburger, sat with them. At the next table gathered what Jazz *assumed* was a family of four—or maybe some kind of freaky cult members, because they were all dressed in matching homespun cotton outfits. The father of the matching misfits stared hard at Jazz and Michael's clasped hands, and Jazz managed to repress a shudder. The young man chewed his thumbnail, looking lost in his own world, and the two women wore identical bland brown dresses that didn't complement their mousy hair.

Jazz indicated the women with his eyes after they slid into the booth. When Michael checked them out, Jazz whispered, "Sister wives?"

Casually glancing back, Michael whispered with amusement, "Nothing would surprise me. With the Acoustic Music Festival in town, I'm sure there's a banjo or two involved."

Before Jazz could make a *Deliverance* joke, Gruff lumbered up to their booth and set menus and table settings before them. "Hey there, Dilworth."

"Since when do they let you out of the kitchen?" Jazz teased. "Where's Hattie tonight?"

"Off visiting our sister in Wisconsin." Gruff shook his head. "Never work with your sibling, trust me on this. You know how long since I've been to Wisconsin?"

"Five years?" Jazz asked in a flat tone of voice. He'd heard this complaint before.

"Five years," Gruff said as if Jazz hadn't spoken. "Guess the cook doesn't get to take days off." He gave Michael a once-over. "You're new, but you look familiar."

"Oh. Well, yes, I'm new *here*, but I do live in town. I'm Michael Fleishman."

"The mortician?"

Jazz watched over the top of his menu as Michael's blush spread bewitchingly across his cheeks. *So freaking cute.* Jazz had to admit, he really was a lucky man. Even if his past romantic experiences made it seem otherwise.

"Yes. I own Fleishman's Funeral Home. That's me."

"You're the county coroner too, right?"

The blush deepened, and Jazz almost couldn't stand the level of adorable coming off Michael in waves.

"That is also correct. You seem to know a lot about me, but I don't even know your name."

Gruff frowned at Jazz before speaking to Michael. "I'm Gruff."

"That's your given name?"

"That's the name I'm givin' you, so yeah, it's my given name." Gruff turned to Jazz. "The usual?"

"Yeah."

"How about you, County Coroner? Don't tell me you're gonna order a salad like those vegan-folk-singer types over there."

Jazz looked where Gruff indicated. It was the table of three, with the miserable-looking couple and the *Happy Days* throwback. The couple appeared thin and sallow as they picked at their garden salads. Despite the summer heat, the woman shivered like she was cold. Naturally one would be miserable and cold surviving off twigs and berries in a burger joint.

"Are they performers at the festival?" Jazz whispered.

Gruff bent down and motioned them closer. Jazz and Michael leaned over the table, and then Gruff said in what was more or less a normal tone of voice for most people but passed as a whisper from him, "Yeah. Bit of tree-hugging, antifracking folk singers have been coming in since yesterday, asking why I don't offer quinoa and if everything I make is gluten-free."

Jazz did an elaborate eye roll for Gruff's benefit. "The nerve of some people."

"Right?" Gruff straightened up and jerked a thumb toward the table of four who were all dressed alike. "And don't even get me started on the von Trapp wannabes over there."

Michael's face was so red Jazz worried he might burst into flames. He took pity on him and spoke up. "Hey, Gruff? Michael will have the same as me."

Gruff looked between them with a critical eye. "Burger medium with a basket of fries and a Coke?"

"Yes," Michael said, giving Jazz a relieved smile. "That sounds lovely."

"All right. I'll get that going for you."

Gruff stomped back toward the kitchen. Jazz noticed all the diners Gruff had been loudly gossiping about were now giving him and Michael the stink eye. But he chose to ignore them and focus on his date.

Michael was tall and incredibly fit, with a cock to write sonnets over. His dark brown hair was neat and tidy, just like everything else about him.

Jazz was incredibly lucky to have met such a great guy.

Michael had admitted to Jazz he had not dated much—in fact, he'd only had one serious boyfriend and a handful of lovers, unlike Jazz's wild past. But Michael did not cease to *wow* the socks off Jazz in the sack. He could go from being a power bottom to a cuddly submissive in one day. Or even the dominant man who bent Jazz over the kitchen table and insisted he keep the kitchen apron on while he pounded Jazz's ass. After those encounters, Jazz typically had trouble walking and standing behind his salon chair the next day.

Sexual compatibility aside—and oh *Lord*, were their bodies compatible!—Jazz could not believe how wonderfully their relationship was going. It had been almost two months, and they hadn't had a single argument. They liked many of the same things and pretty much always agreed on which TV show or movie to watch. Jazz hoped his active social life wasn't too much for his shy new lover, and though he knew they were still in the honeymoon phase of their relationship, he felt like he was living in a romance novel and every day was a happily ever after.

He never wanted this book to end.

"What?" Michael asked, touching his face. "Is there something on my face?"

Jazz grinned, not embarrassed in the least to have been staring starry-eyed at his beau. "Nope. Just admiring my handsome boyfriend."

Michael cheeks pinkened again and his gaze darted away. "Oh."

"I hope I didn't interrupt an exciting evening when I called."

"No, I was listening to part two of that new podcast I was telling you about."

"Frozen Forensics?"

Michael smiled, and Jazz could tell he was trying to downplay his enthusiasm. "*Frigid Forensics* with Blake Hanson. He's investigating a cold case about a woman's husband she reported missing five years ago. The police never found anything suspicious, but apparently very recently, she sold her house and moved to Ho Chi Minh City, of all places. The new homeowners have done some excavating and discovered human remains."

"Of course they have."

If Michael wasn't a detective with Scotland Yard in a previous life, he was making up for it in this one with his love of a good murder mystery. His obsession with mystery novels was how they'd met—Michael waiting in line to have ten Brock Hammer novels signed.

"Lemme guess?" Jazz said. "The wife killed her husband, chopped him up, and buried him all over her flowerbeds?"

"I suppose I'll find out when part three is released."

"Think she'll pay for her crimes?" Jazz asked wistfully.

"It's unlikely, unless she returns to the States. Vietnam won't extradite to the US, which is doubtless why she went there. But Blake Hanson has a lot of fans who call in or use social media to share clues, loopholes, etcetera, in order to bring people to justice."

Jazz gave Michael a teasing smile. "And do you ever call in with a clue?"

He glanced down in a fetching way at his hands on the table. "Maybe."

"You are so damn adorable."

His blush reappeared. "Don't tease."

"Totally not teasing," Jazz assured him with a smile. "Not to change the subject from murderous widows and how utterly freaking adorable you are, but you're still free for Misty's block party Sunday?"

"Barring a mass influx of bodies, yes. Should I bring anything?"

"Just your delectable self," he quipped. "And I don't wanna overbook your weekend, but do you wanna go to the festival tomorrow after I get off work too?"

Michael's brown eyes lit up. "Sure, if you want to. But won't that be a late night for you, having to get up so early on Saturday?"

"Yeah, but I'll manage. Misty has some shirt-tail relatives performing tomorrow night. She met them through one of those ancestry sites and wants us to meet them. I'm not much of a folk music fan, but I do love all the food trucks and wineries that usually come."

"That sounds lovely," Michael said, then lowered his voice as he added, "even if most of the performers are pissing off Gruff."

"It doesn't take much to annoy him."

"How long have you known Gruff?"

"Oh, I don't know. I met him when Russell and I started coming here for the summers. I think we recognized the easily annoyed side of each other, and since then he's tolerated me pretty well."

The mention of Russell's name sent a wash of sadness through Jazz, and he suddenly felt very tired.

Russell Withingham.

Jazz's almost ex-husband.

Famous author.

And sociopathic murderer.

As it did every time Jazz allowed himself to think about Russell, his stomach knotted.

Four phone calls had come to his apartment from the prison where Russell was being held while he awaited trial—no bail had been set because of Russell's potential flight risk. Jazz had denied the charges every time.

If Jazz was the type to seek therapy, he imagined a shrink would tell him he should talk to Russell. Get some closure.

But how could he face talking to the man he once loved, knowing Russell had deviously plotted to kill Dylan Roberts, the twenty-three-year-old twink from Russell's favorite bar, who Jazz had cruelly thought of as just another one of Russell's fuck toys. Lord knew, Russell had had plenty when they were together. But Dylan had been a young man in his prime, and he'd written a mystery novel that Russell stole and published as his own. That alone was terrible.

But to systematically plot how to murder and get away with killing Dylan, his own lover? And cutting his hands off for no apparent reason other than a plot misdirect?

That was a whole different level of crazy.

And Jazz used to sleep next to Russell, make him breakfast, suck his dick, hold his hand, and watch movies....

No. Don't think about it.

Before Jazz could shake himself out of the mood—*I'm on a date with Michael!*—it plummeted even further when the door opened and an all-too-familiar figure stepped in. The man was tall and painfully thin, with a swoop of blond hair across his forehead that stood out from the raven-black color of the rest of it.

Norbert Farthington.

"What the actual fuck?" Jazz whispered.

Michael looked over his shoulder and jerked in surprise when he saw Russell's PR rep in the doorway. He turned back to Jazz with wide eyes. "What is Norbert doing here?"

"Haunting my life?"

Norbert appeared worse for wear, his tacky hair color in dire need of a touch-up, dark circles under his eyes, and his skin the exact color of boiled chicken. His narrow, pointed face was pinched in an expression of distaste as he surveyed the diner.

7

Jazz's body wanted to react, to stand up and stride to Norbert and punch him in his narrow-lipped mouth. The last time Jazz had the displeasure of the guy's skin-crawling company, Norbert had offered to help Russell kill not only Jazz, but Michael, the town sheriff, and Dylan's uncle.

Before Jazz could even move, the couple at the first table gave simultaneous gasps of surprise.

"What the blue blazes are you doing here?" the man demanded. He was already anemic-looking—probably all that rabbit food—but at the sight of Norbert, he seemed to go even paler.

Norbert glared down at them. "Do I know you?"

"Yes, Norbert, you do," the woman said. "Or you did before you left the group back in college, cheated on Bill, and never paid us the five grand you owed."

"This is him?" From the sound of the voice, the androgynous greaser was a young woman, and she glared up at Norbert with open hostility. "Are you fucking kidding me? *This* is him?"

Jazz was satisfied to see Norbert's face blanch. He looked completely stunned, and maybe even a little bit guilty? A moment later, however, his features shifted back to his standard expression of something just short of a glare.

"Bill and Sonya," Norbert said, a chill to his tone. "How utterly retro to see you again."

"Well, it's real shitty to see you, Norbie," Sonya snapped, arms crossed over her chest.

Norbert made one of his insufferable grunts of superiority that had Jazz clenching his teeth. "Are you two still together and singing?" Norbert asked, and then he tittered a condescending laugh. "And is this your offspring? Don't tell me, Bill, that you disappointed all your male paramours as badly as you disappointed me so you decided to settle for Sonya's desperate attentions. How gauche."

Norbert sounded so much like Russell that Jazz actually flinched as if slapped. He closed his eyes and shook his head to erase the sensation. Fuck Russell and fuck his loser PR rep! Why were they even still a part of Jazz's life?

Jazz was glad Michael had shifted in his seat, openly watching the exchange along with everyone else in the diner, and hadn't noticed Jazz's reaction. Michael had asked Jazz more than once how he was holding up after the whole Russell debacle, and Jazz always insisted he was fine. He didn't want Michael to worry or allow Russell's bullshit to tarnish their so-far so-damn-good relationship. But it had proved quite difficult in the days following Russell's arrest, when it seemed that every blogger and minor-market reporter had been hounding them for some kind of sound-bite or quote. Thankfully attention spans were crazily short these days and someone else's misfortune had drawn that circus out of town.

At least until today.

The sound of a hand slapping a table and rattling the dishes made Jazz jump and look back at the argument.

"This is Ally Roberts," Bill snapped, his hands flat on the table and high color in his cheeks. "She's our new lead guitarist." Bill sat back, crossing his skinny arms as he glared up at Norbert. "And we perform all over the country now. I'm sure you've heard our music. One of our biggest hits is a song about a no-good, cheating, thieving, lying boyfriend. It's titled 'Skinflint Norbie and His Walkabout Shoes.'"

Jazz's snort of amusement surprised him, and was unfortunately loud enough for Norbert, Bill, Sonya, and Ally to hear. All four looked in Jazz's direction, and he felt a smug sense of satisfaction at the quick flash of fear that crossed Norbert's face.

"He likes it." Bill chuckled. "Might have sold another CD."

"Better get the cash up front from that one," Norbert said with a sniff. "He's as dishonest as they come. A real snitch too."

"With that endorsement from you, then we like him already," Sonya said, flashing a smirk.

When Norbert sniffed a second time and turned his nose up at Jazz, Jazz's hands tightened into fists without any thought. He glared at Norbert, who glared right back, both of them shooting daggers, lasers, cannons, mortars, and boulders from catapults with their eyes.

"Jazz...." Michael's voice was calm and quiet. "He's not worth it."

"It might be worth it," Jazz muttered. "One little punch would take him down a peg or two."

Michael reached across the table and rested his hand on Jazz's forearm, and by doing so, he might have saved Norbert's life. At the very least, he saved Gruff's chair, which Jazz had been envisioning breaking over Norbert's head.

Norbert had always been a thorn in Jazz's side, and a creepy one at that. As Russell's PR rep, he'd always been lurking around during their marriage. The day of that big storm, after Russell had been caught red-handed, Norbert had lied to the police that he'd been playing Russell to defuse the situation and maybe get the gun away, and that he'd never intended to side with Russell to help murder them all. The authorities had oddly believed him, but Jazz knew better. The little weasel would've gladly helped Russell put a few bullets in Jazz and Michael. He'd always had a boner for Russell, and he'd even known about Dylan's plagiarized book.

Norbert deserved a swift kick in the—

Michael's gentle touch and warm eyes halted Jazz's rising fury and stopped him from causing a bigger scene. It wasn't worth it. And neither was Norbert. He unclenched his fists and sat back. Crossing his arms, he glared at Norbert.

Norbert seemed to take that as some sort of victory. "See? He'd never have the guts to do it," he said, then directed his glare at the couple still sitting down. "And as for the two of you, I beg to differ on owing you money. I was the one who started the band. I was the one who revitalized the entire folk-punk movement, if you'll recall."

That got a few scoffs, but Norbert wasn't deterred.

"If you'll also recall, you two never paid me for gas the whole time I drove us to those dumpy bars in those godforsaken small towns." He gave Ally a frosty smile. "Make sure you get any money they promised you up front."

Jazz frowned and looked at Michael, his anger slowly being replaced by curiosity. What was Norbert talking about? He'd been in a band with these two? Book industry PR rep Norbert? And just what the hell did "folk-punk" even sound like? Whatever it was, Jazz was pretty sure there was no such thing as a "folk-punk movement."

Bill pushed to his feet, fists clenched at his sides and his jaw set. To Norbert's credit, he didn't flinch or take a step back, rather he stared Bill in the eye.

Jazz hated to think it, but Norbert might've grown a spine since Russell was arrested.

"You take that back," Bill said, his voice low and threatening. "That was my van you were driving. And we agreed that you would pay for gas while we put miles on it."

"I don't recall that agreement at all," Norbert said. "I think you made it all up since you're obviously still harboring deep feelings for me. You wouldn't worry about a petty debt all these years if you weren't still in love with me."

"You were a warm body in the night. Nothing more," Bill snapped. Sonya fidgeted, apparently too furious to even watch the two men facing off.

If Jazz wasn't imagining it, he would've sworn Bill looked a little strained. Good Lord! Did this guy still have the hots for *Norbert*?

Unbelievable!

Jazz noticed the von Trapp family exchange peculiar glances before returning their attention to the confrontation. They seemed as uncomfortable as Jazz at the notion of anyone pining for Norbert.

"You haven't changed one bit." Sonya stabbed angrily at her salad. "Norbert Farthington never bothered to remember anything that made him uncomfortable."

"From what I've heard," Ally sneered, "all you cared about was finding some guy to suck your dick in an alley."

"Charming," Norbert said. "And completely off, just like Sonya's vocals."

"Like this conversation?" Michael grumbled.

Jazz managed a smile and reached out to take his hand. "You always know exactly what to say."

"My vocals are off?" Sonya cried, finally looking up, her cheeks flushing with color. "You couldn't carry a tune in a bucket, Norbie."

"Oh, Sonya, give it up with that hair color—it really washes you out," Norbert said with a sneer.

Bill lunged forward and grabbed the front of Norbert's shirt.

The stocky and muscular young von Trapp man shot to his feet. His cheeks sported patches of dark blond whiskers that had Jazz thinking he might be sixteenish. When the young man took a step toward Bill and Norbert, the younger sister wife put a hand on his arm. Her touch appeared

11

to calm him, and he returned to his seat even though he continued to closely watch the confrontation.

The kitchen doors swung open, bumped by Gruff's big ass as he carried two plates out into the dining area. He headed toward Jazz and Michael's table, all smiles until he noticed Bill holding Norbert by the shirt.

"Hey! No roughhousing inside!" Gruff shouted.

Everyone froze, and Michael let out a startled gasp.

Pounding over to Jazz and Michael, Gruff set the food down before them with a clatter. Half of Jazz's fries fell off the plate—his waistline but not his taste buds would appreciate that later—but Jazz didn't care about the fries as he and Michael watched Gruff stalk over to separate Bill and Norbert.

"He started it!" Norbert insisted, brushing off his shirt when Bill released him.

"You're a complete dickhead," Ally said, and got to her feet. "I should kick your ass for what you did to Bill and Sonya and—" She stopped herself abruptly from saying anything further.

"Ally, stop," Sonya said, her voice sounding tired and used up.

Gruff gave Ally a gentle push back into her seat, then glowered at Norbert. "I don't like people messing with my customers."

Sputtering but determined, Norbert pointed at Jazz. "That man egged this lunatic on!"

Gruff looked at Jazz over his shoulder.

Jazz calmly gazed back at Gruff and ate a fry off his plate.

Gruff faced Norbert and growled deep in his throat. "Nobody comes into my restaurant and insults my friends. And when they do, I show them the door."

"I will not stand—"

"I don't care if you stand or sit," Gruff said. "You won't be doing it here."

And with that, he spun Norbert around, grabbed him by the belt and the back of the shirt, and hustled him to the door.

"Oh my God," Jazz said, his heart pounding and a light sheen of sweat coating his body. "Oh my God."

"Jesus," Michael whispered and turned to sit sideways in the booth again to be able to see better.

As Gruff tossed Norbert out of the diner, Jazz's smile was so big it made his cheeks ache.

But then a nibble of guilt poked its way through the joy at Norbert's comeuppance. Something had definitely changed about Norbert since Russell's arrest, and maybe Jazz shouldn't feel quite so good at seeing Norbert treated so badly.

Then again... it *was* Norbert. The guy was such a snake in the grass. And apparently a cheater and a thief. Not to mention the father of the "folk-punk movement," whatever the hell that was.

The creep.

"Show's over folks," Gruff said, dusting off his hands as he headed for the kitchen. He paused beside their table and winked at Jazz.

"Thanks, Gruff."

"My pleasure." Gruff tipped his head toward the door. "You know him?"

"I did once," Jazz said and gave Michael a sad smile. "In a previous life."

"When you were with that writer?" Gruff asked.

"Russell. Yeah."

Gruff looked at Michael, then back. "I'd say you traded up."

And with that, he stomped back to the kitchen.

"I can't believe that skinny puff of a pantywaist actually showed up this weekend," Ally said with a long glare at the door where Norbert had disappeared. She sat back with a huff and screwed her face up at Bill. "Get over him already, Bill. He's like a big cocksucking zero."

"I *am* over him," Bill snapped, but even from across the room, Jazz could hear the lie in his tone.

Michael and Jazz exchanged glances. Michael's brows shot up as he whispered, "There's no accounting for tastes, is there?"

Jazz made a disbelieving sniff of agreement and ate another fry.

"What a jerk," Sonya said. "Who would have guessed Norbert would be in Lacetown."

"Do you think he'll be at the festival?" Bill wondered.

"Who cares?" Ally said confidently. "You guys just focus on performing this weekend. I'll take care of ol' Norbie if he comes around again. Don't you worry about it, Bill."

The diner fell quiet then, except for some whispered conversation between the von Trapp clones, but Jazz didn't pay them any attention. He reached across the table to take Michael's hand again and gave him a smile.

"Don't I know how to show you a good time?" Jazz said.

"Always." Michael had a decided glint in his brown eyes that made Jazz wish he could cancel the rest of his customers and go home to play in Michael's giant walk-in shower.

Jazz released Michael's hand, but not his gaze as he picked up his burger and reveled in the anticipation of salty, meaty, greasy heaven. "How's your burger?" he asked before taking a huge bite of his own. *Perfect.*

Flinching adorably, Michael pushed his glasses up his nose. "Oh! I haven't even sampled it yet. Too busy watching the show." He took a bite and nodded appreciatively. "Delicious."

Chuckling, Jazz put his burger down and wiped the grease from his mouth with a napkin. Then he sobered and leaned forward. "Why the heck do you think Norbie is in Lacetown?"

Always so in tune with Jazz's moods, Michael quickly took his hand once more, and Jazz squeezed back, feeling suddenly off-balance. "It doesn't matter," Michael assured him. "He's none of our concern anymore. Let's focus on enjoying our impromptu date, okay?"

"Yeah, okay. Dinner and a show, right?"

Michael smiled at that, then picked up his burger.

Jazz tried to enjoy the pleasure in Michael's expression when he took another bite, but his mind flooded with questions. Was Norbert in Lacetown snooping about Dylan's murder case, gathering evidence to help his precious Russell? Jazz had hoped to never see either of them again, at least until he and Michael testified at Russell's trial. Maybe Jazz could request a private testimony? Was that a thing? Hopefully the prosecutor would offer a plea and there wouldn't even be a trial, just a long prison term for Russell.

Michael touched his hand again, and Jazz looked up.

"You sure you're okay?" Michael asked. "Seeing Norbert has to bring up bad memories."

He hadn't realized he'd been bouncing his knee, clenching his teeth, and staring off into nowhere—he'd been doing that a lot lately. He forced a smile, which was easier than it should have been with all the hamster-in-a-wheel thoughts running on a loop in his head.

"Yeah, I'm okay." Jazz knew he sounded as convincing as that Bill guy, but he was grateful when Michael nodded his acceptance. Jazz wrapped his other hand over Michael's. "As long as I've got you by my side, I'll be simply grand."

The older man from the table of von Trapp clones stepped up to their booth, startling Jazz. Michael and Jazz both looked up at him in surprise. A black shirt with a preacher's collar hung from broad shoulders, and brown cotton pants hitched halfway up his belly were held in place by leather suspenders. He wore a black broad-brimmed hat, and his weathered face was creased in a scowl as he stared down at their entwined fingers.

Michael quickly pulled his hand free. "M-may I help you?" he stammered.

The man stared at Jazz, who suddenly found himself sitting up straighter.

"I saw you on TV. You were in an unlawful union with that homosexual writer who killed a young man right in this town, weren't you?" the man said.

Jazz blinked twice before the words registered. "*Excuse* me?" he said with the biggest head bob he was sure he'd ever made. Surely this guy wasn't another reporter, because he came across more like a backwoods preacher.

The man fixed his watery gaze on Michael next.

Jazz bunched a fist. If he insulted Michael, Jazz would "escort" the man out the door, far less politely than Gruff had booted out Norbert.

"Repent, brothers," the man said simply and placed a pamphlet on the tabletop before turning away to usher the rest of the von Trapp clones out of the diner. Jazz noticed that the boy was blatantly staring at them as he followed the creepy preacher man—his father?—out the door.

Michael picked up the pamphlet and made a face.

"Is it telling you that meat is murder?" Jazz asked.

"Nope. It's telling me we're sinners and going to hell."

Michael turned the pamphlet around and showed Jazz the front. THE ROAD TO HELL screamed the bold-type headline. Three columns of type were set beneath it, listing all the burnable offenses. From just a cursory glance, Jazz discovered he was pretty much doomed, even if he miraculously turned straight.

"Good thing you're Jewish and don't believe in hell," Jazz said dryly. "Looks like I'm screwed."

"Yes, a boon for me, eh?" Michael frowned at the door, where the family had disappeared. He slid the religious tract out of sight under his paper placemat.

Jazz reached out to take both of Michael's hands. "Aren't you glad you left your comfortable abode and had dinner with me?"

Michael smiled and squeezed his hands back. "Nothing, not even all that nonsense, would make me regret it."

CHAPTER TWO

Michael pulled his Toyota into a parking spot behind the Holland Harbor Lofts where Jazz lived above Misty's salon. He glanced up to the second floor of the old brick building and saw white curtains fluttering in an open window to the loft apartment Michael had gotten to know well.

The old chandlery building was on Lacetown's historic registry, the town quite proud of its rich fishing and shipping history. Right on Steelhead Avenue, the redbrick structure housed businesses below and the lofts above, all of them with a view of Lake Michigan across the street.

"Here you are," Michael said.

"Yup, back to the grind. You going home to listen to your podcast to see if they found the hubby's leg under the azalea bushes?"

Michael chuckled. "No, part three comes out next Thursday."

"You'll have to let me know what happened." Jazz glanced at his watch. "I've got twenty minutes before my next client."

Jazz's wheat-colored hair was pulled back in a low ponytail, and his eyes sparkled like whisky in a crystal decanter. Michael never tired of gazing at Jazz. Sometimes his heart would leap in his chest like it had the first time he'd seen Jazz, taking him by surprise.

And you're dating him. You get to make love to him....

Michael's heart skipped again, and he gave Jazz a smile. "Twenty whole minutes?"

"Yup."

Off and on during dinner and on the drive back from Gruff's Grub, Jazz had complained about seeing Norbert again, a sure indication he was very preoccupied with the incident and trying not to be.

I've got just the thing to get Jazz's mind off all that drama.

Michael placed his hand on Jazz's bouncing knee. "You can do a lot in twenty minutes."

Jazz's wide mouth crooked into a knowing smile. "You can. You can cook a frozen pizza."

"You can pay bills or do the dishes."

Jazz nodded seriously. "You could even work out in twenty minutes."

"Know what else you can do in twenty minutes?" Michael said, his pulse thumping even as his groin stirred.

"What's that?" Jazz licked his lips.

"Play truth or dare."

"Oh, I like that game," Jazz said.

On their first date, Jazz had initiated the teenage girl slumber party game as a way to get to know each other, and it had worked surprisingly well.

He wasn't sure what it was about Jazz—maybe his open, accepting nature?—but Michael had never felt so confident with any of his other lovers. At least not confident enough to say what he said next. "Would you like to take a dare?"

"Always."

"I dare you to invite me up to your apartment."

Jazz let out a throaty growl and hastily fumbled with his seat belt. "Dare accepted. And dammit, there's only nineteen minutes left now."

"We'd better hurry."

Michael killed the engine and quickly got out of the car. His hands trembled with excitement as he locked the car with a *beep-beep* and pocketed his keys.

Grinning, Jazz entered his code for the interior stairway that led to his trendy loft. They climbed the stairs two at a time, and since they were alone in the hallway, Michael pressed his body against the length of Jazz's back as Jazz unlocked his door.

With a sigh, Jazz leaned into Michael, thrusting his ass against Michael's hardening dick. Michael wrapped his arms around Jazz's solid waist and inhaled the sweet herbal scent of his boyfriend's glorious hair.

His every fantasy had now become fixated on Jazz's beautiful hair. He really hoped Jazz never got the notion to cut it all off.

The warmth of Jazz's body seeped through their clothing and heated Michael's blood. Any lingering thoughts about Jazz cutting his hair faded as passion flooded Michael's senses.

"So what do you have in mind, Mr. Fleishman?" Jazz purred, pushing his door open but not stepping out of Michael's embrace.

Michael nibbled Jazz's earlobe, his pride swelling like his cock when Jazz shivered. That was definitely one of Jazz's hot spots. The other was.... Michael pressed the flat of both hands on the front of Jazz's hip bones, then to the soft fleshy areas before hip, thigh, and cock met.

Jazz groaned.

"What would you like?" Michael purposefully tickled the skin below Jazz's earlobe with his lips.

Jazz walked forward, and Michael went with him, never releasing him. Using one foot, he kicked the door shut behind them.

The second the latch clicked, Michael cupped Jazz's balls with one hand, then slid his other hand under his T-shirt and over warm skin until he had one of Jazz's delicious nipples between his fingers. He squeezed and pinched, kissing and nibbling up Jazz's neck. Gently humping him, Michael relished the way Jazz melted back into him, dropping his head onto Michael's shoulder and exposing more of that strong neck for Michael to taste and explore.

"That's a good start," Jazz muttered, voice rough and breathy. He pushed his ass back harder. "God, I want you inside me."

"Not enough time." Michael took charge, spinning Jazz in his arms to claim those lips in a heated kiss. He cupped the back of Jazz's head, tugging on his hair tie. "Take your hair down while I suck you."

Jazz's hands roamed all over Michael's back, groping his ass. "Yes, sir."

"Sir?" He flashed a cocky smile. "I like the sound of that. Now take your hair down. There's no time for you to play coy with me."

When Jazz chuckled, Michael made a *tsk* ing sound as he loosened Jazz's belt. "Be a good boy and do as I say. Good boys who do as they're told get rewards."

Grinning wide, Jazz reached behind his head and untied his hair. He shook it loose, fluffing it with his hands, all the while his eyes twinkling with mischief. "Have I been a good boy?"

Michael *tsk* ed again. "You've been a very, *very* bad boy."

"Will I have to be punished, sir?"

Michael pushed Jazz's pants down, and a mind-numbing heartbeat later, he had that warm, hard cock in his hand. "Yes, most severely."

With one longing caress of Jazz's hair, Michael fell to his knees and took Jazz into his mouth. The scent of his body—the sweat of the day and his natural musk—inundated Michael's senses, making him moan. Jazz shuddered and held on to Michael's shoulders as Michael sucked and bobbed on a cock he'd memorized every inch of, each contour, ridge, and vein. From the rough velvety texture of Jazz's cockhead to the hard line of muscle at the bottom of his shaft. Michael fisted Jazz's cock up and down, sucking hard on the head, not taking his time, but pumping the pleasure out of Jazz as fast as he could.

"Oh fuck... your mouth," Jazz moaned above him.

Nothing brought greater pleasure to Michael than making Jazz happy, in every possible way. He recognized Jazz's rising need the moment Jazz began to thrust, his hands digging into the muscles of Michael's shoulders. They were rushed for time, so there was no holding back for either of them, no time for finesse or romance. Just the raw need to get off together. Michael cupped Jazz's balls, cradled and gently massaged them—Jazz was ultrasensitive there.

Jazz hissed through his teeth. "Close... so close... right there...."

Michael felt the pulse before Jazz's rich cum flooded his mouth. As he continued sucking and stroking Jazz while he orgasmed, a surge of precum escaped his own cock. If he let go of Jazz and touched himself once, he'd come too. But he stayed with Jazz through the whole thing, wringing all the pleasure out of his lover he could.

"Fuck," Jazz panted.

Michael sucked his head a little longer, loving how different it felt after Jazz came—softer, more delicate, still so hot. He lifted his gaze to watch through the steamed-up lenses of his glasses as Jazz's chest and belly heaved for breath, his beautiful hair falling forward around his flushed face. Reluctantly, he pulled off, and kissed the tip tenderly before pushing to his feet.

Smiling, Jazz took his hand and helped him stand. "If that's how you punish bad boys, I don't think I'm ever going to be good again."

Michael laughed, dipping his head to kiss Jazz slow and deep. He coiled his fingers in that hair, and their tongues danced for a moment.

Jazz withdrew, wearing a sleepy, contented smile that made Michael's heart swell with such an overwhelming sense of affection and love that he sucked in a breath of surprise.

I love him, he realized suddenly.

"I love tasting myself in your mouth," Jazz whispered.

Michael's heart jumped until the second half of Jazz's statement soaked into his brain after his own personal realization. *I love Jazz....*

Of course he didn't say that. It was too soon, wasn't it?

Losing himself in those rich, burnt-sugar eyes, Michael stroked Jazz's face with a thumb. His heart pounded, and an undeniable sense of warmth, joy, and fear washed over him, spreading down his scalp, neck, and torso like drops of ink seeping across paper. He kissed Jazz again rather than say anything stupid. This time the kiss was more fervent, desperate for... for what, Michael didn't know. He only knew his heart and cock ached for the man in his arms.

Panting for breath, Jazz pulled back and pushed on Michael's chest. Michael blinked a few times, disoriented somewhat when Jazz let go of him.

Jazz was smiling, bouncing as he pulled up his underwear and jeans. "I do believe it's my turn. I wouldn't want to get punished too much for not doing what's expected of me."

He forced himself to give Jazz a predatory smile, to get back into the little game he'd started, though his mind reeled with discovery.

I love Jazz. This is it—I finally love someone.

But now was not the time, so he nodded and said, "Yes, you'd best be a good boy. Get to it."

"Get to it," Jazz repeated with a laugh, his knees cracking audibly when he knelt and began tugging Michael's belt loose. He buried his face in Michael's crotch, inhaling so deeply Michael's dick and balls cooled. Jazz ran his hands up Michael's stomach, down his hips and over his thighs. "Damn, I love your body," he murmured, face still pressed to Michael's crotch. "So fucking sexy."

Lovingly, Michael gazed down at Jazz, glasses slipping down the sweaty slope of his nose. He fingered Jazz's hair, cradling his head in his hand. There was something so perfect about having Jazz on his knees before him, the way

Jazz seemed to savor or worship Michael's body. No one had ever wanted Michael like this, with such passion and hunger. He didn't know what he did to deserve it, or what he would have to do to keep it, but he knew then that Jazz meant *everything* to him.

It should have scared him, but it didn't. It felt right.

Jazz lowered Michael's trousers and pulled out his cock. Michael's heart pounded, his breath coming so fast he knew it wouldn't take long.

Jazz took Michael's cock in his hand, stroking and studying it while Michael cupped the back of Jazz's head, waiting breathlessly.

"So fucking perfect," Jazz muttered. With a starved moan, he swallowed Michael down. Michael buckled over, gasping at Jazz's fervor as he rode the wild rhythm of his mouth.

He clutched tightly at Jazz's hair and gave himself over to the pleasure. His lover could take him all the way in, and Michael didn't hesitate to meet Jazz's mouth, thrust for thrust. Jazz moaned his approval at that, and the vibration was all it took.

"Oh, Jazz!" he cried out as he spilled over the edge and into rapture.

He emptied himself into that willing mouth, his body shaking as pleasure trembled throughout his every limb.

Still lost to the throes of ecstasy, Michael stood very still, clinging to Jazz, and barely registering when Jazz tucked his spent cock away, zipped him up, and then fastened his trousers.

Jazz stood and kissed him.

Damn, Michael liked the taste of himself in Jazz's mouth.

"That was awesome." Jazz kissed Michael's cheek, then looked at his watch. "I have three minutes. Just enough time to brush my teeth and fix my hair."

Michael laughed. "You'd better hurry."

With a wave, Jazz sauntered to the bathroom. "My evening clients expect me to be running behind by this time of the day. It'll be fine." He tucked his T-shirt into his jeans and buckled his belt as he stepped into the bathroom.

Michael followed, adjusting his clothing as well.

Jazz's apartment was full of refurbished antiques, plants, books, colorful fabrics, and a pair of purple velvet couches. It was long and narrow, flanked on two sides by east- and west-facing tall windows, the western offering a view of the lake. The evening sun glared in, making Michael squint before he stepped into the small bathroom with the claw-foot tub and pedestal sink.

Jazz studied himself in the mirror, then Michael's reflection. "Oh, we have FFL hair, don't we?"

Michael wrapped his arms around Jazz from behind, needing to touch him every chance he had. "What's that mean?"

"Freshly Fucked Look," he explained, reaching for his toothbrush. He squirted some toothpaste on it. "Can't be doing hair with cum breath."

Michael laughed, watching Jazz brush his teeth in the mirror.

Indeed they both were flushed, hair tousled, and their knowing smiles giving away what they'd just done.

"Want some?" Jazz held up the toothpaste tube. He made no move to leave Michael's embrace, as if being joined like this was right where he belonged, even while performing such a mundane task.

"I wanna taste you a little longer," Michael whispered, burying his face into the crook of Jazz's neck when he spied his own blush in the mirror.

Jazz chuckled and spit out toothpaste. "My kinky mortician."

He swayed their bodies a little, only mildly embarrassed. "You bring it out in me."

"That's because I'm a very, very bad boy," he teased, rubbing his butt over Michael's groin.

"You are," Michael agreed, his body stirring even though he'd just come. He gripped Jazz's hips tight and stilled his teasing. "And you keep doing that with this juicy ass of yours, you'll be more than a couple minutes late to work."

Jazz threw back his head and laughed. When he bent down to rinse his mouth directly from the faucet, Michael let him go and leaned against the doorjamb, crossing his arms.

Humming a tune, Jazz splashed water on his face. He let it drip down as he studied the sides of his face closely in the mirror. Satisfied by whatever he found, he dried his skin and then the edges of the pedestal sink where he'd splashed water. He hung the towel and picked up a hairbrush from one of four baskets tucked into the cubbies of a small storage stand between the sink and toilet. Michael enjoyed watching him brush his hair and wondered if Jazz would ever let him do it.

Somehow Jazz always managed to take his hair down and put his hair band around his wrist in one practiced move. He did the same thing in reverse as he tied his hair back again, folding it into a man-bun—a term his sassy boyfriend hated but described the style nonetheless. Michael had never paid so much attention to a man's hair before, but with Jazz it was only one of the many things Michael was becoming obsessed with.

I'm in love.

Michael had never been in love before, and he had no idea what the rules were. Should he tell Jazz? Was it too soon? What was the protocol? Should he plan a romantic moment to tell Jazz or tell him after sex? What if Jazz didn't love him back?

Squirming a little and feeling grossly out of his league, Michael remained silent and watched his boyfriend get ready.

Boyfriend.

The word seemed to ping around his mind. After a few failed attempts at finding someone, Michael was still surprised to have met Jazz and fallen in love right there in Lacetown, standing in line while waiting to see one of his all-time favorite authors.

Who just so happened to be a murdering sociopath.

And Jazz's soon-to-be ex-husband.

What a small and weird world it could be.

To Michael's surprise, Jazz grabbed a black pencil from the medicine cabinet and began lining his eyes.

"Makeup?" Michael questioned. He liked it when Jazz wore eyeliner.

Jazz winked at him, then opened a tiny pot and smeared something shiny and tinted on his lips with his pinky finger. "Liner and gloss to go with my FFL."

"Ah, I see."

Jazz came up to him, his gaze on Michael's hair. Without asking, he reached up and smoothed it into place. "There, you're almost presentable."

"Almost?" Michael wrapped his arms around him, and Jazz's hands rested on his waist.

"When are you gonna let me get my hands on your hair?"

"Well, um...." Michael flushed. He'd always gone to Elmer Washington over in Bridlestop. Did Jazz not like his hair? Was it not stylish enough for his trendsetting boyfriend? Was Jazz embarrassed by how conservative Michael looked?

"Don't worry," Jazz said, kissing his cheek and stepping past him and out of the bathroom. "I won't change your hairstyle unless you want me to. I just think good ol' Elmer's vision is going, and he's not blending your sides all that well."

Relieved Jazz wasn't interested in changing how he looked— *he's not embarrassed by me*—Michael squinted at his reflection in the mirror. He *had* been using more hair gel to make his hair behave lately.

"Besides, why should you pay for a haircut when your boyfriend can do it?" Jazz called from the living room.

When Michael joined him, Jazz was fishing in the basket of scarves and other various accessories he kept on the floor beside the door for last-minute outfit details. Once, when Michael and Mr. Pickles—his large black-and-white cat—came to visit, the cat had taken a nap in them. Jazz hadn't minded at all. When he found a black-striped tie, still looped and knotted, he pulled it over his head, then flashed a grin at Michael. "I gotta fly, sweetie. Can you lock up and get the lights for me?"

"Of course."

Jazz gave him a quick kiss, then hurried out the door with a "Later, sweetie!"

As Michael switched off all Jazz's lights, he felt warm inside. Jazz trusted him even though Jazz had been horribly betrayed in his last relationship.

Well, Michael was not going to betray that trust or ruin his chances with Jazz. Russell had been such a selfish fool. If an idiot like Russell could be lucky enough for Jazz to marry him, maybe Michael did have a chance at something lasting and genuine with Jazz. Because unlike Russell, Michael loved Jazz and would never take their relationship for granted.

CHAPTER THREE

Indignities!

Norbert Farthington seethed as he sped along the two-lane blacktop.

He clenched and released the steering wheel, wishing he was strangling Jasper's neck instead.

Jasper Dilworth.

He should have known he'd run into that tired old queen at some point this weekend. But he hadn't expected it to happen quite so fast.

And seeing Bill and Sonya again after all this time had really thrown him for a loop. It was like he'd stepped into an episode of *The Twilight Zone* written specifically about wicked people from his past. And that new guitarist Ally really had a mouth on her. Norbert had never met her, and yet she seemed to have some kind of dispute with him. And how dare Bill try to take credit for the "folk-punk" sound.

I put that genre on the map!

No one had ever heard of folk-punk until Norbert put the band together. Now Bill and Sonya were acting like they'd started it all. While frustrating, the whole incident had felt rather gratifying in a way too.

Bill still holds a torch for me. How delightfully unexpected!

Until that giant bear of an owner had literally thrown him out the door of that nasty fly-and-rat-trap place he called a diner.

Outrageous!

Norbert took a deep breath and let it out. As much as he'd dreaded coming back to Lacetown, he needed to make this weekend a success. Down to his last bit of cash, credit cards maxed, he had no more options. His very life depended on making connections at this festival, whether or not Jasper would be there. Whether or not Bill and Sonya would be smearing his name to everyone they met. Or that bitch dyke Ally said any more hateful things to him. He already hated her.

But this weekend, he had to forget about them all. He would have to enchant anyone he might be able to represent. Despite what Bill and Sonya thought, Norbert had scheduled every gig for their group, The Lanky Balladeers. If he'd been able to find places for their folk-punk trio to sing with Sonya's awful vocals, then he'd be able to do the same for any singer or group with a modicum of talent. He just needed to be calm, steady, and charming.

To be able to get to that place from his current mood, however, would take a lot of mental exercises. And he would need some space where he could be alone. But where? He didn't relish the idea of sleeping in his car again.

A thought occurred to him, and he smiled as he sped through the downtown. Then he forced himself to slow down—the last thing he needed right now was to be pulled over by that asshole brute of a sheriff or one of his dimwit deputies.

Perhaps the cottage Russell had rented was still considered a crime scene. What could it hurt if Norbert spent a night or two there? Slept in the bed where Russell had once laid his head? Maybe the pillowcases still held his special scent.

Yes, that just might work. He could park the Oldsmobile down the road in the Bluffs at Lake View retirement community's visitor lot and walk to the cottage. It wasn't very far, and he didn't have much luggage with him anyway.

Yes, Russell's cottage would work perfectly.

Grateful to have a game plan, Norbert sneered as he drove past the sign reading Visit Historic Downtown Lacetown!

If there was one place Norbert had *not* wanted to return to, it was Lacetown, Michigan. Not only was it ridiculously small in size, but its residents were ridiculously small-minded. Sitting in a cove on the shore of Lake Michigan, the town tried to sell itself as the next Saugatuck or Muskegon or even Traverse City. Norbert snorted as he thought about it. As if anyone in Lacetown had any concept of what it took to be a successful summer resort town. They didn't even have a decent beach! When he'd left this hellish town, he'd vowed never to return. But even though he was returning a broken and desperate man, he sure as fuck wasn't going to let anyone know that.

Especially not Jasper I'm-A-Motherfucking-Asshole Dilworth, his creepy mortician boyfriend with the continuous lost-puppy-dog expression, or that laughingstock homophobic Sheriff Musgrave. The blame for everything that had crumbled around Norbert's once successful life rested squarely on them, the Terrible Trio.

They had all conspired to put his beloved Russell in jail for killing Dylan Roberts. *Who cared about that nasty little twink?* Norbert had thought.

His damn uncle, Wilson Roberts, that's who.

Wilson had exposed Russell's plagiarism, which made Norbert appear culpable too.

That had put the final nail in Norbert's career in the literary world. Printed Screams fired Norbert without any mention of a thank-you and with only a month's severance after all he'd done for them.

Once Russell had been arrested and hauled off to jail to await trial—no bail, courtesy of some bitchy judge who apparently wanted to make an example of him—Norbert had floundered, crying and alone in his tiny New York City apartment.

He'd lost Russell and his career in one fell swoop.

He'd tried to find work at other publishers. But the large publishers had never responded to his calls or emails, and the medium and smaller houses must've been poisoned by those haughty and jealous bitches at Printed Screams and their legion of online trolls. No publisher wanted to be associated, even secondhand, with a plagiarist seen as an accessory to murder.

Norbert had been blackballed. He would never work in publishing again.

With no work and even fewer prospects, he eventually packed up what few belongings he owned and set off in the Oldsmobile he'd bought used from his uncle ten years ago. He would have been evicted in a few weeks anyway. His rent was atrociously high for such a small, shitty apartment, even by New York City terms. He would start fresh somewhere else, someplace less cutthroat and more open to his particular brand of PR.

He just needed to figure out exactly what that entailed.

Since he was going independent with his skills, and the literary world was no longer an option, going back to the music biz had been the logical choice. He'd always had an ear for music, so he'd set off for Nashville.

But Nashville wasn't as welcoming as he'd hoped. Especially not to someone with his background. Every call to set up a meeting had not been returned. And when he'd dropped in at a music label to wait out an executive, *any* executive, he'd wasted hours sitting and looking pathetic until security finally escorted him out. The cost of a motel was ridiculously expensive as well, so two days after arriving, he'd packed up the Olds once more and headed north.

While he'd been sitting in one of those waiting areas, he'd overheard some musicians talking about a large acoustic music festival touring the Midwest, so he had decided to give it a try. It wasn't until he was at the border between Ohio and Michigan that he really looked at the festival's website on the cracked screen of his five-year-old cell phone and realized the festival's next stop.

Fucking Lacetown, Michigan.

The scene of the crime, so to speak.

He tightened his grip on the smooth plastic of the steering wheel, knuckles whitening with the force. Taking a calming breath, he flipped on the radio, and the rich sounds of Vivaldi washed over him. The CD was stuck in the radio, but at least it was one of his favorites.

Small blessings, he supposed. But he would take what he could get.

Music had always been a balm for him, soothing and quieting the thoughts zooming and colliding in his busy, chaotic mind. Just like it had back in college when he, Bill, and Sonya had toured as The Lanky Balladeers. Norbert should've known better, even at the time, that popping Bill's gay cherry would turn Bill so clingy. But when Norbert grew tired of Bill's incessant neediness, the breakup had ended the band with Lindsey-and-Stevie-Fleetwood-Mac-sized proportions.

And dammit if Bill and Sonya hadn't stolen the band name and kept touring together.

He'd have to see if there was some sort of legal recourse to get royalties over the name of a band he created.

That little Ally with her greasy hair wouldn't be so cocky then, would she?

He lifted his pointed chin, gritted his teeth—which were nearly worn away from years of grinding in his sleep—and aimed his Oldsmobile toward the cottage.

His stomach clenched and his bowels quivered when the curvy street turned and Norbert was once more looking at Russell's lakeside cottage rental. Police tape fluttered in the breeze, and the curtains were drawn. Norbert had a free place to stay for the weekend after all.

A weary sigh slipped from his lips, and his shoulders sagged.

It seemed such a short time ago that Norbert had pulled this very car into the driveway, lavender lattes with a dollop of honey in hand, only to find that bastard Jasper had broken in and attacked poor Russell.

His groin stirred at the memory of Russell's beautiful pale flesh spread-eagle on the floor of the living room, his every secret part exposed to Norbert's hungry gaze for the first and last time.

He would have been mine, Jasper, if you hadn't ruined everything!

Norbert shook out his hands and took several deep breaths. He had to get past his feelings about Jasper if he wanted any chance of focusing on his career these next few days. When he felt sufficiently settled, he continued past the cottage and down the road to the old-fart apartments, where he could hopefully park his car unnoticed. He arrived at the huge parking lot surrounding the main building of the Bluffs at Lake View, and found a space in a back corner. As he hauled his two bags out of the trunk, he heard a man's voice raised in anger and nervously looked over his shoulder.

It was no one he knew, just a big man with thinning brown hair, berating an elderly woman with fluorescent orange hair who sat in a wheelchair.

"Now, I—"

"Can it, you old bat," the man snapped, pushing her chair roughly. "I've had enough of your mouth. I told you this afternoon, I've had it with your complaints too. You keep...."

As their voices faded, Norbert wondered if that kind of treatment was mentioned in the community's brochure, then realized he didn't much care. He grabbed the handles of his suitcases and set off across the parking lot.

He could do this.

He would get himself into a better place and change the trajectory of his life.

As he pulled everything he owned along behind him, he heard the man still shouting at the elderly woman.

I'm probably a lot better off than she is.

Deciding it would look strange if someone saw him standing at the cottage door with two suitcases in tow, Norbert stashed the cases in the bushes and approached the back door as casually as possible. He glanced around, then tried the knob. Locked. What a time for that buffoon of a sheriff and his posse of idiots to start acting competent.

Russell had mentioned the spare key was inside a fake rock the last time they were here, so Norbert checked each rock surrounding the dead flowers in the small patch of garden until he found it. Another look around, and then he unlocked the door. He hurried back to his suitcases and carried them inside. After closing the door, he leaned against it and let out a long, quiet breath.

It felt strange to be here again. Especially without Russell.

Norbert hesitated a moment. He was nervous and, he had to admit, more than a little turned-on. He was being bad, and he was going to sleep in Russell's bed.

He finally managed to convince his legs to move, and walked slowly through the cottage. The place was a mess, having been photographed and torn apart for evidence. It made him angry to see what careless disregard the sheriff and his yahoos had for private property. If Norbert had more time, he might consider putting things back the way they had been. But he wasn't supposed to be in the cottage in the first place, so he left it all alone.

The bedroom was a complete disaster. The king-sized mattress had been stripped of sheets, and every dresser and nightstand drawer was open, the contents piled in the center of the bed. Norbert poked through the items but didn't find one sex toy. Not even a tiny butt plug he could use and pretend it was Russell.

Apparently the electric bill was still being paid, because the power was on, which meant the well pump was working. He stripped and stepped into the shower stall for a long hot shower, keeping his gaze averted from the large tub where Russell had been attacked by Dylan's psychotic uncle.

Russell's favorite bodywash was still in the shower, and Norbert lathered his whole body three times. He was hard the entire time, and after the third lathering, he quickly jerked off onto the shower wall.

If only it had been Russell's face.

After a final rinse, Norbert shut off the water and grabbed a towel from the cupboard. He walked barefoot through the cottage, which felt so empty and lifeless without Russell.

Jerking off should've calmed him, but it had the opposite effect, and he was hornier than before.

I need to get laid for real.

But with no one special in his life— *Russell, darling Russell*—he would have to rely on a hookup app.

Norbert opened Grindr and hesitated. What if he discovered Jasper trolling around on the site? Or better yet, that I-think-I'm-so-smart mortician? How he would love to throw that knowledge back in Jasper's smug face. This might be more fun than ever.

He scrolled through the images of men, surprised by the number nearby looking to hook up. Must be because of the festival. He paused on a picture of a man's thin, pale, and hairy torso. A small mole was visible to the side of his left nipple, and Norbert slowly smiled.

"Well, hello, old friend," Norbert said as he tapped on the profile picture. "Let's see where this takes us, shall we?"

CHAPTER FOUR

The salon door opened and Jazz looked up to see Michael, the Friday midday sunlight sparkling behind him and instantly brightening Jazz's crummy day.

"Hi," Michael said, a nervous flutter in his voice. "I know you're busy today...."

"Actually, I happen to have a few minutes." He smiled and walked toward Michael. "It's good to see you, sweetie."

"Hi, Michael!" Misty called from the other side of the salon, flashing a bright smile. Hot pink highlights streaked through her red curls, which were currently in a sweeping up-do.

"Oh, hi. Hello, Misty. I like your hair that way."

Misty patted her hair, and her smile brightened even more. "Why, thank you!" She was a bohemian woman, always wearing flowy, colorful clothing. A devout yogi, she had earthy ways and a kind heart Jazz adored. He'd not only gotten lucky in the work environment, but he was also lucky enough to count her as a close friend.

Michael stepped up to Jazz and handed him a takeout cup of coffee from Coffee, Tea, and Thee, the only coffeehouse in town. "Last night you said you had a really full schedule today, so I thought I'd get you something to help you through it."

"What flavor this time?" Jazz asked, loving how Michael enjoyed surprising him with different beverages.

Michael beamed, a hint of mischief behind those glasses. "Caramel macchiato."

"Oh, my new favorite!" he declared as he did every time Michael brought him a coffee.

Jazz started to lean in to kiss Michael but noticed every set of eyes in the salon had zeroed in on the two of them. Instead of delivering a kiss, he took Michael's hand and led him toward the back room.

"Back in a jiff, Misty," Jazz called over his shoulder.

"Sure thing," Misty replied, a hint of disappointment in her tone.

Why did everyone always want to watch the gays make out?

He closed the purple door to the back room, the hinges squeaking loudly and drawing a few snickers from out in the salon.

"Remind me to get some WD-40 for that," Jazz said as he took the coffee and set it on the break table. Then he gathered Michael in his arms and gave him a hot and heavy kiss.

"Oh, hello," Michael murmured against his lips. He pulled back and took a trembling breath, his eyes crossed a little as he gazed at Jazz.

Craving the comforting touch of his lover, Jazz answered by kissing him again. Michael made a slight whimpering sound when Jazz ran his palms down the flat, muscular planes of Michael's back, ending his caress by gripping that tight ass he loved fucking. Fingers tangled in Jazz's hair, Michael responded by deepening the kiss.

Damn, Michael's so passionate, so responsive to every touch....

Lots of tongue and a fair amount of groping later, Jazz stepped back and smiled. "You are a sight for sore eyes."

"I guess so." Michael adjusted the very visible hard-on inside his suit pants. "I had no idea a caramel macchiato got you so worked up or I'd be bringing one to you every day!"

"Oh, it's not the beverage, though that's always welcome. It's definitely the delivery man." Jazz gave him another kiss, but softer and sweeter than the previous. He ran a hand down Michael's firm chest, savoring the muscular feel of his boyfriend's amazing body. If people only knew what a sexy, passionate man lay beneath Michael's reserved, stoic exterior.... Jazz loved being the one trusted with the secrets Mr. Fleishman the funeral director kept hidden.

Michael kissed the tip of Jazz's nose, his hand playing with Jazz's long hair. "That's nice to hear. I love it when you wear your hair down."

"I know." Jazz smiled. "I can't wait until tomorrow evening, when I can have you all to myself for three whole nights." Jazz didn't go back to work on

Tuesday until three o'clock, and as long as Michael had no funerals, they'd become inseparable from Saturday afternoon until then.

Michael grinned. "Sounds lovely." They gazed into each other's eyes for a moment.

"We're still on for the festival tonight?" Jazz clarified. "Misty keeps asking."

"Folk music, tourists, food trucks, and wine?" Michael said. "Wouldn't miss it." He wound his fingers further in Jazz's hair, holding on and not letting go of his gaze. "How's your day been so far?"

Jazz sighed heavily and rolled his eyes as he reached for the drink. He took a sip, savored the sweetness a moment, then said, "Does everyone in this town go a little crazy before a festival kicks off? Because it's been a crappy day."

"You know, people have seemed a bit edgy lately. Maybe they're remembering the bloodshed from the last town festival?"

"Let's hope acoustic musicians are a little more tame than authors," Jazz said, thinking of their unfortunate Norbert sighting last night. "I had to start my morning with a color correction, and it was a doozy. She liked it in the end, but was pissy about having to shell out three hundred bucks. I refrained from mentioning that's what she gets for coloring her hair at home and trying to fix it herself three times. Before I even had a chance to recover from that, our favorite sheriff chewed my ass three ways to Sunday. And not in a hot porn kind of way either."

"Uh-oh. Did you park Beulah between parking spaces again?"

"No," Jazz said, and thought lovingly of his blue-and-cream-colored scooter, currently chained up in the back parking lot. "I cut his daughter's hair the way she requested."

Michael's eyes went wide. "Amanda Rae?"

"She wants to be called Rae now."

"Oh. Okay. What kind of cut did she want?"

"A fauxhawk."

Michael frowned. "I'm not sure what that is."

"Like a mohawk, but blended nicely." When Michael looked confused, Jazz explained, "You know, shaved on the sides and long on the top. Pink, Rihanna, and Adam Lambert all have worn them before."

"Oh," Michael said, brown eyes wide with understanding now. "Oh, my. She's always had such long hair."

"Yeah, we cut off over eighteen inches. I almost did a Sioux warrior cry because I basically scalped her."

Michael furrowed his brows in worry. "You didn't do that in front of Musgrave, did you?"

Jazz laughed, regretting throwing away the opportunity to shock the uptight sheriff now. "Oh no, I didn't."

Michael sighed in relief. "That's probably good. I know he's doted on his daughter since Jenny left them, so I can't say I'm surprised he'd be upset."

"She's nineteen years old!" Jazz exclaimed, then lowered his voice and crossed his arms. "She can join the armed services and defend our country, for God's sake, but she can't wear her hair in a cool style? You should've heard what he said to her too. Said her hair looked like a dyke haircut, and since apparently she *is* gay, he added the helpful 'I'm tired of this lesbian phase.'"

"Oh no, he didn't?"

"He did. The whole salon heard. Thankfully Misty calmed everyone down."

Michael rubbed Jazz's arms and gave him a gentle kiss. "I'm sorry. I know how difficult Musgrave is. And especially with you."

"I'm his favorite."

"You're *my* favorite," Michael insisted with a smile that washed away the last remnants of Jazz's stress. After seeing and talking with Michael about it, things didn't feel quite so bad. It was all just the sheriff being who he was and Rae being who she was and Jazz being a dynamite artist, if he did say so himself. And wasn't art, even in hair, subjective?

"I guess I'm used to Musgrave hating me, but the worst part about it for me was he stomped out without paying." Jazz sipped his drink again.

"Oh, I'm sure he'll come back when he realizes."

"Like I want to see him again anyway. I'm glad he goes to your barbershop in Bridlestop."

"Are you sure you're okay?" Michael asked, hand caressing Jazz's bare forearm. "Especially after running into Norbert last night. That had to bring up bad memories."

Setting his coffee down, Jazz gave him a smile and then stepped closer to steal another kiss. "Most definitely. Don't worry about me."

"I'll always worry about you." Smiling, Michael hugged him tight and kissed him back. "But I should get going and let you get back to work."

Jazz kissed those lips once more. "Thanks for the drink."

"My pleasure." Michael didn't let go, rather took the kiss to such a slow and deep place it made Jazz's toes curl.

Purring, Jazz drew back. "Give Mr. Pickles some pets for me."

"I will." Another kiss and a firm grope of Jazz's ass. "I wish it was Saturday night."

"After we hit the festival for some wine, we'll have time for a quickie." Jazz wouldn't mind a repeat of last night at all.

Michael grinned. "I'll never say no to that. But I do like waking up to you. I sleep better when you're with me." He blushed, and his gaze flitted away shyly.

"Oh, that's so sweet. I like waking up to you too." Jazz thrust into him, loving those hands on his ass and wishing Michael could be deep inside it right now. The man fucked like a dream, and his cock... Jazz actually shuddered thinking about it. But that would have to wait. With working until nine or possibly ten sometimes on Thursday night, then taking clients at the butt-crack of dawn on Friday and Saturday, the last three days of the week didn't allow for much socializing or lovemaking with his hot new boyfriend. "But I have to be here early tomorrow, and it's so hard for me to get out of bed when you're right there next to me, all warm and sexy and delicious. If my morning ladies cancel, maybe I can sleep over tonight."

Wishful thinking with his Saturday regulars.

"I'd hate for you to lose out on all that money, but I'd do my best to take your mind off the losses," Michael whispered, fingers lingering on the crack of Jazz's ass and pressing in.

"I'm sure you would."

Reluctantly, and after another hot kiss, they broke apart. Jazz checked his watch. "I have a client coming in any minute."

"Then I should be going."

Jazz led the way out of the back room.

When they stepped into the main salon area, all heads turned toward them.

"At no point was any article of clothing removed, so you all can just calm your filthy minds right now," Jazz announced, not letting go of Michael's hand despite knowing how embarrassed his boyfriend might be.

Everyone laughed.

Offering Michael a smile, Jazz walked him to the door. "Thanks for the coffee."

Michael licked his lips, looked over Jazz's shoulder to the watching women, then blushed adorably. "See you tonight?"

"Counting the minutes, sweetie."

Michael's gaze dipped to Jazz's lips, but he didn't lean in for a kiss. He gave Jazz an awkward wave and left, the jingling bell on the door dancing cheerily behind him.

Jazz watched Michael until he was out of sight, then turned back to his chair. He took the broom and began sweeping up Rae's hair, though the bulk of it was in the ponytail he'd cut off for her to send to one of those places that made wigs for kids with cancer, which Jazz noticed she'd left behind. With a sigh, he tossed the bound ponytail into his drawer. He'd have Lisa Ann call Rae and see if she still wanted it. Then he laid his favorite shears, several texturizers, a razor, and a comb on a fresh towel for his next client. The methodical tasks helped him push away the negative thoughts that had been growing louder lately.

Thankfully those sensuous kisses from Michael and the considerate coffee run had all but erased Jazz's dark mood.

It was a little surprising how different his relationship with Michael was after all the men Jazz had lived with, dicks he'd sucked, and boyfriends he'd had. Things had never felt this easy with another man before, not even with Russell, the man he'd married! Every day with Michael was a new adventure or a new flavor of coffee, leaving Jazz so completely happy, comfortable, excited, and surprised, all at once.

Hindsight being what it was, Jazz knew he'd only been infatuated with Russell and the men who'd come before. While he understood that he and Michael were still in their honeymoon phase, so to speak, no other honeymoon phase had ever lasted this long—not even his real honeymoon.

Misty came up to him. "Don't worry. I'll call the sheriff and get it all taken care of."

"What?" Jazz shook his head in confusion.

"The haircut he didn't pay for?" she prompted. "I don't mind. I'll call him."

It took Jazz a moment to process what she was talking about, and then he blinked a few times and nodded.

God, I'm getting old and losing my mind.

"Yeah, sure. That would be great, Misty. Let him know Rae left her hair here too."

"Will do." Then she cocked her head to the side, studying him. "You seem out of sorts."

He forced a smile. "Just woolgathering."

Misty made a funny face at that. "You should have a session with me. Get some movement. Realign your chakras."

"Maybe I should," he agreed. Misty taught private yoga classes in a small room at the back of the salon, and chair yoga at the Bluffs.

She patted his arm, then swept back to her client. Jazz leaned on the broom handle for a moment and surveyed the salon, taking in all the smiling faces, the familiar sounds and smells. Then his gaze alighted on the picture taped on his mirror. On their first date, he and Michael had posed for a make-believe book cover, donning cowboy hats and riding atop green-screen sawhorses. They'd drunk white wine and played truth or dare. It had been such a perfect date.

Until that big goon Rocko had shot at them outside Michael's funeral home.

Last Jazz heard, that trio of cat-napping, drug-dealing misfits had gotten off on some technicality. Apparently the girl's father had survived the Canadian drug dealers and used his big bucks and good lawyers to get them all off.

I wonder if in the end Russell will get away with what he did to Dylan.

Before his mood soured again, he pulled out his phone and swiped open his text messages.

Just seeing Michael's name made him smile.

He tapped out a quick message with his thumb: *Thinking of you... still. Thanks again for the coffee. Caramel was exactly what I needed today.*

He added the kissy-face emoji and a few hearts, then closed the screen, and slipped his phone back into his pocket. Michael was probably back at the funeral parlor by now, since it was only a few blocks away. He didn't keep his phone on him when he was working downstairs in the preparation rooms or meeting mourning families, so he would respond to the message whenever he looked at his phone next.

Jazz whistled as he finished cleaning his station. Being with Michael had a way of really putting Jazz in his happy place. Over the last six weeks, they'd spent almost all of their spare time together, making love or sitting around talking and drinking white wine on Michael's straight-out-of-a-designer-magazine back patio. While reality sometimes intruded—usually in the form of Russell Withingham trying to contact him from prison or a reporter looking for some kind of gossip—Jazz had been living inside an ideal bubble.

He only hoped it wasn't going to pop any time soon.

"You guys are coming to the festival tonight?" Misty asked. "My cousins are performing at eight, remember?"

"Yes, I remember. You've only reminded me seven times today. We will be there." Jazz loved being a "we" with Michael.

As Jazz continued to sweep around his station, thoughts of Michael put a spring in his step.

Misty walked her client Marlene to the door, chatting and laughing.

As Marlene left, Jazz heard her gasp and say, "Oh, excuse me! I didn't see you there."

"I'll thank you not to touch us, please," a woman snapped in reply.

Jazz paused in his sweeping to see who the brusque woman might be, but the retail shelf distorted his view.

"Oh," Marlene said, obviously caught off guard by the woman's attitude, and she hurried off down the sidewalk.

"Come in!" Misty exclaimed and threw her arms open wide. "I'm so glad you're here."

Jazz went back to his cleanup until Misty called out, "Jazz! I want you to meet my first cousin, Dottie, and her daughter, Beatrice."

Grinning, he looked up at the woman Misty led to her chair. The younger woman followed, holding tight to her mother's hand.

Only decades of being in the beauty industry and seeing some *weird* shit enabled Jazz to keep a straight face.

Misty's two cousins were the "sister wives" from Gruff's yesterday.

Recognition flashed in Dottie's eyes. Her husband had noticed Michael and Jazz having their *sinfully homosexual* hamburgers and left that stupid pamphlet.

Well, Jazz would play nice for Misty's sake.

Introductions were made as Misty got Dottie and Beatrice settled in chairs, and then she left for the back room to mix color. He wondered if whatever colors she planned for the two sister wives were von Trapp Daddy approved, or if he'd think their new dos might lead them down the road to hell.

No matter, because Jazz would have to hold his tongue on this at least. Misty was excited to have family in her life again. Her mother had been from somewhere in Appalachia and ran away to California, where she met Misty's father. Misty was born and raised in SoCal, where she'd picked up her hippy-dippy ways—as he was sure Musgrave would call them. But after her mother passed away, her father moved back to his hometown, Lacetown. When he got sick, Misty moved here to take care of him before he passed, but then she never left. Several months ago, she'd been excited to find these musician relatives through some ancestry website.

Jazz excused himself and resumed sweeping up around his chair before his next customer arrived. He did a sweep of the room to pick up Misty's hair from the floor too.

"Eek!" Dottie jumped, lifting her feet like a cartoon woman who'd seen a mouse.

"Oh, don't mind me," Jazz said. "Just cleaning up." But when he swept under her chair, she squealed again, clutching her knees to her chest, eyes wide.

"I'm scared of brooms," she said in a breathless pant.

Jazz chuckled, and then he realized she was being dead serious. "Sorry about that," he said, quickly collecting the rest of the hair and hurrying to the garbage can.

Good Lord. I thought I'd seen everything in this business!

Jazz went into the back room and told Misty what happened. He also told her that Dottie's husband had given them a Bible tract the day before, after Norbert had arrived and caused a scene.

"Not sure about these relatives of yours," Jazz went on. "And they're staying at your house? Hide the good china and *don't* lend them money."

Misty—of course—was understanding and told Jazz, "Be nice. Dottie has had a tough time of things. On the phone last week, she told me that her first husband, Gregory, died in a freak accident in their home ten years ago, leaving her with five-year-old twins, a boy and a girl. Such a tragedy the way he died." She leaned in and lowered her voice, though no one could possibly overhear them. "He was doing some work out in the garage and got his scarf caught in the chain of the door opener. It hung him right there in the garage, and Dorothy and the twins found him when they came home from grocery shopping."

"Oh my God."

"I know, right? So awful. Not long after that, she married Herschel, the preacher. I get the feeling Herschel might be a marriage of convenience. He was Gregory's best friend, you know, that kind of thing. She never had a job outside the home when Gregory died. And Herschel seems... well? He gave me his credit card this morning and told me to let the girls have anything done they wanted. Taylor is going to give them mani-pedis too."

"Tell her to hide the brooms."

Misty widened her eyes seriously. "I will."

Jazz quirked his pursed lips to the side in a half smile. "Well, they're different, I'll say. Never seen a person afraid of a broom before. Maybe somebody beat her with one."

Misty gave him an airy gesture. "All the more reason to be nice. I know they're different." When Jazz's brows shot up, she nodded. "Okay, very different, but that's not such a bad thing. They're excellent musicians. Dottie's son, Oslo—"

"Oslo?" Jazz interrupted, but Misty never stopped talking.

"—is incredibly talented. They're playing tonight. Will you still come see them? Even though Herschel left that pamphlet?"

"I promised you we would. And I promise to drive my scooter, not my broom."

"You are such a witch," Misty said, obviously trying not to laugh.

"You know it!"

Leaving her to mix the rest of her color, Jazz went up to the front desk to wait for his next customer. There was a man in the waiting room, whose eyes widened when he spied Jazz.

"Are you Jazz Dilworth?"

"One and the same," he quipped, hoping in the back of his mind his schedule wasn't messed up and he'd been double-booked. His next client was Trish Johnson, the mayor, not a men's cut. "How can I help you?"

The man handed him a manila envelope, and Jazz reached for it. When Jazz had it in his hand, the man stepped back and nodded. "You've been served."

CHAPTER FIVE

"Fleishman?"

Michael looked up from his desk and over his glasses, startled to see Sheriff Hilton Musgrave standing in his office doorway. "Hilton," Michael said, setting down his pen. "What brings you in today?"

Please don't let it be a murder.

Musgrave lingered in the doorway, spinning his sheriff's hat in his hand. If Michael didn't know better, he would say the sheriff looked nervous. Scared, even.

"What can I help you with?" he asked again.

Musgrave took a big gulp of air and stepped into Michael's office a little too quickly for normal. He was a very large man, the kind who actually shopped at a big-and-tall store because he more than fit those requirements.

Mr. Pickles had been napping atop the kitty condo in the corner, and he raised his head with a curious meow.

When Musgrave shut the door, Michael sat back in his chair, somewhat startled. The sheriff's movements were jerky and awkward as he reached into his pocket and pulled out his wallet. He withdrew a couple of bills and tossed them on Michael's desk. The money scattered a bit, and Mr. Pickles let out a warning hiss of displeasure.

Michael shook his head in confusion. "What's this?"

"Jazz cut my daughter's hair this morning, and I forgot to pay him."

Michael collected the bills and stacked them together. "Oh. Well, you could've taken it directly to Jazz."

"Figured you would see him before I did," Musgrave said. "Ain't you two living together?"

Michael's face warmed. "No, we keep separate households." *Dammit, why do I always sound so stuffy?* "But I'll see that he gets this."

It was common knowledge that the new hairdresser who had moved to Lacetown last summer was dating the mortician. Michael generally didn't like to be the subject of gossip, but when it came to being connected to Jazz, somehow it seemed more bearable.

Musgrave stood in the middle of Michael's small office, his large bulk taking up a lot of space. Mr. Pickles's wary green eyes watched his every move, tail swishing when it seemed Musgrave wasn't leaving.

Michael had been schooled well in grief counseling and could always tell when a person was desperate for conversation or to spill some truth they were holding in. Many spoke of the deathbed confession, but the bereaved confession was almost more notorious.

"Is there something else I can help you with, Sheriff?"

"It's Amanda Rae," he said in a rush. He sat down on the edge of the chair, and it creaked when he leaned forward, his face urgent. "She got her hair cut off like a bull—" He stopped himself short and sat back, chewing his lip.

"Were you going to say bull dyke?" Michael asked, not sure if he was offended or amused.

The sheriff ran a big paw over his face and scratched at his curly buzz-cut hair. "I was, and I shouldn't have. I know that. It's just that... I don't know what to do."

"About?" Michael prompted.

"She said she's a lesbian now. And she wants me to call her Rae."

He glanced at the fat black-and-white kitty watching them, then leaned forward and said in a conspiratorial whisper, "Like a *man's* name."

Michael sat back in his chair and steepled his fingers.

So the sheriff's daughter was gay or bi. Was he seeking advice on how to handle it from Michael? Well, Michael was probably one of the only two gay men in town that Musgrave knew. Obviously Musgrave wasn't comfortable with Jazz if he was paying Michael for the haircut, and Michael had gone all through school with Hilton.

"All right," Michael began hesitantly. "Would you like to talk about it?"

He felt somewhat disingenuous to the rainbow by employing the calm tone he used on the bereaved, but the sheriff seemed genuinely distressed. While that should have annoyed Michael—it was long past high school for them, for God's sake—Michael found a well of patience to draw from.

The sheriff's very presence here signified that, while he was having trouble accepting his daughter's orientation, he came to the source, so to speak, asking for advice. He was making an effort, and so Michael needed to do the same.

"How can she even know?" Musgrave said, sounding like the punk he'd been in ninth grade math class, telling the teacher that he'd never use algebra. "She's nineteen. She's a kid. She can't know. I never should've let her go to college in Chicago. Girls always do this lesbian thing in college to get attention."

While Michael knew that to be *somewhat* true, he didn't say as much. After all, hadn't Steve Childress—Michael's supposedly straight employee—implied he'd had some bi-curious adventures in his youth? Experimentation and orientation, however, weren't mutually exclusive or defining either. Human sexuality was a complicated topic, not that he intended to go in-depth with Musgrave.

"Be that as it may, it might not be that," Michael said.

"Amanda Rae's never even had a boyfriend. She doesn't know what she wants."

"Did you know what you wanted when you had the entire football team pick up Heather Reynolds on their shoulders and march her through the hallway so you could ask her to prom?"

Musgrave chuckled at the memory and then frowned. "That's different."

"Is it?" Michael countered. "Were you confused about your attraction to Heather? Was it a phase? Did you need to date a few men to figure out that you liked women?"

"Of course not, but...." He squirmed, some of his confidence deflating.

"Then why are you so quick to assume it's a phase for Amanda Rae?" He chose to use her full name to ensure Musgrave was listening.

"I guess," he said, face screwed up in thought. "But you took Christy James to prom. So obviously you had doubts."

Michael chuckled and shook his head. "Of course I did. I wanted to like girls."

"You did?" He looked surprised.

Michael sighed.

He'd never vocalized that before, not with Jazz or any other gay man. But the way the sheriff was hanging on Michael's every word, if it could help Hilton understand his daughter, maybe it was time to share something he had never told another soul.

"I didn't want to be gay," Michael admitted. Mr. Pickles let out a plaintive meow, and Michael half imagined his beloved pet saying, *Daddy, don't be sad.* His kitty always seemed very intuitive. Michael studied Musgrave before he continued. "Why would I want my life to be harder? Why would I want people to think I'm different or even more weird than being the mortician's son? Why wouldn't I rather be like ninety percent of the people on this planet? Why would I want my father to yell at me in a crowded beauty salon?"

The sheriff flinched at that.

Michael leaned forward. "*That's* why I dated Christy in high school and took her to prom. Not because I couldn't make up my mind or being straight was a phase. I was trying to see if I could change what I already knew and felt because I was afraid of the truth. But dating her didn't change who I really was on the inside."

The sheriff's eyes widened, and he sat back, Michael's quiet words like a slap in the face.

"Shit," he muttered. "Shit, shit, shit." Then he stood up so fast Michael flinched back.

Mr. Pickles hissed from his perch on top of the kitty condo, then scurried inside one of the cubbies. Michael could see his fluffy tail swishing in agitation below his new vantage point.

The sheriff began pacing the office like a giant bear in a small cage Michael had seen in a nature documentary once. "Shit, shit."

He stopped and glanced at Michael. "Shit." Then he began pacing again.

Michael assumed his point had gotten through the sheriff's thick skull, so it wasn't really a surprise when Musgrave turned and looked at Michael again.

"What the hell am I supposed to do now?" he asked, his big hands all but crushing the hat he held. "She thinks I hate her."

"Tell her you don't. Tell her the haircut just surprised you and that, given time, you'll learn to like her hair. Don't say 'I still love you.' Those words will make things worse, trust me on that. Tell her you love her no matter what."

I love you no matter what, Michael," Dad had said when Michael came out to him, and Michael loved him dearly for such genuine words. The unexpected memory of his father's kind eyes and his soft voice stung Michael with a startling pang of loss. Oh, he missed Dad. Dad really would have liked Jazz, so very much.

The sheriff put his fists on his hips and shook his head at himself. "She never got over Jenny leaving. And now she's gonna think I've abandoned her too. Shit, shit, shit." With each subsequent curse, he jerked his head.

Michael stood and walked around the desk. He thought about patting the sheriff on the arm, but decided against it. Instead, he positioned himself in front of the man, clasping his hands in front of him. "Why don't you stop saying *shit* and go find your daughter and talk to her?"

Musgrave pursed his lips and nodded, that gruff sheriff expression back. "Yeah, I'll do that," he said, sounding like a man on a mission. "Fleishman, thanks."

He returned his hat to his buzz-cut curls and nodded at Michael with determination.

Before he turned to go, the office door burst open.

Steve Childress, the all-around fix-it man for the funeral home, stood there with wide eyes.

"Captain, come quick!" Steve cried, using the nickname he'd given Michael years ago. He gripped the doorknob so tightly his knuckles whitened.

"What the hell, Childress?" Musgrave snapped.

"There's a body." Steve's chest rose and fell rapidly as if he'd run there.

"It's a funeral home," Musgrave said with a sigh. "Of course there's a body."

"In the hearse." Steve looked at Michael. "Captain, someone's left a dead body in the hearse!"

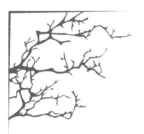

CHAPTER SIX

"*What?***"** Michael said.

"There's a dead body in the hearse," Steve repeated, blue eyes wild. "I-I opened the door.... Looks like he's been strangled or something."

Musgrave's expression tightened. "Show me."

They rushed through the funeral home and out the back entrance, which opened onto the parking lot. Steve strode across the asphalt with Musgrave right behind him and Michael hurrying to keep up. Having helped Michael pick up bodies for years, Steve knew enough to stay out of a crime scene and stopped just outside the door to the garage, but he looked particularly disturbed by the finding.

Michael put a hand on Steve's shoulder as Musgrave slowly entered the three-car garage. "Are you okay?"

"It's a shock, Captain," Steve said and licked his lips. "Really got to me for some reason."

Stomach sinking, Michael gave a determined nod. "Okay. Thanks for the warning. Sometimes no amount of training can prepare you for a shock like that."

The lights were on in the garage when Michael stepped inside. There were three vehicles parked in a row, his personal Camry, a Cadillac hearse, and the county coroner van—all kept polished and shiny, courtesy of Steve. Musgrave stood on the driver's side of the hearse, the door open as he frowned down into the seat. With great trepidation Michael made his way over.

He sucked in a breath at the sight of a man with his head slightly askew, sitting in the driver's seat, his hands positioned on the steering wheel in a macabre fashion. Overcome with a morbid curiosity, Michael leaned in very close, careful not to touch anything.

"Dispatch," Musgrave said into his radio, making Michael start and flinch back. "This is the sheriff. I need all hands at the funeral parlor, stat."

As Musgrave communicated with his team of deputies, Michael resumed his visual examination of the body.

"Skin's bruised and slightly broken around his throat," he said calmly. "Some blood, but it doesn't look like the carotid has been cut. Most likely strangulation with a thin ligature of some kind. If he was killed in the hearse, he would've had to have been strangled from behind, and the murderer would've had to be on their knees and short. There's not a lot of height in the back." Michael glanced around his garage. With all three vehicles, there wasn't much space for a struggle, and everything seemed perfectly in order. "Or perhaps the victim was murdered elsewhere and transported here?"

But why here? Why my business?

"How the hell did he get inside your locked garage, Fleishman?" Musgrave asked.

Michael shook his head. "My question exactly, but I have no idea. I would've heard the garage door opening last night, if that's when he was murdered." The driver side of his Camry was mere feet away from the body. Steve always backed the vehicles into the garage, but Michael didn't. "He wasn't here when I got home at seven thirty. I would've seen him."

Musgrave nodded at the positions of the vehicles, both drivers' sides facing each other. "You got an alarm system?"

"On the house and the parlor. I have security cameras, but the motion sensors are only aimed at the house and parlor entrances. If anyone moved through those areas after the alarm was set, I would've gotten an alert on my phone."

After the attempted break-in by some bumbling drug dealers who cat-napped Mr. Pickles, Michael and Steve had upgraded the security to a high-end alarm system with cameras, motion sensors, and phone-synching capabilities.

"But you didn't," Musgrave surmised. "Must mean there's a blind spot in your security."

"I never thought anyone would bother with lawn equipment, and the vehicles are insured," Michael said, his mind whirling. "Why arm a garage?"

Never in his wildest dreams would Michael have imagined a scenario such as this!

His gaze drifted to the window on the north side of the garage, above the workbench where Steve stored all the gardening tools, fertilizers, and such.

"Someone could've broken in through the door or that window," Michael said aloud. "They either brought the body, or two people broke in and only one of them left."

He hoped there were fingerprints.

"What's all the fuss about out here?" Kitty asked as she joined Steve outside.

"Don't come in," Michael instructed her. "This is a crime scene. We can't contaminate it."

"A crime scene?" Kitty exclaimed. "What's happened?"

"Someone left a body in the hearse," Steve said.

"Isn't that where bodies usually go?" Kitty asked. Michael could all but imagine the buxom blonde quirking her brows in tandem with her sarcasm.

"Not the driver's seat," Steve said.

"Oh," Kitty said, her tone grasping the severity. "Who is it?"

A few clacks of her heels on the concrete floor of the garage made both Michael and Musgrave look up sharply.

"Keep back!" Musgrave's stern demand echoed through the garage before Michael could say anything. "I don't want this scene contaminated any further!"

"I was just trying to see if I recognized the victim," Kitty said, pouting as she backed out of the garage. She fixed Musgrave's broad back with a glare, and Michael wondered how either of them managed to get through a holiday dinner since Kitty had married Hilton's younger brother, Marty, which was short for Marriott.

Musgrave's parents had named all their kids after the hotels in which they'd been conceived: Hilton, Marriott, and their younger sister, Holiday. Jazz had once called the Musgraves the poor man's Howard family, since Ron Howard's kids had middle names based on the location they were conceived too.

"You don't want to see him," Steve said quietly to Kitty.

"So it's a man?" Kitty leaned left and right, craning her neck in an effort to see the body more clearly.

Michael studied the victim. The man looked familiar, but he couldn't place how he knew him.

Then it clicked.

This was the man who Norbert had been arguing with last night at Gruff's Grub.

The one still pining for Norbert....

Michael straightened up, his vision spinning a little. He shook his head to clear it, like he'd just walked into a wall, and then took several stumbling steps backward, bumping into his car. He leaned his weight against it, thoughts and questions tumbling around in his brain.

Could it be a coincidence that Norbert had shown up in town the day before a body appeared in Michael's hearse? The man's very presence felt like a harbinger of death. But he wouldn't have killed this man, would he? Strangulation was a crime of passion, though, and they'd been former lovers, or so Michael and Jazz had understood from the argument. And this man had stolen Norbert's band, or so Norbert had claimed.

A flash of déjà vu hit Michael hard, transporting him back to Hardscrabble Beach, kneeling on the rocky sand and staring down at a drowned young man with missing hands. Once more he knew just enough of the victim's identity that a cold slick of sweat worked down his spine, like a warning, sharp and personal.

"I-I saw this man last night," Michael stammered, forcing a deep breath. Norbert had said his name more than once, but Michael couldn't recall it. Jazz might be able to remember, if Michael could get a minute to give him a quick call. And the sound of Jazz's low and sexy voice would help him calm down. Unfortunately he'd left his phone in his office.

"Where'd you see him?" Musgrave demanded.

"He was talking to Norbert Farthington."

"Farthington? He's back in town?" Musgrave turned in a circle, one big hand tightening into a fist. "You saw him *and* the vic, last night? What is it with you knowing murder vics all the time, Fleishman?"

"Twice is hardly all the time, Hilton," Michael bristled, the sheriff's brusque demeanor helping him get ahold of himself. He pushed off his car and stood straighter. "And it was a coincidence that we even saw them."

"It's a helluva coincidence. We've only had two murders in town. Now, tell me how you know the vic *this* time? And who was the other part of your *we*? Dilworth?"

"Yes, and I don't know this man." Gesturing to the body, Michael shook his head. "But Jazz and I did see him and Norbert have a disagreement last night at Gruff's Grub." He then explained, with as much detail as he could remember, an accounting of the argument between Norbert and his former lover and bandmates.... "The Lanky something or other. That was part of the name of the victim's band," Michael said, wishing he had Jazz's affinity for remembering names. When he wrapped up his story, Musgrave, Kitty, and Steve were chuckling about Gruff tossing Norbert out.

"Wish I would've seen that." Musgrave shook his head in mirth, and then he sobered. "Looks like I need to track down our favorite snake of a PR rep and question him thoroughly. Unless you have any other ideas on perp or motive."

"My first choice for perpetrator would be Norbert," Michael replied. "The victim was his jilted lover, and there appeared to be bad blood between them still. As for motive, it could be a crime of passion."

Musgrave sneered. "A crime of *passion*?"

"Yes, sheriff," Michael said with more edge than he'd intended to his tone. "No matter what you'd like to think, there can be passion between two men."

Outside the garage door, Steve coughed and Kitty muttered, "Uh-oh."

"I understand that, Fleishman," Musgrave said slowly. "I just didn't like imagining Norbert in any kind of passionate activity."

Before Michael could reply, a new voice joined Kitty's and Steve's.

"What's going on?"

"Someone's been murdered," Steve replied, voice tight.

Michael turned as his apprentice, Ezra Glum, arrived and stood alongside his other two employees, poking his head inside like an adorable puppet, an undeniable gleam of excitement in his eye. "Someone was murdered in your garage?"

Kitty scowled at him. "Don't you have floors to wash or something?" she said snappishly.

Chastised, Ezra pushed his glasses up his nose, mumbling something Michael didn't catch. Kitty crossed her arms and chewed on her long red pinky nail.

"Yes, Ezra," Michael said calmly. "There's been a murder. Again."

"Not to bring the mood down even further, but Elaine called from the Bluffs," Kitty said.

"Oh no, not another one," Michael said. "Who is it now? We already have Grace Murray here."

"I'm afraid it's Ruth Blankenship. She was found in her apartment this morning. Looks like she died in her sleep."

When it rains it pours. Michael sighed. "I'm sorry to hear that. She's one of Jazz's clients. She missed an appointment with him yesterday."

The mention of Jazz and his clients made Musgrave flinch, and Michael figured he was feeling a twinge of guilt for confronting Jazz earlier about his daughter's haircut. Good. Maybe it would make Musgrave think twice in his future dealings with both Jazz and his own daughter.

"So many dying over at the Bluffs lately," Michael said with a shake of his head.

"Kind of expected, isn't it?" Musgrave grumbled. "I mean, it's an old-folks home."

"It's a retirement community, not heaven's waiting room." Kitty threw her brother-in-law a cool glance.

"Any chance we can get the van out to pick up the body?" Michael asked Musgrave before the man could fire off a sharp retort.

Musgrave turned his glare from his sister-in-law to Michael. "After my deputies get here, dust for prints, and photograph the scene, yeah, you can take it out. Shouldn't take that long."

"That's fine," Michael said with a nod. He looked at his staff. "Everyone, back inside. There's work to be done."

Musgrave turned away to bark into the radio on his shoulder, "Tanner, where the hell are you already? There's been a murder!"

"I'm here, sir!" Tanner answered in person, stepping inside the garage. He was a polite young ginger-haired man, and had been a part of the team who'd rescued Mr. Pickles. It felt reassuring having him there, though he was sure Jazz would have something snide to say about that.

While Musgrave filled Tanner in and Michael's employees left, Michael looked over the man in the hearse.

Norbert's old lover, a jilted one apparently. Had Norbert killed him? If so, for what reason?

And why kill him, then prop him up in Michael's hearse? To frame him?

Norbert had seemed shocked to see his old lover, but was there more to their history? Something so sinister it was worth killing the man? *What's his name again?*

This appeared to be a case cut out for someone like Michael's fictional hero, Brock Hammer. The thought was exciting, but also made Michael's insides twist with guilt.

He had not yet told Jazz he was rereading the Brock Hammer series from the beginning. It felt dishonest, but he couldn't help loving the books all the more after he'd had a hand in solving one horrendous murder. It was like he was reading them for the first time, Russell's words laying out even more subtle clues toward Dylan's death. Michael had been keeping a file of everything within the pages similar to the way Dylan had been murdered, and he hoped to present it to the prosecution to see if it would help their case.

The sharp whine of police sirens announced the arrival of more deputies, startling Michael from his thoughts.

"The rest of the team is here, sir," Tanner reported. He smiled, like an excited puppy, eager to please.

"I have ears," Musgrave muttered, then followed that up with, "Tanner, check the victim for ID."

Tanner went a little pale, but he pulled latex gloves from his pocket and approached the hearse. Michael watched the deputy carefully check the victim's pockets before straightening up and shrugging. "No wallet or phone."

Musgrave turned to Michael. "All right. Looks like we should start with Farthington. Any idea where he might be?"

"I have absolutely no clue," Michael assured him. "But apparently the victim's band was scheduled to play at the festival sometime this weekend.

Perhaps examining the list of acts will provide a name to our John Doe, and a clue as to Norbert's location. Right now, I should retrieve my kit and have Steve bring a gurney for the victim."

"Yeah, go ahead. My team will get started collecting evidence." He met Michael's eye. "Looks like we have another murder, Fleishman. Let's hope it's less high-profile than the last one, eh?"

"Indeed."

Halfway back to the funeral home, Michael spied a small group of onlookers. The police activity at the funeral parlor had piqued his neighbors' curiosity and brought them out to gawk already.

Michael really disliked the negative light a murder might land on his business, and he made his way over. The group consisted mostly of his neighbors, with a few people from town and some strangers interspersed. A particularly tall man with blond wavy hair and a bold yellow hawaiian shirt caught his eye. He seemed to be staring right at Michael rather than all the police activity. Michael had never seen him before. A tourist maybe?

"Ladies and gentlemen," Michael began, approaching the onlookers with his hands raised in a placating manner. "This is a police matter. Please let our deputies take care of it and go about your business."

"What's going on?" Rob Wilkerson asked. He lived in the bungalow on the alley directly behind Michael's house, with Michael's upper deck overlooking the back of his garage.

"I am not at liberty to say."

"I heard on my police scanner that there was a murder," Rob insisted. "Someone was strangled."

Startling Michael a bit, the tall man in the yellow shirt spirited away, pulling a cell phone out of his pocket.

How bizarre.

Michael dismissed him and turned back to his gawking neighbors. "I'm not at liberty to say," he repeated.

Mrs. Merriweather grumbled, clutching her Pomeranian, Reginald, which always barked like a savage beast when Mr. Pickles sat in the window. "Lacetown used to be a nice place. All that riffraff coming in from Chicago and Detroit is ruining it."

After a few more minutes of discussion, Michael managed to calm and corral his neighbors to return home. Then before he headed inside, he stopped by the garage and asked Musgrave to have a deputy keep the pedestrians away.

Musgrave cursed. "Damn rubberneckers. Tanner!"

The ginger deputy snapped to. "Yes, sir?"

"Why aren't you keeping the civilians away from our crime scene? Use your head!"

"Yes, sir!" The man scurried away, and Michael resisted the urge to make a comment about Musgrave's less than polite management skills.

With a wave to the sheriff, he returned to the funeral home, hoping examination of the body might provide a clue as to why the man was killed and left in Michael's garage. In his hearse, specifically, propped up like he was driving somewhere. Randomly, he thought of the religious pamphlet handed to them at the diner.

The road to hell, indeed.

He had to agree with Mrs. Merriweather. What on earth was happening in Lacetown?

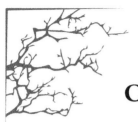

CHAPTER SEVEN

Having such a gruesome body left inside Michael's hearse felt like a warning. But a warning of what?

During their investigation of the crime scene, Musgrave's deputies had circled the outside of the garage and discovered some disturbed mulch and broken petunias beneath the garage window. That was the most likely point of entry, but they'd found no prints—not even Steve's or Michael's—which meant it had been wiped clean. But how did the murderer get a body inside? Did he drag it? Was there an accomplice? Or had the victim followed his killer willingly?

As expected, Musgrave had been overbearing to Michael and his staff, telling each of them *"Everyone's a suspect until Sheriff Musgrave says they're not."* They all cooperated—although Kitty had some choice words for her brother-in-law—and overall Michael chalked the whole thing up to typical dealings with their county sheriff. But he didn't think Musgrave believed any of them were involved.

At least he hoped not.

Naturally, Norbert was a prime suspect until they had more information on the victim and his life. Some people had a morbid fascination for death and everything around it, and outwardly Norbert fit the profile of someone with a death kink. Had Norbert lured his former lover here, maybe to have sex in the hearse and then kill him? Was this an illicit tryst gone wrong?

All of it was speculation at this point.

Michael shook his head, trying to focus on the task at hand. He had three bodies to attend to. Grace Murray was already in the cooler, and Ruth Blankenship would be arriving soon. Thankfully, his facility was large enough to handle the sudden influx. Most funeral parlors subbed out embalming, but Michael still ran an old-fashioned business. A "one stop shop" as Grandpa often said. In the parlor's basement, he had a large storage room with traditional caskets—some people liked to custom order one, but most were content with classics—a preparation room for embalming, and a separate area specifically for autopsies. In order to keep the chains of evidence intact and to isolate the criminal or unusual cases requiring an autopsy from the day-to-day functions, the two work areas were divided by a locked door.

The man from the hearse lay on a gurney in this secured area, contained within a body bag. As he washed up, Michael looked over his shoulder at the black bag. Just yesterday this man had been living and breathing, having dinner with those two women. He was a member of a band, and he harbored bad blood over an old relationship with Norbert.

Norbert Farthington was still managing to be a pain in the ass. Jazz had insisted yesterday he was fine, but Michael knew seeing Norbert again had rattled him.

Hell, it had rattled Michael too.

Even though he'd had an epiphany last night that he was in love with Jazz, his dreams had been a swirling mix of blood, gunfire, Russell's airy laughter at the signing, and poor Mr. Pickles in that goon's grip.

Maybe Michael should lay off the Brock Hammer novels before bedtime. Listening to *Frigid Forensics* and tweeting professional tips to the host probably didn't help his overactive imagination either. But he really did love hearing about those left behind receiving some kind of closure.

After drying his hands, Michael pulled on a pair of gloves and solemnly approached the gurney. He eased the zipper open and spread the flaps apart to look at the man's face. Blue eyes clouded by death, a Roman nose that appeared to have been broken at least once in the past, maybe twice. Blond hair threaded with silver. He had been handsome, something Michael had overlooked during the commotion at Gruff's.

"I wish I knew a name to call you," Michael said and crossed his arms. "This feels very strange. I feel as if there is some kind of connection between us, yet I don't know who you are and have no idea how to refer to you. Therefore, my apologies if this feels impersonal. But I've been thinking about you. Well, thinking about you since yesterday evening. Or more specifically, since about two hours ago when you were found dead in my hearse."

He started to pace alongside the table as he continued to talk.

"There are a lot of possibilities for the reason you were left in my hearse. I can't help but take it personally of course, even though it could have merely been an act of convenience. Perhaps you were murdered nearby and the window in my garage provided an easy way to quickly get you out of sight.

"Then again, it may be more personal, a kind of vendetta if you will, against myself or the business. Either way, you were discovered on my property, and, though it pains me to say this for several reasons, I feel it's only fitting that I recuse myself from performing your autopsy."

With that finally said, Michael stopped pacing and looked at the man. "This is nothing personal against you, so please do not take it as such. I would rather be the one to uncover the identity of whoever did this to you. But instead, I will turn you over to Parker Trevino from Bridlestop." He held up a gloved hand as if to stop the corpse from protesting. "I know you may have heard that Trevino and I have a bit of bad blood between us, but do not let that concern you. He is a skilled coroner for the neighboring county, and he will treat you well and work with law enforcement to solve your murder."

Michael zipped the bag closed and rolled the gurney across the room to the double storage cooler, confident in his decision. With careful movements, he transferred the body to the stainless steel drawer, slid it into the cooler, then closed the door.

After peeling off his gloves and washing his hands, Michael headed upstairs to call Trevino, already dreading the anticipated smug tone of the man's voice.

Parker Trevino was the Ottawa County coroner. He also ran a funeral home and crematorium, and while Michael referred his clients to Trevino for cremation, he really disliked the pompous man. He should have been a peer Michael could bounce ideas off, but Trevino deigned to dislike Michael the day he'd taken the Harbor County coroner position after Michael's grandfather had retired. Grandpa despised Trevino as well, and after years of dealing with the petty man, Michael had to agree.

But personality aside—like he'd told Norbert's old lover—Trevino *did* know his way around an autopsy.

As Michael dialed Trevino from his office phone, Mr. Pickles leaped up on the desk, seeking attention with curious meows.

"It's been a hectic day," he said. "I know you didn't like the sheriff in here, blustering, did you?"

Michael stroked his fat kitty's back while he waited for the phone to be answered, the rings grating on his nerves while Mr. Pickles's contented purrs soothed the irritation. He always brought his cat to work.

Naturally reticent like most cats—except around his preferred humans—Mr. Pickles was a staple in the business, and clients found his presence calming. He always seemed to know which person to befriend during arrangements or showings, and Michael just adored him.

"Trevino Funeral Home, how may I assist you?"

Michael rolled his eyes. Even the woman answering Trevino's phone sounded smug.

"Hello, this is Michael Fleishman, the Harbor County coroner. I need to speak with Parker Trevino, please."

Perhaps his own tone carried some annoyance, as at the sound of Michael's voice, Mr. Pickles jumped from the edge of his desk onto the kitty condo. Once there, he meowed, swishing his tail from the curved perch he'd taken, big green eyes watching Michael.

"He's with a client at the moment, Mr. Fleishman...," the woman started, but then stopped. "Oh, wait, I hear him coming down the hall. Can you hold?"

Without waiting for a response, she put him on hold. Soothing classical music began to play, marred by some kind of staticky interference. Michael's nerves tightened even more with each burst of static, and when Trevino finally picked up, it almost pushed him over the edge.

"Michael Fleishman. What can I do for you?"

Trevino's voice was deep and smooth, lacquered, it seemed, to a honeyed tone from years of dealing with the grieving public. For Michael, the sound of Trevino's voice invoked thoughts of used car salesmen and insurance agents. He really hoped he never sounded like that. If he ever did, he supposed Jazz would call him out on it.

There's that anticipated domesticity again.

"Find a job too taxing for your older equipment?" Trevino asked.

"No," Michael said, unable to keep the competitive edge from his voice. He hated the fact that Trevino knew all the buttons to push when it came to him too. *Bastard.* "I've come into a murder case that I need to recuse myself from."

"You're suspected of murder?" Trevino's voice went up at the end, and Michael desperately wished he'd phrased things better.

"Not in the least, thank you very much," he said with a sniff. "But a body has been found on the property of my funeral home, and I feel the right thing to do is for me to step back and have someone else take over."

"Oh, my, my," Trevino said. "I'm sure it galls you to have to ask me, doesn't it?"

"Parker, I don't know why you think there's some kind of competition between us," Michael said with a sigh. "I respect your work and was devastated to learn about the recent fire in your crematorium."

Trevino blustered, and Michael buried a smile.

The fire had been a blunder on Trevino's part. Michael might not have a crematorium of his own, but he knew better than to stuff a five-hundred-pound man into an oven without allowing for proper air circulation.

"Yes, thank you for your concern," Trevino snapped, his cool shattering for just a moment.

Michael spun in his chair, very much enjoying the flustered sounds on the other end of the line. Taunting the man was almost fun. He waggled his brows at Mr. Pickles, but his cat merely licked his paws, not amused by the funeral parlor gossip chain. Their industry was a small community, and the story had managed to make its rounds, and Trevino had definitely been the brunt of a joke... or ten.

"We'll be completely rebuilt soon," Trevino finally said, obviously having gotten himself under control. "The smoke damage meant our display rooms will be updated as well. We'll soon have the premier location for families celebrating the lives of their loved ones."

A thought whipped through Michael's mind, and he sat up straight. Had Trevino intentionally stuffed poor Mr. Jones in the furnace, hoping for a fire in order to have insurance remodel his outdated parlor?

How utterly disgraceful!

"And convenient," Michael muttered. His display rooms were circa 1995. But still... at the expense of treating a body with such disrespect? Totally unthinkable!

"What was that, Fleishman?" Trevino demanded.

"Nothing," he quickly said. "So do you think you can come over to my facility and perform an autopsy, or should I call U of M?"

"No, no," he spit out. "Don't call the university. I can be there later today. Will seven work?"

"Yes, that will be fine," Michael said. He bit back his irritation and spoke in a serious voice. "I'll be assisting with the investigation where I can, so I appreciate your assistance in keeping everything on the up-and-up."

"You simply need to say thank you," Trevino quipped, smug once more. "But I'll be there. No need to worry now. My work is without equal."

Michael hadn't been *worried*, but he didn't argue. It wasn't easy. "I'll make sure that Sheriff Musgrave is here to inform you of all the details thus far."

After hasty goodbyes, Michael hung up the phone with Trevino—that ass. Jazz would probably come up with some hilarious but apropos nickname for the man, but idiot, ass, and bastard were as original as Michael could get at the moment.

I need to talk to Jazz.

Michael had his cell phone out and his texts open before he thought better of it. Jazz was at work. He shouldn't bother him. This was a conversation best had in person—if Jazz hadn't heard the gossip already.

With slow movements he scrolled through their recent text messages, smiling as he remembered the moments.

Early in the week, Jazz had sent: *How's my mortician on a hot tin roof 2day?*

And later that same day: *Having inappropriate thoughts about u while working on my clients. Hopefully ur not doing the same!*

Just seeing those texts and all the playful emojis Jazz added soothed some of the disquiet niggling at the back of Michael's mind.

No, he would tell Jazz about everything tonight.

Fingers itching to get to work on the mystery, Michael fired up his laptop. He might not be able to perform the autopsy, but his hands weren't tied.

An ID on the man would be an excellent place to start. He pulled up the Lacetown website and found a list of festivals on the city's activities and events page. Michael looked over the band names for the current festival, hoping something jumped out at him so they could piece together who might've wanted the man dead and why.

And more importantly, why they would leave the body in his Caddy.

Dammit, Musgrave is going to have to impound my hearse!

As he scrolled, a name on the weekend schedule popped out to him—The Lanky Balladeers!

"That's it!" Michael said with a rush of excitement.

He clicked on the band's links and was led over to a Facebook page. He read their bio.

The Lanky Balladeers is a folk-punk band from Chicago....

Michael read on, scrolling through pics and posts.

Bill Denton, that was their victim's name.

With a wan smile, Michael clicked on his picture.

"Why were you left in my hearse?" Michael asked the image.

Denton was on stage with his guitar and the photographer had caught him with a huge smile that made him look very handsome. It seemed he'd really loved playing music. Sad he'd never get another chance.

Michael surfed the page and found the other bandmates.

Sonya Metcalf and Ally Roberts. All of their personal profiles were private, and the images they used in their profile pics and banners didn't provide much information. It did seem that Ally had joined the band recently. The Lanky Balladeers had a string of recent guitarists, actually.

Michael supposed in and of itself that wasn't fishy.

How many musicians would really want to stay with a folk-punk band?

Michael clicked on a link to the song Denton had mentioned last night, "Skinflint Norbie and His Walkabout Shoes."

What an absurd way of getting even with an old lover.

The slash of electric guitar cut through the twang of a harmonica, and a strumming banjo kept the beat. Michael cringed as a crooning male bluegrass voice began to sing:

"*You played the part, you broke my heart... all with those walkabout shoes... I was a boy, it was your ploy... all with those walkabout shoes....*"

"What in the name of Glen Campbell's ghost are you listening to?"

Michael looked up and found Kitty standing in his office doorway, face scrunched up like someone had tracked dog poop across the carpet.

He turned the volume off. "Just some investigating."

"On what?" she asked seriously. "Hillbilly torture techniques?"

That made him laugh. "No, but I found the name of our victim." He quickly scratched the names of the three bandmates down for Musgrave, along with the link to the Facebook page.

"How are you holding up?" Kitty asked.

Michael looked up at her, noting the perfect red lips and flawless blonde hair. She was the picture of beauty and true concern.

"I'm okay," he assured her.

She arched one brow like a knowing mother whose son was withholding that he ate the last of the cookies.

Chuckling, he raised his hands. "Okay, I'm still in shock, but now I'm more curious about why a body was left here, in my hearse."

"I'm totally freaked out about it," she admitted. "Those beer tents at the festival can't pour me one fast enough."

"Indeed."

"Are you and Jazz going tonight?" she asked, then waved airily in the direction of the garage. "Despite all this."

"We planned to."

"Good. I like the two of you together," she decided, as if she had been the matchmaker. "He's loosened you up."

It was Michael's turn to raise his brows. "And I was so uptight before?"

Kitty made a very unladylike snort, then opened the adjoining door between their offices and sauntered to her desk. "Shouldn't you be preparing for the autopsy?"

Michael's amusement faded as he realized he'd have to tell Kitty about Trevino. She wasn't going to be happy about having her space invaded. Trevino really had a way of getting under people's skin.

Michael pushed to his feet, the names of the victim and his bandmates clutched in his hand. He headed for his office door, calling out behind him, "Trevino will be conducting the autopsy. He'll be here tonight at seven."

"What!"

Michael hurried to the back entrance, knowing he was taking the chicken's way out, but not wanting to hear a Trevino-tirade from Kitty.

He slipped out the door, only marginally guilty for dropping that bomb on Kitty.

CHAPTER EIGHT

A night out with Jazz is exactly what I need after today.

Michael could have waited to greet Trevino personally—maybe should have—but he had plans with Jazz. Besides, Ezra had been more than excited to show Trevino where he'd be working—no doubt hoping to assist in the autopsy in some way. Michael didn't want to hang around while Trevino was in his business, doing his job for him. He knew it couldn't be helped, given the situation, but that didn't mean he needed to witness it.

After a much needed brisk walk, Michael arrived at Misty's Makeover Palace to pick up Jazz for the festival. Smiling and eager to see his boyfriend, he stepped inside, only to discover Jazz pacing laps in the center of the salon. Misty was there too, applying lipstick to a woman while another looked on. An unusual tension hung in the air.

"Hi?" Michael gave a tentative smile. "Everything okay?"

"Oh, it's fine," Jazz said and flapped a hand as he made another lap. "Just, you know, great. No worries. All good. At least, it will be. Once it all gets figured out. It's a start. That's a good way to say it, right?" Jazz looked over at Misty.

"That's right, Jazz. It's one step closer to freedom." She smiled at Michael. "It's okay. Things are fine. He'll be right as rain once he gets something to drink."

"I see." But Michael didn't.

"Jazz, go ahead to the festival, and I'll meet you there after I finish up with Dottie," Misty said. "Oh, Michael. How rude of me." She spun her chair so her client faced him. "Michael Fleishman, this is Dorothy Rafferty. She's my first cousin on my mother's side. And her daughter, Beatrice, who turned sixteen last month. Dottie, Bea, this is Michael, Jazz's boyfriend."

Though they had on makeup and their hair was more stylish now, and maybe even different colors, Michael recognized both women. The sister wives of the Bible-tract-distributing preacher.

Oh my, *these* were the relatives they were supposed to watch perform tonight? At least they didn't have to talk to them while they were on stage. But if Misty's relatives would be at her cookout Sunday, things might be awkward.

But more used to being awkward than not, Michael gave her a polite tip of his head and said, "Hello, Dottie. Nice to meet you." He nodded at her daughter. "Bea."

Dottie shook her head at her daughter, and the girl immediately stared at her hands flat on her lap, saying nothing. Long auburn curls hid most of her sad face. She seemed older and broken somehow, out of place in her bland brown dress and sensible black shoes. The only thing to indicate that she was a teenager was her sparkly blue nail polish.

Apparently satisfied her daughter wouldn't communicate with a gay, Dottie pursed her glossy pink lips and gave Michael a single nod. Perhaps she had recognized him too. "Hello. *You* can call me Dorothy."

Dorothy it is!

The atmosphere in the shop grew even more chilly, and Michael could think of nothing else to say, so he turned toward Jazz. Something was definitely bothering his boyfriend. Could it be the presence of these two women? "Ready to go?"

"More than you'll ever know." Jazz walked past Michael and opened the door before waving goodbye to Misty. "See you down there."

"Save some wine for me," Misty said.

"No guarantees," Jazz said and walked out.

Misty laughed and spun her cousin back around to face the mirror. Michael could see Dorothy's face in the reflection, and she had fixed him with a hard stare. Beatrice was looking at her nails, smiling softly. Michael felt a pang of empathy for her, but he hurried after Jazz and closed the salon door behind him, glad to be out of Dorothy's presence.

"What's going on?" Michael asked as he hurried to catch up.

Jazz whirled, and Michael drew up short, his stomach dropping at the fury in Jazz's cognac-colored eyes.

"That fucking fucker served me fucking divorce papers!" Jazz shouted. "Can you believe it?"

It took a moment for Michael to process that Jazz's fury was not aimed at him. For two terrifying heartbeats Michael had feared he had done something to anger Jazz. But no. This was about Russell, Jazz's murderous husband. Or apparently, soon-to-be ex-husband.

Michael took a fortifying breath and glanced around. Several people had turned to stare at Jazz's outburst, but Jazz didn't seem to care as he paced a small section of sidewalk.

"You fucking believe that shit?" Jazz snarled. "Fucker's in jail and he serves *me*! I'm gonna take his ass to the cleaners for this. Fucking *fuck*!"

Michael placed a comforting hand on Jazz's arm. "How about we find some vino, eh? I'll tell you about my nightmarish day, and you can tell me about yours."

Jazz's eyes widened, and concern crossed his face. "What do you mean nightmarish day? Did something happen? Are you all right? Oh my God, is Mr. Pickles okay?"

"He's fine," Michael assured him, linking an arm with Jazz and leading him toward the festival. "The same cannot be said for the murder victim Steve found in the driver's seat of my hearse this afternoon."

Jazz stopped dead. "What did you say?"

"Yeah." Michael sighed. "I'm surprised the gossip hasn't circulated to your chair yet."

"It could have," Jazz admitted. "I wasn't even listening to my clients with half an ear after I got served. My tips are probably shit."

"I hope not. Remember the man Norbert was arguing with at Gruff's?"

"Bill, right? Ol' Norbie's ex-boyfriend."

"Right. Bill Denton." Michael smiled. "You have a great memory. I couldn't recall his name and had to find it on the band's Facebook page."

"People still have Facebook pages?"

Michael frowned. "I have one for the funeral home. Kitty actually fields a number of questions and inquiries from it."

"That makes sense, I guess, seeing as how most people coming to your business are older."

"Hmm," Michael said. "We've gotten off topic."

Jazz made a face. "Sorry. My fault. My head is all over the place today. Tell me about this body."

"Not certain of the cause of death, but I would say strangulation from a first look. The body was placed inside my hearse, propped up like he was driving. I don't know exactly how he got there or why. Since he was found on my property, I recused myself from processing the body."

"Oh my God, are you a suspect?"

"According to Musgrave, *everyone* is a suspect until Sheriff Musgrave says they're not."

"Ugh, I hate when people talk in third person."

"Indeed," Michael agreed. Mention of the sheriff sparked a memory, and he pulled cash from his pocket. "Musgrave came by to talk to me about the scene he caused in the salon this morning over Amanda... oops, she wants to be called Rae now. That'll take some getting used to. Anyway, he wanted me to give you this."

Jazz accepted the money and pocketed it without counting. "That was big of him. Too scared to come see me himself, I assume."

"Most likely," Michael said.

"So are you a suspect?"

"Oh, you know how Hilton is. He talks a big game, but I know he doesn't believe I did it."

At least Michael hoped not.

"I don't even know if my brain can process what you just told me," Jazz said, sounding blown away. "C'mon. Let's walk some more. I really need wine now."

They continued on to the festival in silence, only a couple of blocks away. Across Lake Shore Drive, to the west, beautiful Lake Michigan churned big waves up and over their rocky bit of coastline, splashing across the boardwalk that stretched the length of town. A cool breeze off the lake kept the air from being too muggy.

"Norbert is our main POI," Michael said after a time.

"A what?"

"A person of interest."

Jazz scoffed. "Of course he is."

"Musgrave sent Tanner to check local hotels and motels for him so he can be questioned. And they also need to locate the two women who were with Denton at Gruff's. If they haven't heard that he's dead, they'll be looking for him, I'm sure. Sonya Metcalf and Ally Roberts are his bandmates. They're not listed on the festival schedule to play tonight... well, or again, so it would seem. But perhaps we can keep an eye out for them this evening. Maybe they have a clue to provide as to why Bill was murdered and left on my property."

"Isn't that a job for Musgrave and his band of merry nincompoops?"

Michael grinned and bumped Jazz's shoulder as they got in line at the entrance to the festival. "You go from saying fucking fuck to nincompoops? I do love your range, my dear."

"Oh, if you like that, you're going to love what I've got in mind for you later."

Michael's cock took notice of the predatory tone in Jazz's voice. "Oh? And what's that?"

Jazz leaned in close and whispered, "You'll find out later." He dabbed the tip of his tongue quickly into Michael's ear before straightening up and turning to smile at the woman in the small ticket booth, collecting entrance fees.

"Hi, Hilda, two please," Jazz said.

Hilda waved his money away and affixed paper bracelets to their wrists. "You boys have a nice time. The mayor's making the rounds and passing out wine tickets."

"You're the picture of regal poise and beauty," Jazz said. "Thank you, my dear."

"Yes, thank you," Michael said.

Hilda's bright smile only dimmed a touch when she met Michael's gaze, which he had to admit was a better response than he was used to receiving at town functions. No one felt comfortable around the local mortician.

Since he and Jazz had started seeing each other, however, Michael had noticed a subtle shift in the way people in Lacetown reacted to him. Maybe some of Jazz's exuberant outgoing personality had rubbed off on Michael. Most likely, though, he figured that people thought if the well-liked and extroverted Jazz had found something in Michael worth exploring, perhaps they could too.

No matter the reason, Michael had to admit he enjoyed the change.

The Acoustic Music Festival, like all other festivals hosted by the town, was held in Lacetown Park, a large, rectangular expanse of grass behind the police station and bordered by Main Street, Pike Street, Route 551, and Lake Shore Drive. A stage had been set up at the far end of the park, with the performers facing away from Lake Michigan. This allowed the festival attendees to enjoy the performances while observing glorious sunsets over the lake.

"Jazz!"

Lacetown's mayor, Trish Johnson, grabbed Jazz in a tight hug. She wore a top hat decorated like the American flag, a star-spangled glitzy blazer, and a navy blue skirt. She carried a roll of tear-away tickets in each hand, the ends swaying along Jazz's back as she rocked him back and forth. She might have been using some of those drink tickets for herself, if Michael wasn't off his mark.

"Lady Mayor," Jazz said once he'd finally freed himself. "You're looking fine, as always."

"Lady Mayor, oh you." Trish lightly tapped his shoulder with a roll of tickets before turning to Michael. "Hello, Michael. Good to see you, as usual."

"Thank you. Nice to see you, as well." *So now I'm Michael,* not Mr. *Fleishman? How lovely.... Maybe someday I'll receive an exuberant hug.*

Trish gave Jazz a critical once-over. "You still seem stressed."

"I do?"

"I can feel it pouring off you in dark, noxious waves. I could tell you were off this afternoon when I got my haircut. I thought that...." Her gaze drifted to Michael, and then she looked a tad apologetic. "Well, never mind what I thought. I see the evening hasn't brought your usual sparkle back. We can't have you polluting the rest of the festival-goers, so my recommendation is wine." She pulled a long rope of tickets off a roll and handed them to Jazz. "Lots and lots of wine."

"Lady Mayor, your keen sense of style is overshadowed only by your insightful study of character." Jazz held up the tickets. "Michael and I both thank you."

She looked between them, and Michael could practically read her thoughts as though they were being broadcast across her forehead: *I don't get the attraction, but if it works for them....*

He smiled and stepped closer to link arms with Jazz. "Yes, thank you, Madam Mayor."

"Call me Trish. And you're welcome, Michael. It's nice to see you taking part in the town festivities." She winked at Jazz. "Enjoy the music." She leaned in close and lowered her voice. "But you might need to use all of those tickets to do that, if you know what I mean. It is a third-tier festival, you know. You didn't hear that from me."

With that, Trish walked off, calling out to someone else she had spotted in the crowd.

"Everyone loves you," Michael said. "You've really made an impact on this town since you moved in."

"Oh? Just the town?" Jazz arched an eyebrow. "No one in particular?"

Michael grinned down at his handsome boyfriend, his heart swelling with love at the teasing smile Jazz wore. If only Jazz knew how much impact he'd truly had on Michael's life, and how madly he'd fallen in love with him. It was on the tip of his tongue to tell him something to that effect, but his response was drowned out by a screech of violin strings. The sound put Michael's teeth on edge, and a group standing nearby jumped and gave shouts of surprise. A young woman stood on the stage, sawing frantically on a violin.

Michael exchanged an alarmed look with Jazz, who held up the tickets. "Shall we?"

"Most definitely."

They got in line just before a crush of people who apparently realized they would need a lot more alcohol to handle the wide-ranging talent on display. A few minutes later, they each carried two clear plastic glasses of pinot grigio into the crowd.

"Mikey!"

Michael turned as his grandfather, Joel Fleishman—the only one in existence who called him Mikey—hurried over to them, his lady friend Mona on his left arm. In his right hand, to Michael's shock, he had a white plastic cup with Great Lakes Brewing Co. emblazoned on the side.

"Are you drinking beer, Grandpa?" Michael asked in surprise. His grandfather only drank manhattans, as far as Michael knew.

"Hell no," Grandpa said with a laugh. "Not that it'll convince you two lovebirds to switch teams, but one of the best things about dating a lady is that she never leaves the house without her handbag."

Mona had a clear plastic cup similar to Jazz's and Michael's, only filled with red wine. With an impish giggle, she showed them the contents of her purse. There was a whisky bottle—Grandpa's brand—and a jar of maraschino cherries inside. "I mixed Joel up a fresh batch of manhattans before we headed out."

Jazz laughed loudly, his mood obviously lightening.

"I think you're a keeper, my precious puddin' pop," Grandpa said, smooching the delighted woman on the cheek.

Though Michael was grinning, he said, "And I hope the two of you plan to call an Uber."

"Nah." Grandpa waved that off. "Deputy Tanner is working security tonight and promised to take us home. Even said Mona could blow the siren if she wanted."

"Oh dear," Michael said.

Then Grandpa grew serious. "Now, Mikey, why in the heck didn't you call me this afternoon? I had to hear it all from Tanner. Who the hell put a body in our Caddy?"

A few faces turned their way, and Michael quickly guided their group toward the quieter side of the park, where the local gossips had less chance to overhear. At least that horrendous violin shrieking would drown out their words.

Hillbilly torture techniques, indeed.

They found a newly vacated picnic table and sat.

"Firstly, it's my Caddy, and you're not the coroner anymore. It would've broken protocol to call you," Michael said.

"Protocol shmotocol." Grandpa blew a raspberry. "You were gonna tell your boyfriend, why not me too?"

Jazz gave Michael an encouraging smile. "Yeah, sweetie. Tell us what happened."

"Who found the body?" Grandpa asked.

"It wasn't your creep-tern, was it?" Jazz said with a sniff before drinking his wine. "Because if it was, you might want to have the sheriff give him a more rigorous questioning."

"He's not an intern—"

"Creep-tern," Jazz corrected gently. "It's a Jazz-ism."

"He's an apprentice," Michael continued patiently. "I really don't know why you and Kitty don't like Ezra."

"He's a fine young Jewish boy," Grandpa said, and Michael smiled in thanks. "Not creepy, just awkward like Mikey used to be. He'll find his groove one day. Look at our Mikey now."

Michael frowned at Grandpa's unnecessary overshare. He knew he'd been awkward most of his life, but did it bear constant repeating?

"Mr. Pickles doesn't like him either." Flashing a saucy smile, Jazz sipped his wine with his pinky out. "But that's beside the point. Tell us about the body."

Michael described the discovery, and Grandpa had a dozen questions. Michael sort of wished he had called him to the parlor that afternoon, if only for efficiency. Finally he wrapped it all up by telling them Parker Trevino would perform the autopsy.

"Wait." Jazz made a face. "Parker Trevino as in Trevino Funeral Parlor and Crematorium in Bridlestop?"

"That's right."

"Your sworn nemesis?"

Michael chuckled, gaze darting around before he took a drink. "Well, you make it sound like some kind of superhero movie or something...."

Jazz reached across the table and took Michael's free hand. "To me, you are a superhero. And he's obviously a nemesis. I mean, he's totally jealous that you have an elevator and three display rooms, right? And your hearse is a newer Cadillac with a fancier coach package—so you've reminded me more than once. I never knew the funeral parlor biz was so cutthroat," he said in an aside to Mona before he squeezed Michael's hand and smiled at him. "Trevino is obviously your nemesis. And I'm sure he's jealous of how hot you are too."

"You're sweet," Michael said, feeling the warmth of a blush even through his irritation. He really disliked Trevino, and now he'd be in the parlor tonight, and possibly tomorrow.

"This is true." Jazz grinned. "I'm cavity-inducingly sweet. Just don't tell anyone. Don't wanna lose my street cred."

"Gotta maintain the street cred," Mona quipped. She and Jazz toasted their wine.

Grandpa frowned at Michael. "Do you trust that putz to do a good job? Look what he did to Mr. Jones."

"Who's Mr. Jones?" Jazz cocked his head curiously.

Knowing his boyfriend had a twisted sense of humor, and seeing as his sarcasm bordered a nine out of ten tonight, Michael grew serious. "Now, Jazz, don't laugh."

Jazz cracked a smile. "Okay?" he ventured.

"Now, I know you're going to want to laugh, but it's not funny. Not one bit." Michael took a breath and let it out. "Mr. Jones had a heart attack and died recently."

Jazz furrowed his brow. "That's not funny."

"Yes, well," Michael hedged, knowing his beau's dark sense of humor too well. "You should know that Mr. Jones was a very large man. Almost five hundred pounds probably. Once he and his equally large wife had to be de-wedged from the tub by the friendly Bridlestop volunteer fire department when they decided to share a common bathing experience."

Jazz let out a bark of laughter.

"Now don't laugh, Jazz," Michael admonished, feeling like he should've known not to add that last detail. "Apparently, when Trevino put Mr. Jones in the cremation oven, the buffoon miscalculated his body mass ratios. He was so tightly lodged in the oven that he clogged the flue to the crematorium chimney. The smoke and heat caused part of the funeral parlor to catch on fire. They managed to turn the burner off, but—now don't laugh—but they couldn't get him out of the oven because he was stuck."

Brows raised, Jazz covered his lips with his fingers. "Oh my God! Are you serious? That's awful!" Mona didn't bother to hide her giggles.

"Jazz. Mona," Michael warned them. "There's more, and remember, I told you not to laugh."

"No! There's more?" He schooled his features, but a snicker escaped him. "How did I not hear about this?"

"No idea, but the whole town turned out to watch the firemen put out the blaze. After the fire was extinguished, Mr. Jones's remains were still intact, but...."

Grandpa rapped his knuckles on the table. "They had to cut poor Mr. Jones in half and cremate him a second time!"

Michael scowled when Jazz and Mona burst with laughter. "It's not funny. At all. Come now, be serious."

Wiping a tear of laughter from his eye, Jazz patted Michael's arm. "No, it isn't funny, sweetie. It's awful. But you can't tell a story like that, telling us not to laugh, and then expect us to keep a straight face. That's not fair."

"I suppose not," he admitted. "But it truly was a tragedy."

Jazz did an admirable job of faking a somber expression. "Yes, a tragedy."

"Poor Mr. Jones." Mona giggled.

"That's why I said Trevino's a putz," Grandpa declared, polishing off the last of his cocktail and handing the decoy beer cup to Mona. "Shoddy workmanship all around. And now he's in our parlor."

Mona slipped the cup and her purse under the picnic table, then she glanced around very suspiciously as she refreshed Grandpa's manhattan. Michael was glad Tanner would be watching over the two of them later.

Jazz released Michael's hand, and Michael wished he'd held it a little bit longer. Jazz finished his first cup of wine and gave Michael's practically full cup a critical look. "Don't let me be the only giddy drunk one, sweetie."

"Want a topper?" Mona asked, holding up her purse. "We'll just have to get you a beer cup and dump it out so the popo doesn't know what you're up to."

"I'll stick to my vino." Jazz chuckled, and Michael took a healthy swallow of his wine, relishing how it smoothed over some of the rougher edges left by the stress of his day.

"Very good," Jazz said to Michael as he started on his second cup of wine. "So, Nemesis Trevino will obviously need to use your examination room since his joint burned down. How do you feel about him traipsing around your place and touching your things?"

"That's fine. It's fine." Michael heard the lie in his voice even as Jazz made a face. "Okay, so I'm a bit agitated by it. But there's not much I can do for it."

Jazz lifted his cup in a toast. "There's wine."

Michael chuckled and lifted his first cup. "Yes, there is that."

"L'chayim," Grandpa said, and they all took a drink.

"I think I better *unexpectedly*"—Grandpa did air quotes—"stop by and make sure that sticky-fingered putz doesn't steal any of our good equipment."

"Trevino's an ass but not a thief," Michael countered.

Grandpa mumbled something in Yiddish around his cocktail.

When Jazz and Mona finished their wine, the group headed to the nearest vendor. Michael polished off the rest of his second cup while they waited in line.

"So when does he arrive?" Jazz asked.

Michael glanced at his watch. "He's probably there right now. He said he'd be over at seven."

"He's there unattended?" Grandpa cried, drawing a few looks from a couple walking by.

Michael gave his exuberant grandfather a shushing gesture. "Ezra is there. And the sheriff is meeting him too."

That seemed to appease Grandpa. "Oh, well, that's good. Ezra's a good boy."

Jazz rolled his eyes at that but stayed silent. He used their tickets to get three wines, two white and one red. They wandered back into the festival, and Jazz coiled his arm with Michael's, leaning closer than necessary.

Michael fought a shiver. He'd never been one for PDAs, though in all reality he hadn't had much opportunity. But being with Jazz melted away some of the walls Michael had spent years building.

In many ways, Michael was envious of his boyfriend. Jazz was social and outgoing and seemed to know the right thing to say in every situation. Everyone was happy to see Jazz—who didn't love their hairstylist? And Jazz was adept at making small talk that didn't feel small. He managed to finesse tiny personal tidbits from each of his clients and send them off not only looking beautiful, but feeling refreshed and good about themselves.

As a child and through the majority of his adulthood, Michael had always been quiet and more of a loner. He'd never excelled at sports, he wasn't musically inclined, and he seemed to have the perfect thing to say to bring any conversation to a lurching halt. Many of the kids in school had avoided him, too creeped out by his family's business to risk picking on him. There had been some nasty bullies, as would be expected in Michael's situation, but for the most part he was left alone. A couple of the more macabre kids tried to establish a connection, but Michael had seen through their intentions pretty quick and put an end to it.

He'd spent a lot of his younger years alone, and that had carried over into his adult years as well.

Until he'd met Jazz.

For some reason, Jazz had taken a shine to him. And it seemed that shine might have been just the thing to pull Michael out of his shell, making him a bit more outgoing and socially adept. It would never change the way people viewed him or felt around him—that was a natural byproduct of his business. But Jazz's interest and attraction had boosted Michael's confidence, and he felt more secure and less self-conscious.

"I've been neck deep in my own drama today, sorry," Jazz said, and squeezed Michael's biceps. Every touch from Jazz sent a gentle spark straight to Michael's groin. "How are you doing with what happened to you, sweetie? Are you holding up okay?"

"It's upsetting for a number of reasons, and troubling as well. I can't help but feel like I've been targeted in some way, but I've no idea why or by whom." He shook his head as he thought about Bill Denton sitting behind the wheel of the hearse. He agreed with Musgrave that Norbert should be a suspect, but would Norbert really have murdered Denton and left him there to taunt Michael? Why?

"Is Trevino staying with you?" Jazz asked after he put a big dent in his third drink. "Like sleeping in your guest room?"

Michael choked on his own wine. "Good Lord, no. It will be hard enough to have him in the funeral parlor, let alone sleeping in my home."

Jazz smirked. "There's an honest look into how you really feel about all this."

"Yes, well, like I said, there's not much I can do about it. And he needs to be here so Bill Denton's companions can identify his body."

"You think they'll do that tonight?" Jazz asked.

"The sheriff had Tanner out tracking them down this afternoon, so it's very possible."

Jazz gave him a skeptical look. "You're talking about the same deputy who worked on Dylan's case? And when Mr. Pickles was abducted? Tanner's nice but such a mimbo."

Grandpa laughed and slapped his knee. "He is!"

Michael cocked his head and frowned. "A what?"

"Mimbo, a male bimbo," Jazz explained. "Remember that *Seinfeld* episode?"

"I loved that show," Mona said. "Jewish boys have the best sense of humor."

"That's not all they got, bubbeleh." Grandpa winked, and they both giggled.

Michael chuckled as he remembered the episode where George had a man-crush on Elaine's gorgeous but dimwitted boyfriend. "Ah, yes."

Jazz waved his almost empty wine in an airy gesture. "And Tanner thought Mr. Pickles was a person when he went missing. His detective skills are about as fine-tuned as our Sheriff Motel 6."

While Grandpa and Mona laughed, Michael didn't join in. Jazz's joke on Musgrave's first name was a norm, but the comments about Tanner felt a tad meaner than Michael was used to from his boyfriend. Jazz was still on edge from the divorce papers, seeing as his sarcasm had been amped up to a new level, and that worried Michael a little bit.

"I need more wine," Jazz announced, upending his cup and making a sad face as two drops trickled from the rim and onto the grass.

"We'll catch you boys later," Grandpa announced suddenly. "I see Trish. There's some parking tickets I need her to fix for me, and her husband owes me a favor. She does too, for that matter."

Mona and Grandpa laughed conspiratorially at some inside joke, and then Grandpa all but dragged a tipsy Mona away as he flagged down the mayor.

Jazz smiled after them. "I love your grandpa."

"Everyone does," Michael agreed as they got in line again. At this rate Jazz was going to burn through their tickets in no time. He was obviously upset, and Michael wanted to help with more than just wine. "So now it's your turn. Tell me about these divorce papers."

Jazz's expression clouded. "I want a divorce, you know that. But with all the media attention Russell's attracted, I was hoping to wrap it up quietly. Maybe make an agreement privately, then have lawyers make it official." He sighed. "Of course, I'd have to answer his calls if I wanted to do that."

Michael's brows shot up at that aside. "He's called you?"

"Yes, and I'm sorry I didn't tell you. I never accepted the charges."

"Oh, that's all right," Michael assured him but wondered why Jazz had kept that detail from him.

"I think that's why he served me papers like I'm the bad guy in all this. That's what pisses me off. I know he did it on purpose just to get to me."

"He being Russell."

"Yes, your favorite author."

A thread of guilt stitched through Michael's gut, and he couldn't help looking away. *Jazz will understand why I'm rereading Russell's books, right?*

But now was not the time for that conversation.

"He's not my *favorite* author...."

Jazz waved his words away. "Oh, it's fine. I get it. You like his mysteries and his stocky, macho private investigator character. Which I guess is a good thing, since you seem to have gotten yourself involved in another murder."

"Not through any fault of my own," Michael said, then noticed over Jazz's shoulder someone waving to him from a very long line at the beer vendor. "Oh, there's Kitty and Marty."

"Oh?" Jazz turned to look. "I should give them some tickets. Are you getting another wine too?"

Michael hesitated, then remembered Trevino was currently using his equipment. "Sure, why not?"

Jazz tore off the correct amount of tickets for Michael to pay for their drinks, then hurried over to Kitty and Marty, calling out, "Hey, Kitty Litter!"

Michael smiled. Kitty and Jazz got along famously and liked to give each other amusing nicknames. Jazzercize was Michael's favorite of Kitty's creations. Jazz had run the gamut of cat-related names such as Kitty Litter and Kitty Kat. Michael had gotten a good laugh when Jazz had come up with Itty Bitty Gritty Kitty.

Michael let his gaze rove the length of Jazz's body as he walked away, focusing on the lovely swell of his ass. Desire burned through him as he thought about spreading those firm, hairy cheeks and feasting on Jazz's hole. Michael wouldn't press him for sex, but he sincerely hoped Jazz had meant his sexy innuendo earlier. After he'd received that paperwork, sex might be just what Jazz needed. Hell, what they *both* needed. Michael could remind Jazz how much better off he was with Michael than Russell. And also that he'd substantially traded up in the length and girth department as well.

A familiar figure cut across Michael's line of sight, startling him out of his thoughts.

Norbert!

Michael's heart pounded.

Per their last conversation, Musgrave and his deputies hadn't located Norbert yet. Should Michael follow Norbert?

Norbert stopped and looked around, completely blocking Jazz from Michael's view. It seemed almost intentional. The line Michael stood in moved a few feet closer to the wine booth, and he shifted position. From his new spot, Michael lost sight of Norbert behind a group of loud, and clearly drunk, young men. Anxiety tingled in the center of his chest. What if Michael lost Norbert and he left town before Musgrave could question him?

With a glance at the wine booth, followed by a long look at Jazz, standing yards away talking and laughing with Kitty and Marty, Michael pocketed the tickets clutched in his now sweating hand and stepped out of line. He dodged around the group of loud young men, some wearing fraternity letters on their shirts, others designer clothes, and all of them half in the bag on craft beers. Their cocky attitudes and brash laughter ignited a fear-based flinch he hadn't experienced since his school days.

Must be cellular memory. The instinct to avoid pain and stay alive, learned in the halls of Lacetown middle and high schools.

Once he'd left the drunk college guys behind, Michael spied Norbert striding across the park. He wasn't very far ahead, his tall, thin frame shrouded in a leather duster coat too heavy for the hot summer air. His glossy black-and-yellow hair made him stand out as he slipped through the crowd.

Michael hung back a bit. Pulling his phone out, he sent a quick text to Musgrave. *Spotted Norbert in park at the festival. Have you questioned him yet?*

Musgrave's response was nearly immediate: *No! Keep him in sight, but do not engage. I'm on my way.*

Excitement joined with Michael's anxiety, and his hand trembled slightly as he sent *okay* back to Musgrave.

Michael was involved in another murder mystery. He was following a suspect. It was so much like a scene from a Brock Hammer novel, Michael wanted to stop and shout with giddy glee.

But he needed to remain cool and focus on not letting Norbert give him the slip.

When Norbert stopped to talk to a man sitting in a camping chair and tuning a guitar, Michael took the opportunity to text Jazz: *Over near the staging area. Norbert is here, so I'm keeping an eye on him until Musgrave arrives.*

Jazz wrote back: *OMG! Stay right there. I'm on my way!*

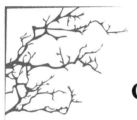

CHAPTER NINE

Jazz couldn't help grinning as he made his way through the crowd. More clue hunting with Michael. Clue hunting that might land good ol' Norbie in the slammer, or at the very least questioned rigorously by Musgrave.

He shouldn't be delighted by that notion, but he couldn't help it.

Jazz met up with Michael quickly, surprised to realize he was slightly out of breath. Was he really that out of shape or just that excited to trail another suspect with his boyfriend?

"Where is he?" Jazz asked.

Michael jerked his head, and Jazz looked that direction in time to see Norbert put his nose in the air and stomp away from a seated man tuning a guitar. Shaking his head, the musician frowned at Norbert's back.

"I wonder what transpired there?" Michael mused.

"Let's find out."

They shared a grin, then walked toward the guitarist.

"This reminds me of our first date," Jazz said fondly. "Though last time, I was avoiding the hell out of Norbert, not following him."

"Well, we didn't know what a snake in the grass he was then."

"I did," Jazz countered. "Speaking of a snake in the grass, I can't sleep over tonight—got an 8:00 a.m. client—but I would be open to some snakes playing in the grass after we're done doing Musgrave's job for him again."

Michael chuckled. "You're bad."

"The worst," he quipped as they neared the guitarist. Maybe Michael would dole out some of that decadent punishment he'd showered Jazz with last night in his apartment. That blowie had really gotten his creative juices flowing when he went back to work.

Norbert was still in sight up ahead. What the hell was he doing back in Lacetown? Had he just come for the *Deliverance*-esque, squeal-like-a-pig music, or was he up to something? Jazz never would've pegged Norbert for a killer—a conniving sleazeball, yes. Murderer, no. But after his actions in the cottage, Jazz wouldn't put anything past him. But if he did kill Denton, why leave the body at Michael's? What the hell was his angle?

"We'll have to be subtle," Michael whispered, a gleam of excitement in his eyes.

Jazz smirked as he studied his boyfriend. "You're all lit up with the thrill of this. You look really sexy." Jazz licked his lips suggestively, delighting in Michael's resulting blush.

"Focus." Michael nudged him gently with his shoulder. "How should we handle this?"

Though the phrase he'd overheard a man say once—"find yourself a living room lady who's a bedroom slut"—flitted through his mind about Michael, they needed to focus on the situation at hand. "Looks like the guy wasn't too impressed with Norbie. Let's play to that."

"Good idea. Which of us talks to him first?"

Jazz grinned. "You started this mystery-novel-role-play game, you take the lead."

"Okay. Let's go."

Michael moved toward the man, who still glared at Norbert's back, and Jazz followed. They only had a few minutes before they would lose sight of Norbie, so they would need to work fast.

"That guy, huh?" Michael said and followed it up with a quiet, rueful laugh.

"What?" The man stopped tuning his guitar and frowned up at Michael and Jazz.

"That guy you were talking with. He's a piece of work, isn't he?"

The man huffed a laugh. "Yeah. He thinks so. He hit you up too?"

Hit him up? Like for sex? Eew!

Jazz and Michael shared a look, and Michael shrugged, obviously not knowing what the guy meant either.

Michael cleared his throat nervously and continued. "Oh, yeah," he said noncommittally. "You know how it is."

"Yeah," Jazz agreed. "Totally."

"Yeah, guys like him are all over these festivals." The man plucked a string and winced, continuing to talk as he tuned his instrument. "They keep promising more than the last one, but when it comes right down to it, all they want is a cut of whatever you're getting paid."

Jazz's brows shot up knowingly, and he saw Michael's do the same. So Norbert was in town trying to find someone to sign with him. Obviously the publishing world had booted his scrawny ass out for hiding Russell's plagiarism, and apparently Norbert was now trying to slither into PR for musicians. At least something was starting to make sense.

"Well, you can't be too careful," Michael said.

Jazz looked around. Shit! They'd lost sight of Norbert. He tugged on Michael's shirt and then smiled down at the musician. "Good talking with you. Good luck up there."

They hurried off through the crowd, Jazz in the lead, until they spotted their quarry once again. After that they slowed down, careful to keep out of sight. Norbert led Michael and Jazz on a full circuit of the festival, finally stopping in front of the stage to watch the performers.

Michael passed over the last of his wine to Jazz so he could text their location to Musgrave. Jazz wondered what Musgrave would have to say about the two of them following a suspect again. Most likely it would have a low number of syllables.

"It's fun playing private dicks with you again," Jazz said, then sipped Michael's wine.

Michael chuckled. "Later I'll show you my telescope I use for spying."

Smiling, Jazz people-watched as they kept Norbert in view. The crowd consisted of a wide variety of people, so he had a lot to occupy him. A bright yellow hawaiian shirt in the crowd caught Jazz's eye, and he frowned. The man was tall and stood looking over the heads of those in front of him, watching the performers. Though he drank from a beer now and then, he didn't move at all to the music like the rest of the crowd. He just stood and stared at the stage, intently watching the performers. He looked familiar, but Jazz couldn't place where he'd seen him before.

"We really need to ride your scooter more often," Michael said out of the blue.

"That's random, sweetie," Jazz said. "You must really be feeling horny. Imagining yourself as Brock Hammer, are we?"

Michael's blush gave him away, even as he said, "Hardly. More like remembering riding behind you the last time we tailed a suspect."

Placing a hand on the small of Michael's back, Jazz let out a little grunt that sent a shiver he could feel down Michael's spine. "I've never wanted to see Musgrave so badly in all my life."

"Why?"

"The sooner he gets Norbie in custody, the sooner I can be in your custody."

Michael let out a bark of laughter, then slapped a hand over his mouth. They both looked toward Norbert, but the weasel's attention was riveted on the stage as he bobbed his head. Jazz checked out the band flailing on their stringed instruments.

"No accounting for tastes," Jazz remarked.

"Indeed," Michael said with a nod. "But this group is at least playing in the same key."

A flash of red hair by the stage caught Jazz's eye, and he smiled. Misty. Then he studied the performers and realized the two musicians in the back were Dorothy and Beatrice.

"Misty's up there," Jazz said.

"Where?" Michael asked, looking around.

Jazz pointed to the stage. "Her cousins are playing right now. I wonder if they call themselves the Ancestry Website Relatives," he said dryly. "Remind me never to do that. If sister wives afraid of brooms and Bible-thumpers who play the squeak-box might be on my tree, I'd have to shoot myself."

"We wouldn't want that."

"No, that would put the cherry on top of this shitty day."

That came out harsher than he'd intended, and by Michael's expression, it had caught him off guard. Jazz was joking around, but the resentment he harbored for Russell and his crony Norbert was seeping in. Though very justified in nursing his bitterness for them, Jazz didn't want that negativity to bleed over into his current relationship. Michael was far and above a better person than Russell could ever hope to be, and Jazz didn't want his attitude toward his ex to send his current boyfriend running for the hills.

Maybe following Norbert hadn't been such a great idea.

A cursory glance back at the stage showed the old fart who'd given them the Bible pamphlet standing stage left, playing a stand-up bass. Dorothy and Beatrice looked like they had wiped their makeup off already. *Figures.* Daddy Dearest probably didn't like it. The teenage son was center stage, sawing away on a violin with apparent dexterity and skill—if the happy audience was any indicator. Strings flew from his bow, and people actually cheered.

"I'm not a fan of country music," Michael said, "but you have to admit he's quite gifted."

Jazz snorted. "I guess, sure." His gaze drifted away from Misty's relations and back to Norbert. *Why are you really here, Norbie?*

A thought zinged through his mind with breathtaking speed.

It couldn't be a coincidence that ol' Norbie was in town at the same time Russell served Jazz papers, could it?

Shit! Was Russell at the heart of all of this?

It wouldn't be outside the realm of possibility for Russell to have convinced Norbert to come back to Lacetown and clean up any witnesses to Russell's murderous plagiarism. Did the dead guy in Michael's hearse know something Russell needed to remain hidden? But what?

Jazz let out a frustrated sigh. None of it made any sense!

Michael turned to study him, brows raised in concern. "Everything all right?"

"Sunshine and roses." Jazz forced a smile and sipped Michael's wine.

Michael had been asking Jazz a lot lately how he was doing, and Jazz had been responding with jokes, quick barbs, and pithy sayings like, "I'm right as rain, baby." Though they had not been together long, Michael and Jazz were in tune with each other—both in bed and in life—and Jazz knew Michael suspected he wasn't really okay.

But now was not the time for that conversation.

Michael's phone pinged, and Michael rolled his eyes when he read the text.

Jazz chuckled. "What's the good sheriff telling you to do?"

Michael shook his head. "Three exclamation points. Really?"

He held his phone out to show Jazz the text: *DO NOT approach the suspect!!! I sent Tanner to question him. Be there ASAP.*

"What a dumbass," Jazz said with a snort.

"Well, we're almost through."

Offering a tender smile, Michael caressed Jazz's back. It felt good, comforting, and before Jazz realized it, he was smiling.

"This can't be fun for you, stalking Norbert, but thank you for joining me."

"And let you have all the fun," Jazz said, trying for a joke but hearing how flat and hard his voice sounded.

Misty's relatives came to a rousing finish, and Jazz looked back at the stage as they all took a bow. Norbert and the rest of the audience cheered and whistled. The tall man in the yellow shirt only stared at the stage. *Curious.*

Jazz noticed Michael looking over his shoulder, frowning as he scanned the crowd.

"Who do you see?" Jazz asked.

"It's who I *don't* see," Michael replied. "Where the hell is Tanner?"

"Probably trying to figure out his right from his left," Jazz said, then made a face and took another swallow of Michael's wine. "That sounded mean as fuck. Sorry. I'm in a mood."

Before Michael could reply, they were both startled to hear Dorothy's husband at the microphone.

"Acts 3:19 reads thus." The man removed a leather Bible from his coat and opened it. The passage was marked with a long, brown, and mottled bookmark that looked like braided rope. He spoke in a loud, resonant voice that had no need of the microphone before him. "Repent ye therefore, and be converted, that your sins may be blotted out, when the times of refreshing shall come from the presence of the Lord."

His preaching almost drowned out the crash and fold of the lake's big waves, and a grumble of discontent filtered through the crowd.

"Oh, just when I thought this festival couldn't suck any worse," Jazz muttered.

Michael pointed ahead of them. "Norbert seems to agree with you."

Norbert gave an elaborate eye roll, then turned away to slink into the crowd.

"Suspect is on the move." Michael hastened forward and Jazz hurried to keep up. Damn, his boyfriend really did love a mystery. And Jazz had to admit Michael's excitement was contagious—and sexy as hell.

They skirted the stage, neither keen to catch the preacher's eye. Misty's cousins were fricking weird. The whole time Misty had been coloring their hair, Dorothy had been quizzing Beatrice with Bible trivia, oblivious to the awkward glances they received from other customers.

Jazz pointed at the son picking up violin bow strings from the floor as the old man droned on with another scripture. "He sawed on that squeak-box so hard he broke all his strings. I don't know who to feel sorrier for, my ears or that bow, ya know—"

"You motherfucker!"

Jazz was cut off midsnark by the outburst, and he wasn't sure which was more shocking, the words themselves or the vicious tone of voice. He and Michael drew up short.

Norbert jumped a bit and turned to look back. Jazz tugged Michael out of Norbert's sightline and craned his neck to see who had shouted.

"What's going on?" Michael asked.

The crowd parted for two figures, and Dorothy's husband went silent as everyone stared.

"Shit," Jazz said. "That's Bill's band members, Ally and Sonya, right?"

"This won't be good," Michael muttered.

Ally stomped toward Norbert, her short hair combed back like Danny Zuko from *Grease*. Trailing behind her was Sonya, wearing an expression of concern as tears streamed down her cheeks.

"You killed him!" Ally shouted.

"What are you—"

Norbert was unable to finish. Ally planted both hands on his chest and shoved him hard. The force sent Norbert stumbling backward, and he fell into the midst of a group of loud frat boys.

"Oh no," Michael said in a low voice. "I saw those guys earlier. They look even more drunk now."

"Fight! Fight!" one of them chanted as they hauled Norbert to his feet.

Most festival-goers scattered, but others closed in, forming a circle around those involved. Primal excitement ran through the crowd, and cell phones went up to record the action while no one bothered to intervene. The tall man in the yellow shirt was still there, watching with anticipation like everyone else. Jazz could practically taste the bloodlust in the air. A woman standing near them said to her male companion, "I'm going to get so many likes on Instagram with this video."

Jazz and Michael pushed their way to the front of the onlookers. Ally stood on one side of the circle, glaring at Norbert as the drunk frat boys shoved him back toward her.

"Fight, fight!" two of the frat boys resumed chanting.

"You get him, girl!" a familiar voice shouted.

A few feet away from Jazz and Michael stood Christy James, the woman who ran the marina in town bearing her name and who Michael had dated in high school and taken to prom. Michael had told Jazz all about Christy, how they'd lost their virginity to each other, and how Michael had foolishly shared secrets with her that she'd gleefully spread around town after he told her he was gay. The most damning secret had been that when he was twelve, he'd peeked at a naked woman in the preparation room just to see what all the fuss was about boobs. Jazz had thought it was an innocent and rather funny epiphany along Michael's journey to discovering his sexuality, and the sweet way his father had handled it warmed Jazz's heart and he'd wished he'd had a chance to meet the man who made his boyfriend the wonderful man he was.

But the man-hating Christy had layered on lots of embellishments to Michael's innocent story, which landed her big butt smack onto Jazz's nemesis list. He had declared very firmly, "There will be no redemption for Christy after spreading rumors to besmirch my man's character," and promptly made Michael swoon.

"Figures she'd cheer to see a woman kick a man's ass," Jazz muttered. He really didn't like Christy. Not one little bit.

Dismissing bitter ol' Christy, Jazz returned his attention to the scene unfolding before them.

Norbert jerked free of the frat boys, his face bright red and a smear of dirt across his forehead. "Unhand me!"

They laughed and shoved him toward Ally, and Norbert flailed his arms to keep from face-planting.

When Christy laughed meanly, a strong and surprising burst of compassion rattled through Jazz. Horrible as Norbert was, and as much as he really deserved a beatdown, Jazz hated to see anyone suffer this kind of public humiliation. It also awakened memories of the times he'd been bullied in school, events he'd tried hard to bury in the past.

He sensed the same internal conflict going on in Michael, who stood stiff and tall beside him, hands tightened into fists at his sides. If Jazz was considering stepping forward to get between Norbert and his aggressor, Ally's next words rooted him in place.

"I know you murdered Bill," she said, rage glittering in her eyes and fists clenched.

"Ally, don't."

The soft words, layered with pain, came from Sonya. Jazz thought she looked weak and defeated, too grieved to calm her bandmate.

"You know it was him," Ally said without taking her gaze from Norbert. "You said so yourself. Bill was with him last night. You know he did it!"

"What?" Norbert spat, eyes wide. "Bill's dead? How?"

Jazz didn't think the shock on Norbert's pinched face was fake. So Denton had been with Norbert last night? What for? An argument over the band again? A booty call? Had Norbert tried to reignite an old flame, only to be rebuffed, and decided to lash out in a most deadly manner? Musgrave would find that very interesting, to say the least.

And, most likely, pretty gross. Jazz would have to agree.

"This won't fix anything," Sonya said, resting a hand on Ally's arm but not pulling her away. "Let the police handle it."

"Dammit," said the Instagram-hopeful girl, her cell phone trained on the action. "I thought they were going to fight."

"Let's go, Deirdre," the girl's friend said. "I don't want to see this."

"I need something big on my feed," Deirdre said, waving her friend off. "Let's wait a bit longer."

"You never know what'll happen in a group," Christy muttered, and then she spotted Michael and Jazz. She wore her graying brown hair long and parted down the middle, a style that did nothing for her round face, which was currently scrunched up in some semblance of a polite smile. "Hello, Michael." She gave Jazz a head to toe. "Michael's friend."

"I thought I smelled fish," Jazz said, barely glancing at her.

"Excuse me?" Christy growled.

Facing her, Jazz gave her his best believable smile. "Don't you own the marina? Such an accomplishment." He considered telling her that 1994 called and wanted its fashion back, but he figured Michael would receive the brunt of any payback, and he didn't want that.

"Oh," Christy muttered, unsure if Jazz was mocking her or not. She adjusted her shirt, smoothing the front of the untucked flannel. "Thanks."

The smile Jazz gave her felt like one of Michael's best mortician smiles, and he turned away. God help that bitch if she started any more rumors about his man.

Jazz looked around for Deputy Tanner, but the mimbo was nowhere in sight.

Seriously, what was up with the law enforcement in this town?

He let out a heavy sigh and decided to take matters into his own hands and rescue Norbert before things got further out of hand. In an odd way, Jazz felt a weird and unsettling kind of responsibility for Norbert. Like someone's wicked pet they'd set loose in the neighborhood when they moved away. Damn his sense of duty.

Jazz stepped forward—

But Ally moved fast. She turned and lashed out, her fist catching Norbert on the chin and sending him staggering back into the midst of the drunk frat boys. Once again, they cheered and chanted, "Fight! Fight!"

Jazz flinched, and Deirdre screamed, "Yes! Get him, girl! Beat his faggot ass!"

Christy seemed as excited as the rest of the crowd for a fight.

"What is the matter with people?" Michael muttered, peering around at the people raging like Romans at the Colosseum.

Kitty and her husband, Marty, pushed to the front of the onlookers directly across from them, joined moments later by Joel and Mona. Kitty and Marty held plastic cups of beer and both looked surprised.

Ally stomped after Norbert, fists up and jaw clenched.

"Ally, no!"

Sonya rushed in and tried to hold her back, but Ally shrugged the skinny woman off.

"Get up," one of the frat boys demanded. The young man had perfect hair, attractive features, and designer clothes—but the sneer on his face was anything but handsome.

"Get him up, Brad!" one of his cronies cried, and the college group cheered. "Make him fight back!"

Laughing like a bully, Brad hauled Norbert to his feet. "You scared of a girl?"

Norbert pulled free and snapped, "More so than I am of you."

"Big words for someone getting their ass kicked by a girl," Brad said with a sneer.

Ally reached Norbert and grabbed the front of his shirt. She drew back a fist and hit him right in the nose. Jazz flinched, and the people around him cheered and pressed forward. Jazz shifted position in an effort to see better, and lost sight of Michael among the throng. When he searched for their friends, he discovered they had moved out of sight too.

Jazz was jostled by the strangers around him, making him feel alone and vulnerable, a feeling he didn't like one damn bit. He turned back to Norbert in time to see two of Brad's preppy friends pick Norbert up and hold him so Brad could look him in the eye.

"Scared of me yet?" Brad asked, then punched Norbert in the face, sending him back into Ally's arms.

"Come on, Norbie," Jazz whispered. "Fight back, goddammit."

But Norbert simply stood between Ally and the frat boys, possibly stunned by the direct hits to his face. Brad and his friends advanced on Norbert. This was just like fifth grade when Andy Fox and Jason Rawlings had ganged up on Jazz behind the school. The bloodthirsty jeers and taunts around him rang in his ears, the echo of long ago but never forgotten laughter making his stomach clench. His hands shook, and he realized he'd crushed the plastic wine cup in his hand.

This had to stop.

"We won't mess him up too much," Brad said, apparently to Ally. "We'll leave some for you to finish." He shoved Norbert, knocking the stunned man onto the grass.

"Enough!"

The word came up Jazz's throat as a deep, shouted command.

He hadn't intended for it to carry so far, but it momentarily quieted the crowd and halted the frat boys in their tracks.

Everyone turned to look at Jazz, and he caught sight of Michael's wide and shining eyes among the faces. The pride and adoration in Michael's expression gave him the fortitude to step into the circle and say, "Everybody back off! Now!"

Tossing his empty cup so his hands were free, Jazz placed himself between Norbert and the obnoxious frat boys, chin up and gaze defiant as he stared them down. His stomach was knotted with nerves, but knowing Michael was close by helped.

"This isn't your fight," Jazz said. "Back off."

"Who are you, his boyfriend?" one of the guys said with a sneer.

Some people in the crowd laughed, and Jazz distinctly heard the word *fags* muttered by someone—possibly Christy. Jazz tamped down his rage and let out a derisive snort. "He should be so lucky."

Brad was fueled by the crowd's support. "Get out of my way, fag. This isn't your fight either."

Oh, hell no. I'm not that scared little kid anymore. Jazz clenched his fists.

Brad lurched toward him, but Jazz was ready for the drunken swing. He dodged the blow and landed a solid jab to Brad's face. The crowd gasped when the guy tripped backward and landed on his ass.

Jazz took up a defensive stance, fists up and knees bent. *Bring it, motherfucker.*

Brad cupped his face. "That was my nose, asshole!"

"Let's teach this faggot not to mess with Sigma Chis!"

Three of the frat boys advanced, big fists raised, and Brad pushed to his feet, growling.

Michael rushed forward and stood at Jazz's side. Jazz turned to him, grinning and wild-eyed. "Hiya, sweetie. Do I know how to show you a good time or what?"

A high-pitched scream of rage rent the air, drawing everyone up short. Ally had escaped Sonya's grip and crashed past them, knocking both Jazz and Michael back as she lunged for Norbert on the ground.

"You're dead!" Ally jumped onto Norbert, who was still sprawled on the grass. She straddled him and punched him repeatedly in the face and body. He shielded his face with his arms, and she just whaled on those.

"Get off me, you crazy bitch!" Norbert screamed.

Jazz moved quick, grabbing the girl by the waist and yanking her off, her legs and arms still flailing.

"Get off me! Lemme at him!"

The frat boys laughed uproariously at the whole thing.

Jazz somewhat forcefully shoved the girl at Sonya. "Get ahold of her!"

Sonya had Ally in a death grip, and Ally's screams turned into quiet sobs as the weight of her grief finally hit her. Her rage gave way to exhausted defeat. "He killed him.... I know it.... If he'd been in jail where he belongs, Bill would still be alive...."

"I'm not finished with you, fag," a voice snapped.

Dammit, I forgot that I broke Brad's nose.

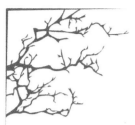

CHAPTER TEN

"Call him that one more time," Misty growled, coming up to stand beside Michael and Jazz. The menace in her usually sweet and open expression shocked the hell out of Michael.

"We don't tolerate that talk in this town," a familiar voice said, and Steve stepped forward. He gave Michael a curt nod. "Need a hand, Captain?"

Then to Michael's utter shock, several more people stepped forward: Kitty, Marty, other Lacetown residents he recognized by face only. Grandpa and Mona came forward as well, though Michael had no idea what they intended to do.

It was Mayor Johnson who stepped out of the crowd and spoke next. Trish pointed at the frat boys. "You need to get the hell out of my town."

Brad wiped the blood from his nose with the back of his hand. "Do you have any idea who my father is?"

"Another asshole like you?" Jazz threw out.

"I'll—"

But Trish was having none of it. "I don't care if your father is the king of England. You don't act like this in our town. You go and call an Uber that your daddy will pay for, and get the hell out of Lacetown, or I'm calling the sheriff to haul the lot of you to jail!"

Gobsmacked, that's what Michael was. All these people had jumped to their aid?

"He's already on his way," Tanner announced, stepping forward. He spoke with authority, his uniform giving the trust-fund brats pause.

"Dude, let's get out of here," one of them muttered, grabbing Brad by the arm.

Brad was all but pulled away by his fraternity brothers. "You'll hear from my father about this!"

"With relish," Trish snapped as they all slunk into the night.

"I had to break up three other fights trying to get here. Now what the devil is going on?" Tanner assessed the situation, looking between the sobbing Ally and Norbert, bloodied and dirty on the ground. He pointed at Norbert. "We've been looking all over for you. The sheriff needs to talk to you."

"Why? I'm innocent in all this!" Norbert spit blood and gestured up at Ally. "That creature assaulted me. I want to press charges." His arm did a wild arc, pointing at everyone still gathered. "On all of you! You're accessories to an assault!"

Jazz let out an exasperated sigh and held his hand out to Norbert. "Give it a rest, Norbie. Here, lemme help you up, get some ice—"

"I don't want *your* help!" he shrieked.

Everyone flinched at that.

Norbert spat blood again, then wiped his mouth with the back of his hand. He glared evilly up at Jazz and Michael, hatred seething from his every pore. Amazingly he had the strength, if not the grace, to stagger to his feet.

"You keep away from me, Jasper! And you too!" He shot an evil look at Michael, then let out a nasty chuckle, his yellowed teeth red with blood. "Tell me, Jasper. Does your new paramour pretend he's embalming you when he comes? Does he ask you to hold really, really still?"

Fire heated Michael's face and shock rendered him immobile. Blood pounded in his ears, but it wasn't loud enough to drown out the crowd's gasps and snickers. Michael recognized Christy's laugh all too easily. He could feel the weight of her smug gaze upon him, Norbert's words new fodder for her gossip.

Deirdre, still recording everything, let out a quiet "Oh snap!"

"You fucker!"

Jazz's growl made Michael jump. Norbert's eyes went huge as if he realized he'd gone too far when Jazz lunged for him.

Though Jazz was shorter, Norbert let out a cry when Jazz seized him by the lapels of his long duster coat and gave him a rough shake. "Say something like that again, and I will fucking kill you! What Russell did to Dylan will pale in comparison to the shit I'll do to your skinny carcass."

Michael gasped right along with everyone else, only not from shock, but red hot lust.

"Y-you all heard t-that... right?" Norbert stuttered, eyes wide in panic as he scrambled to escape Jazz's grip. "He threatened t-to k-kill m-me!"

"Everybody calm down," Tanner said, but no one was listening to him.

Jazz shook Norbert again and got inches from his face. "Not a threat, fucker. A promise. Say one wrong word about Michael, or just look at him funny, and I will fucking empty my .45 in your stupid fucking face!"

"What in the name of everything hot and holy is going on here?"

Musgrave parted the crowd and stepped into the middle of it all. The frat boys were long gone, but a crowd still lingered, all of them seeming excited about the way the events were unfolding. Two deputies trailed after Musgrave, the twins Greg and Grace Tompkins, both managing to look simultaneously alert and nervous.

"Break it up!" Musgrave shouted. Michael could see the surprise on his face. "Dilworth? What the hell?"

Jazz shoved Norbert away from him and turned, not looking as apologetic as he should. He flashed a grin that had a tinge of the maniacal to it. "Just trying to keep the peace, Sheriff," Jazz said, and blew a strand of hair out of his face.

"By getting into a fight?" Musgrave said. "Threatening people?"

"He didn't start it."

Kitty stepped out of the crowd. Musgrave gave her a dubious look, until her husband, Marty, appeared behind her, holding what Michael assumed were his own and his wife's beers.

"You too?" Musgrave shook his head in disappointment at his brother.

"We haven't even finished our first beers," Marty said, sounding a bit defensive. He was as big as his brother, with that same high and tight curly blond hair, but leaner through the chest and far less surly.

"Those men were shooting off homophobic slurs," Misty announced, glaring up at Musgrave.

The sheriff jerked his head back and stared down at Misty as if startled. "You have pink in your hair."

"And the fiery passion to defend my friends to match it," Misty threw back, flipping her red-and-pink curls over her shoulder. "We were all bystanders when those two started fighting." She pointed at Ally and

Norbert, then toward the street where the frat boys had disappeared. "You need to go after those homophobes who ran off."

Michael swore Musgrave let out a gasp as a flash of lust crossed his eyes. But it switched so quickly back to a glower, maybe he had imagined it.

"Tanner, round up the POIs we've been looking for," Musgrave growled.

"Convenient they all came to the festival, isn't it?" Tanner said with a smile, walking toward Norbert.

"Shut up, Tanner." Musgrave looked at his brother. "Who else was involved?" Then his gaze drifted back to Misty for a moment.

Marty sipped his beer, calm as a cucumber under his brother's brash attitude. "The girl attacked the skinny guy, and those frat guys made it worse. Jazz was trying to stop an all-out brawl, and the skinny guy insulted...." His voice trailed off awkwardly, and Michael felt his face flame under Marty's quick glance. Then Marty frowned and shrugged. "Well, he was being a real homophobic jerk," he finished with a scowl at Norbert.

"And then we kinda ended it, didn't we, Lady Mayor?" Steve waggled his brows and winked at Trish, who smiled and blushed a little.

"We did."

A Brock Hammer line flitted through Michael's mind: *Escaping the deadly ebb and flow of a riotous crowd with your skin in one piece makes a man damn grateful to be alive, and itching to fight or fuck.*

Not one of Russell's more eloquent lines, but rather apropos, apparently. Michael was still aroused by Jazz's fierce display.

"I've half a mind to run all of you in for public fighting," Musgrave said.

Michael was impressed that neither Kitty nor Jazz made a comment about Musgrave saying "half a mind" about himself.

"So much for crowd control, Tanner," Musgrave remarked, and then he looked at Greg Tompkins. "Help Tanner clear these bystanders out of here."

Tompkins started moving people on with the familiar phrases, "Nothing to see here. It's all over. Move along. Come on, now, move along."

"I don't know if it's enough to go viral, but I'll post it," Deirdre said as she walked away.

"I don't think so," Misty said, and snatched the phone out of her hands.

"Hey!" Deirdre cried when Misty deleted the video.

"Show some class," Misty told her, handing the phone back.

Musgrave approached Ally and Sonya, both still crying. "The two of you are bandmates with Bill Denton, correct?"

Sonya nodded, wiping her tears away with her sleeve.

"I take it you're aware that Mr. Denton has died," Musgrave said flatly, probably his idea of sympathy.

"Y-yeah," Sonya muttered. "We heard about an hour ago."

"We'll need you two to ID the body, and then I'm going to have to ask you to come down to the sheriff's station with me," Musgrave said. "I have a few—"

"But he's the murderer!" Ally shrieked, pointing at Norbert.

"She attacked me for no reason," Norbert said, and spit blood into the grass.

"You murdered Bill!" Ally shouted. "You should have been locked up with Withingham!"

"How dare you!" Norbert shouted back, and then he addressed Musgrave. "I didn't even know Bill was dead until she attacked me. I had nothing to do with his death."

Michael exchanged a look with Jazz. "She just mentioned Russell," he whispered.

Brows up, Jazz only shrugged, appearing as confused as Michael.

"Now come on, emotions are running high, I know," Musgrave said, hands up. "Everyone needs to cool their jets or you're all under arrest."

"You should've arrested him when he tried to help Withingham cover up killing Dylan, but you let him go," Ally said and pointed again at Norbert. "He's a fucking killer!"

"Watch your language!" Musgrave snapped, then scowled at her. "And how do you know so much about the Dylan Roberts case?"

Ally spit and glared at Norbert. "He's my cousin. Or he was, until Withingham murdered him. That asshole tried to kill my dad too."

"Cousin?" Musgrave and Jazz said at the same time and then gave each other dirty looks.

"So you're Wilson Roberts's daughter, cousin to Dylan Roberts," Musgrave clarified. When Ally nodded, he planted his hands on his hips, looking at Norbert and then Michael. "Well, shit."

The plot thickens, Michael mused. He might have recused himself from Denton's autopsy, but now Michael wondered if his death was somehow connected to Russell. That seemed like a stretch, even for his mystery-novel-fed mind.

"Dad? What's going on?"

Musgrave's daughter, Rae, pushed into the clearing. She was as tiny as her father was huge, and her new fauxhawk haircut surprised Michael. He'd heard Jazz and Musgrave both talk about it, but he had yet to see her in person. It was a drastic change from her previous style, and he felt a twinge of sympathy for Musgrave trying to navigate the unpredictable waters of raising a young woman.

Rae put a hand on Ally's shoulder. "Hey, what are you doing here? I just heard the news about Bill. Are you okay?" She turned on her father, eyes wide. "What did you do to her?"

"I didn't do anything to her," Musgrave said, his tone defensive. "How the hell do you know her?"

"This is my girlfriend." Rae glared up at her father, and when her face screwed up in anger, the tiny blonde actually resembled Musgrave. "I told you about her!"

"Try and keep up, Hilton," Kitty said, glowering at her brother-in-law, then smiling at the two girls. "Hi, Ally. I'm Rae's Aunt Kitty, and this is my husband, Marty."

"Hi, Amanda... sorry, Rae. Hi, Ally," Marty said with a quick lift of his two beers and bashful smile.

Musgrave gaped at them all, then at Rae. He flipped a thumb at Ally. "*This* is your girlfriend?"

"Oh, Hilton," Michael muttered when he saw the disgust in Musgrave's face. It's like he hadn't heard a word Michael told him that afternoon.

"She assaulted me," Norbert shrieked, halting whatever Rae had been about to say. "I demand you arrest her. And Jasper. He threatened me. I fear for my safety."

"What?" Rae said, clutching Ally's arm. "Dad, no!"

"She's a menace and needs to be taken off the streets," Norbert declared, looking surprisingly arrogant even as his face started bruising up.

Michael approached Jazz and took his hand. Jazz hissed in pain, and Michael quickly released it. "Sorry!"

"It's okay." Jazz gave him a small smile. "I'm bummed it's my scissor hand. Guess I'm not used to punching guys in the face."

"You were very brave," Michael said and leaned in closer. "And hot."

"Oh yeah?" Jazz grinned, but it looked sad and tired to Michael. "You like butch fighter-type men?"

"Just so you know, we can hear everything you two are saying," Marty muttered from where he stood a couple of feet away.

"You are the biggest tattletale," Kitty said as she shot a dirty look her husband's way before smiling at them. "Please continue, Jazz Hands and Boss Man. Don't mind us."

"I think I need to put some ice on my hand," Jazz said, then cocked an eyebrow at Kitty. "And you obviously need to read more gay romance novels."

"No one leaves yet," Musgrave declared. "I need statements from each of you. Again."

"At least it's not about a murder this time," Jazz said, then bit his lip as he turned to Michael. "Oh, wait. But it was for you earlier, wasn't it?"

Musgrave approached them, shot a glance over his shoulder at Rae and Ally, and grumbled, "These festivals bring in all the weirdos."

Jazz pursed his lips and narrowed his eyes. "And by weirdos, I'm sure you don't mean people of an LGBTQ persuasion."

To his credit, Musgrave got a stricken expression. "What? Oh, no. I meant.... Forget it." He adjusted his gun belt and peered over his shoulder. "Tompkins!"

The twins answered simultaneously. "Yes, Sheriff?"

"Each of you take a statement from one of these two." He jerked a thumb toward Michael and Jazz. Musgrave surveyed the immediate area where most of the crowd had thinned. "Where the hell is Tanner?"

"Here, sir!"

Musgrave whirled and jumped back when the ginger-haired deputy stood directly behind him. "Dammit, Tanner! I told you not to bunch up in my space."

"Sorry, sir!"

Musgrave glared at Norbert. "Tanner, have Farthington cool his jets in my squad car. You stay with him till I get there. Call the EMTs and get his face looked at. Then I'll take him to the station for questioning."

"The indignity!" Norbert stomped his foot. "What do you need to question me for? I did nothing! They attacked *me*."

A faint grin teased the corner of Musgrave's scowl. "You told me that you fear for your safety. Nowhere safer than the back of my squad car."

Norbert huffed, speechless as Tanner led him away. As the crowd parted, Michael saw two squad cars parked in the middle of the street, their red-and-blue lights flashing.

"What about them?" Grace asked, indicating Sonya and Ally.

"Put them in your car, then when you're finished with Dilworth and Fleishman, take the ladies to ID Denton and then bring both of them back to the station," Musgrave said.

If Michael wasn't mistaken, the sheriff grimaced a little when he used the word *ladies*.

"She didn't do anything!" Rae shrieked, clutching her girlfriend's arm.

A flash of uncertainty crossed Musgrave's face, but then his expression hardened. "Just doing my job, Amanda Rae."

"I told you to call me Rae!" she shouted back.

Musgrave's expression tightened even more. "I'm sorry. It's tough to.... Fine, Rae. You happy?" Without waiting for a response, he directed his attention at Grace Tompkins. "Put them in your cruiser, Deputy."

When Grace hesitated, Musgrave frowned. "You have your orders, Tompkins."

She jumped and then hurried over to Sonya and Ally. "If you would come this way, please."

"This is total bullshit, Dad!" Rae shouted, not letting go of Ally's arm as Grace herded them toward the squad cars. Norbert was already in the back of one car, Tanner standing guard and waiting for the ambulance.

"Sheriff, I trust that you have all of this under control, then?" Trish asked, looking quite authoritative despite her colorful Uncle Sam hat and bedazzled blazer.

"I do, Madam Mayor," Musgrave assured her.

Trish nodded, then announced to everyone nearby, "The night is young, and there are still plenty of drink tickets and more musical performances. Let's all enjoy the festival." She blew a kazoo Michael hadn't seen her pull from her pocket. "Let's get this party restarted!"

That seemed to break up the last remaining onlookers. Grandpa and Mona sidled up immediately to Trish, whispering in hushed tones as they slipped back into the crowd.

"We should go too," Kitty said to Michael and Jazz. Then she glared up at Hilton. "You can be such a giant ass clown, ya know that?"

With a wave of disgust, she followed Rae.

"I'll come with you, Kitty," Misty called after her. Then she paused and placed a gentle hand on Musgrave's arm. His anger disappeared in a flinch. "Patience, Hilton. Patience."

She flitted away, and Musgrave gaped after her before turning to his brother. "What the hell did I do?" he cried, throwing out his hands.

Marty, still holding the two beers, opened his mouth to say something, glanced at his retreating wife, then shrugged. "Gotta go, Hil. Call me later." Then he rushed after Kitty.

Musgrave shot a look at Michael. "This whole thing is a nightmare," he declared. And then he stomped off toward his squad car, where Norbert awaited.

"Well, that was a rather dramatic exit for ol' Hotel Boy," Jazz remarked.

"Indeed."

"Guess I'll see you in the morning, Captain," Steve said with a wave.

"Steve," Michael began, halting the man. When Steve faced him expectantly, Michael fumbled for the right words, finally settling on, "Thank you. And I'll see you tomorrow."

Steve flashed a wink and gave Michael a tiny salute. "No problem, Captain." Then he too disappeared into the festival.

Jazz and Michael turned to find the Tompkins twins standing directly in front of them.

Jazz flinched. "Boy, you two just came out of nowhere."

"Been standing here the whole time," Greg said.

"Did your parents like '80s new wave pop music with a lot of synthesizer?" Jazz asked.

The twins frowned as they looked at him.

"Ever hear of the Thompson Twins?" Jazz continued. "Band from the '80s? 'Hold Me Now'? 'Doctor, Doctor'?"

Michael snickered and wished he could whisk his man away from the festival and into his bed. Now that everything had settled down, visions of his brave boyfriend standing up to all those bullies were dancing salaciously through his mind. He wanted nothing more than to be alone with Jazz, kissing a path down his body as he undressed him.

"You don't think we've ever heard that joke before?" Grace asked.

"Pretty much every day of our lives," Greg said.

Jazz gave them an elaborate, wide-eyed look. "Even when you were babies?"

Michael let out a laugh, then cleared his throat and turned away as the twins gave him the evil eye.

"I'll take the one who thinks he's so funny," Grace said.

"Guess I get the mortician," Greg said, and pulled out a small notebook.

It didn't take long for them to give their statements, and by the time they'd both finished, a new musical group had taken to the stage. The sun hung low over the lake now, and the mosquitos were out in force. A cloying mix of bug repellent, citronella, sunscreen, body spray, and patchouli floated over the crowd, the strong aromas kicking off a headache for Michael.

Misty came up beside him and rubbed his back. "You okay, Michael?"

"Oh, I'm fine." He looked over to where Jazz had apparently finished giving his statement to Grace and was talking to her about possible hairstyles. "It's him I'm worried about."

"He would hate for me to say this, but I am too. He's been through a lot this year." She wrapped an arm around Michael's waist and pulled him close to her side. "You're the brightest spot in his life right now. I'm so glad you found each other."

Michael gave her a side-armed hug in return, overcome with affection for his new friends. "I am too."

She stepped back and patted his arm. "Give him some time. He's going through a lot of changes."

Something in Misty's tone made Michael want to ask what she meant, but at that moment Jazz approached, so he let it go.

"How's Rae?" Jazz asked, and they all watched the squad car with two grieving women in the back fade into the night. A bright red ambulance took its place, bringing EMTs to check Norbert for serious injuries.

Misty sighed. "She'll be fine. I talked to her and Hilton."

"And?" Michael questioned. He had hoped Musgrave would think twice when it came to Rae, because his usual brusque manner wasn't helping.

She waved airily. "They'll figure it out. Hilton is just doing his job, and I think Rae knows that. Ally isn't under arrest or anything. They need them to identify the...." Her voice trailed off. "Well, you know. *Bill.*" She whispered his name. "They'll be finished in an hour or so. Rae is going to bring Ally by the salon tomorrow so she can pick up her braid. I think they want to get pedicures."

"Can't be all that upset if they're planning spa services," Jazz remarked.

"What do you mean, pick up her braid?" Michael asked.

"When I cut her hair, we kept a foot of it so she could send it off to a place that makes wigs for kids with cancer," Jazz explained.

"How nice."

"Oh, there's Dottie," Misty said, her face brightening. "Did you get to hear them play before the commotion? Oslo was amazing, wasn't he?"

Michael and Jazz exchanged looks, and Michael answered for them, "Yes, we saw them. He's quite talented."

"He is," Misty agreed, then waved good night. "Jazz, I'll see you in the morning. Michael, you're coming to my block party Sunday, right?"

"Wouldn't miss it." Since Jazz came into his life, Michael had developed quite the social calendar, and he rather enjoyed it.

Misty hurried over to her cousin, Dorothy, who hovered near the stage entrance with a disapproving expression. Dorothy had her arm around her daughter, and her husband stood behind them, his expression condemning, as he held a Bible with a long bookmark against his chest. Behind them, Oslo was dutifully collecting the broken strings from his violin bow off the stage floor. Yeah, they were weird, all right.

"Nice save, sweetie," Jazz said, and then he frowned and shook his hand. "Do you mind if we leave now? I should get some ice on my hand."

A banjo player currently on stage hit a sour note, making them grimace.

"I don't mind at all," Michael said. "Let's go."

"I hope you have wine at home," Jazz said.

"I do."

"A lot of wine."

Michael chuckled. "Oh, I do."

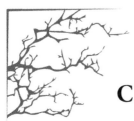

CHAPTER ELEVEN

Jazz held the ice pack wrapped in a dish towel against his knuckles as he sat on a stool at the granite-topped island in Michael's kitchen. His hand ached, but not too bad. He just hoped it wouldn't swell. It would be hell trying to hold a pair of scissors with swollen fingers.

Michael puttered in the kitchen, putting together something for them to eat. Jazz leaned down to sip his wine through the bamboo straw Michael had added to the full-to-the-brim wineglass he'd set in front of Jazz.

Of course Michael would have reusable drinking straws instead of plastic. And of course he would be considerate enough to not only provide an ice pack wrapped in a dish towel, but the straw itself to allow Jazz to drink hands-free. Jazz wasn't sure what he'd done to deserve meeting such a thoughtful, caring, patient man—with a hot body and a cock to match—but he hoped the universe saw fit to keep them together.

"This has been a crazy night," Michael said with a sigh.

"Yup," Jazz agreed.

"I can't believe we were almost in a fight...." He looked over his shoulder. "Well, you did dodge that guy's punch and throw a good one yourself. Where'd you learn to fight?"

"It was a big place back home called Being Gay in the Midwest," Jazz said with a sigh.

"At least we didn't end up in jail."

"You don't think you'd like to stay at the Hilton?" Jazz said, referring to the Lacetown jail's nickname.

"Not especially." Michael turned and leaned on the island. "I can't believe how everyone stood up for us when that homophobe started name-calling."

Jazz smiled at Michael's shocked expression. "That was pretty cool, huh?"

"And surprising how *many* people stood up." With a disbelieving smile, Michael shook his head. "Trish was amazing."

Jazz recalled Michael telling him once that he didn't have much in the way of friends. Michael's own self-deprecating personality did not allow him to see how wonderful he was, or how much everyone who took the time to get to know him adored him.

Why, that odd and creepy little apprentice, Ezra, even followed Michael around like a puppy dog!

Jazz watched Michael get out some plates. He loved the domestic bliss of evenings like this. Over the past couple of weeks Michael had kept up with Jazz's active social life—something he had been a little concerned about in the beginning. Michael was reserved, but he didn't seem to mind being with other people... if Jazz was there. And while Jazz still liked to go out and be with people, he socialized for a living, so he treasured the quiet evenings spent inside with his shy mortician.

But the man *certainly* was not shy in bed.

"Well, sweetie," Jazz said. "We apparently know how to have enough of a good time to make the cops show up but not get arrested." He sipped more wine. "Poor Ally. Can you believe that she's Dylan's cousin and Wilson's daughter? I can't imagine what she's been through. She must've been really close to Dylan to lose it like that. I hope Musgrave isn't being a dick to her."

"It's Musgrave," Michael countered, then looked thoughtful. "Kind of makes sense why she's got it in for Norbert."

"Do you think she's been stalking him?" Jazz asked. "Kind of a coincidence that she's part of his old band, and then just *happens* to show up here in town as he's trolling for musicians to represent."

"I wondered the same. Could she have hired a private investigator or something?" Michael wondered aloud. "Someone to track Norbert's movements?"

"Who knows? Does any of this shit in Lacetown make sense anymore?" Jazz asked. "I mean, if they declared that Roswell aliens were here first... shit's so crazy here now... how could I argue?"

Michael chuckled, though there was always a little bit of truth in a joke. "Indeed."

Indeed. Sooooo.... "Any word from the nemesis?" Jazz asked, his gaze on Michael's strong arms. He was tired of talking about Norbert and all the bad memories he'd surfaced.

Michael looked over his shoulder in the direction of the funeral parlor. "Nothing yet. He's here, though. That's his truck in the parking lot."

Jazz slid off the kitchen stool and walked to the sliding door that opened onto the back patio. He peered next door and saw a large, black pickup parked outside the back entrance. It's freshly waxed surface gleamed in the last of the daylight.

Mr. Pickles sat at the door, gazing out into the yard, the tip of his tail slowly twitching. Jazz made quiet smooching sounds until the cat looked up at him.

"How's my favorite big kitty?" Jazz crooned.

Mr. Pickles gave him a slow blink before returning his attention to the oncoming night beyond the glass.

"He loves me," Jazz said and returned to the kitchen stool. "So the nemesis has a shiny black pickup, huh? Is that what he uses to harvest the bodies?"

That earned him the laugh he was fishing for.

"Harvest. Ha!" Michael turned from the counter and set two plates on the island before Jazz. One plate held reheated chunks of the pot roast Michael had slow cooked the day before, and the other was a selection of cut vegetables.

"But no," Michael continued as he settled onto the stool next to Jazz. "He just likes to drive a big truck. He's also got a Cadillac hearse, unless that was lost in the fire."

"Along with Mr. Jones," Jazz said, fighting a chuckle. He knew Michael had been matter-of-fact when he'd told them about Trevino's fire and the subsequent swelling of the obese Mr. Jones, but that whole "now, Jazz, don't laugh" routine had been funny, whether he meant it to be or not. Jazz had intended to tell Kitty when he gave her and Marty drink tickets, but tracking Norbert had interrupted his chance.

Michael shook his head. "Such an unnecessary tragedy."

"It got the job done." Jazz sampled the pot roast and sighed. "You do know how to work with meat."

Michael blushed as he selected a cube of roast. "How's your hand feel?"

Jazz flexed his fingers. "Still a little sore, but better than it was." He set aside the towel-wrapped ice pack, and Michael immediately scooped it up and returned it to the freezer.

"Thanks for taking care of me," Jazz said. Since he'd been a teen, Jazz had taken care of himself. His mother had worked all the time, and no man—not even Russell—had doted on him like Michael did. Michael was always doing such nice things for him, and it made Jazz glow with happiness. Honeymoon phase or not, Michael was a damn fine catch.

"I'm happy to do it." Michael returned to the stool beside him. "To be honest, I was a little surprised earlier when you stepped in to protect Norbert."

Jazz nodded. "No more surprised than I was myself. No idea what came over me."

"Human compassion," he offered. "Which is just one of the things I like about you."

"Oh, just one of the things?" Jazz smirked. "What are the others?"

Michael returned his smirk. "We can cover those later. Seriously though, the way you stood up to that group of guys was really impressive."

He held up his hand. "Or foolish."

"I prefer impressive." Michael took Jazz's hand and placed a gentle kiss on the knuckles. "And sexy."

A longing trembled through Jazz, and his cock started to respond. What kind of craziness was he into when a simple kiss on the hand was enough to get his blood flowing south? Russell had never had that fast of an effect on him.

Russell. What a primo raging and inflamed asshole.

And no one he needed to be thinking of right then. He turned his mind away from thoughts of Russell and back to the moment at hand before all his negative juju ruined the evening.

"What you said to Norbert afterwards was a little...." Michael paused, searching for the right word. "Dark."

Jazz sighed. "After that shit he said about you, I couldn't help myself. He's a hemorrhoid-afflicted, stretched-out asshole."

Michael made a face. "That's, um, graphic."

"Thank you." Jazz smiled. "Speaking of pains in the ass, any idea where Nemesis Trevino is staying in town?"

"Nope. If I know him like I think I do, I would assume the Inn on Windswept Point."

Jazz raised his eyebrows. "That fancy-schmancy bed-and-breakfast out near the lighthouse?"

"The very one."

"He really does go all out, doesn't he?"

Michael shrugged. "He tends to pamper himself."

"How do you know so much about him?" Jazz crunched a carrot and selected another cube of roast. "Did you two date or something?"

Michael's eyes widened so much, Jazz worried he might hurt himself.

"No! I can't...." Michael shuddered. "Just, no. Trevino has always been competitive with his peers. First with Grandpa, because Trevino was younger and had something to prove, and then with me because I'm younger than him and he thinks he can intimidate me."

"So you never fucked on one of those cold steel tables?"

Michael made a face of disgust. "That's gross for a number of reasons. And as far as I know, he's straight. Like, really straight. Frankly I don't care to know because I don't want to think about him in any kind of sexual way."

"Which you're doing now because you can't help yourself," Jazz said with a smirk.

When Michael blustered further, Jazz laughed. God, he loved teasing his uptight mortician. Being with Michael was so much easier than being with Russell.

Michael gave him a gentle glare. "You're asking for trouble."

Jazz blinked in feigned innocence. "Who? Me?"

Moving slowly like a predator stalking prey, Michael approached. A flush of excitement heated Jazz's face and the mild throb in his hand melted away.

"You know what happens to guys who don't know when to quit?"

Michael's voice was soft and deep, and he leaned in to press the hard line of his cock against Jazz's leg.

"They win?" Jazz whispered.

Michael smirked. "Yeah, they do."

And he leaned in for a kiss. It was soft at first, almost sweet, but quickly turned more eager. Michael's tongue swiped along the seam of Jazz's mouth, and Jazz opened for him. The kiss deepened, became more forceful, and Michael growled hungrily.

"Bedroom?" Jazz asked.

"Glad you got the hint," Michael said, and took Jazz by his uninjured hand to lead him to the stairs.

In the bedroom, they kissed as they fumbled with each other's clothes. When that became too complicated, Jazz stepped back and locked his gaze with Michael's as they stripped. He enjoyed the slow reveal of Michael's body beneath his layers of clothing. The pale skin of his torso, which practically gleamed in the soft glow of a corner lamp, covered with fine dark hairs that traveled south to a thick dark patch at the root of his dick. And that cock, that glorious, throbbing cock that stuck out toward Jazz as if reaching for him. Jazz's mouth watered and he licked his lips as he released his hair so it fell around his shoulders in gentle waves.

"You're beautiful," Michael said, his tone almost reverential.

"And you're hotter than a man has any right to be," Jazz said, then got on his knees and took Michael into his mouth.

Michael's hand curled into the loose strands of Jazz's hair, and he said through a drawn-out sigh, "Oh God."

Jazz sucked him slowly, dragging his lips up the length to purse around the soft cap. Michael's legs trembled and his hand tightened in Jazz's hair. There was nothing more arousing to Jazz than getting his quiet mortician to open up and let go. And over these last few weeks, he'd learned quite a few of Michael's pressure points.

"I need to taste you," Michael said after a gasp and stepped back. He pulled Jazz to his feet, kissed him firmly, then turned him around and directed him toward the bed. "On the bed, on your hands and knees. Now."

Oh my! Jazz's cock jumped at Michael's commanding tone, and a long string of precum dribbled out. Michael made his cock think it was seventeen again! He climbed up on the bed and positioned himself on all fours with his feet just off the side of the mattress. Michael placed a hand on either asscheek and spread them apart.

"I love looking at you like this," Michael murmured.

Jazz shivered when Michael leaned in close and blew a gentle breath across the sweat-damp crack of his ass. The shiver grew to a tremble when Michael ran the flat of his tongue slowly over his hole.

"Oh, Michael, what you do to me."

Michael set his glasses on the nightstand, then said, "I've got a lot more in mind."

And Jazz was more than ready to entertain whatever Michael intended. He loved this more intense and yet somehow playful side to his lover. From what Michael had revealed in conversations about past relationships, he'd never really felt free to indulge in his fantasies until he'd met Jazz.

Lucky me.

Michael spread Jazz's asscheeks wider and leaned in close. The brush of a day's growth of stubble across his tender ring coaxed a gasp out of Jazz. And when Michael pushed the tip of his tongue into him, Jazz moaned and lowered his forehead to rest on his uninjured hand. As Michael tongue-fucked him, Jazz groaned and grunted and pushed his hips back against Michael's mouth.

With wet and sloppy kisses, Michael soaked Jazz with spit. As he slid his tongue down from Jazz's anus to his balls, Michael eased a long, slender finger into him. Jazz moaned and spread his legs a little wider. He wanted to do something for or to Michael, but he was behind him and out of reach.

Another finger joined the first inside of him, and Jazz's dick jumped and pumped out another runner of precum. Michael licked and spit around the edges of Jazz's hole as he pushed his fingers in and pulled them out. Jazz could tell Michael was more intense this time, deeper into his fantasies, and it made him feel good that Michael could be this open with him.

The fingers eased out of him and were replaced by Michael's tongue. He'd curled it tight at the tip, a trick he'd demonstrated on Jazz more than once, and which no one else had ever done. Not even Russell, who loved eating things like frozen strawberries and circus peanuts out of Jazz—and all his other men he'd had on the side.

But Michael wasn't anything like Russell. Michael was steady and true, and he'd never made Jazz feel second best to anyone or anything else.

And why was he thinking about Russell at that moment? Oh, right, the fucking divorce papers.

Fuck, why couldn't he get Russell out of his mind once and for all? Wasn't there a pill or a surgery or something that would remove those memories for good?

Michael pushed a finger into him again, and Jazz imagined Michael's expert finger-fucking was a damn fine start to erasing Russell from his mind. Then that finger nailed Jazz's prostate at the same time Michael dipped down to suck Jazz's balls. A practical flash flood of precum surged out of Jazz and pooled on the sheet.

"You've got me so worked up," Jazz said with a moan. "I need more than that inside me."

Michael kissed up along Jazz's spine, making him tremble as he fingered him, working him open. When Michael arched over him, he bit gently on Jazz's shoulder, whispering in his ear, "Damn, I wish I could just be in you, my dick, your ass, skin to skin. Nothing in between."

Jazz's stomach leaped. "Oh yeah?"

But Michael was purring, inhaling Jazz's scent as if in a daze, lost to the pleasure he was doing to Jazz's ass.

Through the wave of euphoria, questions bounced in Jazz's mind. Did Michael really want to take that next step? With Jazz? Even after everything?

"Um," Jazz began, brought slightly out of the moment by Michael's suggestion. "FYI, I don't have anything, if you really wanted to. I mean, I got tested after...."

He didn't want to say Russell's cheating, but Michael seemed to know what he meant.

Michael withdrew his fingers, and their eyes met. "I always get tested, every year too. Trust me?"

Breathless with sudden want, and an overwhelming need to have Michael like this—just the two of them, open and honest—made Jazz tremble. "Yeah, I do."

Michael flashed a wolfish grin. "Then do you want to go bareback?"

Jazz smiled back. "Yeah. Let's do it."

"Oh, baby," Michael said, his voice deep with lust. He slapped each of Jazz's asscheeks lightly, and followed that up with gentle bites before pushing to his feet and moving to the nightstand.

Jazz watched from under one arm as Michael opened the lube and squirted a generous amount along his thick, bare dick. He applied some to the end of his fingers, and then moved back between Jazz's legs. The mattress dipped as Michael climbed behind him.

"God, the sight of you open and waiting like this is so fucking hot." Michael's voice had an edge to it that Jazz had never heard before, and it tightened his stomach with anticipation as Michael slicked him up.

He'd never felt this connected with Russell. Never.

Stop fucking thinking about Russell Fucking Withingham!

The crown of Michael's cock touched Jazz's hole, hot and slick. It stayed there, just pressing against the threshold, and Michael leaned down to gently kiss Jazz's back. Then Michael placed the palm of his hand right over the spot he'd kissed and eased his dick into him. It was a slow, steady thrust that opened Jazz up and filled him.

Purring from the new shared sensations, Michael pulled back and pushed in again, and then again, moving faster with each stroke. "So warm...." He groaned and Jazz was too lost to reply.

It had been a long time since he'd made love like this, but then nothing had ever felt quite as fantastic as Michael's perfect cock thrusting inside him, hitting his gland. Michael braced himself on Jazz's ass, fingers gripping each cheek tight enough to leave marks. His cock hit all the right spots, thick, solid, and oh-so warm.

This was way better than it had ever been with Rus—

Jazz let out a cry when Michael's fingers twisted in the back of his hair, grabbing tight, the sting of pain bringing Jazz fully into the moment. Suddenly his only thought was Michael and the rhythm of their bodies. Michael gripped his asscheek, his other hand holding Jazz by the hair. Jazz was completely consumed, wrapped up and united with Michael. Jazz's skin prickled with heat and it felt like every nerve ending was alight. Michael filled him perfectly, touching all the places deep inside him. And not just with his naked cock or his skilled fingers. Michael lit up the shadowy spots inside of Jazz, the dark corners where all the bad memories and thoughts lived.

It was liberating, and more than a little frightening.

"You feel so good around my dick," Michael said, and then smacked Jazz's asscheek hard as he pulled back on his hair.

"Oh, damn, ride that ass!"

Slap, slap!

Michael had never pulled his hair and spanked him like this before, but he seemed deep in the pleasure of their bodies, finally united the way it should have always been. Nothing but the two of them, flesh to flesh, passion and heat.

When Michael delivered a fast staccato of slaps to the bottom of his ass as he pounded him, Jazz let out a wild cry. "Michael... ugh...*fuck*!"

Jazz pushed up to all fours again as the sound of sweaty skin slapping quickened. He was close, and from the speed of his thrusts, Michael might be as well.

How long had it been since Jazz had felt so in tune with a partner? Had he ever felt this much in sync? He closed his eyes and let Michael take control of him, riding his ass like a rodeo cowboy, his hair the reins. When he brought the flat of his hand down on Jazz's other cheek, Jazz gave up, collapsing onto one shoulder, exposing himself to Michael in every way, body and heart.

"Oh God," Michael gasped, strong hand gripping Jazz's heated ass and pounding harder. "I'm close. So close."

Barely propped up, face pressed into the bedding and Michael still holding his hair, Jazz reached down to stroke himself, the sticky-slick precum allowing his hand to glide along himself. "Me too. Just fuck me! Don't stop!"

Michael's hips sped up even more, banging against him. The fingers tightened in his hair and sent tingles of pain across his scalp, but Jazz didn't care. The pain kept him focused on the moment, his mind firmly rooted in the present with Michael.

"I'm there, oh God," Michael practically screamed, and hammered at Jazz as he grunted through his orgasm.

Jazz felt Michael's hot load filling him deep, and he came a moment later, eyes rolled up and cum splashing onto the sheets. He collapsed on top of his spunk, and Michael slipped out and dropped down on his back beside him.

"Oh my God," Michael said between panting breaths. "I'm seeing stars." He turned his head to look at him. "Was it okay for you? It wasn't too much, was it?"

Jazz smiled. "It was great."

A bright smile was his reward, and Jazz cherished it.

For all the light Michael had brought into Jazz's life, he wished he knew what Michael got in return. Other than amazing sex, of course, Jazz had gotten Michael tangled up in a twisted murder scenario, his cat abducted, and both of them nearly killed. Not to mention all the police statements.

And now with Norbert stomping around the festival and Dylan's relatives showing up, it was like a recurring nightmare they couldn't awaken from. Michael had made him forget in the moment, but now it all came flooding back to the fore.

"Hey, you all right?" The sweet concern in Michael's voice sent a shot of guilt straight into Jazz's gut. "Your expression got kind of sad there. You sure I wasn't too rough?"

Jazz rolled onto his back and took Michael's hand. The fingers of his injured hand had gone quiet during sex, but now they were aching something fierce. And his mind kept running in a loop, trying to think up something good he had done for Michael but coming up empty. What exactly was Michael getting out of this relationship? Jazz brought a lot of baggage from his time with Russell. That made it sound like past tense, though, and it wasn't even close. With the goddamn divorce papers he'd received today, Jazz was going to be "involved" with Russell for months to come. And that didn't even take into account what roles they might play in the trial.

Was that fair to Michael?

And why the hell was his brain doing this to him when all Jazz really wanted was to bask with his man in the afterglow of some hot sex? Especially after such an important first step of ditching the condoms. Was there any possible way his brain would be able to switch the channel away from thoughts of Russell?

"Jazz?" Michael's voice intruded on his thoughts. "You haven't said anything."

Michael rolled on his side and propped himself up on an elbow. His expression was serious and concerned, and Jazz's heart fluttered a bit at the sight.

Russell had never looked at him that way.

Not once.

For fuck's sake, stop thinking about Russell! You're here with Michael. Enjoy it.

But there was no turning back now. Memories of them walking in on Russell trying to drown Dylan's uncle—Ally's dad—in the tub came roaring back, along with the brutal fight afterward that nearly got them killed. And then the memories morphed into seeing the panicked agony on Michael's face as they searched for Mr. Pickles, who had disappeared while they'd been having sex for the first time.

I'm ruining our honeymoon phase....

"Jazz? Did I hurt you?"

The tremor in Michael's voice brought Jazz back, and he managed to smile as inside his head every bad thing he'd brought upon this sweet man played on a loop.

"You could never hurt me. But I do need to get back to my own apartment. Tomorrow's an early day and I want to settle in with another glass of wine and ice my hand. You understand, don't you?"

The smile looked genuine, but Jazz could see concern in the tiny crease between Michael's eyebrows. "Yeah. Of course. Have you had enough to eat?"

"Everything was perfect." Jazz rolled onto his side and gave him a soft, lingering kiss. "Just like you. I hate to fuck and run, but I really do need to get home. It's been the longest day."

"Yeah, sure, sure."

They got off the bed and dressed in awkward silence. It was so different from how things usually ended between them, but Jazz had no idea what to say to make Michael feel better. Losing the rubbers was a big step, one they'd made so easily, but what did Jazz really have to offer Michael? He wanted to say something, but what could he say that might return the ease they'd shared earlier that day when Michael brought him a coffee?

Shit, had they lost that?

Jazz didn't know.

At that moment he needed some space to get his head on right.

As Jazz zipped his jeans, Michael stepped up and slid his arms around his waist. "You're sure I didn't hurt you? The whole... you know?"

It was cute how Michael couldn't voice his actions when the heat of the moment was over. Jazz wanted to tell Michael he had done quite the opposite: opened up his closed and tired heart. But that would lead to more questions and more conversation, and Jazz had too many thoughts of Russell barging through his mind to be able to pull off any of that the way he needed to. The way Michael deserved for him to.

"I'm positive, sweetie." Another quick kiss and Jazz slipped from Michael's arms to head for the bedroom door. "I just need to get home and get settled and ice my hand. It's been a strange evening."

"To say the least," Michael said and followed him out of the bedroom and down the stairs.

Jazz gathered his house keys and cell phone that he'd casually tossed on the kitchen table and pocketed them. A hardcover book lying open caught his eye. "Is that...?" Jazz had to catch his breath.

"What?" Michael came over and quickly looked like he'd been caught in a lie. "Oh, yes, um...."

"You're reading Russell's books again?" Jazz wasn't really surprised. Michael was a longtime fan, after all, but Jazz was... disappointed.

"Yes, I'm searching them for clues to help the prosecution build a case that Dylan's death was premeditated," Michael said in his mortician's voice, making Jazz flinch.

Might as well have been saying *I'm sorry for your loss.*

"Did you know that Russell is pleading insanity, claiming amnesia?" Michael told him.

"No, no, I didn't know." Jazz shook his head, trying to shake loose all thoughts of his murdering, lying, soon-to-be-official ex-husband. Michael's words were perfectly logical, and looking in Russell's books for clues was very intelligent. But still....

Why the hell couldn't Russell just disappear? Why was he ruining things between Jazz and Michael?

And why was Jazz letting him do it?

Michael touched his arm. "I'm sorry I didn't tell you. I thought it would upset you. I know you say that you're okay, but everything that happened, what Russell tried to do... just know that I'm here to talk when you're ready."

Sweet, thoughtful Michael. If I tell you everything in my head, you'll realize how badly I'm ruining your life and you'll drop me like a hot potato. But I'm selfish, and I want to keep you for as long as I can.

Of course he didn't say that out loud.

Instead, Jazz smiled up at him, grateful to see Michael's real smile, not the mortician one, and hear his real voice. Michael cared for Jazz—though Lord only knew why—and Jazz had to stop letting Russell fuck with his head. Russell was in prison, out of his life.

He pulled all of his strength to give Michael a genuine smile. "Thanks, sweetie." He gestured airily to Russell's book. "And I get it. Makes total sense. Gotta build a case. Did you find anything good in those pages that'll keep his ass in jail and away from me forever?"

He tried to make that sound like a joke, and judging by Michael's pitying look, he'd failed epically.

"Quite a few things, yes."

"Cool, cool."

Jazz tried to make everything seem normal after that, and crouched down to bid Mr. Pickles goodbye and give him some pets. But nothing felt normal about this. It felt like Jazz had fucked something up, and he didn't know how to fix it.

Fucking Russell.

Stop thinking about Russell!

He rose and kissed Michael once again, then took a moment to meet his gaze. "Sleep well, sweetie."

"You too. I'll talk with you tomorrow?"

"It's a date." After a final kiss, Jazz turned away and slipped out the sliding door into the humid night.

He walked quickly along the streets, wanting nothing more than to be back in his apartment. His ass was tender from that hard fucking, asscheeks still alive from Michael's slaps, and he could feel the slickness of Michael's cum leaking out of him. The sensations should have made him smile, or at the very least urged him to send a naughty text to Michael about it, but he couldn't shake off the toxicity—the dark, noxious waves, Trish had called it. A few people were walking down Main Street, couples mostly, all hand in hand, and Jazz looked away from them. He seemed to bring darkness to those closest to him.

That sounded way more dramatic than he'd intended, even in his own mind, and he chastised himself for being such a drama queen as he approached the chandlery building, which housed Misty's Makeover Palace, the Robichaux Bakery, and Yvette's Haberdashery on the ground level, and Holland Harbor Lofts above. Jazz's apartment was right above the bakery, and he loved waking up every morning to the smell of their baked goods.

The only thing better was waking up beside Michael.

But maybe he needed a bit of a break from that. Nothing too long, of course, merely enough to allow him to clear his head of the troubling memories of Russell. And let him read through the divorce papers or hire a lawyer to do it, and make sure he wasn't going to be fucked by Russell one more time. Michael deserved Jazz at 100 percent, not this current state of negative, distracted, hot mess.

He rounded the corner of the building to the back parking lot and headed for the residential entrance. When he was a yard or so from the door, movement in the shadows down by the back entrance of the salon made him stop. A chill went through him, and he reached for his phone in his back pocket.

A figure moved into view beneath the parking lot lights, the motion tripping the sensor for the light over the back door.

Ally Roberts!

She must've finished giving her statement over at the police station.

Was it a coincidence that she was hanging around outside the salon, or was there something more sinister afoot? Jazz thought about calling out, but Ally scurried away, maybe scared off by the sudden flood of light, and he lost sight of her in the surrounding darkness.

Well, that was interesting.

Jazz approached the back door of the salon and tried the knob. Still locked. Maybe she'd just been looking for a place to smoke a joint or something, get some time to herself. Jazz could more than understand that. He had a key, but he didn't see a need to let himself in. He'd be there soon enough for his 8:00 a.m. client, Kevin Raines, the director at the Bluffs at Lake View retirement community. Since Kevin got kinda pissy if Jazz ran late, he always made sure Kevin was first on his schedule—which made a craptastic start for the day—and never at the end of his day.

Not only would Kevin be disgruntled when Jazz was inevitably running late after a full day of clients, but if Kevin was last on the schedule, Jazz had a hard time ending the appointment politely since Kevin was always trying to flirt and ask him out, no matter how many times Jazz insisted he did not date his clients and that...

He. Had. A. Boyfriend.

Whatever, Jazz thought. At least Kevin was a good tipper.

He returned to the residential entrance and keyed in the entry code. Once inside, he climbed the steps and drew up short when he saw a tall man in a yellow hawaiian shirt step out of Kurt and Sarah's apartment. It was the man he'd seen at the festival earlier, the one who'd been watching Misty's cousins perform.

Suspicious, Jazz asked, "Oh, hi. You a friend of Kurt and Sarah?"

The man shook his head of thick blond hair. "No, I found the room on Airbnb. Great place. I'll be giving it a five star."

A tourist, then. Jazz fought a frown. "Yeah, we like it here."

Those millennial twits. They were gonna get themselves kicked out when the landlord discovered they were renting out their loft. It was a direct violation of their lease.

Jazz was really too tired to give too many fucks about it at this point. Waving at the tourist, he let himself into his apartment. It felt familiar, but not as warm and inviting as Michael's place. Jazz had become spoiled being with Michael. He hoped it hadn't clouded his judgment. Maybe he shouldn't have agreed to losing the condoms tonight. That was a big step, and Michael deserved a lot more connection than what Jazz had been able to provide him tonight.

Maybe Michael deserved someone better than Jazz overall.

A sigh slipped out before he realized it, and Jazz switched on the television, then headed for the kitchen to get an ice pack for his hand and a glass of wine for his troubled mind.

CHAPTER TWELVE

"Stupid fucking sheriff," Ally groused, throwing her wallet on the motel bed.

"He's doing his job, trying to find who killed Bill," Sonya said as she followed Ally into the room and closed the door. A forgotten box with a slice of vegan pizza, discarded paper plates, and napkins littered the small hotel table, and their instrument cases and suitcases took up much of the floor space in the cheap room.

Ally glared at her new bandmate. "You *know* who killed him. We both sat here and watched Bill pace this floor and talk about that fucking Norbert all afternoon and evening. And then he went out for a 'walk,' which we both know is code for him getting on Grindr and finding a hookup."

"You don't know that." Sonya sat on the end of the bed, facing away from Ally, shoulders defeated. She looked tired, used up, and Ally knew she was grieving deeply. Sonya and Bill had toured together a long time.

Ally snorted. "I asked him where he was going, and he acted guilty. He went for a hookup. I know it, and you know it. Then he never came back."

If the damn sheriff had found Bill's phone, they'd know for sure.

Sonya turned toward her, tears in her eyes and a fierce expression on her drawn and pale face. "And you barely know us. You only joined the band a few weeks ago. You don't know what it was like all those years ago when we were playing with Norbert. To see him again after all this time. It was quite shocking for me, and I'm sure even more so for Bill."

Sonya placed a hand on the pillow where Bill had slept two nights before. A tear ran down her cheek, and she wiped it away before getting to her feet. "Anyway, we need to let the sheriff and his deputies do their job. They'll figure out what happened to Bill."

"I know what happened to him," Ally said with a sneer. "That fucker Norbert killed him, just like he helped that fucking hack writer kill my cousin."

"I can't believe that you know Norbert too," Sonya said. "What a small, cruel, cruel world."

Not such a small world, but definitely cruel.

A ball of grief wedged in Ally's throat, making it difficult to breathe. Losing Bill had brought all the pain of losing Dylan rushing back, like she was learning about his murder for the first time all over again.

"I can see you're upset," Sonya said, tears flowing freely now. She wiped them away and grabbed her purse. "I'm going to that bar down the street for a drink. Care to join me?"

Ally was crying as well, and she vehemently shook her head, unable to speak for fear the word "no" would come out as a sob.

"I think we both need some time on our own," Sonya said and left the room.

Ally fell onto the bed, burying her face in her arms as she wept.

Dylan had only wanted a chance to show the world what he was capable of, to prove his talent as a writer. When Russell Withingham had started hitting on him, Dylan had confided to Ally that he intended to make the most of the relationship while it lasted. Poor Dylan wasn't used to staying with a guy for longer than six weeks.

But the six weeks had come and gone, and they'd still been together. Then once Russell had separated from his husband, he'd asked Dylan to move in with him. Dylan had been pretty much head over heels by then, and although Ally had warned him to take things slow, he'd jumped at the chance for a happily ever after.

And now he was dead. No more writing, no more dancing, no more late night phone calls and video chats. No more listening to podcasts about cold cases and brainstorming as she helped Dylan plot his mystery novel. A novel stolen as swiftly as his life. All of that was over with, and all because Russell had wanted Dylan's book.

And Norbert had helped.

Ally concocted her plan for revenge weeks ago. Using her meager savings, she'd paid a private investigator to dig into Norbert's life. She'd seen

Norbert's post on Instagram that he was headed to the Acoustic Music Festival—only forty-six followers. Pretty sad. Her ex-girlfriend's hamster Puffball had two thousand. The PI had told her about Norbert's old band, The Lanky Balladeers, and as luck would have it, they'd posted on Facebook they needed a new guitarist. It hadn't taken much for her to be hired. She'd always been good at guitar. Ally had casually mentioned the festival to Bill and Sonya over dinner one evening, and when Bill got excited about the idea, she almost felt guilty about not mentioning Norbert would be there. The poor guy still had feelings for Norbert, no matter what Sonya tried to tell Ally after the run-in at that greasy diner. The foolish woman had been pining for Bill. It was more obvious than the nose on her face.

"It's been a few years since we did the festival circuit, Sones," Bill had said. "We're a trio again. Let's get out on the road and let our folk-punk flag fly. Come on, what do you say?"

Sonya had taken more convincing, a lot more, but in the end she'd relented to Bill's enthusiasm, and they'd packed up Bill's old Subaru and headed for Michigan.

The closer they got to the state line, the more snappish and irritable Ally had become. She needed to see Norbert face-to-face, finally confront the scumbag who had helped Russell take her cousin from her, and nearly took her father as well.

When she'd come out, she'd lost everything. She had been living with her mother at the time, and Mom shoved her out the door without so much as a toothbrush. She hadn't even been able to take her cell phone with her since her mom paid the bill and snatched it from her hand before slamming the door in her face.

For a few nights, she'd stayed at a shelter for LGBT youth, until she'd talked her way into a ride with a lady trucker to Chicago, damn close to where Dad lived. She'd walked the rest of the way, flipping off carloads of guys hollering at her out windows as they passed, and running through the woods to escape those who pulled over. When she arrived at her dad's place in Gary, Indiana, he'd welcomed her with a hug and a hot meal. He'd loaned her a pair of sweats as he washed her filthy clothes, and then let her sleep in his bed as he took the couch.

Things with Dad had been good for a while. She and Dylan chatted more often, and Dad kept her fed and clothed and got her a cell phone and a new guitar. She'd met Rae at a bar near the college, and they'd hit it off.

Then Dylan had been murdered, and her world went gray. Sweet, wonderful, and talented Dylan, suddenly gone. And in such a horrible way.

And then Dad had nearly met the same fate.

Norbert Farthington might as well have held both of them under that tub faucet, the simpering idiot.

From what Dylan used to tell her during their chats, and what her father had seen when he'd gone to Lacetown to look for Dylan, Norbert had been obsessed with Russell and would have done anything for him. Hell, Dad said that Norbert had offered to help Russell get rid of all the witnesses when that hairdresser and mortician had caught him.

Those two weren't very high on Ally's list either. While they had saved Dad, they shouldered blame for Dylan's death too. Dylan had called Ally shortly after the hairdresser had caused a big scene at Russell's book signing. The incident had embarrassed Russell, and Dylan as well.

That could have set Russell off, since he had killed Dylan that same night.

And the body count was still rising.

Ally knew deep down that Bill had met up with Norbert last night. She'd argued with him about it as he got ready to head out the door, and then he was found dead. And in the mortician's hearse, no less. Norbert had the heart of a killer. Even if he hadn't actively murdered Dylan and mutilated his corpse, he'd intended to help Russell kill Dad and the rest of them. Norbert was an accomplice then and a murderer now.

If the fuckwad sheriff of Lametown couldn't figure that out, Ally would see that he paid the price.

But Rae's father being the fuckwad sheriff put a real crimp in Ally's plans. Why hadn't Rae said anything about it on any of their dates? Things here in Lacetown had already spun out of control. All she'd wanted was to destroy Norbert, then Bill had to get in the way and mess it all up.

Ally sat up and angrily swiped away tears. She sniffled and snuffled a bit before getting up and stomping into the bathroom, where she blew her nose on a mound of rough motel toilet paper. *Jesus Christ, how much wood pulp is in this stuff?*

After splashing cold water on her face, Ally sat on the foot of her bed and swiped through photos of Rae. Her hair had been so long and beautiful when they'd met, she couldn't believe Rae had cut it all off. Ally had loved running her fingers through those long, soft waves. Such a waste to lose all that beautiful hair.

That's what she got for dating a newly out lesbian. She should have known better.

She closed the photos app and set her phone aside. Her stuff with Rae would have to wait. Sonya's absence couldn't have come at a better time. It wouldn't take Sonya long to put all the pieces together, and then Ally would have a shitload more to explain than she did already. And Ally didn't think Sonya would like what she had to say.

Come to think of it, the fuckwad sheriff probably wouldn't either.

But fuck them.

Ally grabbed her phone and wallet and left the motel room.

Bill was already dead, and while regrettable, it couldn't be undone. The plan had to carry on. She was meeting with someone tonight who would solve all her problems. And after that, she had something important to take care of. Ally had always been good at lying, so she didn't think Sonya would be too much trouble. But she wasn't in the mood right then for lies. First, it was time to get everything in motion. Then she'd deal with Sonya... carefully of course. Bill's murder had put the town on edge, so people would be extra cautious. She couldn't afford to screw up now after all the work she'd done to get here.

Ally slipped off into the night.

The rendezvous was in twenty minutes. If she'd been stuck at the sheriff's station any longer, she would have missed it. She had a lot to do tonight before she met up with Rae again, and she couldn't make any mistakes.

Ally couldn't take the car, so she walked fast. The Lacetown Light had seemed as good a place as any for a clandestine meeting to plot revenge.

The lighthouse grounds were closed to automobile traffic, but Ally easily slipped between the padlocked gates. Shallow woods surrounded it, and a paved path snaked through them. When she stepped out of the trees and into a patch of moonlight, she looked up the side of the tall concrete lighthouse. It had recently been painted and stood with a pale glow on a point of land.

The light on top moved in a 180 degree arc, keeping the bright beam from shining in the windows of nearby homes.

"Are you Ally Roberts?"

The man's voice made her jump, and she took a step back as a tall man in a hawaiian shirt stepped out from behind the building.

"Whoa, I didn't mean to scare you." He held up his hands.

Ally's pulse calmed. "You didn't," she snapped.

"So, I did what you asked," the man said. "Now what?"

Ally punched her fist into her palm. "Now we finish what we started. Norbert is next."

CHAPTER THIRTEEN

After a night of fitful sleep, Jazz barely managed to make it downstairs and let himself in the back door of the salon on time. He was the first one in, as usual on Saturday, and he headed down the short hallway for the break room to start a pot of coffee. The sun had been up for an hour or so, and sunlight lit his way, allowing him to keep from turning on the lights. Once the coffee was brewing, Jazz stretched the fingers of his right hand, still a little sore from the punch, but better than last night. As he waited for the coffee to finish, he spent a few minutes inventorying the hair color in his locker, making a note in his phone about any supplies he needed to order.

As he looked at the boxes, Jazz became aware of a lingering odor even the fresh-brewed coffee couldn't mask. It was strange and unsettling, and he wondered if some rodent had gotten into the walls and died there. Or perhaps someone had dumped out food in the trash.

He peered into the trash can but discovered the bag was clean and empty. Most likely Misty had taken it out the night before prior to leaving for the festival.

Thoughts of the festival made him think of Norbert, and he sneered and made a fist, flinching a bit at the ache that produced. But then he thought about Michael caring for him, icing his hand, doting on him. And then opening up even more and showing his dominant side with some of the hottest sex Jazz had ever experienced. His sweet mortician was a bundle of surprises, with a lot of pent-up sexual energy waiting to be released.

Too bad Jazz had brought so many strange threats to Michael's life. He was afraid to ask what more could happen, because he might just find out.

The coffeepot gave a long final burble, and Jazz poured himself a cup. He added sugar and sipped it as he left the break room and walked into the salon.

The bad smell was stronger in here.

He stopped and sniffed as he made a face. *What is that?*

Something else was off, and Jazz stood in place as he looked around. His salon chair was turned away from him, and from where he stood, he could see the back of someone's head.

Somebody was sitting in his chair!

The chair was facing the front of the salon, so all Jazz could see was a shadowy silhouette. A cold shiver went through him as he stared at the back of the person's head.

"Who's there?" he called, then cursed himself for acting like every dimwit character in a two-bit horror movie.

He puffed out his chest and set his coffee on a nearby counter.

Pulling his cell phone from his back pocket, he moved slowly toward his chair. Obviously Misty had forgotten to lock the front door and Kevin had let himself in.

"Why didn't you tell me you were here, Kevin?" Jazz asked, mentally adding, *instead of sitting here all quiet and creepy in the dark.*

Intending to text Misty and tell her about the unlocked door, Jazz gave his chair a wide berth as he moved around to face the intruder, putting his back to the windows. His arm holding up the cell phone dropped, and he drew up short when he recognized the man.

He snorted with disgust. "Norbert, what the...?"

The words died in his throat.

"Oh...," Jazz breathed with shock and sudden understanding.

Norbert still wore the clothes he'd been in the night before, hands resting casually on the arms of the chair, and his legs splayed open. His head tipped back as he stared sightlessly at the ceiling, his mouth gaping and his pale skin putting the injuries he'd received during the fight the night before into stark relief.

A runner of blood had dried from a long, gruesome cut across his throat.

"Oh fuck. Well... fuck."

Jazz took a couple of steps back and jumped when he brushed Misty's chair. He dropped down into it and stared at Norbert's body.

Someone had murdered Norbert.

Someone had murdered Norbert and left his body in Jazz's salon chair.

What the actual fuck?

Sounds at the front door brought him to his feet. His heart pounded, and his brain locked up, sending out questions but no answers.

Who was here? Was it a client? Was it Jazz's client? Wait... who was his first client again? Why couldn't he think of a name?

Some kind of reasoning kicked in then, and he realized that no one should see Norbert's body, but he didn't know what to do. Should he cover him? Should he move him?

No, I need to call the cops.

He squinted at the figure outside the door. Correction, two figures, both in silhouette. One was short with hair piled atop her head, so it had to be Misty, but the figure behind her was tall and broad-shouldered. Who could that be?

Jazz heard a high-pitched giggle and recognized it as Misty's flirty come-on laugh.

"Oh, bother with this lock," she said and giggled again.

"Here, let me try," her companion said, his voice deep, sultry. And oddly familiar.

Jazz's logic and mobilization centers had shut down, so he turned away from the door and simply stood and stared at Norbert's body, cell phone in hand at his side. There was nothing left for him to do. And even if there was, he didn't think he'd have the energy to get it done.

He suddenly felt very, very tired.

The door finally opened, and from the corner of his eye, Jazz watched Misty glide into the salon. Her head was turned away as she smiled at the man following close on her heels.

The new arrivals saw Jazz, and both gave a start.

"Dilworth? What the fuck?" the man said, and Jazz realized why his voice had sounded so familiar, and also why he hadn't recognized it.

Misty's male companion was Sheriff Hilton Musgrave. And the only tones of voice Jazz had heard the sheriff use were gruff, impatient, or mocking, never flirting and kind.

"Jazz?" Misty asked. "What's—oh my God! Oh dear God." Her keys clattered to the floor.

"What the fuck? Is that Norbert Farthington? Is he *dead*? What the fuck did you do, Dilworth?" Musgrave was next to him, grabbing him by the arm and giving him a shake.

That snapped him out of his daze.

Jazz yanked his arm free and turned on the sheriff. "I didn't do this! I just found him like this." He held up his phone and pointed it at Musgrave. "I was about to call you when you happened to show up here." Jazz looked at Misty, who was staring wide-eyed at Norbert's body, and then back to Musgrave. "What are you doing here so early?"

"I'm going to give him a haircut," Misty said in a dull, flat voice. "He and I talked about it last night at the festival."

Musgrave waved toward Norbert's body. "You've been found at the scene of a murder. Focus on what's important."

"I-I...." Jazz had no words to argue.

"And you threatened to kill him last night," Musgrave sneered. "The whole town heard you." He reached for his hips, frowning when no cuffs or gun met his search. He stepped forward. "Why the hell did you do it, Dilworth?"

Jazz's mouth opened and closed a few times, again having no words to defend himself. *I didn't do it* just seemed so hollow and cliché.

"Oh, Hilton, you know Jazz was only defending Michael when he said all that," Misty said dismissively. "He didn't do... this."

"I don't know anything," Musgrave blustered.

Jazz couldn't even muster a zinger for that.

Misty approached and stepped carefully between them, facing Jazz and putting a hand against his cheek. "Jazz, honey," she said in a soft voice. "Look at me."

Jazz dropped his gaze from Musgrave's angry expression to Misty's one of concern.

"What happened?" she asked.

"I came in and found him there. I've only been here a few minutes."

"You didn't see him when you came in?" Musgrave said, his tone hard and dripping with doubt.

"Not from the back door," Jazz snapped. "Then I was in the back room, making coffee, and I smelled something...." His stomach rolled, and he lost any shred of bravado he'd regained.

"Hilton, perhaps you should do something about"—Misty gestured toward the body—"that unfortunate man. Let me get Jazz settled a bit."

"Settled a bit? What the fuck does that mean?" Musgrave said with a growl. "He's a suspect!"

Misty shot him a look over her shoulder, and Jazz was surprised to see Musgrave take a step back. His cheeks turned pink, and he dropped his gaze to the floor.

"Fine. Get Dilworth settled a bit, and I'll secure the scene." He pointed at Jazz. "Don't you dare try to flee."

"I didn't do anything!"

Musgrave scoffed and jabbed himself in the chest with a thumb. "Everyone's a suspect until Sheriff Musgrave says they're not."

Before Misty or Jazz could reply, the front door opened, and Jazz's client stepped inside. At the sight of him, the man's name popped into Jazz's mind— *Kevin Raines, that's right.*

Kevin frowned at them. "Quite a gathering of people right here up front. What's going on in here, Sheriff? I thought you—" Kevin's eyes shifted, and he frowned at the body. "Hey, who's that? I'm Jazz's first appointment."

"Never mind that, citizen," Musgrave said, spreading his arms to keep Kevin back and block his view.

"What's going on? Why's there another man in Jazz's chair?" Kevin demanded. "Wait... is that blood?"

Rather than answering, Musgrave quickly switched into sheriff mode and escorted a protesting Kevin back outside, talking to him in a low, calming tone that Jazz knew would never be directed at him.

"Let's get you something warm to drink," Misty said and tugged on Jazz's arm, leading him toward the break room.

"What the fuck is wrong with my life?" Jazz said, not really expecting an answer.

"Seems someone has their sights set on you for some reason. Come on, I'll make you some tea."

"I made coffee," Jazz said.

"Thank you for doing that. But I think a soothing cup of herbal tea is just the thing you need right now."

Misty directed Jazz to one of the cheap padded chairs at the tiny lunch table, and then she began puttering around near the sink. She fumbled one of the cups, and it broke on the tile floor. Jazz jumped and his heart pounded hard enough for him to hear the whoosh of blood in his ears.

"Well, Satan wearing a crocheted poncho, that was my favorite mug." Misty gave a quiet, shaky laugh and glanced over her shoulder at Jazz. "That body right here in my salon has got me a bit worked up. I think we both need some herbal tea."

Musgrave appeared at the door of the break room, his expression a concerned glare.

"What happened? What broke?" He looked between them and settled his gaze on Misty. "You okay?"

"Oh, I'm fine. Just broke a mug, that's all." Misty pushed the pieces aside with her foot. "Did you get Kevin rescheduled?"

"What?" Musgrave frowned and glanced at Jazz before looking back at her. "Well, no. I told him the shop would be closed for at least today and to call for another appointment. I don't... I didn't know how to reschedule him."

Misty turned to face them and leaned her butt against the counter. She put a hand on her chest, tipped back her head, and gave a girlish laugh. "Oh, I'm ridiculous. Of course you don't know how to do that. You don't work here. I'm sorry, Hilton. I guess I'm a bit more shaken by all of this than I thought."

Jazz stood and took her hands. They were very cold and trembled in his. He gently led her away from the counter and over to the chair he'd vacated. "Misty, sweetie, you sit down and let me clean up the broken mug and make the tea, all right?"

"Are you sure?"

"I'm really sure. First of all, we didn't have that many mugs to begin with. Can't have you dropping more," Jazz said, and was rewarded with a faint smile from Misty and a deep scowl from Musgrave. Undaunted, he continued to talk as he selected a couple of tea bags and two new mugs. "Besides, being busy helps me stay in the moment, you know? So this is good for me."

Jazz was glad when Musgrave returned to the front of the salon. Nothing worse than a big bear of a lawman hovering in the doorway when he suspects you of murder. Jazz grabbed the broom standing in the corner and started sweeping up the mess. He thought of Misty's cousin Dorothy and her fear of brooms as he swept. A snorting chuckle escaped him.

The sound seemed to startle them both, and their eyes met. "Sorry," he mumbled. "Just thought of something, is all."

"What happened to him?" Misty asked. "His throat was...." She drew her finger across her throat and grimaced. "Was it cut? Do you think he knew what was happening? And why would he be here in the salon? How did he get in? And who was with him?"

Jazz dumped the ceramic pieces into the trash can and filled the electric kettle with water before flicking the switch on. He really needed to get one of these for himself. He wondered if Michael liked herbal tea, and was sorry he'd never asked.

Oh wait, Misty had asked him a question.

Focus!

As they waited for the water to heat, Jazz leaned back on the edge of the counter and faced Misty. He crossed his arms and tried to put the image of Norbert out of his mind. But it was there, in full high-def color. He could still smell the blood....

He cleared his throat. "Those are all very good questions, and I wish I could answer even one of them. If we had a video surveillance system in here, we might be able to figure things out faster."

Misty nodded and looked down at her clutched hands on the tabletop. "I know. But what brought him here to the salon? Or, better yet, who brought him here? Norbert didn't like you very much, so I don't think he'd be hanging around here."

Her choice of words sparked a memory, and Jazz gasped and pushed up from the counter.

"What is it?" Misty got to her feet. "Do you know something?"

"I saw someone outside the back door of the salon last night when I came home. I thought it was weird at the time, but that was all. I made sure the door was locked and then went up to my apartment. Oh my God, what if she's the killer? What if she murdered Norbert and left him here to throw Musgrave off her tracks?"

"Her? It was a woman? Which woman?"

The water reached a boil and the kettle automatically clicked off. Jazz stared at Misty with wide eyes.

"Rae's girlfriend, Ally," he said in a quiet voice. "She was sneaking around behind the shop last night. And she's Dylan Robert's cousin. Her dad was the guy Russell was trying to kill when Michael and I caught him."

Misty's eyes grew very wide. "That's a pretty big motive. Oh, poor Amanda Rae."

Musgrave stepped into the break room, his expression even more cloudy. "Did I hear my daughter's name?"

Before they could answer, Michael appeared right behind Musgrave, his gaze dancing around the small space until it locked on Jazz. Michael wore a polo shirt, uncharacteristically untucked from a pair of blue jeans, and loafers with no socks. His chest rose and fell rapidly, brow damp with sweat.

"What's happened?" He squeezed past Musgrave and walked up to Jazz. He started to reach for him, glanced over his shoulder at Musgrave and Misty, and then dropped his arms to his sides. "Are you okay? What's happened?"

"How'd you get here so fast?" Musgrave asked. "Tanner just called you."

Michael kept his gaze on Jazz. "I ran."

"Oh," Jazz said. "You ran all the way here?"

Michael nodded, his hair slightly askew. "Tanner said there was a body at the salon we needed to pick up. He didn't say who it was or what had happened. No one else was in yet, and I didn't want to waste time getting the van out, so I ran here and came in the back door."

Michael blushed deeper as he explained, and the sight of those delightfully pink cheeks nearly pushed Jazz over the edge into chest-rattling sobs.

He ran here for me....

How did Jazz deserve someone so good and kind and decent when all he'd ever had in his life was darkness and deceit? And now that darkness and deceit was seeping into Michael's life, and Jazz didn't know what to do about it. He ached at the thought.

"Well, it's not me." Jazz smiled and gave Michael's arm a gentle squeeze. Simply touching him seemed to quell the rising panic. He gazed in Michael's brown eyes and smoothed the hair off his brow, settling it into place. "But it's someone we know."

Michael frowned and looked over at Misty and Musgrave before turning back to him. He placed his hand over the one on his arm. "Who? Is it a client?"

"It's Norbert," Jazz said.

Michael's mouth dropped open, and he took a step back, letting go of Jazz's hand. Jazz tried not to think he'd stepped away because he was afraid of him, but it was difficult to keep his mind from going to that place.

"Norbert?" Michael looked between the three of them, ending up back at Jazz. "But... how? Why? How'd he get in here?"

"All very good questions that my force will find the answers to," Musgrave said and fixed Jazz with a cold, steady stare before turning to Michael. "Come on, let's check out the scene."

Michael's gaze had gone a little glassy, and Jazz could practically hear the gears and wheels frantically spinning as his thoughts raced. Michael blinked a few times, then stepped closer and took Jazz's hand. "Are you okay?"

Jazz gave him a squeeze and a smile that felt pretty feeble. "I'm fine."

"You found him?" Michael asked.

"I did. Hadn't even had my first sip of coffee." Jazz sighed, then remembered he hadn't yet made tea for himself and Misty. "And now I haven't even had my tea. Do you like tea, Michael?"

"Um...." Michael shot a concerned look at Misty, and Jazz wasn't so addled he didn't notice.

Jazz shook his head. "I don't know why I asked that. I'm fine. Really."

"Okay. I'm going to examine the crime scene," Michael said and leaned in for a quick, sweet kiss. Jazz heard Misty sigh and Musgrave grumble something.

"I'll be back soon," Michael said, his brows knitted close. "Are you really sure you're okay?"

"Positive. Just fine."

"C'mon, Fleishman," Musgrave said. "We got rubberneckers at the window already."

Jazz smiled in reassurance at Michael, then said, "And before you say anything, Sheriff, I'm not going anywhere until I give someone my statement."

"Good to hear," Musgrave said, then led the way out of the break room and Michael followed with a quick final look over his shoulder.

When Michael was out of sight, Jazz took a deep breath, held it, then let it out. "How about that tea?"

"Did you really see Ally at the back door last night?" Misty whispered.

"I did." He turned away as he prepared their cups of tea. "I only caught a glimpse, but I recognized her. You know how bright that light is in back. And that hair. Whew, it's hard not to notice."

With the tea steeping, he faced her again as she slowly shook her head. "Oh my."

"I know."

"You have to tell Hilton about it," Misty said.

"*Hilton*, not Sheriff Musgrave?" Jazz narrowed his eyes and crossed his arms, seeking a distraction from his own thoughts and trying to appear as calm as Michael always was when things went to shit. "You seem to be acting very friendly with the good sheriff. What's going on?"

"What?" She dropped her gaze and fussed with her hair. "Oh, well, I.... Nothing to speak of. And besides, it's nowhere near as important as a body ending up in the salon."

Jazz nodded and didn't pursue his line of questioning, but he knew there was something brewing between Misty and Musgrave. And he wasn't sure how he felt about it. At the moment, his brain couldn't seem to find the space to contemplate the idea. It kept stuttering back to the image of Norbert like some kind of faulty film clip.

Jazz shuddered but tried to piece the facts out in his head.

Russell had murdered Dylan and was now in prison.

Norbert had been Russell's PR rep long before Jazz had come into the picture. Did Russell know Bill Denton, the man killed yesterday and left in Michael's hearse? Now Norbert had been murdered and left at Jazz's work. What did that mean for Jazz? For Michael?

Was Russell somehow lashing out from prison?

But then there was Ally Roberts.

Russell had killed her cousin and tried to kill her father. Based on her reaction at seeing Norbert at the festival, she blamed Norbert too. It couldn't be chance that she was in town and seen creeping around the crime scene, could it?

But what purpose did she have putting Norbert in *Jazz's* chair? A sick joke? Because he had intervened on Norbert's behalf last night? It made no sense!

The murders were too similar to be a coincidence, but why would Ally kill her own bandmate and prop him up in Michael's hearse?

Was someone targeting them? Tormenting them? Were these bodies being left in Jazz's chair and at Michael's some kind of warning that one of them was next?

"It's so obvious, Jasper dear!" Russell's airy laugh echoed in Jazz's mind.

Russell... it all keeps coming back to Russell. But what—

"Hey, did you hear me?"

Misty's voice broke through the chaos spinning inside his head. Jazz rubbed his hands up and down his face, then gave her a smile he hoped looked more steady than it felt. "Sorry, my dear. I was woolgathering, as Michael puts it. What did you say?"

"I said you need to go home and relax."

Michael's cozy bed flitted through his mind. "I don't think I can leave—"

"Damn right you can't leave," Musgrave said as he crowded into the break room.

Misty turned on him, hands on her hips and a surprising ferociousness burning in her eyes. "Hilton Musgrave, you change that tone right quick, do you hear me? Jazz has received a terrible shock, and he needs time for his mind to process it fully."

Jazz turned wide eyes toward Musgrave and watched with interest as emotions wrestled for dominance in the sheriff's expression. First he looked angry—the man's default expression—quickly followed by shocked, which was replaced in turn by some kind of lewd attraction.

Oh God, it was true. If they weren't doing it already, Sheriff Musgrave and Misty were really close to getting hot and heavy.

Now Jazz hoped like hell he was allowed to go back to his apartment, if only so he could do a couple of shots of whisky in an effort to burn away the mental images frolicking inside his overwrought mind.

It took a few seconds for Musgrave to tear his gaze from Misty—seconds that felt like years to Jazz as he stood there being drenched in their pheromones. When the sheriff finally addressed him, his expression had softened slightly.

"Dilworth, give your statement to Deputy Tanner right now, and then you can go. But—"

"Don't leave the city limits," Jazz said with a bored tone. "I know the drill."

Musgrave grunted. He delivered a long, hot look to Misty before turning to leave. Before Jazz could think of a single thing to say about any of it, Tanner appeared at the door, looking attractively all-American in his short-sleeved uniform shirt and nicely fitting pants. He seemed a bit nervous.

"Sheriff said you're ready to talk?"

"I'm ready to give my statement, if that's what you mean."

"Right. Yeah." Tanner pulled a notepad from his shirt pocket, then a small nub of pencil missing an eraser.

"You don't make mistakes?" Jazz asked.

"What?"

"Your pencil doesn't have an eraser. Does that mean you don't make mistakes?"

Tanner chuckled and that seemed to relax him. "Nah. I chewed it off. Nervous habit, I guess."

"Lots of fiber in pencil erasers?"

"I don't know, probably chemicals and some kind of glue."

"Okay, where do you want to do it?" Jazz watched Tanner's face turn bright red and wondered what the hell was wrong with everyone. Or maybe it was just him?

"How about my office?" Misty suggested. "Here's your tea. Now take the deputy into my office and both of you sit down."

Jazz accepted the cup she passed to him, and then led the way to Misty's office, situated across the short hallway from the break room. He kept his gaze on the office door and away from where Michael inspected Norbert's body in the salon. When he tried the knob, it didn't budge. "It's locked, Misty. Do you have the key?"

"Oh shit and shinola, I think I dropped them up front after I came in and saw.... Well, after I came in."

She stepped past them, and Jazz's gaze followed her up to the front of the shop. The Tompkins twins were taping up newspaper over the front windows to block the view from the rather large crowd gathering outside. Michael was taking photos of the body, and apparently his employees had clocked in, because his creepy apprentice, Ezra, lurked behind him, and Steve leaned against a wall, his expression serious and arms crossed tight over his chest.

A lot of people had arrived in short order, and Jazz hadn't heard any of it.

Misty bent to pick up her keys from the floor. Jazz turned away when he caught Musgrave checking out her ass from the other side of the salon.

Gross. Just... gross.

"Hell of a Saturday morning, eh?" Tanner said.

"Yeah," Jazz agreed with a nod.

"First all of that excitement last night at the festival, and now this."

Misty returned, keys jingling, and unlocked the office door. "It's a mess, but it'll give you a place to sit and talk." She leveled a somewhat stern look at Jazz. "Talk about everything. *All* the information you have."

Jazz scowled at her in return. "I'm very familiar with how to give a statement to the police. And I think both of us could stand with talking to people about everything and all the information we have." Jazz looked over to where Musgrave stood behind Michael, and then back at her. "Don't you?"

Misty flushed and played with her hair as her gaze darted around, landing on everything except for Jazz's face. "Well, I don't know. I just meant that you should be as honest and open as you can be with the nice deputy. That's all."

"Where do you want to sit?" Tanner asked. "At the desk or in the chair in the corner?"

"I'll take the corner," Jazz said with a sigh. "That feels pretty appropriate at this point."

Tanner sat at Misty's desk and scribbled notes as Jazz related the events that occurred after he and Michael had left the festival. He was glad he had

Michael for an alibi for a portion of the evening. If only he'd spent the night with him, he would be free and clear right now.

"I walked home from Michael's house around eleven or eleven thirty, I think," Jazz said. "I don't remember the exact time, sorry."

"No worries. And you two were together the entire time prior to you leaving?" Tanner asked. "You didn't step out to the store or he didn't have to go to the funeral home?"

Jazz gave him a direct stare. "We were together and otherwise occupied the entire time."

Tanner blushed a deep crimson and looked down at his notepad, scribbling furiously. Jazz wondered if he was writing *They fucked long and hard until suspect left between eleven and eleven thirty.*

Tanner cleared his throat, back on business. "You have a concealed pistol license, is that correct?"

"I do, but I'm not carrying. You need my license?"

He nodded and after Jazz fished his CPL out, Tanner wrote more notes on his pad, then returned it. "Were you carrying last night?"

"I was on a date." He stuffed his wallet in his pocket.

"You didn't answer my question." Tanner narrowed his gaze, and Jazz could all but imagine him practicing Musgrave intimidation tactics in his bathroom mirror. He still had a long way to go.

"No, my gun is in a case in my bedroom closet," he replied.

"You and the vic had a history. And not a good one," Tanner remarked.

"That's not a secret. But I didn't kill him." He ran trembling hands over his face, pushing his hair back. "Jesus, someone murdered him, cut his throat or choked him or something. Even I didn't hate him that much."

Saying the words aloud did nothing to erase the surreal insanity of the morning.

Norbert was killed and left in my chair. What the fuck?

"But you threatened him," Tanner countered. "I heard you and it sure sounded like you hated him."

"If you heard me, then you also heard what he said about Michael. It pissed me the hell off, and I reacted. Poorly, I'll admit, but there ya go." He actually had meant the threat at the time, but now... Jazz shuddered.

Tanner pursed his lips, thinking hard enough Jazz almost told him not to hurt himself. "Yeah, that was a very mean thing he said about Mr. Fleishman. He's a nice man. Just has an unusual job, ya know?"

He flinched at the astute observation. "Yeah."

"So you have no alibi after eleven thirty, and a long, bad history with our vic. You threatened to kill him, and the next day he's dead. That's motive and opportunity, Mr. Dilworth."

Jazz forced a chuckle. Since when did Tanner actually act like a real cop? "Why would I leave him at my place of employment if I killed him? And second, what about Bill Denton? Do you think I killed him too? Then left him at my boyfriend's house? I never met that guy. Obviously the same person killed them both."

They didn't actually think Jazz did this, did they?

"True," Tanner said, nodding slowly. "The murders are too similar to be coincidence."

"Exactly."

"Two murders less than a day apart." Tanner finished writing and then furrowed his brow. "There's been a lot of that kind of thing happening around town this year."

"You never know what kind of people these festivals will bring in," Jazz said. "Speaking of which, when I came home last night, I saw someone loitering by the back door of the salon."

Tanner sat up straighter. "Who was it?"

Jazz hesitated, then said, "It was the young woman fighting with Norbert at the festival, Ally Roberts."

Tanner's eyes widened, and he nodded. "The girl with the slicked-back hair, related to our last vic, Dylan Roberts. Yeah, I remember her. She's pretty tough." He started to make a note, then stopped and slowly raised his head, eyes wide. "Isn't she dating the sheriff's daughter?"

"Yep," Jazz said with a nod.

"Oh balls."

"Yep," Jazz said again.

"Oh balls," Tanner repeated. "This is going to cause a pretty big scene."

"I know." And Jazz felt only a teensy-weensy bit guilty that Tanner would be the one to tell Musgrave about Ally. *Better him than me.*

"Oh balls."

Jazz nodded. "You said that already."

"Okay, yeah, you're right. Okay, I've got this. Anything else?"

Jazz shrugged. "Not really. I had a glass of wine, then went to bed and was asleep before my head hit the pillow. When I got to the salon this morning, I found the body in my chair."

The body.

The words seemed to echo around his brain.

It wasn't just a body, though.

It was the body of Norbert, someone he had known—and, yes, not really liked—for years. The man had been infuriating, annoying, and downright terrible for as long as Jazz remembered. He'd done everything he could to undermine Jazz's relationship with Russell, and had even offered to help Russell kill Jazz, Michael, and Musgrave and cover up the murders.

But he'd been living and breathing and thinking and talking yesterday, and now he was dead. Granted, he'd been talking shit, like usual, but still, he'd been alive and aware, and now he was... gone. And his exit from this world had not been easy, it appeared.

Things had definitely gotten much darker in Lacetown lately, and Jazz couldn't help but feel more than a little responsible.

CHAPTER FOURTEEN

"I can't believe this," Musgrave mumbled to Michael.

"Indeed." Weary, Michael sighed as he looked at the gruesome scene, the tiny yellow markers for the photographs littering the floor. Michael was assisting Musgrave by taking pictures with the camera Ezra had brought him, until Trevino arrived to officially collect the body. Michael hated being on the outside, especially when this seemed like a personal attack on himself and his boyfriend, but he knew it was the right thing to do.

"He was my prime suspect, and now he's dead."

"No other leads?" Michael asked casually.

"Your friend is looking awfully suspicious," Musgrave grumbled.

"Jazz?" Michael couldn't contain his nervous chuckle. "Surely you must be kidding. Jazz could never do this."

"Everyone's a suspect until—"

"Yes, yes, I know," Michael said dismissively, not in the mood for Hilton's third-person dramatics. While Michael had entertained notions of Jazz's guilt when Dylan's body washed up on Hardscrabble Beach, even then, before they'd gotten to know each other, he'd dismissed Jazz as a suspect. And now? "You must know Jazz had nothing to do with any of this."

"He threatened the vic."

"And he had never even met the first vic," Michael countered.

Musgrave seemed to be in actual pain as he admitted, "That's true."

"There's a killer on the loose in Lacetown," Michael said, a shiver working down his spine at the words. "Was Norbert the only lead on Denton's death?"

"Yeah." Musgrave sniffed. "Was hoping it was a crime of passion, as you suggested. Guess he hooked up with Denton at HPP the night of his murder on some phone app called Grind Him."

Michael had lived in Lacetown pretty much all his life, and had only learned about Heavy Petting Point—or HPP to those in the know—back in May. He was, however, a second away from asking what sort of app that was, when he recognized the sheriff's gaffe. He buried a laugh and reminded himself to tell Jazz. "I believe you mean Grindr."

Face wrinkled, Musgrave shot Michael a look. "That makes no sense. Farthington said it was a *gay* hookup app. Why would you guys use an app called Grind Her?"

Oh, Jazz would have a field day with this!

A sneeze cut off Michael's reply.

Parker Trevino strode into the salon, blotchy and red, and appearing to be in a foul mood. "Sheriff, are you divulging information?"

"I'm not divulging shit, Trevino. Fleishman and I work together."

Trevino walked up to them, his dark, almost black hair slicked back from his low forehead. Ordinarily so impeccable, today his eyes were watery and red, and little hives peppered his neck.

Musgrave sneered as he took in Trevino's appearance. "What the hell happened to your face? You look like a pimple cream commercial."

Trevino blustered. "I seem to have come down with an allergic reaction. Probably the soap at the inn."

Michael had managed to avoid Trevino last night while the man had performed Bill Denton's autopsy, and it had felt like a feast of the proverbial crow when he'd had to call the man back to another murder scene.

"Hello, Parker," Michael said. "Thanks for coming over so quickly."

"Well, it doesn't take long to get from one end of your quaint little town to the other, now does it?" Parker gave him a cool smile as he inspected the salon with barely disguised distaste and approached Norbert. Just like Denton had been staged to appear driving, Norbert's feet and hands were deliberately placed so he appeared to be waiting for a haircut in the chair.

Jazz's chair, Michael thought. Where his boyfriend— *lover*, his mind corrected—stood all day and talked to people and made them look good. Because that's what Jazz did. He talked with people and helped them become the best they could be.

He'd even helped Michael come out of his shell, and Michael longed to return that kindness by being there for him now. He should have hugged Jazz earlier, Musgrave be damned.

"Well, you've gotten yourself into quite the pickle here." Parker's voice broke into Michael's vortex of thoughts as he looked Norbert's body over. "This appears to be the same handiwork we saw in the body found in your hearse." Parker frowned at Michael. "Shame about that nice upholstery. And that it's impounded as evidence."

"Yes, a shame," Michael agreed, bristling.

"There are larger contusions, blood this time. This victim must've struggled more." Trevino straightened up, eyes still on Norbert. "It would seem our killer has a bit of a sense of humor, staging the bodies."

"Not very funny," Musgrave muttered.

Smirking, Trevino gave Michael a sideways glance. "And it appears someone is targeting you and your lover, eh?"

Musgrave made a sound of agreement and Michael found himself at a loss for words. He had no clue how Trevino even knew of his relationship with Jazz, but he was more annoyed by the astute observation, which mirrored his own worries.

But who would target them and why?

Russell.

The name popped immediately into his head, but after what they'd all witnessed at the festival the night before, Ally Roberts couldn't be ruled out. In light of the revelations about her familial connections, she had an obvious motive, and the most passionate reaction to Norbert.

Whoever the killer was—be it Ally, or someone Norbert had possibly offended at the festival—the macabre mystery of it all seemed like something from a fictional world.

"Didn't your lover have an altercation with our victim last night?" Trevino asked.

Michael stiffened. How the hell did Trevino know that? Jazz's violent and swift reaction coming to Michael's defense had roused primal lust within Michael. But now, in light of this, Michael wished the whole thing had never happened. And why did it make his skin crawl the way Trevino said the word *lover*?

"My deputy is questioning Dilworth right now," Musgrave said.

Michael frowned at both men, but directed his words to Musgrave. "I imagine Ally Roberts is on your list to question, then," he said, confident in Jazz's innocence.

Musgrave looked like he'd just tasted something gross. "She is."

"The cousin to your previous murder victim," Trevino stated rather than asked. "How intriguing."

Although Michael had a lot of questions about the murder, his thoughts pinged about his brain like a frantic game of pinball. He couldn't seem to focus on anything at the moment. All he could think about was Jazz. What was happening with the man in his life? Was someone targeting him in some way? Was Jazz in danger?

Jazz, Jazz, Jazz. It was like the name was a song on repeat in the back of Michael's mind, echoing among his every thought and lying unspoken but intermixed with everything he said. Last night, Michael had worried about Jazz's distant behavior, fearing his own actions had upset his boyfriend. And now this?

Needing to talk to him, Michael glanced toward the back of the salon, where Deputy Tanner stood in the hallway outside of Misty's office. Where was Jazz?

When he realized Trevino was still smirking at him, Michael frowned. "Could you please just process the scene and take the body back to my funeral home for the autopsy?" Michael said. "Ezra and Steve will help you with the transportation."

"Yes, very good. I'm already familiar with your simple facility. Once they deliver the body, I will no longer require their services." Trevino gave them all a dismissive wave, his focus on Norbert.

I wasn't going to allow you to use their services whether you wanted them or not, Michael thought irritably but wisely didn't say aloud.

"Very good," Michael said. "I'll be back at the funeral home shortly."

"Oh? Have someplace else you need to be?" Parker asked as Michael walked toward the back of the salon.

"Yes, as a matter of fact, I do."

Michael resisted the urge to turn around and flip the man off. Instead, he focused his energy on moving forward, moving toward Jazz. He approached the short back hallway, where Deputy Tanner was now talking quietly with Deputy Tompkins—the woman, not her twin brother.

"Are you finished taking Jazz's statement?" Michael asked. "Is it all right if I speak with him?"

Deputy Tanner shifted his weight and rubbed a hand across the back of his neck. "Oh. Um, yeah, it's fine."

Michael looked around but didn't see Jazz. Of his two employees, Ezra stood the closest, so he waved him over so as not to be overheard by Trevino. "Have you seen Jazz?"

"Oh, he left without saying goodbye?" Ezra said. "I'm sorry."

The remark hit Michael like the sting of a wasp.

"Well, I'm sure he's just unsettled by all of this," Michael blustered, unsure why Ezra's words triggered such a reaction. *Jazz was understandably upset, and I was busy working the crime scene.*

"Yes, I'm sure that's all it is."

Michael schooled his expression to something he hoped looked relaxed and natural. "It is."

Michael sighed. He was allowing Trevino's chigger-like presence to make his skin itch and his temper flare. Jazz was obviously upset about the murders. He had a personal connection to Norbert, and he was now a suspect in the man's murder. This all had to be bringing up memories and thoughts of Russell. Michael really needed to talk with Jazz, but there hadn't been a spare minute.

"Are you doing all right?" Ezra prompted. "You did know the victim, after all."

"Yes. Well, I'm fine, thank you. Go ahead and take the body back to the funeral home when Trevino is ready. I'll meet up with you there."

Ezra frowned but then offered Michael that puppy-dog smile. "Yes, of course, whatever you need, Michael. And good luck with Jazz." Ezra hesitated, appeared to be about to say something further, but then gave a single nod and went back to work.

Michael was about to say something too, but Parker Trevino was looking at him with a smug expression. There really would be no getting past the man without hearing a cutting comment.

And Michael wasn't sure he'd be able to hold back from returning a Jazz-worthy comment of his own. Which would not help the strained situation he was already embroiled in. He'd be working in close quarters with Trevino for a couple more days. At least with Trevino working the scene, Michael had the time to check on Jazz.

He faced the deputies once again. "May I use the back door?"

Deputy Tompkins shook her head. "Nope, the techs are checking for prints now."

Great, he would have to go past Trevino and through all the gawkers out front.

Michael nodded his thanks before he left the salon, not meeting Parker Trevino's keen eyes. Trevino was complaining to Steve how cold Lacetown was with the "biting wind off the lake." Michael barely suppressed an eye roll.

Cold? It was supposed to be ninety degrees today.

The sun was high and baked the asphalt street, two of the angled parking spaces outside of the salon taken up by police cruisers with light bars flashing. The other Tompkins twin had set up yellow tape, and he was currently trying to keep gawkers back. Greg Tompkins shouted out to two deputies several feet away, "Hey, make sure mine is a double shot!"

The deputies Michael recognized by face only waved to Greg in acknowledgment, then headed to the coffeehouse across the street.

Coffee! Jazz mentioned he hadn't had any coffee yet, and seeing as Jazz lived off caffeine like manna, Michael would get his lover a latte before he went to his loft to check on him.

A flash of orange caught Michael's attention in the crowd. Tall and familiar, a man in an orange hawaiian shirt typed frantically on his cell phone and then quickly followed the officers.

It was the same man he'd seen eyeing the scene at his funeral parlor yesterday.

Michael's heart skipped.

When their eyes met, the man flinched and looked away.

Suspicious.

More than curious, Michael crossed the street as inconspicuously as possible and entered the coffeehouse behind the two officers and the mystery man. Inside Coffee, Tea, and Thee, the officers waited in line, laughing about some show on Netflix. The suspicious man had taken a seat at an empty table and picked up a discarded newspaper. Michael got in line and watched the whole situation for clues.

This man had been at both crime scenes, yet Michael was sure he'd never seen him in Lacetown before.

While sitting in a coffeehouse and reading a newspaper without ordering anything was no more illegal than being a gawker, it was definitely fishy. And Michael wasn't mistaken—the man had definitely followed the deputies.

What for? Hoping to hear a clue about the murder? Or was *he* the murderer, satisfying his ego by watching his crimes be discovered?

Michael scolded himself. He really shouldn't be listening to that podcast about unsolved crimes or fixating so much on Brock Hammer novels. His imagination was really going wild.

The deputies' conversation moved onto the weather, and then they paid for their tray of drinks. They refused to explain what had happened at Misty's to the curious baristas, and if Michael wasn't reading it wrong, the tall man in the hawaiian shirt looked disappointed.

After the deputies left, the man casually got up and left too.

Okay, it was not his imagination. That was *totally* suspicious.

Should I pursue?

"Help you?"

Flinching, Michael made a quick decision.

A comfort coffee for Jazz was more important than some odd man in a hawaiian shirt. He was probably just being nosey like the rest of the citizens trying to peek through the covered windows of the salon, hoping to gather a tidbit of gossip.

He smiled at the barista, Josiah, who waited patiently.

"Something chocolaty," he ordered. They were used to his random orders, and Michael suspected they knew it was for someone in the salon by the way they always smiled and watched him deliver it across the street.

The tall stranger stood outside the coffeehouse while Michael waited. Then he took a quick left as Michael was paying. Trying not to be obvious, Michael took his coffee and hurried out after him.

When he was back on the street, he glanced this way and that, but he'd lost sight of the man.

"Damn," he cursed quietly under his breath.

"So what's going on?"

Michael jumped at the voice, turning to find Kevin Raines, one of Jazz's clients, standing beside him. Raines's thinning brown hair fluttered in the breeze off the lake, and his green eyes were narrowed suspiciously. He had an Ace Hardware bag in his hand, stuffed full with a large coil of nylon rope.

Michael had never been comfortable around Kevin. He'd been eerily happy at his grandmother's funeral several years ago, and he was aggressively persistent in always asking out Jazz, despite knowing Jazz and Michael were an item.

Then Michael realized he was staring at Kevin. "Excuse me?"

"What's going on?" Kevin asked again, sounding perturbed. "I was supposed to be getting my haircut this morning, but there was a dead body in Jazz's chair. Now I don't know when I'm going to get back in."

Michael was a bit taken aback by Kevin's selfish spin on the morning's incident, but schooled his face and spoke in a professional but firm tone. "I cannot comment on an ongoing investigation. And as for my boyfriend's schedule, I don't have the foggiest when he can fit you in for your haircut. You can call the salon once they're open again."

Kevin flinched when Michael said *boyfriend*, and Michael wasn't quite sure if he'd intentionally or accidentally put emphasis on the word, but Kevin rubbed Michael the wrong way—like sand in his ass crack, as Jazz had once said.

Frowning, Kevin shook his head. "No, Jazz will have to find a spot for me. That receptionist is always lying about his schedule and giving me a hard time and moving my appointments around willy-nilly." Grumbling to himself, he stalked off.

Michael dismissed the man and decided not to mention the encounter to Jazz. He had enough on his plate that he didn't need to be reminded about obnoxious clients.

Needing to check on Jazz, Michael hurried back to the loft before the coffee cooled.

Skirting the small crowd of curious citizens, he found no sign of the tall man among the people still lingering near the salon, wanting to know what was going on.

MURDER MOST DESERVING

Maybe the man was no one of import.

It didn't matter. Jazz was his number-one priority right now.

CHAPTER FIFTEEN

Coffee in hand, Michael stood at the back entrance for Jazz's loft. They hadn't gone so far as to give each other keys to their homes, and Jazz hadn't shared the entry code for his building, therefore Michael had no way to get in. He rubbed the pad of his finger against the hard plastic of the buzzer button, not pressing it but trying to see if he could feel Jazz's presence. He felt an urgent need to be near Jazz, even if they didn't talk, just to hold him and comfort him and make sure he was doing okay.

But now that he was at the door, nervousness itched at his mind.

Maybe that was the *real* reason he stalled by getting Jazz a coffee.

He'd all but flown down the street when he thought Jazz might be the body they found—irrational—but all the deaths lately had put his imagination in full swing.

But Jazz was okay.

Physically, anyway.

Emotionally might be another story.

Everything had been going so well between them, and then the shit had hit the proverbial fan. First the return of Norbert's trying presence, then divorce papers from prison, followed by two murders, which seemed to be a message specifically for them.

And in the midst of all that, Michael had instigated a major change in their relationship in the heat of the moment. What if Jazz had only agreed to lose the condoms because it felt better, not because of some imagined commitment? Had Michael somehow pressured him into making their relationship exclusive?

His stomach dropped.

Jazz *had* been distant when he'd left last night. He hadn't told Michael that Russell had been calling. He kept insisting he was okay, but was he?

And just now, he didn't even tell Michael he was leaving the salon.

Was he upset with Michael?

You're rereading Russell's books and didn't tell him, a voice whispered, sending Michael's mind into a tailspin.

Jazz had been oddly calm when he'd spied the book, but did he see it as a betrayal?

Admittedly, Michael had been feeling sentimental, wanting to say goodbye to his favorite character. But he also intended to do anything in his power to help lock Russell away so he could never hurt Jazz again. Michael wasn't being selfish. He wanted to keep Jazz safe. He was doing this for Jazz.

That spanking was all about you, the treacherous whispers argued back.

But Jazz enjoyed it, hadn't he?

Unless that's just what he told you....

The door opened.

"Michael?"

With a squawk of surprise, he jumped, and managed not to spill the coffee.

"What are you standing here for, sweetie? Why didn't you buzz?"

Michael shook his head. "I did ring the bell." *Hadn't he?*

"No, you didn't, sweetie," Jazz said with a sleepy smile. "Misty texted that you were on your way up. I was keeping an eye out for you, but you took so long I peeked out and you were standing down here like a deer caught in the headlights. Everything okay? Aside from ol' Norbie dead and bleeding two doors down."

"Woolgathering, I suppose."

Jazz stepped aside. "Well, you can do that in here."

Michael cursed himself. He was worrying about nonsense in his head, and he wasn't sure why. He and Jazz were in a good place, but in light of everything happening around them, Michael should dial it back. Any declarations of love would have to wait until all of this blew over. To add an *I love you* would put too much pressure on Jazz after such a shock. Michael didn't want to cause him any undue distress.

Right now, the most important thing was making sure his boyfriend was okay.

"I brought you a coffee." Michael held up the drink.

"I adore you," Jazz said, smiling and taking the drink with both hands before leaning in for a chaste kiss. "Come on, let's go up to my apartment."

Being near Jazz had a calming effect on his mind. Michael followed Jazz up the steps to the second floor, drinking in each flex of his ass.

"You looking at my ass?" Jazz asked without turning around.

Michael blushed. "Yes. Sorry."

"Don't be sorry. I was hoping you were doing it."

Jazz smiled over his shoulder as they reached the second floor, making Michael's heart flutter like the first time. His apartment door was propped open, and he led the way inside. Michael closed the door behind him and locked it before joining Jazz on one of the purple velvet couches that suited Jazz's effortless style so perfectly.

"How are you?" Michael asked.

Jazz shrugged. "Surprisingly all right. Maybe still in a bit of shock. It's a ghastly way for someone to go out, and a really awful way to find them."

"It must be bringing up a lot of memories for you," Michael said. "Being Norbert and all."

"Yes, imagine that: Norbert reminding me of a bad time in my life." He sighed and shook his head. "It's a terrible thing, but I can't say I'll miss the man. Does that make me an evil person?"

Michael touched his forearm. "Not at all. Things between you and Norbert were... very complicated."

"At least," Jazz muttered, then fell silent a moment. He shifted and placed his feet on the cushion, facing Michael with his back against the padded armrest. He sipped the coffee. "Mmmm, peppermint mocha. My new favorite."

Michael felt warm all over at that smile, as if the hot coffee were working through his every limb. "I'll make a note."

Jazz's smile faded. "You know, with everything that's happened these last couple of days, I can't help but feel like the man you found in your garage and now Norbert sitting in my salon chair is some kind of message."

"I thought the same," Michael said. "But from whom?" With Jazz's bare feet so near, Michael scooted closer and placed them in his lap.

Jazz arched an eyebrow when Michael began to gently massage his feet. "Who do you think should be on the top of our list?"

Michael frowned and pressed his thumb deep across the arch of Jazz's foot, delighting in the satisfied sigh he brought out of him. "I will admit that Russell came to mind. But he's in jail awaiting trial."

"Oh, and no one's ever managed to hire a killer from behind bars," Jazz said, then groaned. "Fuck, that feels good."

His tone was so sexual, so decadent, that a spike of arousal went through Michael, despite the conversation topic. "Feet sore?"

"Ten hours behind the chair yesterday," he answered, eyes closing as he enjoyed Michael's touch for a moment. Then he let out a weary sigh and looked right at Michael. "I know it sounds like I'm paraphrasing one of Russell's Brock Hammer books, but it's got me thinking these murders have hit a little close to home. Don't you think so?"

A twinge of guilt over rereading the books hit him, but he devoted his attention to Jazz's foot. "I do see your point. But if Russell is involved, why did he murder Bill and leave him in my hearse? What kind of message is that? He's a complete stranger to us."

"Hard to understand the mind of a psycho. No one knows why he cut off Dylan's hands either." Jazz gave Michael a sideways glance.

"Unless you discovered a clue rereading the books."

Jazz's not-so-casual tone was like a knife in the heart.

"Actually, I think I did discover a reason for that," Michael admitted. *He is upset I'm reading them!*

"Oh?"

"In every book, there's a major foreshadowing for the next murder. His last book, *Sea of Discontent*, drug mules transported heroin in their rectums with condoms. And in Dylan's book, the one Russell stole for his own, the last victim has his hands chopped off for no apparent reason. Perhaps Russell cut Dylan's hands off in homage to Dylan's book, or perhaps it was a clue for the next book. We may never know."

"Oh snap," Jazz muttered. "Guess it's a good thing you're reading them, huh?"

Michael concentrated on massaging Jazz's foot. "Are you upset I didn't tell you?"

He shrugged. "Honestly, yes, but I do understand why you're doing it. I probably would've tried to talk you out of it, but it's obviously turning up clues, so you were right, and there's no sense worrying about it now. Too bad Russell didn't write the next book so we could have the clues we need to solve these murders."

At Jazz's casual but oh-so-honest reply, the rapid spiral of panic that had plagued Michael began to quiet to a dull murmur. "Musgrave told me that Norbert and Bill Denton hooked up at the HPP."

"What?"

"Yes, via a *gay hookup app*." Michael did air quotes before returning to his massage. "It's one I never heard of before. Grind *Him*, Musgrave called it. Because why would we gays use an app called Grind *Her*."

Jazz stared blankly for a moment, and then a bark of laughter escaped him. "You shitting me? Musgrave said all that?"

Pleased he'd been able to bring a light to Jazz's eyes, Michael nodded. "Yes, he did. Norbert hooking up with Bill made him the prime suspect. Obviously he isn't now."

Jazz sobered. "The crimes are so similar, they have to be the same killer, right?"

"Or a copycat killer," Michael mused. "But that doesn't make much sense, because they knew each other, and we know each other. There must be a connection."

"Russell."

It keeps coming back to him, doesn't it?

Focusing on Jazz's foot and the current case, Michael contemplated what they knew of Russell's attention to detail. "At least with Norbert being killed, there's some kind of personal connection to Russell and to us," he said aloud, and then he had a thought and paused his hands to stare straight ahead. "Unless...."

"Uh-oh," Jazz said with a smile that looked even more tired than when he'd opened the door downstairs. "I know that expression. Michael Fleishman, Mortician Detective, is onto a scent. Unless what?"

"Well, let's step back. Russell is in prison, and as possible as it might be for him to orchestrate something from behind bars, what if it was someone else with a connection to both victims."

"You're thinking about Ally."

"I am," Michael said with a nod. "She only recently joined Denton and Sonya Metcalf in the band. And we know about their connection to Norbert. It's an unlikely coincidence, her being with Norbert's old friends in Lacetown at the same time Norbert was here."

"True," Jazz said. "She really was going after him last night. And for good reason. I mean, it sounds like she and Dylan had been really close." His eyes went wide. "Oh my God! I totally forgot to tell you that I saw her last night outside the back door of the salon!"

"What? When?"

"When I got home from your house. Ally was lurking near the door, and the motion sensor light spooked her or something because she ran off. I checked the door, but it was still locked."

"That's pretty damn suspicious," Michael said. "And it's shifting my thinking even more to Ally being the killer."

"But why would she kill Bill? Acting out a Tarantino movie?"

Michael gave him a grim smirk. "That is darkly funny. But maybe Ally was following Norbert the other night and saw him meet up with Denton and became angry at him for getting back with Norbert? Maybe she saw Denton's act as a betrayal to her?"

"It's possible." Jazz gave a tired shrug. "But why would Ally target us?"

"As for me, perhaps she finds me culpable during the investigation. Like I didn't find Dylan's killer fast enough so she almost lost her father. And last night, you mentioned Dylan when you threatened Norbert, saying what Russell did would pale in comparison to what you would do to him. And you're married to Russell."

Jazz waved the last statement off. "I was defending my man's honor, not besmirching Dylan."

"Which I appreciated."

That gifted Michael with a genuine, albeit brief smile. "Anytime, sweetie. But if what you say is her motive, why not target Musgrave as well? Unless that has something to do with Rae." He sighed. "But when it comes right down to it, I'm a suspect as well. You should've heard Tanner questioning me. He actually sounded like a cop."

Michael made a face. "And I can't be your alibi. If it's any consolation, I don't think Musgrave believes you're guilty. Not truly."

"But I doubt he thinks I'm innocent either. Musgrave's had it out for me from the beginning, everyone knows that. Which leads me to believe that this was all staged by Russell. He's trying to frame me for Norbert's murder."

"And Denton's?"

"Maybe that was a mistake?" Jazz looked across the room as he talked through his thoughts. "What if whoever Russell hired to kill Norbert followed good ol' Norbie to the HPP and witnessed their hookup? Maybe he got them mixed up or Bill saw him or something, and he had to kill Bill first? Russell probably told him about your funeral home, so he decided to put Bill in your hearse to throw things off a bit? Russell would probably pay a bonus to know he's framing both of us."

"That's a lot to consider. There was a tall fellow acting suspiciously outside the salon when I went to get your coffee. He followed the deputies into the coffee shop and lingered long enough to eavesdrop on their conversation. If this is being orchestrated by Russell, he could be the hired killer." Michael paused, then switched feet, digging his thumbs into Jazz's arch. "Although wearing brightly colored clothing isn't helping him blend in."

"Fuck that feels good." Jazz groaned, lost to bliss. Eyes closed, he asked, "You going to tell everyone's favorite sheriff about our theories?"

"I might mention them to him."

"Probably should, huh?"

"Probably. All he can do is call me names and roll his eyes, right?" Michael grinned.

Jazz grinned back. "Our tax dollars at work." He sipped his coffee again and stared down at the lid.

"Something more on your mind?" Michael asked, feeling a trickle of concern.

"Yeah, there is." Jazz took a deep breath and let it out in a sigh. "I don't really know how to say it, though."

The trickle of worry he thought had ended became a heavy downpour. "Oh?"

"I need to talk to you about something," Jazz said seriously. "You're not gonna like it, but...."

Ezra's words echoed in the back of Michael's mind. *Oh, he left without saying goodbye?* Fast on the heels of that were all the other fears his own mind taunted him with.

Panic ignited inside him like a brush fire. It was like a physical thing, expanding rapidly and pushing against his lungs, making it difficult to catch his breath. As the panic filled him, it pushed the words up his throat and out before he could even try to stop himself.

"Are you mad at me?" Michael blurted.

"What?" Jazz flinched. "No! Why would you think that?"

"I-I...." What could he say? His panic deflated a bit, and all he could do was shrug and stare down at Jazz's foot in his hands. "I dunno."

From the corner of his eye, Michael saw Jazz cock his head. "What would make you think I was mad at you?"

Michael's palms grew sweaty. Hastily he dried them on his pant legs and devoted his attention back on Jazz's foot. Michael was so bad at this kind of relationship thing. He focused on massaging each curve of Jazz's sole, the length of his toes, and not the whirlwind inside his mind.

Jazz asked you a question.

Cheeks flushing hot, Michael kept his face down, unable to look him in the eye. "Last night when I...." His throat tightened, and he barely whispered the words. "I wonder if I pressured you into sex with no condoms. Maybe you really don't want that much commitment with me? And then I... I spanked you. Hard. Did I take things too far or—"

The deep rumble of Jazz's laughter made Michael's stomach knot and his throat tighten.

Mortified, Michael summoned the courage to look at Jazz.

His smile was not mocking or critical.

"You were worried about that, sweetie? Oh, I wish you hadn't. That was fantastic! I loved every second of it. It was so hot, knowing you were inside me with nothing between us, that when you came you left part of yourself in me. And I was really turned-on by the spanking. I totally want you to do that again." Jazz waggled his brows. "Harder next time, actually."

Michael stared at him stupidly, his mouth agape. "You really liked it?"

"Yes. It was so hot," Jazz assured him. "Just what I needed."

172

Hearing Jazz's words were almost impossible to believe. "You're really sure?"

"Were you actually worrying about this after I left?"

Michael barely managed a nod.

"Oh, sweetie. When have you known me not to say what I think? If you're ever doing something in bed that I don't like, I'll tell you. Deal?"

He nodded again.

"And for the record," Jazz said with a smile. "That hasn't happened yet, and I highly doubt it could. I wanna be the man who helps you live out all your fantasies."

Those sincere words quieted his doubts. It was only with Jazz that he ever felt comfortable enough to let his guard down and be himself. To know Jazz wanted to learn the secret side of Michael he'd never revealed to another made his heart swell with happiness. But he paused, knowing now was not the time to profess his love. "You're very important to me, Jazz. I've never been this invested in a relationship, and sometimes that makes me nervous. I have no confidence whatsoever when it comes to you."

"*You* not confident?" Jazz repeated in disbelief. "The way you saved Mr. Pickles from armed criminals, or how just now, you ran all the way here for me. How can you say that? I've seen you confident. In fact, I've been on the receiving end of your confidence in bed." He pointed to his kitchen. "Over there the other day. In the shower. On my couch. And in your car."

Michael's cheeks warmed with pleasure, but he shook his head. "Maybe. That's because you make me comfortable enough to be myself, especially when we're making love." He whispered those last two words. "That's something I've never felt with anyone. Literally no one."

"Oh, sweetie," Jazz cooed, brushing Michael's cheek. "You can always be yourself around me. Even when you're feeling unsure or nervous."

"Thank you for saying that, and I believe you. Honestly I do. But there are still a lot of insecurities in my head. I'm working on that."

Jazz gave him a soft, sweet kiss. "We'll work on it together, sweetie. For future reference, though, I don't want you worrying about our sex life. It's perfect. You're the best part of my life right now."

Michael's head popped up. "I am?"

Jazz nodded seriously. "You are. Why else would I toss the jimmy hats? You're all I want."

The trickle that had become a downpour of concern suddenly shifted to a rush of joy and excitement. "I am?"

Jazz smiled, though it didn't sparkle his eyes per usual. "Yes, though honestly, I don't know how you put up with all this drama I've thrown into your life."

"You haven't done a thing," Michael assured him, his mind still dancing with the sweetness of Jazz's casual declarations. *"You're the best part of my life right now."* He felt like Sally Field just then: "You like me, you really, really like me!"

"Haven't I?" Jazz countered.

"It's not your fault what others do around you."

"So says you." Jazz gave him a tired smile. "Regardless, what I wanted to talk about isn't us. Well, it kinda is since it's about me and I'm part of us." He hesitated and sat back.

Michael held his breath. He was here with handsome, sweet, sexy Jazz, and what he wanted to talk about sounded like it was important to him. Michael needed to listen and be ready to support whatever Jazz said next, not allow his own imagination and insecurities, or Ezra's simple off-hand remark, to invent a problem with their relationship.

Jazz let out a weary sigh. "I need to go see Russell."

CHAPTER SIXTEEN

"**O**h." Gaze shooting up and hands stilling, Michael blinked as every thought seemed to slam to a halt. He couldn't form any words other than what he'd already said, so he said it again. "Oh."

"Yeah, oh."

It wasn't anywhere near what Michael had expected, but it was a hell of a lot better than what he'd been imagining. "Well, I can clear a day whenever—"

"No, I need to do this by myself."

"Oh," Michael said, his thoughts jamming once again.

Jazz flashed a tired smile. "You're saying that a lot."

"Oh?"

Sighing, Jazz pulled his feet back, but Michael was only disappointed for a moment because Jazz set his coffee down and straddled Michael's lap. Smiling softly, Jazz put his hands on Michael's shoulders and rubbed. "It's been a long and emotional morning for both of us."

Michael managed a humorless chuckle, savoring the familiar, easy way they fell into touching each other. "It has at that. Yes, indeed."

"Do you understand?" Jazz asked, eyes searching, brows creased.

"Which part?" Michael placed his hands on Jazz's hips, squeezing gently. "The fact that you want to see Russell, or the part where you don't want me to go?" He couldn't stop the hitch in his voice when he said the last part and he hated himself for such weakness and insecurities.

Jazz rested a warm palm on his cheek. "Both, sweetie."

Though they were so close, his gaze darted all around the room rather than looking at his boyfriend's face. "Kind of?"

"That sounded more like a question than a statement," Jazz said. "Let me try to explain it better."

Lips pursed, Jazz studied Michael's face, as if thinking about what to say. Michael watched the tip of his tongue skate along his lip. He leaned in for a soft, sweet kiss that tasted of coffee and sent a warm rush of security and love through him.

"That was nice. What was that for?" Jazz said.

"Couldn't help myself," Michael admitted, blushing.

"My romantic mortician," Jazz said with a sigh, scooting his hips deliciously closer. "How lucky am I?"

"You were going to explain better?" Michael prompted, heart racing at Jazz's nearness and the conversation. *Why doesn't he want me to go with him?*

"If you'd quit distracting me with romance and your hot bod, I might be able to think more clearly." Jazz dramatically turned away from Michael and held a hand up to block his view even as he shimmied his hips playfully. "I need to remove you from my sight until I collect myself."

A moment later, Jazz looked back at him with another weary smile. He pressed their foreheads together and Michael's eyes crossed keeping him in view.

"Okay, I'm collected." He sat back, his weight both uncomfortable and welcome on Michael's thighs. "I need to go see Russell because that fucker is still in my head. We just sat here and talked about how he could be sending us death threats from prison, and.... Well, I need to talk to him face-to-face and see if there's anything to this idea that he's responsible. Plus, I need to do this to close the door on that part of my life."

Michael's heart perked up at that last bit. "Oh?"

Jazz gave him a soft smile. "There's that word again. But yeah. I want to put all my energy into looking to the future. And us. I need to get Russell out of my head for good. Do you understand?"

"I do," Michael assured him. "Looking to the future... that's what I want too."

Knowing it wasn't the right time to say those three words but wanting to convey them through touch, Michael embraced Jazz tight.

Jazz's arms coiled around his neck and they held each other close, sharing breaths and relishing the connection.

As Michael breathed in the woodsy, sweet scent of Jazz, his mind calmed. He loved Jazz. It wasn't a surprise to him, not really. It had been less than two months since they'd met, but he knew he loved him. Had known for a while now. He had yet to say the words aloud, even to himself or Mr. Pickles.

While Jazz was still sorting through his complicated feelings about Russell, Michael shouldn't expect Jazz to simply fall in love again so soon.

Yet Jazz's words about a future gave Michael hope. He said that Michael was all he wanted. *You're the best part of my life right now*, Jazz had said.

Maybe visiting Russell would help Jazz put the worst part of his life behind him so they could move forward.

Michael shifted, pulling Jazz tighter, hoping to convey his love and support. Being so close, his body stirred. When Jazz arched against him, Michael could tell he was working himself into a similar state.

Jazz drew back. "Wanna get our minds off all this?" he said at the same time Michael said, "Bedroom?"

They both chuckled.

Jazz climbed off and held out his hand, drawing Michael to his feet.

Smiling and heart thumping with a never quenchable need for Jazz, Michael followed Jazz into his bedroom.

Whereas Michael's bedroom was all precision and order, clean lines, whites, grays, and dark woods, Jazz's bedroom was as colorful and as complex as the man himself. To the east, large windows with drawn white curtains faced the back parking lot, while discarded clothing littered the plush lavender chaise lounge sitting beneath the opposite windows offering a view of the lake. An antique vanity painted a distressed white with a tiny stool covered in black and white polka dots sat beside the chaise, Jazz's hair products all lined up neatly atop it. Jazz had somehow managed to cram a king-sized bed into the small room and it faced the door, a focal point with two large canvases of a colorful landscape in lieu of a headboard. The giant bed was unmade and beckoning.

Inching around the bed, Michael set his glasses on the end table, and they kissed.

Michael's heart ached for everything Jazz had gone through, from the way Russell hurt him and now to this horrible day. He wanted, no, he *needed* to make Jazz feel loved, cared for. Appreciated. Hungry for Jazz, but eager to make sure Jazz got what he wanted, Michael whispered, "What would you like?"

"Anything," Jazz breathed, hands caressing Michael's chest. "Everything."

The trust in Jazz's eyes washed away the niggling doubts in Michael's mind. Jazz had assured Michael he'd been on board with the spanking—*damn, he'd said he wanted it harder next time!* A surge of confidence swept through him. "Everything, eh?"

Jazz gave Michael a sleepy smile as Michael reached for the button of Jazz's pants.

"Are you going to undress me?" Jazz whispered.

"Yes, and I'm going to do my damnedest to make you forget everything that's going wrong right now."

Jazz brushed his hand across Michael's face. "I'd rather think about everything that's going right in my life... at least right now."

Michael nodded and pushed Jazz's slacks to the floor, a delighted thrill whipping through his body when he discovered, once again, his boyfriend had gone commando. He gripped that semihard erection, eyes locked on Jazz.

As Michael slowly stroked, he memorized Jazz's face: every flinch, every nibble of lip and faint sigh while Michael brought him to full hardness. When a small pearl of moisture brushed across Michael's palm, he released him.

Jazz let out a sigh, and Michael knew it was not one of disappointment. Jazz understood that Michael was devoted to his pleasure... always.

Jazz assisted him ever so slightly as Michael removed his shirt. When Jazz stood naked before him, Michael pushed the covers of the bed aside.

"Here," Michael said, his voice rough with desire as his own cock pressed hard against his jeans. He relished the denial of his own needs while he put Jazz's before his own. "Lie down. Let me take care of you."

Wearing a sleepy grin, Jazz readily obeyed. His hair spread out across the watercolor floral sheets like rays of sunshine in a meadow of wildflowers.

Michael crawled onto the bed and, as if Jazz read his very mind, he opened his legs so Michael could fit in between. Michael continued his massage, working up Jazz's calves, over his hairy thighs, his gaze alternating between Jazz's rock-hard cock and the dazed look of pleasure in his boyfriend's eyes.

When he reached the soft skin along Jazz's inner hip bone, Jazz twitched and thrust his hips up.

"Fuck, you know that's my hotspot," Jazz gasped, then let out a breathless laugh.

"I do," Michael said, somewhat surprised by his arrogant tone. He dipped his head and kissed that soft unguarded skin, first one side, then the other.

Jazz was whimpering now, and Michael took mercy on him by taking his cock all the way down his throat in one forceful movement. Beneath him Jazz convulsed and let out a cry. Michael sucked with vigor and used the heels of his hands to press on Jazz's hip bones to keep him stationary, letting him know in no uncertain terms who was in charge.

Jazz willingly succumbed to Michael, relaxing and trusting that Michael would see to his every need.

Never before had Michael been so consumed with a desire to take care of another human being. Jazz was his *everything*. Michael needed him to know he would always be there for him. He put all of his love and devotion into the blow job, and lost himself to the heat of Jazz's dick—the curvature of the head, the salty sweetness of precum, and the brush of pubic hair on his chin. He didn't even mind the discomfort in his throat as he took him deep.

Nothing mattered but making Jazz happy.

"Fuck, Michael," Jazz cried out. "Please...." Hands grasped at Michael's shoulders, tugged on his polo shirt.

Michael lifted off Jazz's cock until only the head was in his mouth as he gazed up at him.

Jazz's skin was flushed, his brow and hair damp with sweat, eyes rolling back in his head. He pulled on Michael's shirt again. "Please, now... I need to taste you too," he begged. "I need to taste your cum... want you so bad...."

Unwilling to deny Jazz anything, Michael hastily pushed to his knees and scrambled to reposition while Jazz fumbled for his belt. Between the two of them they got Michael's pants and underwear below his ass.

Jazz grabbed for Michael's firm erection.

Chuckling at his lover's eagerness, Michael gently pushed Jazz back onto the pillows. "Let me get in position first."

When they were lying side by side, faces at crotch level, they both took each other at the same time. Jazz groaned long and loud, the vibration doing things to Michael's body he didn't know were even possible. Being still fully clothed, with Jazz completely naked and writhing against him, was a delightful sensation. Jazz's fingers clutched at Michael's ass, pulling tight and deep-throating Michael with a talent and fervor that probably belonged in *Guinness World Records* for the best cocksucking ability.

Savoring Jazz's expert technique, Michael went back to his worship of Jazz's cock. Then, to Michael's surprise, Jazz hooked his thigh over Michael's head, shifting somewhat on top of him. He began to thrust deep into Michael's mouth, fucking his throat with a passion bordering on frantic.

Now Jazz was in control, with Michael lying there, his mouth being fucked hard and his cock sucked with gusto.

Jazz's promise to act out all of Michael's fantasies with eager support flitted through his mind as Jazz roughly used his mouth, all the while giving Michael just what he needed.

They didn't last long like that, and the moment Michael felt Jazz jerk against him, plunging his cock deep, Michael fell with him, melting, rolling, and tumbling hard through an orgasm that rocked him to his core.

Dazed in afterglow, Michael cleared his throat and coughed a little when Jazz pulled out.

"All right, sweetie?" Jazz asked, his knees popping as he shifted to look down at him.

Damp cock lying exposed and used above his jeans, Michael lay on his back. "Perfect," he managed. His throat felt a bit abused, but he relished the idea of feeling Jazz later.

Jazz shifted and fell heavily against Michael, lying next to him. They turned and looked at each other at the same time, letting out breathless chuckles.

"That was hot," Michael whispered.

"Always is with you," Jazz said, scooting closer so their faces were mere inches apart.

For all the things Michael had worried about, *this*, the two of them together in moments like this? At least he didn't have to worry about that. Jazz had shown him that just now, sating his stress and taking what he needed—which Michael was more than willing to give.

Once more, Michael was delighted with how compatible they were.

The stress of the past few days should not have shaken Michael's confidence in his relationship with Jazz. They'd weathered one murder investigation, and they would overcome this one too.

Michael jumped when his cell phone buzzed in his pocket. "Sorry, let me check on this."

"Sure, sweetie."

Michael discovered quite a few text messages waiting for him: two from Kitty, one from Trevino, and a few from Musgrave. He sighed. "People are looking for me."

"And lucky me has found you." Jazz smiled and leaned in for a quick kiss. "Go do your job like the superhuman you are."

Michael didn't move from the bed as he looked at Jazz. "Will you be okay?"

"I'll be fine. I'm going to have a long nap and a little pamper-Jazz time now that I have a surprise day to myself."

"I wish I could spend it with you," Michael said, feeling a lonely ache at the thought of missing out on spending quality time with his sexy hairdresser. "I wish we could spend all day making love and forget about everything else."

"That sounds wonderful, but to be honest, I don't think I'll be very good company today. If I do leave the apartment, I'll probably go over and help Misty prepare for her block party tomorrow. She's pretty shaken up."

"When were you thinking of visiting Russell?"

"Oh, not until Monday at the earliest. I'm not up to it today, and they don't have visiting hours on Sundays."

So he's already checked into the prison visiting hours. How long has he been planning this? Since the phone calls from the prison he hadn't told me about?

Michael pushed negative thoughts aside— *we're in a good place*—and got to his feet. Jazz needed to do this so he could move forward with Michael. Michael would support him no matter what. "Okay. I'll text you later and see how you're doing. Maybe we can meet up?"

"Yeah, maybe." Jazz stood up as well. "I'll let you know. But don't take it personally if I want to hang on my own tonight, okay?"

Michael tried to act casual about it even as the concern started up again. "Oh, I know. It's fine."

Jazz squeezed his upper arm. "Sweetie, I mean it. I've got a lot to think about, and it's not about you and me. This is all just shit and nonsense from my past. Okay?"

"Okay."

"No more worrying about us, promise?"

Michael smiled. "Promise." *I promise to try....*

"Good." Jazz seemed pleased, relaxed in the afterglow for now. "I will, however, see you at five to style my ladies."

Michael hesitated. "Are you sure you're still up for that? Ezra or I—"

"Your creep-tern is *not* sending off my ladies to the bingo hall in the sky. I'll be there. It's good to keep busy." Jazz leaned in for a kiss, then pushed him toward the door. "Go be amazing."

Michael blushed as he left the apartment. He stood a moment outside Jazz's door, letting his hand rest on the knob to allow some kind of contact with Jazz's place to linger. His phone buzzed again and he sighed. So much for that. He hurried down the stairs and out into the heat of the day.

CHAPTER SEVENTEEN

After a morning of self-pampering that included the hot sex with Michael, a facial mud mask while he soaked in his big claw-foot tub, and a manicure and pedicure, Jazz still felt antsy after lunch. When he normally would've been at work, he had nothing to occupy himself with until he was due at the parlor to style his ladies.

A shiver went through him, knowing Norbert's body would be in the building.

Why the hell was he in my chair?

Michael had a point about Ally having the clearest motives in all of this, but Jazz couldn't help feeling that all the convoluted foreshadowing Russell had always been so fond of in his books— *"It makes for a great page-turner, Jasper dear!"*—pointed to Russell's involvement. But why involve Michael? Jealousy? Revenge for catching him?

Or just to torment Jazz?

That seemed most likely, but why would Russell murder Bill Denton? Maybe the hitman Russell had hired had been forced to kill Denton to cover his tracks. Denton was skinny and pale, just like Norbert. Totally could have been a mix-up if the killer found them at the HPP, the intended target always Norbert. And Russell knew it would get to Jazz the most by going after Michael, which was why the killer had left "Norbert"—aka Bill Denton—in Michael's garage.

Michael said it felt like a personal message to them, and Jazz agreed. Russell was leaving Jazz the message that he could try to move on, or be happy without Russell, but Russell could stop Jazz's happiness if he wanted to.

The sick fuck.

A stunt like that had Russell's stench all over it.

A few blocks away, the music festival had kicked off the afternoon sets, and someone was plucking away at a steel guitar. The sound system must have been amped up, because he could hear it perfectly through his windows, which were closed against the heat, and over the hum of his air conditioner. His nerves tolerated the guitar, but when the singer started to yodel, Jazz knew he had to tap out. No way was he going to sit around his apartment all day and listen to that while Musgrave and his minions worked the crime scene one floor below.

He needed to leave.

His first instinct was to go to Michael's, but Michael was swamped with work and dealing with his nemesis. Though happy they managed some alone time earlier, Jazz didn't want his current bad mood to cause Michael any more stress. He wished he'd been feeling more himself last night after that hot fucking Michael gave him, instead of so stuck in his own head with all the drama. He hadn't meant to give his nervous boyfriend any inhibitions or insecurities about their sex life.

As far as Jazz was concerned, that was one of the best parts of their relationship thus far, like their bodies were perfectly in sync.

To think his preoccupation with Russell had caused Michael any worry or distress broke his heart.

It also pissed him off.

Fucking Russell, fucking my life up even from prison. This is just like him!

After he got home last night, Jazz had realized he needed to talk to Russell. He'd felt better about everything once he'd made the decision.... But then Norbert.

Jazz fought a shiver.

Even that super-hot sixty-nine hadn't quelled his nerves. He did feel better after he'd told Michael his plan to see Russell, but now the visit loomed over his head. Not to mention another murder investigation he was a suspect in. He knew Hotel Boy well enough to know Musgrave would be harassing him once Misty wasn't there to play defense.

Thinking of his friend, he sent her a text to check on her. *How are you holding up?*

Shaky, but ok

Since Misty rarely sent such succinct texts—she totally abused talk to text—Jazz knew she was about as okay as he was himself.

You need any help cooking for your BBQ? I can come over?

At least Misty's cul-de-sac was far enough from downtown, Jazz wouldn't have to hear any more acoustic music.

Misty responded almost immediately: *YES!!!!!*

Jazz chuckled and jumped up from the couch. Minutes later, he locked up his apartment just in time to hear the Airbnb guy talking to someone about the place he'd rented. *Dumb millennial neighbors.* Jazz didn't want to see them evicted, but seriously? He paid to have a security locked building so he didn't have to worry about strangers rolling in and out.

An uneasy feeling settled over him.

A stranger renting the apartment next door on the same weekend of two gruesome murders, and Norbert's body had been staged inside the salon downstairs. Could it be a coincidence? Maybe Russell had something to do with these murders, maybe he didn't. But Russell *did* have a lot of seedy connections and the money to contract a killer. What if the stranger next door was the hired gun?

Suddenly this building didn't feel as safe as it had before.

For a moment, he thought about getting his Colt 1911 out of the bedroom closet, then shook his head at himself. *No, I'll be fine at Misty's.*

He managed to avoid the cops and the gawkers on his way to his scooter. Once he'd straddled Beulah and started her up, he sped down an alley unseen, then turned out onto Steelhead Avenue.

It was a short and refreshing drive over to Misty's. She lived on a cul-de-sac in a little subdivision east of downtown with a cute name, Warbler Glen, which Jazz liked to tease her about, calling it Goblin Glen or Goober Glen.

Jazz saw an unfamiliar large white van, like a church might use.

Oh, great, Misty's new extended family is here.

Jazz parked Beulah right on Misty's walkway and headed into her cute gray-and-white bungalow. Each of the houses in her neighborhood were similar copies, with manicured lawns, shutters, front porches, all creating a sense of community and security.

A false sense of security, he thought bitterly, but forced it down.

Misty's front lawn, however, was wild with tall native grasses and flowering bushes, intermixed with driftwood, most likely found on the nearby shores of Lake Michigan. It was far more free-form than her neighbors', with whimsical lawn decorations and wind chimes that suited Misty to a tee.

Jazz was a "no need to knock" friend, and he let himself in the front door, calling out, "Hey there, Misty Mae, Jazz is here to save the day!" He chuckled. "I'm a poet and I didn't know it."

Jazz was met with two sour expressions, the first from Herschel on Misty's beige suede couch, surrounded by wildly colorful pillows as he restrung a violin bow. The second was from Herschel's young stepson, Oslo, who sat forlornly, as if he'd just been scolded or perhaps had his mouth washed out with soap. Oslo's face brightened momentarily at the sight of Jazz, the boy's fingers dexterously weaving together what looked like severed bow strings into some sort of arts-and-crafts braid. Probably not allowed to play video games like a normal kid. The dream catchers on Misty's lime-green walls, the fluffy white carpet, and tie-dyed curtains—along with the glow from all her himalayan salt lamps—made Herschel's stern black suit and drawn face seem wildly out of place.

"Hi." Jazz gave them a jaunty wave before hurrying into the kitchen.

Bright pink walls and white cabinets greeted him—along with Misty and her grumpy cousin, Dorothy. Daughter Beatrice sat at the island bar, peeling potatoes. Jazz noted the girl's blue glitter nail polish was gone. Ol' stepdaddy must've disapproved of that along with last night's makeup.

Jazz tried not to frown.

"Oh, you're a lifesaver," Misty said when she saw him. She beamed at her cousin. "Jazz is an amazing cook."

Dorothy forced a smile, which Jazz read clearly: *Real men don't do ladies' work.*

Rather than ask *where do you keep the broom*—he refused to sink to their level—Jazz clasped his hands together. "What do you need me to do?"

"Potato salad? Coleslaw, or maybe the marinade for the chicken...."

Her voice trailed off, and Jazz knew he'd arrived just in time. She was frazzled.

"I'm on it," he said, grateful to have busywork. "Don't worry, we'll get it all together. Did you make a menu?"

She pointed at the fridge, where a list of picnic foods were scrawled on a dry erase board. Only pop and beer were crossed off.

"Let's get started, then," Jazz declared. He got a sick thrill at the frowns from her cousins when he unashamedly took one of Misty's frilly kitchen aprons out of her pantry and donned it.

"I look so good in peach," Jazz said to Misty, smoothing the flowered fabric.

"You do!"

Soon he lost himself to the rhythmic act of chopping onions. He noted that Misty's relatives watched his culinary knife skills with obvious surprise and envy.

"You have all this under control," Misty declared after the potatoes were boiling and the coleslaw was done. "Dottie, will you and Bea help me find the centerpieces in the basement?"

Misty and the sister wives headed downstairs. Oslo walked in after they left, drawing up short when he spied Jazz.

Their eyes met, and Jazz noticed his empty glass. He nodded toward the fridge. "Pop is in there."

"Oh, we don't partake in sugary drinks."

Jazz barely refrained from an *Of course you don't* and smiled instead. "Filtered water is at the sink."

Oslo walked around the island where Jazz chopped celery for the potato salad, almost skirting Jazz the whole time. The boy stopped at the sink and opened a container of Clorox wipes, pulling two free and cleaning his hands. A strong smell of chlorine wafted over Jazz, and he struggled to keep from telling Oslo using those would strip his skin of all the natural oils.

Oslo filled his glass at the sink, then surprised Jazz by leaning against the counter to Jazz's left and openly staring at him.

Only allowing it a moment, Jazz stopped chopping and turned to face him.

Oslo didn't flinch. "You're good at that," he said, gesturing to the cutting board with his glass.

"I like cooking," Jazz replied, unsure what Oslo wanted.

Tipping his head, Oslo studied him more closely. "Your eyeliner is interesting. How'd you learn to do that?"

His tone was one of curiosity, not condemnation, so Jazz answered, "I'm a hairstylist. Learning makeup is part of the skill set."

"A hairstylist? That explains your nice hair."

Not immune to a compliment, Jazz offered Oslo a smile. "Thanks. You know, with those big green eyes of yours, a brown eyeliner would really make them pop."

Oslo blushed. "You think so?"

"I do," Jazz said, suddenly feeling sorry for this young man.

"Oslo."

The sharp tone drew them both up short.

Herschel entered the kitchen with the violin bow in hand. "Your bow's been restrung."

"Thank you." Oslo hurried from the kitchen, taking the bow on his way out.

Jazz met Herschel's eye and put as much *fuck you and your fucking brimstone* energy into his stare as possible. Herschel took in Jazz's apron, his disapproval obvious.

Before either of them could speak, Misty, Dorothy, and Beatrice came up the basement stairs, carrying folding camping chairs, red-white-and-blue streamers, and firework foil centerpieces.

"Everything all right up here?" Misty asked, obviously sensing the tension in the room.

"Everything is fine," Herschel said, keeping his watery gaze fixed on Jazz.

"Jazz?" Misty asked.

Jazz gave a single nod and looked away from Herschel. "Everything's jake, Misty Mae." He flashed her a smile and went back to making the potato salad.

"Oslo," Herschel called, and the boy immediately reappeared in the doorway. Herschel waved for his family to follow, and they all exited the kitchen for the backyard.

Misty closed the patio door, no doubt to cut Jazz off at the pass before he could snark about the von Trapps. "How's Michael handling that other coroner taking over the... exams?"

"You mean his nemesis?" Jazz said with a smirk, then leaned in and lowered his voice. "And it's called an autopsy, not an exam."

Misty shivered and waved her hand. "I know what it's called. I just don't like that word. And you never answered my question."

"He's doing okay. It's been a weird weekend, and he's really busy over there, so I'm giving him space to get his shit done."

"Is that what you want?"

"What? Space?" Jazz stopped what he was doing and looked at her. "I don't know. Michael stopped by once he'd left the salon this morning. Gave me a miraculous foot rub and some *other* attention, if you know what I mean."

"If I said I didn't, would you give me the details?"

He grinned. "You know I would, but it would probably bring bolts of lightning down from the sky. Anyway, my brain felt... busy, you know? Like there was a lot of noise, and I couldn't focus. I did some self-pampering, but then the festival music started up, and I really needed to get out of my place. And my own head, I guess. Michael's got a lot on his plate this weekend, so I'm letting him do his thing and taking care of myself because it's what I've always done."

"But now you've got a handsome and caring man who wants to take care of you," Misty said. "Don't you think you should let him? Or even open up a bit and *ask* for what you need?"

"Oh, I do, when I really need him to do something."

But do I really do that? Or do I just do things on my own like I'm used to? He wanted me to come over tonight, but I said I needed to be alone. Why?

Jazz didn't really feel like being psychoanalyzed, so he changed the subject.

"I didn't get a chance to ask why you were with Sheriff Musgrave this morning. You never schedule appointments that early." Jazz stopped mixing the potato salad and looked at her as his mouth dropped open. "Did you spend the night with him?"

"Oh my God, no!" Misty's face was bright red, and she wouldn't meet his eye. "But we did meet for breakfast at Silvia's. He asked me out after that mess at the festival last night."

Silvia's Breakfast and Lunch Spot was a small but well-appointed diner a few miles outside of Lacetown on the lake. Michael had taken Jazz there once on their way to the outlet malls in the middle of the state.

"That's interesting. A nice little diner just far enough outside of town to not be seen by any locals." He smirked. "And on the water too. How romantic."

"Oh, you," Misty said, snapping a dish towel in his direction. "Stop trying to cause trouble." She was quiet for a moment, then said, "Besides, it was my idea to go there."

"Mm-hmm."

"I like Silvia's vegan waffles."

Jazz made a face. "Vegan anything doesn't sound like a reason to get up early, let alone leave the town limits." He gasped quietly and turned to fully face her. "Oh my. Misty Musgrave?" Jazz shook his head. "I don't like how that sounds. If you marry him, you need to keep your name."

"Oh, for the love of modern medicine, we only went to breakfast," Misty said and blew a curly piece of hair from her face with a huff of breath.

"That's how it starts. So did you two have anything to talk about? Or did you just sit and look at his big hands the entire time and wonder if the size of a man's hands really does apply to the size of his dick?"

Misty flicked water at him from the sink. "You're terrible!" She blushed again and glanced away a moment, then moved closer with a secretive smirk. "I must say, I wouldn't mind finding out. He does have big hands, doesn't he? Big, *strong* hands."

They laughed together until Misty's cousins tromped back inside and sucked all the joy from the air. Jazz and Misty exchanged looks with raised eyebrows and returned to their preparations.

In between avoiding more awkward glowers from the relatives, Jazz managed to get Misty's menu on track. By the time he needed to leave to go to the funeral parlor to style his two customers—so much death lately, it didn't seem Jazz could escape it—everything was ready to go for the next day.

Jazz doubted he'd get to spend much time with his mortician while he worked. The two ladies from the Bluffs, his nemesis in town, and two murders darkening their doorsteps was keeping him occupied. With all that

MURDER MOST DESERVING

going on, most likely he'd get to say a quick, "Hi, sweetie, I miss you," and that would be it. But for now, it would be enough.

"Jazz, you were a lifesaver," Misty insisted as she walked him to the door.

"Anything to help."

"It helps to keep busy," she admitted. She looked as strained as Jazz felt.

"I'm going to see Russell on Monday," he told her.

Her blue eyes widened. "You sure that's a good idea on top of everything?"

He sighed. "I think so? I just need this chapter of my life to be over. It's messing with my head and causing stress between me and Michael."

Her brows knitted in concern. "You're having problems?"

"No, no," he quickly assured her. "But Russell is fucking with my head still, and I don't want his shadow over me and Michael. I really care about Michael. Like more than anyone ever before him. He's perfect, ya know?"

"Oh, you're in love." She smiled in a dreamy way.

He'd yet to say such a thing to Michael, but her observation gave him butterflies. "Well," he hedged. "That's why I need to get this monkey off my back, once and for all. I don't want anything to tarnish what we have."

"You'll come have a yoga session with me before you go see Russell, then," she declared. "It will clear your mind."

He smiled at her. "You know, that's not a bad idea."

"None of my ideas are bad," she quipped.

Laughing, he said goodbye, feeling more relaxed despite the situations being thrust upon him.

True friends had a way of making everything better.

On the ride back home to get his stuff before he headed to the funeral parlor, Jazz passed an older model beige car with a stained and faded white vinyl roof headed the opposite direction. He caught only a glimpse of the man driving, but saw the passenger clearly. The short, slicked-back hair, the expression that seemed to be permanently set to "scowl."

Ally Roberts!

The car whizzed past, leaving him with no chance to really ID the driver and with several questions in mind. Jazz considered doing a U-turn and following, but decided against it. Trailing someone wanted for questioning in a murder case two days in a row probably wasn't the best idea. If he'd minded his own business last night, he wouldn't be a suspect in Norbert's murder. Michael might like pretending to be Brock Hammer, but Jazz didn't feel like being victim number three. He'd leave the tracking down of murder suspects to Musgrave and his band of yahoos.

Besides, trailing a suspect wouldn't be the same without Michael along for the ride.

Nothing was the same without Michael.

"Shit," he said aloud to the wind. "Misty's right. I'm in love with Michael."

What a lovely and surprising revelation.

Recognizing his new feelings made Jazz want nothing more than to spend the rest of the weekend cuddling and sexing up his mortician, especially now that they'd decided to go condom-free. But Jazz wanted his heart and mind to be as clear and open as possible when he told Michael that he loved him. Misty's yoga and meditation would help, but Jazz knew he first needed to deal with Russell face-to-face. It wouldn't be fair to Michael for Jazz to make such an important statement while lingering thoughts of Russell tormented him.

Oh, and it might have to wait until after they were questioned for more murders.

Ugh, fuck my life.

At least he had Michael. Warm, sweet, doting Michael.

That was the one thing he couldn't allow to get fucked-up.

CHAPTER EIGHTEEN

"It's got to be the water. That or the subpar detergent that place uses to wash their sheets."

Parker Trevino stood before Michael's desk, scratching his chest through the lightweight cotton of his scrubs. Hives stood out in angry red patches along his bare arms, brighter and more prolific than they had been this morning when he'd been at the salon. He hissed as he scratched them, but Michael couldn't tell if it was pain or pleasure. Perhaps an equal measure of both.

"The water?" Michael said and tried to focus on the invoices Kitty had asked—more like demanded—him to review before Monday. With Ezra and Steve by his side, he'd spent the rest of Saturday getting everything ready for the two visitations scheduled the next day. Grandpa had dropped by too, under the guise of a friendly visit, but Michael knew he'd been checking up on their "guest." Now Trevino's kvetching was distracting Michael from completing his last task for the day.

"It's got to be something around here," Trevino snapped. Even covered with hives and in distress, an air of superiority rolled off him in waves. "Right here on the lake, all manner of toxins could get blown over you from Indiana and Illinois. And who knows what you Lacetownies add to your water."

Michael folded his hands atop the pile of invoices, barely able to suppress a sigh. His expression must have perfectly reflected his frustration, because Trevino took a step back and his eyes widened slightly, even as he continued to scratch his arms.

"There are no airborne toxins blowing in from the lake, and there is nothing different about our water. I highly doubt the Inn on Windswept Point uses, as you put it, a subpar detergent. Perhaps you're experiencing a very strong seasonal allergy reaction, or your body is responding to an insect bite. Now, I'm sorry that you're suffering, but Willet Pharmacy is a few blocks away. Perhaps it would be in your best interest to pay them a visit."

"Well," Trevino said with a sniff and half turned away from Michael's glare. "I have finished the autopsy on Norbert Farthington. I need to update the reports for the sheriff, but I suppose that can wait for a bit. Where is this pharmacy?"

Michael searched through the stacks of invoices for his pen. He really would like to become completely digital, but as most of his customers weren't computer savvy, he still had to use paper and snail mail. When he located the pen, he wrote out a few quick directions on a Post-it Note. He held the note out to Trevino, who took it with a single nod of thanks before turning to leave the office.

"How was Norbert's...?" Michael couldn't seem to bring himself to say autopsy after Norbert's name—the man had been so jaded, snide, and sharp-tongued, it was still a shock to think of him as deceased. "What are your findings?"

"I'm certain whoever murdered the initial victim, also murdered Mr. Farthington. As I told the sheriff, we have one killer and two victims."

Michael resisted the urge to say "duh" like Jazz would have, and instead questioned, "Did you discover anything of import after the second autopsy?"

Trevino lifted his nose and looked down at Michael. "As a matter of fact, yes, there was something." He scratched his upper arms. "Very interesting."

"And that would be?"

Trevino stuck his thumbs in his front pockets as if he needed to keep himself from scratching his hives, and rocked back up on his heels, reminding Michael of Musgrave. "I don't think it's wise that I inform you. You are a person of interest. After all, one victim was found at your place of employment and the other at your *lover's* place of employment."

Michael picked up on the subtle twist of lips as Trevino used the word *lover*.

"If the sheriff thought we had something to do with it, he would've arrested us. So either tell me what you found that was so very interesting or stop gloating and go take care of your hives."

Trevino blustered. "I'm not gloating." He resumed scratching. "I'm trying to abide by the law."

"And victim rights laws state that I have a right to know what happened," Michael said just as firmly.

Trevino scoffed a little bit, and Michael swore he heard a giggle on the other side of Kitty's door.

Trevino missed it, though, and he took a hefty breath through his bulbous nose and relented. "Fine. Both victims' cause of death was strangulation. They were strangled with a fine ligature, which left a residue on their skin and inside the wounds. I've sent a sample to my lab for analysis. What's interesting, however, is that both victims' fingernails were cleaned. By *bleach*. Which indicates premeditation and perhaps a penchant for doing this sort of crime before."

Michael wouldn't pretend the bleach detail didn't disturb him.

Perhaps Jazz's theory about Russell hiring a hitman wasn't far from the mark?

"That is interesting. Anything else?" Michael said with a less confrontational tone.

"While Bill Denton's wound was deeper and cleaner, Norbert Farthington's lacerations were far more irregular, indicating a terrible struggle. Thankfully, fibers were discovered in those lacerations so I sent them off to my lab as well."

Michael didn't mention he preferred to send his evidence to U of M, but mostly that was because Trevino had a better lab than his own, and he didn't like the man's gloating. But now was not the time for such pettiness. Not when they had murders to solve.

"Anything else of import?" Michael asked.

"No, it seems rather cut-and-dried. They were probably strangled by the same person with a similar weapon, then staged. I can't wrap my head around why or who would do this. But you two seem to have been targeted."

The glimpse of humanity in Trevino's expression softened Michael's ire. "Yes, well, unfortunately this isn't the first time we've been through such a thing here in Lacetown."

Trevino furrowed his brows. "Maybe your town should be a little more selective of what kind of riffraff they bring into it with these obscure festivals. Seems to bring out the freaks."

And the Musgrave vibe returned.

"Perhaps I should mention that to the mayor the next time I speak to her," Michael said.

All business once more, Trevino nodded. "Both vics are cooling downstairs. I don't know what their funeral arrangements are, but I suppose that's the next step. As for me"—he scratched even more vigorously at his blotchy skin—"I'm going to visit this pharmacy, then return to my room at the inn to take a nice hot bath with an oatmeal soak and have a big glass of vodka on the rocks. I'll be back tomorrow to finalize all the paperwork for the sheriff. I'll avail myself of the arrangement room for my work."

Though disliking how he stated rather than asked, Michael tamped the irritation down. "Of course you may." He stood and approached Trevino, but didn't offer his hand in deference to the hives. "Thank you for taking care of this in the interest of transparency."

"Of course. I hope the good sheriff can find out who is tormenting you and your *lover*." There was that twisting of his lip again. "It does seem rather deliberate, don't you think?"

Michael's stomach knotted, and he agreed with a curt nod. "It does."

"I should be going." He scratched his arm again.

"I hope the pharmacist can give you something to help."

Before Trevino could reply, someone called from outside his office.

"Michael? You here?"

Michael's heart thumped and a smile blossomed at the sound of Jazz's voice. Trevino narrowed his eyes and idly scratched at the red spots on his arm. Michael headed to his door and opened it. "In here."

Jazz stepped into view in the hallway outside of Michael's office, and his smile at the sight of Michael lit up the room. His gaze shifted to take in Trevino, and the smile dimmed a bit.

"Oh, sorry," Jazz said. "I didn't realize you were busy." He held up a small carrying case. "I'm here to work on Ruthie and Grace, if that's okay."

"Yes, that's fine," Michael said and smiled. "It's good to see you."

"You too," Jazz replied, then nodded at Trevino. "Mr. Trevino."

"Michael's friend," Trevino said, rather rudely, considering he knew damn well who Jazz was.

"Oh, I thought we'd been introduced." Jazz stepped into the office and extended his hand. "I'm Jazz Dilworth."

Trevino dropped his hand to his side. "Sorry, I shouldn't shake your hand."

"Oh?" Jazz looked at Michael. "Sorry. I didn't know...."

"Parker is having an allergic reaction to something," Michael said. "He's not sure what it is. I've suggested he visit Willet's, and he was just about to leave."

"What a shame," Jazz said, his tone making it perfectly clear he didn't feel that way at all. He set his case on Michael's desk and crossed his arms.

"I'll leave you both to your work," Trevino said, his emphasis on *work* providing quotes around it without the need for finger movements.

Trevino brushed past Jazz and disappeared down the hall.

"He's about as fun as an outbreak of the plague," Jazz observed. "Maybe those hives are his personality pushing through to the surface?"

Michael laughed and stepped closer to give him a long, deep kiss.

After they parted, Jazz preened a bit, running a hand down Michael's chest. "Aren't you proud of how I didn't call you sweetie in front of that ass Trevino?"

Michael smiled and resisted the very strong urge to kiss him again. "I am very proud. And grateful." He pulled Jazz into another hug and whispered, "I've missed you."

"Me too," Jazz whispered back. "But it's only been a few hours."

"Feels like an eternity."

Jazz sighed sadly. "It does."

"How are you?" Michael asked, taking hold of Jazz's hands. "Are you doing okay?"

"I'm all right. I spent the afternoon at Misty's, helping her prepare for the cookout tomorrow. The Bible-thumpers were there."

"Eww."

"Yeah, they're a barrel full of monkeys. Although, our fiddle-playing Oslo did ping my gaydar."

"Oh?"

"He asked about my eyeliner and complimented my hair. Nothing overt, but pinged nonetheless."

"I hope he isn't gay. Can you imagine being in the closet and living in a house with that stepfather of his?" Musgrave wasn't reacting well to

Rae's coming out, but he was a damn sight better than Michael imagined Dorothy's husband would be.

Jazz smiled up at him and squeezed their clasped hands. "And that's why I adore you. I see the situation and make jokes, yet you're worried about the poor kid. Anywho, Misty and I—well, mostly me—got all the food ready for her party while the relatives frowned, and glowered, and gave me the stink eye. I'm gonna go over there first thing in the morning and help her clean up her yard. She's pretty rattled still."

"Naturally." Michael wanted to ask Jazz if he was rattled as well, but he knew that he was, just as he knew Jazz would tell him eventually.

Or at least he hoped Jazz would open up.

Jazz released his hands and picked up his case. "I should go get my girls fixed up. They ready for me?"

"Ezra and I have finished. Both of them are waiting downstairs for your magic touch."

Jazz placed a warm palm against the side of Michael's face. "You look tired, sweetie. Like you could use a bit of my magic touch yourself."

Michael pressed his head against Jazz's palm and smiled. "Always."

Jazz gave him a sweet kiss that was over much too quickly. "I'll leave you to your work. I see those stacks of invoices on your desk, and I do not want to be on the receiving end of another feisty rant from the Itty Bitty Kitty Committee again."

"She's threatened me a few times so far this weekend," Michael said. "But I'm done for the day."

"Headed home, then?"

"I need to feed Mr. Pickles. It's his dinner time. But Kitty will still be here while you work. I'll be back to lock up."

"Okay, good to know you haven't abandoned me with all those dead bodies downstairs."

His stomach dropped. "Oh, no, I should stay, I—"

Jazz shook his head, chuckling. "I was teasing you, sweetie. I'm fine. Now go feed Prince Pickles. You know His Highness doesn't like to be kept waiting." Jazz gave him another quick kiss. "When I'm finished, I'll come over to the house."

His brows rose. "I thought you wanted to be on your own this evening," he said, trying not to sound nervous or too hopeful. Jazz had made him promise not to overthink their relationship. They were in a good place, and they didn't need to spend every waking moment together.

Even if Michael wanted to.

"Changed my mind." Jazz shrugged, smiling impishly. "Besides, we have *Jane the Virgin* episodes to catch up on."

"Ahh, an evening of normalcy amidst all the chaos," he said, not allowing his excitement to show but unable to stop his smile. *Jazz might be stressed but he still wants to spend time with me.* "Sounds lovely."

"I'll text you when I'm done."

He stood in the hall and watched Jazz walk away, dropping his gaze to the lovely swell of his beloved's ass. The invoices needed to be finished, he knew that, but both display rooms were already set up, flowers arranged. Kitty would pick up the refreshments on her way in tomorrow morning, and Michael and Ezra could finish folding the programs then. It was a lot of work, but they were well prepared.

Once Jazz disappeared into the hallway that led to the utility stairs to the preparation room downstairs, Michael glanced at his watch. It was indeed time to take Mr. Pickles home for the night so he could eat. He could use something himself, and his stomach growled as he realized he hadn't eaten anything in... who knew how many hours. And maybe he'd bring something back for Jazz.

Michael found the cat curled up on an armchair in the Serenity Room, lying on what looked like a cardigan sweater. He lifted Mr. Pickles, who mewed quietly in protest, and held him in one arm as he picked up the cardigan. Maybe it was Ezra's? It certainly wasn't something Steve or Kitty would wear. Michael would hang it on one of the hooks by the back entrance on his way out.

Carrying Mr. Pickles, Michael checked each room and turned off the lights behind him. He knocked on Kitty's door, then poked his head in. "You're still planning on being here until six thirty?"

"Yes, just finalizing everything for tomorrow and Monday," she replied, not glancing up from her computer as her long nails clacked away on the keys. "Enid's Floral is bringing another delivery after they close at six."

"Okay, I'm taking Mr. Pickles home. Jazz is downstairs."

"Yeah, I heard him come in. I'll go down and say hello in a bit."

"I'll be back to lock up shortly."

"No need. We'll be fine. I'll lock everything up."

"What would I do without you?"

This time she looked up, giving Michael a smirk. "You'd be hopelessly lost under a pile of invoices that you finished for me, right?"

"They'll be finished, I swear."

She harrumphed, and then her pretty face softened. "You doing all right? I mean, these two murders seem to be connected to you and Jazz. Any thoughts as to why?"

He shook his head, stroking Mr. Pickles's soft back to soothe his own mind. "I haven't the slightest clue. But I'm fine. I worry about Jazz, though. I'm surrounded by death every day, and he's surrounded by happiness and light. He's not used to such darkness."

Tipping her head, Kitty regarded him a moment. "Well, if you need to grab a few tequila shooters at the Roost and talk, you just let me know."

The offer startled him a little, but settled like a warm hot chocolate inside him. He smiled at her. "I will, thank you."

"Night, then. See you in the A.M."

"Good night, Kitty." With that, Michael left her to her bookkeeping. He hung the cardigan on a hook near the back door and then stepped outside. Seeing Beulah parked beside the garage made him smile. Maybe he'd ask Steve to make some room in the garage so Jazz could park it out of the elements.

The sun was past its zenith, golden and beautiful as puffy white clouds drifted past. Michael stood on the grass of his backyard and watched the clouds, wishing Jazz was there beside him. But Jazz was coming over to the house when he finished. Michael didn't know what had changed his mind, but he was happy that Jazz didn't want to be alone after such an emotionally taxing day.

Mr. Pickles squirmed in his arms.

"All right, let's go," Michael whispered and kissed the top of the cat's head. "I'm sure you're hungry, Your Highness."

CHAPTER NINETEEN

S unday dawned hot and steamy. It would be one of the busiest days
Michael and his crew had dealt with in a long time. As if the day weren't
hectic enough, a surprise call had come in from the Bluffs early that morning.
Adina Rosenstadt had passed in her sleep, so it seemed, and Steve and Ezra
had just returned from collecting her.

In his office, Michael was completing the last of the invoices before the
two viewings began.

After Jazz had put the finishing touches on his ladies last night, he'd
walked over to the house, where Michael had grilled burgers and a salad
waiting for him. They chatted about nothing in particular, both too tired to
brainstorm theories about the murders.

But they weren't too tired to share a shower and swap soapy hand jobs
before settling in bed to watch *Jane the Virgin*.

Jazz had fallen asleep in the middle of the second episode, so Michael
shut off the TV and snuggled up close against him. They'd been restless,
however, neither of them managing to get a good night's sleep. Michael's
mind had been on a loopty-loop of thoughts flipping back and forth between
the murders, work, and his concern for Jazz's plans on Monday. And Jazz
had most likely been thinking about Norbert in his salon chair and his
impending visit to Russell.

They were up with the sunrise, Jazz giving him a chaste kiss goodbye
before the coffeepot had even finished. He was headed over to Misty's,
having promised to help her do some yard work for the party, and he wanted
to get it done before the heat of the day set upon them. Michael had watched
him go with sweet longing, then turned away to prepare himself and Mr.
Pickles something to eat. Afterward, he'd gotten dressed and headed over to
the parlor before his staff arrived—Mr. Pickles in tow.

He really needed to get these invoices done for Kitty.

Even though tomorrow would be incredibly hectic as well, with two funeral services, Michael hoped Jazz would stay over tonight again. They could use as much alone time as they could get, to connect and support each other before Jazz faced Russell.

Still unsure how he felt about that, Michael tried to focus on the paperwork on the desk before him. But his mind wouldn't settle enough to concentrate.

A knock on the door had him glancing up to find Steve standing there. "Everything all right?"

"No worries, Captain. I'm done with the setups in the Serenity and Harmony rooms for the visitations." Steve stepped into the office. "And Mrs. Rosenstadt's family just pulled in. Kitty's getting them settled in the reposing room. I called the rabbi already."

"Thank you. I'll be right there."

The Bluffs had a large number of Jewish residents—and quite a few Orthodox Jews—all who chose Fleishman's for their final arrangements. Like so many of them, Mrs. Rosenstadt had a prearranged funeral, and her interment would happen first thing tomorrow morning. With the other two clients on display—also former residents of the Bluffs—many guests planned to visit both of the deceased and would probably wish to see Mrs. Rosenstadt as well.

The phrase *kill two birds with one stone* morbidly went through Michael's mind, and he pushed it away.

He'd been pushing a lot of thoughts away recently—like his concerns about Jazz's trip tomorrow to visit Russell. Although he understood the need for it, he wondered if it was wise.

"You holding up okay?" Steve asked.

Michael managed a smile. "We've juggled multiple funerals before."

"I meant about the murders," Steve said softly. "You've got a lot on your plate, Captain. Not that I think you can't handle it, but thought I would check in."

"Oh, yes. The murders are on an entirely different level from the work here."

There was much to do the rest of this weekend, and a killer still roamed Lacetown among the crowds at the music festival. Michael hoped no one else would turn up dead. Worry that it might be someone closer to either him or Jazz had also kept him from sleeping soundly.

Or maybe the killer was after one of them.

Steve turned to leave and nearly crashed into Parker Trevino.

"Excuse you," Trevino snapped.

"Sorry about that, Mr..... Oh!"

Steve sounded so shocked it brought Michael out from behind his desk and to the door. When he caught sight of Trevino, he stopped and said, "Oh my."

The hives had doubled on Trevino's face. One had sprouted on the tip of his nose, red and shining like neon.

Santa might have lost his Rudolph right here in Lacetown.

Trevino's scowl deepened. "Your pharmacy is shockingly lacking in basic medications," he snarled. "As you can plainly see by my worsening condition."

"Parker," Michael said, "I'm so sorry. That must be very painful. You should see a doctor about this. Allergic reactions can escalate rapidly."

Trevino sneered. "Your sympathy is overwhelming, but I didn't come here for that. I have a few things to finish up downstairs, and I've misplaced my sweater." He scratched his arms and his hand drifted toward his face before he dropped it back to his side.

"Sweater?" Michael asked.

"Yes, my cardigan. The breeze is quite temperate this close to the lake. I've been wearing it each morning. I couldn't find it when I was packing, however, and figured I had left it here."

Michael glanced over his shoulder to where Mr. Pickles lay curled up on the top level of his kitty condo. *Oh. Oh dear.*

Returning his attention to Trevino, Michael gestured toward the back entrance. "I did find a sweater in one of the rooms. I hung it by the back door."

"Very good. Thank you. I'll grab it and go downstairs to finish a few things up before I leave."

"Certainly, just...."

Trevino turned back, his impatience clear from his expression. "Yes?"

"My cat was lying on your sweater," Michael admitted. "Are you allergic to cats?"

"Not that I'm aware of," Trevino said, then scowled. "And that sweater is cashmere. If your feline snagged it, I'll be sending you a bill."

Michael watched Trevino's back as he walked away, hives on the back of his neck like angry red eyes staring back at him.

Michael returned to his desk and stood beside the kitty condo a moment. Mr. Pickles lifted his head and regarded him with narrowed eyes.

"Did you do that on purpose?" Michael whispered with a gentle finger scratch on the cat's head. "Did you know he was allergic and lie on his sweater?"

Mr. Pickles blinked a few times, then got up to shift position, turning his back on Michael.

Steve chuckled. "Oh, sweet karma."

"Indeed." Michael sat at his desk again, but any amusement at Trevino's situation faded as his mind looped back to the murders and all his unanswered questions.

If only he was involved with the case.

Michael sighed. "It is frustrating to not be the coroner for these cases. Maybe it's a bit too much of a control-freak nature coming out, but I feel very much out of the loop on this."

"That's the intention, though, right?"

"Yes, I understand the need for me to step aside as coroner, but I'm worried Trevino missed something important because he didn't know to look for it. Does that make sense?"

"You mean since you've got a history with Norbert and the previous case you were all involved in, you think you might have been more qualified to perform the autopsies?" Steve asked.

"That's right. He doesn't have the history I do with all of this."

"And that's the point, right? You have a history with Norbert. Maybe a fresh pair of eyes will find something you might overlook because you would have been focusing on looking for something you *think* you might see."

"That's very insightful."

Steve shrugged. "A blind squirrel finds a nut once in a while, Captain. I must be having a good day, though, because it usually takes a few beers to get me there."

"Well, I think you can pass on the beer later. You've already achieved enlightenment for today," Michael said, and they both chuckled.

Michael's phone buzzed on the desk next to him, and he touched the screen. As it did every time, a rush of warmth went through him at the sight of a text message from Jazz.

"Only one thing makes a man's face light up that way," Steve said. "I'm guessing that text is from Jazz."

"You guess correctly," Michael said as he read the text a second time.

Been daydreaming about that steamy shower last night. Can't wait to see you later at Misty's party. Jazz had added two eggplants, a bathtub, hearts, and two emoji men holding hands to the message.

Smiling, Michael sent back a response: *I'm looking forward to it as well. Seems like forever since I've seen you.*

"You're going to Misty's cookout with him," Steve said, more statement than question.

"That was the plan."

"Good. You need to see him today."

"It would be nice," Michael said with a sigh. He was questioning whether or not it was wise to leave work for fun when there was so much to be done. "Really depends on the flow of visitors, though."

"You'll go," Steve said, crossing his arms and looking handsome and commanding in his gray suit.

Michael envied Steve's laid-back masculinity and coordination. In preparation for his date with Jazz, Michael had laid out a bold-for-him silk hawaiian shirt, shorts, and a pair of sandals he hadn't worn for a couple of summers—no one had invited him to a cookout in a long time. "It's going to be one of our busiest days in a while," Michael said, fingers fidgeting guiltily atop the desk. "I really feel like I should be here."

"Kitty, Ezra, and I can handle cleaning up after the visitations and setting up for services tomorrow. We've all done it before."

"I know, but these two ladies passing so close together, and now with Mrs. Rosenstadt downstairs as well, it seems like a lot to ask."

"Nothing happens with Mrs. Rosenstadt until tomorrow. And the rabbi's coming to sit with her today, right?"

Michael nodded, feeling better about leaving for his date. "That's right."

"So that leaves all three of us available for the attendees. And I'm sure your grandpa won't miss out on a chance to scope out all the widows at the showing. So he'll be here too."

"Funerals as a social event." Michael shook his head. "Will we be like that one day?"

"Most likely," Steve said. "If anything comes up we need you for, we can call you. You won't be far away."

"Yes, but—" Michael began.

"You're going," Kitty said as she breezed past his doorway. "You deserve a life outside of this parlor."

"Told ya, Captain," Steve said with a grin.

Michael shook his head at his employees—his friends?

Smiling, he thought about Friday night, how everyone had come to their defense at the festival. He'd always just considered Kitty and Steve his employees. Yet each of them seemed concerned about how he was handling the murders. And they always had encouraging things to say when it came to his relationship with Jazz. They were genuinely concerned for his welfare... like true friends.

That knowledge settled like a contented warmth inside his heart.

How had he gotten so lucky?

"MIKEY!"

Michael turned as Grandpa made his way up the concrete ramp that led from the back parking lot to the side entrance of the funeral home. He wore another of his seersucker suits he was famous for, this one a peach striped number that could only be pulled off by his grandfather. Mona walked beside him, one arm linked with his, a purse the size of an airline carry-on bag hanging from the crook of the other—probably toting another bottle of manhattans.

"Hi, Grandpa," Michael said. "Mona, you look very nice."

Mona smiled and pushed her big sunglasses up her nose. "Why, thank you, Michael."

"What about me?" Grandpa stopped in front of Michael and opened his arms wide. "Don't I look very nice?"

"You're the very definition of dapper."

"Damn right I am," Grandpa said, then leaned in and dropped his voice. "Did you set out the fruit punch and lemonade? And coffee and hot water for tea?"

Michael nodded patiently. "I did, as usual."

"And the cookies from Robichaux Bakery?" Mona whispered, also leaning in.

"And the cookies," Michael assured her, then leaned in even closer and lowered his voice. "Three different types."

Grandpa made an impressed face as he and Mona looked at each other. "Get this guy," he said. "Putting the 'ancy' in fancy."

He and Mona laughed, and Michael wondered if it was some kind of private joke.

"Why don't you go in and pay your respects?" Michael said, hoping to inject a bit more solemnity into each of them. It was a double visitation after all.

The two tempered their humor, and Grandpa gave a somber nod. "We'll see you inside, Mikey."

"Yes, I'll see you in there."

As they started to step into the funeral home, Michael took his grandfather by the elbow. "Please tell me Mona's not smuggling manhattans in her oversized purse."

Grandpa feigned surprise. "Mikey. Why, I never. This is a very serious day. We're here to pay our respects to our friends who have passed beyond the veil."

"Uh-huh." Michael gave both of them long, pointed looks. "Don't overdo it."

Grandpa nodded and gave a wink as he touched the brim of his hat. "We'll keep things discreet. You've got my word. By the way, good thinking to schedule the viewings at the same time but stagger the burials tomorrow."

Michael watched them walk off arm in arm, and a warm glow of affection burned through any annoyance he might have felt. He loved his grandfather and was very glad he'd found a steady girlfriend to spend time with. Everyone needed someone special in their life, no matter what age, race, or orientation.

He smiled as his thoughts turned inevitably to Jazz. In just a few hours he'd get to see his sexy hairstylist again. Since they'd made the decision to not bother with condoms anymore, Michael had wanted a repeat performance. Last night they'd only had the energy for slow sensuous hand jobs in the shower. He was excited to try some other positions, to feel Jazz come inside him, to be on the receiving end of that shared intimacy. A tremble fluttered low in his belly at the prospect of being with Jazz like that.

A large transport van stopped at the bottom of the access ramp, bringing Michael's attention to the task at hand. Painted across the side was the name the Bluffs at Lake View, and Michael could see a number of elderly women sitting in the back. He descended the ramp and helped each of the women off the van, smiling pleasantly and greeting them all by name.

Only one of them refused his hand, and she glared at him as she slowly stepped out of the van.

"Don't need any help from you, thank you very much," she said in a snappish tone. "You're profiting off all of us at the Bluffs. Until it's my time to lay on your damn steel table, I don't want you touching me."

Michael nodded and kept his hands at his sides. "I'm glad to see you're still so spry, Mrs. Clarence. There are refreshments waiting for you all after you pay your respects."

The group of women smiled and nodded, some of them clasping hands and others linking arms as they made their way up the ramp to the door. Michael watched them go, Mrs. Clarence's gripes fading as she stepped inside.

When he turned, a familiar face beamed at Michael.

"Rabbi Daniel," he greeted the man with a handshake. "It's unfortunate to see you under such sad circumstances."

"Yes, I didn't think I would get to see you again until your annual visit to temple for Yom Kippur."

The flush of guilt was so similar to the way his mother had often manipulated him when he was a child. Granted, Mother had been quick to run away for her new exciting life in California, but she always managed to layer on that stereotypical Jewish mother guilt. Apparently the rabbi was schooled in yenta guilt as well.

Pushing it down, Michael held the door open for the rabbi. "Please, come in."

Rabbi Daniel smiled sadly at him. "This visit isn't as pleasant as seeing you at temple."

"Unfortunately, death is an on-call business and I can't plan as well as I would like to." It was a lie with some elements of truth, and Michael felt guilty again.

He gave Michael a scrutinizing once-over. "How are you doing? Truly?"

Everyone kept asking him that. Did he look that bad?

For a flash, Michael thought about sharing what was going on in his life with the rabbi, but the urge quickly passed. There was no way in all that was hot and holy he'd tell a *rabbi* that he was excited about the new stage of his relationship with Jazz—aka sex without condoms. Or that he couldn't sleep because he was scared and nervous about Jazz visiting his murderous husband in prison without Michael. He had no information about the murders or why it seemed he and Jazz were being targeted either. So what else was he supposed to tell the man? That he really got off on spanking his boyfriend hard, and he couldn't wait to do it again?

Might as well confess about his sex toy collection!

"I'm doing well, rabbi," Michael answered with a smile. "Thank you for asking. Ezra brought Mrs. Rosenstadt to the reposing room for you to sit with her as the shomer."

From the moment of death until burial, the body of an Orthodox Jew should not be unattended. If a rabbi or family member wasn't available, someone from the staff—including, Michael himself sometimes—would act as the deceased's shomer, or guardian.

"Very good. I know the way." He paused and tipped his head at Michael. "I'm glad to know you're observing the customs here, even if you aren't making it to temple as often as you should."

Ah, the guilt!

"Yes, of course." There were a lot of strict Jews at the Bluffs, and Michael always made sure he observed all the customs for them.

209

After the rabbi left, Michael greeted a number of other arrivals before the heat forced him to follow a trio of senior men inside. *And Trevino thinks it's cold by the lake? Idiot.*

"Think Joel is here?" one of the senior men asked.

"He'd better be," another said. "I've got a date later."

"I'm hoping to score a date with one of the fillies here today," a third man said. "Think he can help me out?"

Michael wondered briefly why the men were talking about his grandfather as if he were some kind of dating guru, then recalled how many widows Grandpa had dated before meeting Mona. Michael moved around the men and checked on things in both display rooms, making sure tissue boxes were full, visitors comfortable, and that the video Kitty had put together for one of the families was still playing. The cloying scent of roses, carnations, and lilies filled the air from the extensive floral arrangements sent for both the deceased. Michael tried not to frown when he heard the soft ping-ping of an electronic game a small child played on one of the couches. It wasn't terribly intrusive over everyone's chatter and at least it kept the boy from getting underfoot.

Eventually he found himself in the kitchen, where he noted the cookies had been heavily picked over by the socializing seniors. He moved all the cookies to one tray, then took the empty platter to the employee break room to refill it.

He found Ezra stretching to reach the high shelf where the cookie boxes were—obviously having the same thought as Michael.

Pleased with the thoroughness of his staff, Michael stepped into the room. "Here, let me get that, Ezra." He reached over the shorter man and brought down two boxes.

"Thank you, sir."

"I trust the rabbi is settled?" Michael opened the box, the attractive and delicious baked goods colorful and appealing. Robichaux's really made the best cookies.

"Yes, and Mrs. Feldstein is actually speaking with him." Ezra gave Michael an impish look. "I hope she isn't telling the rabbi what she was complaining to me about."

Michael frowned. Tova Feldstein often performed the rituals of rechitzah and taharah for his Orthodox women clients—the processes of washing and purifying the body prior to internment. "What was she complaining about?"

Ezra leaned in, barely able to contain a giggle. "She said that the Bluffs is full of *nafkas* and *shiskas*."

Michael sniffed with amusement, because Grandpa had said the same once but with decidedly different meaning. "Why would she say that?" He arranged the iced gingerbread cookies on the platter.

Ezra looked at the doorway, then whispered hurriedly, "Apparently Mrs. Goldfarb and Mrs. Rosenstadt both had... um? You know? *Semen* on their stomachs."

Ezra spoke the word so quietly, Michael wasn't sure he heard correctly. Then he froze, transfixed by the globs of white icing on the cookie in his hand. *How unfortunate.*

While his first instinct was to make a funny comment, this wasn't Jazz he was talking to, rather, an employee. "Oy vey," he muttered, setting the cookie down. "Well, old people do have sex. Even if we don't want to picture it."

"Of course." Ezra schooled his features.

Michael thought back to his ice cream date with Jazz. It had been their third try at a complete date, having been interrupted by the break-in at the funeral home first and Dylan's finger landing in their guac during the second—to this day Michael had lost all appetite for anything avocado related. At the Dairy Clipper, they'd joked about Cialis pudding. Michael could hear Jazz's laughter as warm as a caress.

But that easygoing laughter he'd grown to love had become in short supply recently, this weekend making it more scarce. Michael truly hoped the visit with Russell had the desired effect Jazz sought and didn't backfire, causing Jazz to slip deeper into the darkness threatening his spirit.

"Is something wrong, sir?" Ezra asked softly.

Am I that obvious? Maybe I'm not handling all this stress as well as I imagined. He forced a smile. "I think I'm okay."

"Are you? When Jazz came by yesterday to style our clients, he seemed very distant as well. And I didn't see his scooter this morning."

"He left early. It's a busy weekend."

"Indeed," Ezra said with a somber nod. "Was he very close with the man found at the salon? Did they have... a *past*?"

"Not in the way you might be thinking. Norbert was the PR representative for Jazz's ex-husband." Soon to be ex, anyway.

Michael sighed. He wished the whole thing with Russell was over!

"Oh." Ezra went back to straightening the cookies. "I was hoping things were all right between the two of you. I'm glad it's nothing of an intimate problem."

"No, nothing like that," Michael blustered. "He's...." *Stressed?* "We're both just very busy and working through things."

"I'm sure it's difficult, for the both of you."

"Yes. Well, things will get better."

They're going to, I'm sure of it.

"Michael." Kitty popped her head in the door. "There you are."

Grateful to have an out, though curious about what Ezra had been implying, Michael excused himself.

"How are things?" Michael asked her as he took the tray back.

"Pretty standard," Kitty said, and smiled and nodded at a few people entering the room. "There has been some discussion about the sizes of the rooms."

Michael had been afraid of that. "The display rooms are nearly identical in size," he whispered.

"Yes, *nearly* being the key word. Some of the women were whispering that Mrs. Blankenship should've been in this room and Mrs. Murray in the Serenity Room."

Michael really had to fight back an eye roll. "No one can tell the difference of dimensions by the naked eye."

"You and I know that, but I wanted to make you aware of what people were saying."

"Thanks for that."

The volume of conversation was louder than most showings, mostly because of the hearing loss suffered by the majority of the attendees. Michael caught snippets about recipes favored by the deceased, specific pieces of jewelry worn by the two women, and the fate of other residents at the Bluffs.

"Lots of Joel's ex lady friends are popping up dead," the cantankerous Mrs. Clarence was saying.

"You're just jealous he hasn't asked you to dinner," another said as she sipped punch.

"Says you," the old woman snapped back.

Michael arched his brows at Kitty, but a sudden tension quieted the conversations around them. They turned to see Kevin Raines standing in the hallway between display rooms. He wore a brown sport coat over a white shirt with blue checks and a solid blue tie. His thinning hair was long, now that Michael noticed, but it didn't make him look bad. Kevin was handsome, but the aura of exasperation coming off him seemed to quell all other energy in a room. A woman stood beside Kevin, dark hair in a neat bun at the back of her neck. Michael thought she looked familiar, but couldn't place where he'd seen her before.

He decided to take the first step and approached, reaching out his hand. "Hello, Mr. Raines. It's good of you to come."

"Why wouldn't I have come? I work with these people. Of course I'm going to come and pay my respects."

"I meant nothing by it," Michael said. "Simply a statement."

Kevin grunted as he shook hands with Michael. His palm felt wet, almost greasy, and Michael had to resist the urge to wipe his hand on his pant leg afterward.

"This is Susan Gunderson," Kevin said, tipping his head toward the woman. "She's one of the admins at the Bluffs."

"Ah yes, I thought I recognized you." Michael smiled and shook with her. "Pleasure to meet you. I've seen you at the front desk when I've visited my grandfather."

"Nice to meet you too," Susan said. "Your grandpa is quite the character." She turned to Kevin. "I'm going to pay my respects."

"Yeah, sure," Kevin said.

Susan walked off, turning her head this way and that as if she were searching for someone.

"You've got a booming business going, thanks to me," Kevin said, drawing Michael's attention again. He must have heard how his statement sounded, because he paled and looked at Michael with wide eyes. "I meant... I didn't mean...."

Michael waved a hand in dismissal. "No need to explain. I am proud and honored to be able to host the final farewell for so many of your residents. I only hope all of them trust that those of us at Fleishman Funeral Parlor will honor their final wishes with dignity and respect, no matter their spiritual beliefs."

At that moment, a trio of elderly ladies walked by, moving from the Harmony Room to the Serenity Room. As they passed, one of the women whispered, "Ruth looks better now than she has in the last five years."

"It's that new beautician they got at Misty's Makeover Palace," another replied. "He's a magician with hair and makeup."

Michael's heart swelled with pride, and he couldn't keep from smiling.

"I gotta call over there and get on his schedule," the third woman said as she ran skinny and wrinkled fingers through her white hair. "I'd like to look good while I've still got some time left."

"You said it," one of the others replied. "That Martin Firestone has been eyeing me during pinochle. Rumor has it he's got a bit of coal in his engine still. And he's been talking up Joel Fleishman, so you know he's good to go."

The three tittered like schoolgirls and continued into the Serenity Room.

"Jazz has really got a following at the Bluffs," Michael said, then regretted it when he remembered who he was talking to.

Kevin's eyes narrowed, and his face grew red. "This keeps up and I'll never manage to get an appointment with him."

"You know Misty has several qualified stylists working for her," Michael said.

Kevin gave him a smile that looked more like a sneer. "That's funny. Next thing you're going to do is suggest I go to Elmer's Barbershop in Bridlestop."

Michael bristled a bit but decided not to rise to the bait. Kevin probably knew Michael went to Elmer to get his own hair cut. The man wasn't worth the reaction, and Michael definitely didn't want to make a scene here in the hall outside two viewings.

He gave Kevin a thin-lipped smile. "Well, I won't keep you any longer. I'm sure you want to pay your respects."

Before Kevin could respond, Michael turned and walked down the hall to his office. He opened the door and flinched. Grandpa and five men stood around Michael's desk. They all looked up in surprise.

Grandpa grinned wide. "Mikey!"

"What are you all doing in here?" Michael asked, stepping into the office and surveying his space. Everything seemed to be in its proper place. He hated feeling suspicious about his own grandfather, but something about this gathering seemed very clandestine.

"Oh, I was giving the boys here some dating tips," Grandpa said. "Isn't that right, boys?"

Agreements were made all around before the men hurried past Michael and out of the office, leaving him alone with Grandpa.

"Seems a little secretive, you using my office for that kind of pep talk," Michael said.

"Have you seen how many lovely widows are out there?" Grandpa waved toward the door. "You can't swing your cane without knocking one of 'em down. Trouble is they're never on their own, you know? They travel in groups, just like back in school, and it can be real intimidating to try and approach one of 'em. You remember how it was before you met Jazz, right?"

Michael felt a bit flustered as he recalled his disastrous attempts over the years at asking men out. His flub-ups and tangled words had garnered him more laughs and eye rolls than actual dates.

"Yes, all right. I just wish you would have asked first before herding them all in here."

Grandpa scoffed. "Yeah, right. You expect me to sidle up all casual and ask if I can use my old office to give my friends some dating advice?"

"Fine." Michael took Grandpa's elbow and gently led him toward the door. "Let's rejoin the others."

"Yeah, I'm going. I need to track down Mona anyway and make sure Sy isn't making a play for her."

Michael stood at his office door and watched his grandfather make his way down the hall toward the display rooms. He sent a quick thank-you to whatever energy or entity that ran the universe that Grandpa was still able to get around so well at his age. And then followed that up with a wish that he and Jazz would be that spry when they reached that age.

That wish brought up those feelings of anticipatory domesticity again. What he felt for Jazz *had* to be love, because he could easily imagine the two of them as senior citizens, talking about old times and gently teasing each other about all the little habits and quirks they'd come to love about each other over the years.

The whispers of a conversation caught his attention, and he approached the kitchen, surprised to discover Trevino talking with Susan, the woman who worked with Kevin at the Bluffs.

"Oh," Michael said. "I thought you had left town, Parker."

"I was headed out of town but then realized I had forgotten my phone charger and came in to see if I'd left it downstairs," Trevino said, a blush burning beneath his rash of hives. "I, um, was spotted by this kind woman who, um... took pity on me because of my condition and has been telling me about home remedies to help ease the itch."

Susan smiled and nodded. "That's right. Home remedies."

"Very good," Michael said, returning her smile before asking Trevino. "Did you find it?"

Trevino frowned. "Find what?"

"Your phone charger," Michael said, feeling a bit frustrated.

"Oh, that!" Trevino laughed and Susan joined him, but Michael just stared at them with his brow furrowed. After a moment, Trevino cleared his throat and said, "Yes. I did find it. Thank you."

"I'm glad." Michael gave them a nod. "Good day."

As he returned to the visitations, Michael wondered how on earth Trevino got anything done in his own funeral home if he couldn't keep track of his sweater and phone charger.

CHAPTER TWENTY

I t was early evening when Jazz arrived at Michael's house. He'd received a text from Michael asking him to park in the alley behind his house, no doubt to avoid all the guests still packing the funeral home lot. Jazz had already paid his respects to his ladies last night while he styled them, and wasn't dressed for a funeral, wearing cargo shorts and a pink-striped button-down shirt over a black tank-top.

Michael must've liked Jazz's outfit because he gave him an approving head-to-toe gaze, pausing on his feet.

"Toe rings?" Michael observed at the flash of silver on his two longest toes. "That's new."

Jazz beamed under Michael's obvious approval. "You don't miss a detail, do you, sweetie?"

"Not when it comes to you." Climbing on the back of Beulah, Michael looked like a summer dream in his cream-colored hawaiian shirt with red hibiscus and matching red shorts. He had a small cooler bag draped over one shoulder.

"What's in there?" Jazz asked.

"A few bottles of white for our hostess," Michael explained as he adjusted the cooler and scooted closer.

"Such a gentleman," Jazz said. "Hold on!" Then he took off down the alley, Michael wrapping his arms around Jazz's waist tightly—just like he'd planned.

A breeze off Lake Michigan had chased a bit of the heat from the day, and everything seemed perfect as the wind blew his hair back. The scooter was probably only going twenty-five miles an hour, but Michael held on tight.

"I've already been back over to Misty's twice after I cut her grass,"

Jazz said over his shoulder. "Taking bags of ice and margarita stuff, and then the potato chips she forgot."

"You've been busy today too," Michael said.

"It was good to keep my mind off things."

Michael gave him a gentle squeeze in reply and rested the side of his head against Jazz's back. This was perfect. He didn't want thoughts of murder or Russell or funerals to break the spell.

Eventually, Jazz slowed his scooter and maneuvered around a pair of sawhorses set up to block off Misty's cul-de-sac. Tables covered in star-spangled tablecloths dotted the street in the shade of tall trees, and children played games of corn hole, ring toss, and water balloon toss on lawns. Someone had set out a lawn sprinkler at one house and several children ran screaming back and forth through the spray.

"Here we are," Jazz announced and they climbed off.

Michael's eyes widened at Misty's eclectic yard. "I thought you cut the grass?"

Jazz chuckled. "She has a normal lawn in the backyard. Some of her neighbors weren't too happy when she dug up the front lawn and planted all this prairie grass and wildflowers," he whispered in Michael's ear. "But I think it's pretty."

"It fits her style," Michael said, his proximity and warm breath sending a shiver down Jazz's back.

"C'mon, let's get some grub. I'm starving."

A short while later, plates piled high with food, and plastic cups of wine in hand, Michael and Jazz found a spot to eat and observe the party at an unoccupied picnic table.

"Ping, ping," Jazz said when he noticed they had an audience. He lifted his chin toward Oslo, who stood in the shade of a tulip tree nearby. When Oslo caught Jazz's eye, he quickly pretended to be watching some of the younger kids play corn hole. "We're being watched."

Michael had just taken a bite of his hamburger and paused to wipe ketchup from his lips before he looked that way. "Misty's cousin's kid?"

"He's been pretending not to watch us since we got here."

Michael's eyes widened slightly. "Maybe he's never seen a gay couple out in the open before?"

"Hence my gaydar ping." Jazz waved a buzzing fly away from his potato salad.

"Huh." Michael studied Oslo. "He seems a little...."

He trailed off, so Jazz offered up, "Tightly wound?"

"At least. And sad like his sister."

Once again, Jazz was impressed with Michael's observant nature and his compassion.

Jazz took a bite of his own burger—unfortunately, not as delicious as those at Gruff's Grub—when Misty collapsed into the camping chair next to their table and ran a hand across her brow.

"I'm exhausted," she said in a very dramatic tone. Her hair shimmered in the sunlight, and large white sunglasses gave her a movie star look.

"I have no doubt, after you put all of this together," Michael said.

"Oh, I only passed around a sign-up sheet to the neighbors, no big deal," Misty said, then sat up. "I was being theatrical. What are you two talking about?"

"Michael's hot body," Jazz said, then laughed when his shy mortician sputtered. He loved doing that to him.

Misty laughed too as Michael attempted to recover his decorum.

After he gave Jazz a gentle glare, Michael looked between them. "How are you both doing? You each had quite a shock yesterday."

"It was shocking," Misty said with a grim expression. She reached out toward Jazz and he took her hand, giving it a gentle squeeze as they smiled sadly at each other.

"We'll be all right." Jazz gave Misty a nod, and then he told Michael, "Misty's going to burn a hay bale of sage in there tomorrow, so all the bad mojo should be gone by the time we open up again on Tuesday."

"That's right," Misty said, then studied the street, craning her neck to see around groups of people.

"Looking for someone?" Jazz asked with a grin. "Maybe a continuation of Saturday morning vegan waffles?"

"No!" Misty gave him a warning glare. "I'm trying to gauge the attendance."

"I'd say your threats paid off, and you managed to scare everyone into attending," Jazz teased.

Misty gave him a gentle pinch. "You."

"You both plan to work Tuesday?" Michael asked. "Do you think the cleaning crew will be done in time for you to open?"

Jazz managed to avoid a sigh. As much as he adored his handsome boyfriend, Michael was far too analytical for his own good, always thinking like a business owner. He wished Michael could relax and enjoy the conversation, instead of bringing up reality.

Although, to be fair, it had been an unusual weekend for all three of them. Naturally Misty would meditate and burn sage, Jazz would ignore it and make snide jokes, and Michael would revert to his overly practical county coroner self.

"I checked with them yesterday," Misty replied. "They were confident they could get everything cleaned up in time."

Misty's cousin, Dorothy, approached, carrying a pie, Beatrice following along behind like a teenage duckling. All the effort Misty put into making them look colorful and pretty, wasted. Dorothy wore a lightweight ankle-length gray dress and her hair was tucked into a bun on the back of her head. A wide-brimmed hat kept her face in shadow and long sleeves protected the full length of her arms. Beatrice was dressed nearly identically.

They have some kind of allergy to sunlight?

"Oh, hello," Dorothy said, coming to a sudden stop as she recognized Jazz and Michael. Beatrice bumped into her, forcing an undignified grunt from Dorothy as she staggered forward a step. She managed to hang on to the pie, but now stood directly behind Jazz's chair.

Uh-oh, she's probably afraid she'll catch some gay germs!

He twisted around to smile brightly up at her. "Hi, Cousin Dorothy! Enjoying the party? In the spirit of the approaching Independence Day, tell us what freedom you're most grateful for."

She turned up her nose and said with a sniff, "Freedom of religion, of course."

"Oh, that's a good one," Jazz said, then looked at Misty. "How about you, Misty?"

"What? Which freedom?" Misty shrugged. "I guess it would be freedom of speech."

"Another good one. I like that." Jazz turned to Michael. "How about you, sweetie? What freedom are you most grateful for?"

"Uh," Michael said, wide eyes moving from Jazz up to Dorothy's stern expression and back again. "The freedom to vote as I please in elections?"

Jazz chuckled and squeezed Michael's hand, feeling a delicious satisfaction at the sharp intake of breath the action coaxed from Dorothy. "Aren't you cute? I'm grateful for the freedom to love who I like."

Michael's eyes widened even more, but Jazz wasn't really playing things up for him. He didn't give his word choice a second thought as he saw Beatrice peering over her mother's shoulder, eyes big and mouth open. When her gaze flitted over her brother across the lawn, Jazz heard another loud gaydar *ping*. But Mama Bible-Thumper missed the girl's telling look because she was staring so hard at Jazz holding Michael's hand. Maybe gay PDAs were scarier than a broom?

Herschel approached, a broad-brimmed dark hat on his head and a croquet mallet over one shoulder like a lumberjack's axe. His linen long-sleeved shirt was damp with sweat, and leather suspenders kept his black pants up to his waist.

"Mother, have you brought a pie to share?"

Ugh, I hate it when husbands call their wife Mother. How fucking creepy is that? Ring, ring, Doctor Freud calling, your Oedipus complex is showing.

Herschel came up alongside Dorothy, and his smile stuttered when he saw Jazz and Michael. "Oh. Hello." His gaze swept them both up and down, his contempt for Jazz's pink stripes and Michael's flowers evident.

"Hi yourself, Herschel," Jazz said. "How's croquet going? Everyone's balls behaving?"

Misty shot to her feet, arms out and voice far too chipper. "What kind of pie have you got there, Dorothy? It sure looks good."

"Boysenberry," Dorothy said.

Jazz's least favorite of the berry world. Of course.

"Well, let's get it over to the dessert table, shall we? Come along."

Misty herded her relatives into a group and turned them toward the long table where the desserts were arranged. As they moved away, she turned back to shake a finger in Jazz's face.

"You said you were going to behave," Misty said in a stern whisper.

"What did I do?" Jazz asked, trying to act as innocent as possible. "I asked about his croquet game."

"You know what you did." Misty gave her finger a few more shakes before she hurried after her cousin.

"Some people are so sensitive," Jazz muttered.

"You did seem to be provoking them." Michael took another bite of his burger.

"You too? Why does everyone want to begrudge me of having a bit of innocent fun?" Jazz cast a glance to where Misty and her cousin were discussing the various desserts. "I can't gently pester someone about their draconian views on life and sexuality?"

"Well, when you put it that way—" Michael stopped midsentence, gaze caught by something behind Jazz.

"What is it?" Jazz turned but saw only the tall wooden gate leading into Misty's backyard. "What are you looking at?"

"Nothing, I guess. Thought I saw someone from the corner of my eye."

A Frisbee floated over Jazz's head and dropped with a clatter between them onto the wooden top of the picnic table. They jumped, then Jazz looked around, any smartass remark dying on his lips as he saw Oslo staring at them again, his face as red as a ripe tomato.

"Think it was on purpose?" Michael whispered.

"No, he doesn't seem to follow in his stepfather's footsteps."

"I hope he's not suffering any kind of abuse from that man."

Of course Michael would be concerned and sweet about poor Oslo being bullied by his stepfather. He might be uptight in casual situations, but he had a heart of gold and an endless well of goodness and empathy.

Jazz could stand to emulate some of that.

Wanting Oslo to be comfortable, Jazz picked up the Frisbee and got to his feet. He held up the disc and gestured to the neighboring lawn. "Go long, Oslo. I'll throw it for you."

Oslo nodded and hurried to the lawn, then turned back. Jazz threw the Frisbee with a flick of his wrist and it drifted to Oslo in an impressive curve. The teen caught it and, with a tentative smile, lifted his hand in a wave of thanks.

"That was a very good throw," Michael said when Jazz returned to his seat.

"It's all in the very limp wrist," Jazz quipped and wobbled his hand in an overly weak gesture.

"I think it takes more skill than that, but I'll let you have that," Michael said, and they both chuckled.

After finishing their food, they dropped their plates and utensils into a trash can and wandered across the front lawns of the cul-de-sac, checking out the different games at each house. At one of the houses farther down, a group of kids evacuated a bounce house when the hosting homeowner brought out coolers of ice cream treats.

Jazz turned to smile at Michael. "Dare?"

Michael smiled shyly. "You're kicking off our truth or dare game here?"

"Seems that way. Do you accept the dare?"

"Just remember there are children present."

Jazz looked around, pretending to be confused. "There are?"

"All right, smartass, what's the dare?"

"Join me in the bounce house."

Michael surveyed the vacated castle-shaped structure. "Don't these things have a weight limit?"

Jazz feigned offense and patted his belly. "Did you just call me fat?"

Michael laughed, then cleared his throat nervously. "No, that's not what I meant at all. You know I don't think that. I meant that adults—"

"Oh, stop it." Jazz smacked him lightly on the arm. "I'm teasing you. Now, answer the question. Do you accept the dare?"

"Yes," Michael said with a determined nod. "I accept."

"Good. Open those Velcro straps on your DILF sandals and let's get in there before the mob of children return."

"DILF?"

Smirking at his boyfriend's confusion, Jazz leaned close to whisper, "Dad I'd like to fuck."

Michael's face went as red as his shorts and the hibiscus flowers on his shirt.

Jazz kicked off his flip-flops as Michael removed his sandals, and they crawled into the bounce house. Thankfully it had been set up beneath a tree to keep the summer sun from turning it into a rubberized sauna. The rubber floor felt sticky from sweaty little feet, and Jazz forced that thought out of his mind. As long as he didn't fall over and face-plant on the nasty floor, he could deal with it.

Michael stumbled into him from behind, sending them both staggering across the bounce house and into one of the inflated corner supports. They fell together onto the sticky floor, both facedown.

"I'm sorry!" Michael said as he struggled to stand, his movements making the entire thing bounce. "I lost my footing."

Jazz rolled onto his back and ran a hand across his lips. "If I get hand-foot-and-mouth disease because of you, I will not be happy."

"Hey, this was your dare!" Michael wobbled to and fro, feet sinking and rising as if he were trying to straddle two surfboards.

"Fine, I'll give you that." Jazz pushed to a sitting position. "I may not have thought this through very well."

"Come on, I'll help you up." Michael steadied himself as much as possible and took hold of both of Jazz's hands. "Ready?"

"Not at all," Jazz said.

"Here we go."

Michael bounced down and up, using the momentum to pull Jazz to his feet. They held tight to each other's hands and alternated bounces, laughing like children. Jazz miscalculated a landing and sprung up and off to the side, losing his grip on Michael's hands. Michael bounced after him, each of them springing into walls and each other and probably looking like drunk kangaroos. Michael's face glowed with sweat and too much sun, his eyes so bright with joy that Jazz felt a pang in his chest.

How did I get so lucky?

Jazz had a sudden urge to kiss Michael, but before he could issue another dare, loud shrieks announced the return of children. The horde of rug rats piled in through the small opening, eyes wide and voices shrill from sugar rush as they swarmed around Jazz and Michael. Their little hands and faces were gooey with ice cream, and Jazz led Michael toward the exit, where they both slid out of the bounce house. Jazz's legs felt a bit wobbly once they reached solid ground again, and he staggered as if drunk.

Michael laughed, but it died quickly, and Jazz looked around to see what had caused such an abrupt halt to his boyfriend's uninhibited delight. Herschel was a few feet away, glowering at them over the head of his stepdaughter standing directly in front of him. His hands were clamped on Beatrice's shoulders and she stood stiff and unmoving, watching wide-eyed as the children ricocheted off one another and the walls inside the bounce house.

Jazz smiled, but Herschel did not return the gesture. He might as well have been carved out of stone the way he stared at them, and Jazz wondered what life must be like for Dorothy and her kids.

"Gotta have a bit of fun now and then, right, Herschel?" Jazz said.

He might have given the slightest nod, but Jazz couldn't be sure.

"Okay, good talk."

Jazz picked up his flip-flops as Michael grabbed his sandals. Barefoot, they strolled back toward Misty's house. The sun had started to set and the residents were lighting up tiki torches stuck into the lawns to light the sidewalk and keep the mosquitos at bay.

"Herschel's quite the lively character," Michael muttered.

"Probably less so than some of your clients."

Michael pretended to be shocked but soon couldn't help grinning. "That's terrible."

"But funny."

Jazz looked over his shoulder. Herschel wasn't watching them as he'd expected. He'd bent down to speak into Beatrice's ear. The sight of the man rankled Jazz. He had a problem with devout people who felt the spirit so strongly they had to push their views onto others. Not a fan of organized religion overall, he really had a problem with the pushers. A natural rebel, he didn't like to be told what to do and really hated to be told what he should believe.

Ahead of them, Oslo stood with his head bowed and hands clasped tight in front of him. Dorothy stood before him, shorter than her teenage son, but leaning in close and whispering furiously, her expression stern and Oslo's Frisbee clutched tightly in her hand.

"Wonder what that's about," Michael said, following Jazz's gaze.

"Most likely the fact I threw a Frisbee for him," Jazz said. "Probably afraid it'll make him a gay."

"Think we should intervene?"

Jazz arched his eyebrows. "You would do that?"

"I don't like to see anyone bullied, especially by a parental figure."

Jazz glanced at the bounce house, where Herschel still stood with Beatrice. "Parental figures or cult leaders? I really don't like that guy."

As if he'd heard, Herschel turned his head and threw a cold look their way.

Michael caught Herschel's glare too, and he frowned. "Seems like the feeling is mutual. Maybe we should keep clear of that whole family. We don't want to make things worse for the kids, or Misty."

"Good point. Let's go see if Misty's put together the margarita bar in her kitchen. She sent me to the store because she was freaking out about having enough limes earlier for her special recipe."

Jazz kept his gaze averted from the whole musical quartet family as they set a course for Misty's yard. He swung the gate open wide and motioned for Michael to enter first.

"Beauty before age," Jazz said.

"I have to keep reminding myself you're the older one."

"Me too," Jazz said with a chuckle. "Especially when you're wearing those sandals."

"I thought you said they were DILF sandals."

"Oh, I did."

They stepped into the backyard and the gate clicked shut behind them. The sound was loud enough to attract the attention of a tall figure in a red hawaiian shirt. Tiki torches had been lit throughout Misty's backyard, and the stranger stood next to a large forsythia bush in the back corner.

"Over there," Michael said, jerking his head at the man. "The guy in the red shirt. He's the one who followed the deputies to the coffeehouse. And he was in the crowd of onlookers at both murder scenes. Do you know who he is?"

"*That's* the guy you saw? No, I don't know him, but I saw him at the festival, watching Ally and Norbert fight. And he's staying in my building."

Michael's brows shot up. "Does Misty know him?"

"Not that I'm aware of. I think he's just a tourist, renting my neighbors' loft on Airbnb—which I'm not at all happy about, let me tell you."

"What's he doing here?" Michael mused. "And why's he lurking behind Misty's bush?"

Jazz grinned. "That sounded kind of raunchy."

"You've got a dirty mind."

"Which you love." Jazz watched the man inch along the fence behind the forsythia bush, then gave Michael a sweeping glance. "You're both wearing hawaiian shirts."

"So he's got good taste too?" Michael said, then pointed and exclaimed, "Hey!"

Jazz looked in time to see the tall stranger climb up and over the wooden privacy fence.

"What the hell?" Jazz cried.

"That's a little suspicious."

"More than a little." Jazz dropped his flip-flops on the ground and stepped into them. "C'mon."

"What? Where?"

"To the bat-cycle, Robin," Jazz declared.

Michael pulled his sandals on and then followed Jazz back to the front yard. "Firstly, who says you get to be Batman? I'm taller. Secondly, why are we going to your scooter?"

Jazz waggled his keys. "Because Batman always drives. And we're gonna follow that guy."

CHAPTER TWENTY-ONE

"Follow him?" Michael said as he hurried to keep up with Jazz. "I feel rude leaving Misty's party. If he's staying in your building, why don't you just ask him what he's up to the next time you see him?"

"Where's the fun in that?" Jazz said with a wink. "Misty won't even notice we're gone. Besides, he could get up to all kinds of trouble between now and returning to the building. Like strangling someone else we know and propping them up somewhere."

"When you put it that way...." Michael pointed to the driveway. "To the bat-cycle!"

They ran to the scooter and Jazz got on and started the engine. They attracted some looks along the cul-de-sac when Michael climbed on behind and wrapped his arms around Jazz's waist. Herschel was out of sight, but Jazz thought he could feel a cold stare from the man wherever he stood.

Ugh, I am too old to be bothered by such judgmental shit!

Misty waved and hurried over. "You're leaving?"

"Sorry, Misty," Michael began.

"We'll be back in a jiff. Going to check out some guy we saw lurking in your yard," Jazz explained. "I'll keep you posted."

"What? Someone in my yard?" Misty glanced toward the wooden gate. "Are you sure it wasn't one of my cousins?"

"Yeah, he wasn't acting that weird." Jazz smirked as Misty glared, then turned his head to ask over his shoulder, "Ready, sweetie?"

"I'm ready," Michael said, his hand tightening on Jazz's waist and making Jazz smile wide.

Jazz slowly rolled down the street, weaving around people and party games. Just as he reached the sawhorses at the end of the block, a small car drove past on the intersecting road, headed out of the subdivision. It was an older model, beige with a white vinyl roof stained after years of exposure to the elements.

The driver was a tall man with a baseball hat pulled down low.

"That's him!" Jazz said. "I drove past that shitty car last night when I left Misty's house. I didn't notice the driver at the time, but Ally was with him."

"Ally Roberts?"

"Sure as hell wasn't Ally McBeal," Jazz quipped. "Hang on."

Michael interlocked his fingers around Jazz's waist. The touch sparked memories for Jazz of Friday evening, when Michael had ridden him like a bronco buster, complete with ass slapping. As Jazz set off in pursuit, he shifted position on the small seat to let his rising erection have a bit more room. If it brought his ass a little closer to Michael's dynamite package, neither of them minded.

"He's driving pretty fast," Michael said, chin on Jazz's shoulder and lips right behind his ear.

"Beulah's pretty fast too. We won't lose him." As long as the suspect didn't go much over fifty-five, that is.

Jazz opened up the throttle as he turned onto the two-lane blacktop highway toward Lacetown. To their left, a grassy berm led to the edge of a drop-off and the wide expanse of Lake Michigan, now burning orange and red as the sun set behind it. A field of corn just tall enough to block most of Jazz's view of a farmhouse and Misty's subdivision was a blur of green on their right. The scooter buzzed beneath them and Jazz felt the sting of a few bugs on his face. The law didn't require a helmet anymore, but he really should get one with a face shield. Though he seldom opened Beulah up like this, and when he did, it was usually a last-minute decision.

Like pursuing a suspicious character.

This is way too much like one of Russell's goddamn Brock Hammer books.

He suspected Michael had the same thought and was loving every wind-whipped second of it. The knowledge brought with it a variety of emotions. First and foremost, it gave him a bit of a thrill that he could anticipate Michael's thoughts and emotions.

Right behind the thrill came a kind of exhaustion. It had only been a month since Russell had been arrested, he realized that, but he didn't think he'd ever be able to put Russell, or his creation, Brock Hammer, behind him for good.

Maybe the trip to the prison tomorrow will help me get there sooner.

The beige car was half a mile ahead, and Jazz saw the brake lights flash before the driver turned onto another road. Dust billowed out from behind the stalks of corn. *Great, a dirt road.*

"Hang on, sweetie, we're making a turn. Best to close your mouth too. It might get messy."

"What? Why? Oh!"

Michael's grip tightened even more, and Jazz slowed the scooter and turned the same corner.

The beige car idled on the side of the narrow dirt road about fifty yards past the intersection. The driver climbed out, cell phone in hand. Cornstalks formed a solid green backdrop to either side of them, and Jazz wondered if the man had a gun and whether the corn would deaden the sound of a couple of shots.

And I've left my gun back home.

"Oh shit," Michael said.

"Chill out, sweetie," Jazz said in a low voice. "We're on a joy ride, that's all."

Jazz intended to motor right past the car and its driver, but the suspicious tall man had other ideas. He stepped into the middle of the dirt road and extended his arm, hand held up with the palm facing out.

A quick consideration of swooping around the man went through Jazz's mind, but then he worried Michael might get a bullet in the back. At least if he stopped they'd see the shot coming.

Heart racing, he slowed to a stop and put his feet down. Michael squeezed him a little tighter.

"Your Supremes impression is on point," Jazz said.

The man frowned. "Why are you following me?" He squinted and took a step closer. "I know you. You live in the building where I'm staying."

"That's right," Jazz said. "Which, by the way, is against the rules."

"That's not my problem," the man said. "Talk to the owner about that."

"I intend to."

"Fine. But you didn't answer my question. Why are you following me?"

Michael sat up straighter behind Jazz, but did not let go of his waist. "Why have you been lurking around Lacetown?"

"I haven't been lurking," the man said. "There's a festival in town. I've been listening to music like all the other people."

"Why were you in my friend's backyard just now?" Jazz asked.

"It was a block party. I heard about it and thought I'd check it out." He crossed his arms. "Still waiting for an answer to my question. Why are you following me?"

"Because you were in my friend's backyard, and you jumped the fence when we spotted you," Jazz said. "That's suspicious enough to warrant being followed."

"I jumped the fence because... because I thought you were going to let a dog out, and I'm afraid of dogs."

"That sounds like a stretch," Jazz said, then decided to try and throw the guy off. "Why were you with Ally Roberts yesterday?"

"What?" The man appeared startled and then annoyed. "How often have you been following me?"

"She's a suspect in a murder case," Michael said. "You could be arrested as an accomplice."

The sound of car tires on gravel behind them made Jazz and Michael both turn. A sheriff's car had turned onto the dirt road, the headlights flooding the scene. The bar on top burst into life, sending red-and-blue lights dancing across the clouds of dust, the stalks of corn, and right into Jazz's eyes.

Sheriff Musgrave stepped out of the car, and Jazz sighed, hearing Michael do the same.

"Thank you for coming so quickly, Officer," the man said.

"It's Sheriff," Musgrave replied as he walked up and loomed over Jazz and Michael. "And I'm not at all surprised to find the two of you here."

"Hilton," Michael started, but Musgrave lifted a hand.

"That's Sheriff Musgrave, Mr. Fleishman." He puffed up his barrel chest. "Someone called in that they were being followed by two guys on a blue scooter with white fucking flowers on it. Not many other men would match that description. Were you following this man?"

"Yes," Michael and the stranger said in unison.

"What in the hell for?" Musgrave demanded, glaring at them on the scooter.

"Because he's been acting fishy all week!" Jazz cried.

Michael added, "He witnessed the altercation between Ally and Norbert at the festival. I've also seen him hanging around both crime scenes, and yesterday Jazz saw him driving with Ally Roberts. And just now we saw him at Misty's house."

Musgrave took a couple of steps closer, his expression darkening. "He was at Misty's house?"

Jazz nodded. "Yeah, he was lurking around in her backyard. When he saw us, he climbed over her fence and took off. That's why we followed him."

"*Misty's* house?" Musgrave repeated, and it sounded like a threat that time.

"I take it you'll handle this from here, Sheriff," the man said, looking nervous as he backed away.

"Not so fast, Hawaii 5-O," Musgrave said, taking in his bold shirt with a sneer. "I have some questions for you."

Jazz smirked. This guy had no idea what demon he'd summoned by calling the cops on them. And Musgrave's newfound interest in Misty had turned the tables, making Jazz and Michael the good guys for once. It was kinda fun to sit back and watch Musgrave treat someone else, especially this annoying Airbnb guy, the way he usually treated them.

"I didn't catch your name," Musgrave said as he approached the tall man.

"Joe Stinson."

"You from around here?"

"No, but I'm staying at the Holland Harbor Lofts."

"He's subletting one of the lofts in my building," Jazz interjected. "Through Airbnb."

"That right?" Musgrave turned to Jazz. "Frank lets his tenants do that? I would've thought that would be against the rules of the building."

"Oh, it is," Jazz said and gave Joe a tight-lipped smile.

"That's not my problem," Joe said. "I've got a contract with the apartment owner. If you have a problem with it, take that up with him. Right now, I'm able to stay there for another three days."

"Interesting you're staying in that building," Musgrave said. "You wouldn't happen to have seen anyone Friday night or early Saturday morning?"

"You're asking about the murder," Joe said.

Musgrave raised eyebrows that seemed to have been trimmed recently—by Misty maybe? "Did I say the word *murder*?"

"No, Sheriff, you didn't," Jazz said, happy to play along with Musgrave giving someone else a hard time.

Joe rolled his eyes. "Everyone knows about the body found in the salon downstairs. I can assure you, Sheriff, I had nothing to do with it."

"Oh, well, that's a relief," Musgrave said with a snide tone. "Your assurance is saving me a lot of time questioning you. Tell you what, how about you come to the station with me and we'll have a longer chat. That work for you?"

Joe's lips pressed into a tight line. "On what grounds? I'm on vacation and I called you for help, and now you wanna question me? Why? Because I went to a block party? That's not against the law."

"It is if you weren't invited. You got any reason against helping a local officer of the law, Don Ho?" Musgrave said, narrowing his gaze. "Got something to hide?"

"No," he insisted. "And you have no probable cause."

"I'd say fraternizing with a POI in a murder investigation is grounds for a thorough questioning," Michael said quickly.

Musgrave's eyes narrowed even more as he looked at Jazz. "You're sure it was Ms. Roberts you saw in the car?"

Jazz nodded. "She was in the passenger seat when I passed him leaving Misty's house yesterday."

The mention of Misty's name seemed to respark Musgrave's anger. Jazz wouldn't deny he'd hoped it would.

"You drove past me yesterday?" Joe blustered at Jazz. "How could you have seen anyone clearly in those few seconds?"

"I know hair," Jazz said with a sniff. "And Ally's got a unique hairstyle for these parts."

Musgrave crossed his arms and glowered at Joe. "Do you know Ally Roberts?"

"I gave her a ride, big deal," Joe said, running a hand nervously through his hair but holding his ground.

"You know Ms. Roberts's current whereabouts?" Musgrave asked.

"No, I don't."

"Did you meet her through Russell Withingham?" Jazz asked, hoping to throw him off. This guy could be connected to Russell, maybe *be* the hitman—which made Jazz and Michael insane for following him, now that he thought about it.

For once, Jazz was damn happy to have Musgrave there.

Joe flinched. "The writer? No, no. And I don't know Ally, so I don't know where she is now. I ran into her on the street, and she asked me for a ride."

"You often give strangers rides to places?" Musgrave asked.

Jazz had to fight a giggle. He hadn't expected it to be so fun watching Musgrave bully someone else.

As if rethinking his initial answer, Joe shifted from foot to foot. "Look, I'm just an acquaintance of hers, okay? But I don't know where she is or anything about her being a murder suspect. I'll be happy to stop by the station later and answer any questions you may have, but right now I'm late for an appointment."

Musgrave regarded Joe a long moment, then asked Jazz, "You know what apartment he's in?"

"The one next to mine."

Musgrave nodded. He pulled his cell phone from his pocket and snapped a picture of the license plate on Joe's car. Holding up his phone, he took a pic of Joe, who flinched in the bright flash, and then Musgrave held out his hand. "Driver's license."

Joe rolled his eyes but fished his license out of his wallet and handed it over. Musgrave studied it a moment, then walked back to his squad car, throwing over his shoulder, "Don't move." He withdrew a device from the front seat and scanned Joe's license. He waited for the results, then sniffed, as if disappointed. "No warrants," he said before handing the license back. He fixed Joe with a hard look. "Don't skip town."

"That's one of his favorite things to say," Jazz said. "I've heard it a few times myself."

Musgrave ignored Jazz's quip as he held Joe's gaze.

Finally, Joe gave a single nod. "I'm not going anywhere. I've got business to finish here in town."

"That sounds ominous," Michael whispered, and Jazz nodded.

"Good," Musgrave snapped. "Now you've got business with me as well."

Joe shot Jazz a glare before he turned away and got back in his car. He drove off down the road, leaving the three of them in a cloud of dust.

"Asshole," Musgrave muttered as he looked after the car. Then he turned to them with a stern expression. "What the fuck is wrong with you two? I should impound that goddamn scooter to keep from pulling you over so often."

"Technically, you didn't pull us over this time," Michael said.

"No," Musgrave said with a sneer. Then his face softened and he shuffled his feet, the movements kicking up tiny clouds of dust. "Misty doing all right? Handling the investigation and the block party okay?"

"She's doing as well as she can, considering her salon's a crime scene and she's got a house full of zealots," Jazz said. *OMG, he's really into her!*

Musgrave's face wrinkled. "You don't like Misty's new relatives?"

"It's not that I don't like them," Jazz said. "It's just that I want to spend as little time with them as possible."

Musgrave grunted quietly. He stood in place a moment longer, then pointed at them like some kind of scolding parent or teacher. "Stop following people on this goddamn thing. You're going to kill yourselves."

"That sounds like you might miss us," Michael said.

"Nah, I just don't want to have to write up the report about it and oversee the road cleanup. Go the fuck home, and for God's sake—"

"Don't leave town," Jazz and Michael said together.

"Smartasses."

Jazz slowly turned Beulah back toward the paved road and beeped the high-pitched horn twice as they passed Musgrave in his sheriff's car, hopefully annoying the man. As they motored into town, Jazz wondered about Joe and his reason for being in Lacetown. He'd claimed vacation, then said he had business. That was fishier than the smell at Christy's Marina. Could Joe be involved in Norbert's and Denton's murders? He had been at the festival, both crime scenes, he was connected to Ally Roberts somehow, and Jazz had seen him going in and out of the apartment for a few days now.

Michael gave him a squeeze, and Jazz turned his head to smile at him.

"Wanna go back to the party or go home to see Mr. Pickles?" Jazz asked.

"Home," Michael said. "It's been a long day."

"That it has."

After Michael sent a quick "sorry" text to Misty, Jazz took side streets to Michael's house, avoiding Main Street where the festival crowd gathered. He pulled up Michael's driveway and cut the engine.

Michael led the way to the back patio. He paused and looked over at the empty funeral home parking lot, glowing under the lights.

"Come on, sweetie," Jazz said with a nudge. "I'm sure your crew has everything ready for tomorrow. Look, Mr. Pickles is pawing at the door he's so happy to see you."

Michael nodded and unlocked the sliding door. Mr. Pickles meowed as he wound between their legs. Jazz used the half-bath in the hallway, smiling as he listened to Michael's quiet conversation with his meowing cat as Mr. Pickles waited for food. When he returned to the kitchen, Mr. Pickles was happily eating and Michael yawned as he opened a bottle of wine.

"Can you stay the night?" Michael asked through another yawn.

Jazz smiled. "I'd like that."

He accepted the glass of wine Michael offered and followed him into the living room. They sat close together on the sofa and gently clinked glasses.

"Joe's a suspicious sort, isn't he?" Jazz said.

"Yes, and he's been seen at *both* crime scenes." Michael yawned again. "First, in the group of gawkers, so that could mean nothing, but he did seem very interested. And he was at the salon yesterday, and he followed two of the deputies into the coffee shop and seemed to be eavesdropping on their conversation."

"And you know that because you followed these same deputies and listened to their conversation as well?" Jazz smirked.

Michael gave him a narrow-eyed glare. "I was getting you a coffee."

"Just teasing you, sweetie." Jazz yawned and patted Michael's thigh. "I've had enough playing Hardy Boys for one day. How about we see if there's a fun rom-com on one of the movie channels or something?"

"That sounds good. Anything but a mystery."

Jazz found the remote for the new fifty-three inch flat-screen Michael had purchased for his living room, bringing his household TV count up to a more suitable American standard of two. He clicked around the channels and finally settled on *Pretty in Pink*. By the time he looked over to say something witty about Jon Cryer as Duckie, Michael had fallen asleep sitting up.

"My sweet mortician," Jazz said quietly. "What a pair we are, falling asleep in front of the TV, two nights in a row." He assessed the glasses of wine on the coffee table, then dumped Michael's into his own glass. "Shame for it to go to waste."

He got up to fetch a light throw and covered Michael, then removed Michael's glasses and placed them on the coffee table before sitting on the couch beside him. Checking the time on his phone, he was surprised to find it was past ten. Where had the day, and the weekend, gone?

Wine finished and movie almost over, Jazz started to doze himself. Turning off the TV, he yawned and reached over to pull some of the throw he'd spread on Michael onto himself.

Mr. Pickles jumped up onto the couch and kneaded the throw numerous times before he curled into the space between them. As Mr. Pickles purred, Jazz gazed lovingly at Michael and then drifted off to sleep.

CHAPTER TWENTY-TWO

M ichael woke with a start, his neck kinking. "Ow!"

Disoriented, he squinted in the sunlight beaming through the living room window. *Why am I...?*

He smiled as he remembered falling asleep on the couch with Jazz.

"Jazz?" he called out and sat up. "Jazz?"

His blurry vision spied a folded note tented on the coffee table. He slid on his glasses and read it.

> *Sweetie,*
>
> *Left early and didn't want to wake you since you have such a busy day ahead of you. I fed Mr. Fluffy Butt and made you breakfast. Just need to microwave it.*
>
> *Here's a key to my place. Entry code is 1776 because my landlord is a patriot. Off to yoga with Misty. Will text you when I hit the road.*
>
> *—Jazz*

The abundant Xs and Os and hearts filling in the rest of the empty space on the note made Michael feel fluttery inside. But the key?

Anticipatory domesticity at its finest.

But rather than anticipating domestic bliss, Michael was living it.

Rolling the key between his fingers, Michael read the note one more time. He smiled and traced one of the hearts Jazz had drawn.

Even with everything going on, Jazz was thoughtful and worried about Michael's needs.

I love him so much.

A hardcover book sat on his coffee table, a history of the Lacetown Light. He reverently placed the note inside the book for safekeeping. Rubbing his hands along his thighs, he looked around the room, noting the clock on the wall said six thirty.

Just how early did Jazz wake? Had he not slept well again? Little wonder with all they'd been through and the day he had ahead of him. Michael wouldn't interrupt his yoga session, but he wanted to leave Jazz a text so his lover knew he was in Michael's thoughts.

Unfortunately he found his cell phone in the kitchen, dead. He quickly connected it to the charger and set it on the counter. He slid Jazz's apartment key onto his ring, unable to stop smiling.

Mr. Pickles didn't hound him for food, but padded behind as Michael ascended the stairs to take a shower. Once he'd dressed, he headed to the kitchen to see what his lover had left him for breakfast.

My lover. Never thought I'd get to call someone that.

Jazz had left him cheesy scrambled eggs, which tasted so much better than whenever Michael attempted them. What was Jazz's secret?

"That he's perfect," he told his cat with a smile. "I love him, ya know?"

Mr. Pickles watched Michael fork in another mouthful, swishing his tail. Michael couldn't stop smiling.

When Michael left the house, Mr. Pickles meowed his displeasure at being left behind, but it would be too busy to take him along. Michael locked the back door, then crossed the yard and parking lot to unlock the parlor, the first to arrive, per usual. After he flicked the lights on, he plugged his phone into a charger in his office. It had enough battery power now he was able to send Jazz a text.

Thank you for breakfast & taking care of Mr. P. If you need me, just call. You can do this.

He added a few hearts, then frowned at his sent message.

"You can do this?" he questioned aloud. "Sounds like a damn tennis shoe ad, not something you tell your boyfriend headed to face his imprisoned husband. Idiot."

"Michael?" Kitty's voice rang out. He hadn't heard her come in. "Anyone in there with you?"

Mildly embarrassed having been caught talking to himself—again—he cleared his throat. "No, I'm back here in my office."

He set the phone down, then left the room.

They had a very busy day ahead of them.

MRS. ROSENSTADT'S INTERMENT happened first thing that morning at 8:00 a.m. in the plot beside her late husband at Shady Willows Cemetery, on the eastern edge of Harbor County. Out of respect for his clients and their families, Michael left his phone to charge in his office as he and Steve took Mrs. Rosenstadt to her final resting place in a hearse rented from a Cadillac dealership in Grand Rapids. Musgrave had promised his own hearse would be returned as soon as possible.

After the Rosenstadt family finished at the cemetery, and Michael left her in good hands with the staff at Shady Willows, they returned to the parlor to find that, under Kitty's watchful eye, she and Ezra had the parlor cleaned and completely set up for the two funeral services later that afternoon, the first at one, the other at five. There was a quiet lull in activity just before noon when Michael finally had a moment to slip into his office and see if Jazz had messaged him back.

Closing the office door behind him, he saw the blinking message light on his phone. He hastily swiped open the screen, his heart sinking to his feet when he saw that he had seven missed calls from Jazz not an hour ago.

Seven!

And all of them two minutes apart or less.

He checked his voicemail, but found no new messages.

Michael glanced at the clock. It took a couple of hours to get to the prison in the middle of the state, which meant Jazz must have called from the prison prior to going inside. What happened? Had he been refused? Was it worse than they suspected? Or was Jazz nervous and needing reassurance?

And Michael hadn't been there for him when he needed him.

Hands shaking and gut twisting with helpless worry, Michael checked his texts.

There was one from earlier, letting Michael know he was on the road. And then the final message from Jazz: *Headed inside now* Michael couldn't infer his mood from those simple words, and he stewed with worry.

I never should've allowed Jazz to go alone!

Though Jazz had maintained this was how it needed to be, and he was a grown man, capable of making his own decisions, maybe Michael should have insisted he go with him.

And what if he had?

His insistence most likely would have driven a wedge between them. He never wanted to force himself into a situation where he wasn't wanted.

But why hadn't Jazz wanted him by his side?

Michael still hadn't wrapped his head around that one. He'd wanted to respect Jazz's wishes, but now Jazz was dealing with this all alone. And stressing out, if seven calls were any indicator.

He called Jazz, but as he suspected, it went straight to voicemail.

"Dammit."

He thought about what to text, and wrote: *Call me the instant you are finished. I'll have my phone on me at all times. Sorry I missed your calls. I love you.*

He quickly deleted that last part.

There was a knock on his door as he hit Send.

Michael set his phone to vibrate and slid it into his back pocket. "Come in," he called.

Ezra stepped inside, closing the door behind him.

"Yes?" Michael asked, his mind still on Jazz.

"The Blankenship family has arrived. They're in the Serenity Room."

"Yes, thank you." Michael sank onto the edge of his desk, his mind too scattered to think of work at the moment.

"I have the coffee made and seeing as many of the guests will attend both services, would you like...." Ezra hesitated, the halt of his chatter startling Michael out of some sort of worry-filled trance.

Michael looked up at his apprentice, waiting for him to finish asking whatever he had intended. "Yes?"

Ezra furrowed his brow. "Sir? Is everything okay?"

"Yes, yes," he lied. "Just woolgathering."

He took a step closer. "Are you sure? You seem upset. Does it have to do with Jazz?"

Michael let out a snort of surprise at his apprentice's astute observation. "As a matter of fact, yes, it does."

My poor Jazz, at a prison facing his would-be murderer alone. I should have insisted—

A gentle hand touched Michael's arm and he gazed up at Ezra's eyes shining with sympathy behind his glasses. "I thought I hadn't seen his car or scooter next door this morning. You must have spent the night apart. I had no idea."

Michael closed his eyes and took a few deep breaths, trying to focus on work and process what Ezra had said. But all his thoughts were halfway across the state, along with his heart. And there was nothing he could do to stop the swell of worry washing over him.

He felt utterly useless!

"Michael?"

The soft whisper drew Michael's eyes open again, and he looked at Ezra.

Their eyes locked for a brief moment, and Michael realized that Ezra was now touching his shoulder. As if in a dream, he saw Ezra's other hand lift to touch his cheek, his fingertips cool. Michael flinched and stared. Not taking his gaze away, Ezra pulled on Michael's neck ever so slightly.

Their lips came together in a kiss.

A heartbeat later reality slammed into Michael.

"No!" He shoved Ezra away and leaped to his feet. Panic flooded his brain. It felt as if a long, cold blade had been pushed into his chest and pulled down to a low point in his belly, leaving a thin line of emptiness behind.

Ezra looked as if Michael had struck him. "I thought...."

"No! No, I didn't want that! Why did you do that?"

Without another word, Ezra bolted from Michael's office, leaving the door wide open.

"Ezra, wait," Michael called after him but the man had already disappeared. Then he heard Ezra's voice, louder and more pleasant than usual as he said something to Ruth Blankenship's family.

With a groan, Michael buried his face in both hands. What the hell just happened? Ezra had kissed him! Why?

"Oh my God," Michael moaned.

What would Jazz think?

CHAPTER TWENTY-THREE

"Fuck," Jazz cursed and hung up his phone when he spied the Channel Three news van ahead of him as he waited to go through the prison's gate. He'd called Michael several times, but he hadn't picked up. He knew Michael had a crazy busy day ahead of him, but he sure could benefit from hearing his boyfriend's voice.

And now reporters were here? It couldn't be a coincidence, could it?

If they were here for Russell, then surely they would recognize Jazz.

Double fuck.

After a surprisingly refreshing hour of yoga with Misty, Jazz had been brimming with confidence. She'd been right, and having his chakras aligned—whatever the fuck that meant—and moving his body through poses and breathing had really centered his thoughts.

Things had felt really good with Michael too.

Jazz had been worrying about the honeymoon phase fading with Michael, but last night was the first night they had ever spent together when they didn't have sex or get each other off. In his past relationships, that usually meant an end to the honeymoon and the beginning of the end. Even Russell—with his unquenchable libido that rivaled the biggest nymphomaniacs in the history of the universe—had withdrawn slowly but surely, and Jazz had felt the warnings, though he chose to ignore them. But last night had gone a long way toward disproving the past.

With Michael, it was totally different.

Sleeping beside him, with Mr. Pickles curled up between them, had been sheer bliss.

Like happiness, warmth, and home all mingled up with sunshine and snow on Christmas.

And it felt far more intimate and significant than all the nights spent in the throes of hot, sweaty sex with anyone else.

Something *had* changed in their relationship, but for the better, pulling them even closer and making them that much stronger.

Now, all those happy feelings were dampened, replaced by the gnawing apprehension eating him up inside as he stared at the prison.

Behind those walls was Russell. The man Jazz had married, thought he would spend forever with. The man who callously cheated on him and effortlessly planned to kill him. The man Jazz was pretty much convinced had pulled murderous strings from behind bars to fuck with Jazz's new life.

Well, Jazz would get Russell to confess, because if it's one thing he excelled at, it was talking to people. And Jazz knew just what kind of traps to lay for Russell to get him to spill his guts.

"What a fucked-up life you got, Dilworth," Jazz muttered.

He thought about texting Michael that he'd arrived, but changed his mind and decided to try calling again. He desperately needed to hear Michael's voice.

His hands were shaking as he touched Michael's name on the screen and the call connected. It rang three times, and then his stomach leaped when he heard: "*You have reached Michael Fleishman of Fleishman Funeral Home in Lacetown, Michigan. If you require funeral arrangements for a loved one, or wish to—*"

Jazz sighed and hung up before the message had finished.

The news van in front of him moved into the lot and Jazz was next at the guard station. "Name and purpose?" the guard said in a bored voice. Although his muscles, scowl, and side-arm didn't speak to lethargy.

"Jasper Dilworth, here to visit Russell Withingham. I called ahead. I should be on the list," he said, noting with a bemused sniff that it sounded like he was arriving at some snobby high-society party Russell had planned.

"Photo ID," the guard said after he checked something on a computer.

Jazz handed over his license and waited, tapping his fingers on his steering wheel and looking in the lot to see where the news van parked.

"Are those reporters here for Russell Withingham too?"

The guard handed Jazz his ID back, a parking permit, and visitor's pass. "Not for me to say."

Of course.

After he received directions of where to park and what door to enter, Jazz found himself one lane over from the news van. *Just my damn luck.* What were the chances of this prison holding two notorious murderers? Zero to none, most likely.

He called Michael once more before he got out of the car.

Again, straight to voicemail.

Why did Jazz have to date a man with a job?

Ugh!

This time he listened to Michael's boring outgoing message in its entirety, feeling a little calmer by the soothing tone of his voice. But he didn't leave a message.

What would he say, anyway? He knew Michael was worried, which is why Jazz did the chickenshit move of not waking him up that morning and leaving a note instead. Hopefully a key to his loft would calm any panicked thoughts Michael might be having when he saw Jazz had already left, reassure his lover that Jazz was committed to Michael, to them. Jazz had told himself it was kinder that way, but in truth, he hadn't wanted to see Michael worry, not when he had such a hectic day ahead of him.

Now or never, Jazz thought. *You can't move on with Michael if you don't do this. And you can't prove your theory of Russell's role in these murders either if you hide in your car.*

He texted Michael that he was headed inside. Then, in case the news crew *was* there for Russell, he grabbed a hoodie from the back seat and slipped it on. Cell phones were not permitted inside the prison, so he tossed his in the glove box, donned his big Gucci sunglasses, grabbed his notepad, and stepped out of the car. Locking it, he pocketed his keys and carefully made his way to the prison entrance, avoiding the news van by skirting several cars and coming in from the other side.

Fucking just couldn't ever do things the easy way, eh, Russell?

Jazz hadn't known what to expect visiting a prison, but he was glad he'd called to verify if he was even allowed to visit Russell.

As a spouse, yes he was.

A boon for me, as Michael often said.

Michael. As much as Jazz had insisted he needed to do this by himself—and he *knew* that he did—it sure would've been nice to have Michael holding his hand on the hours' long drive.

Processing through the security points to the visitor area was pretty much what Jazz had seen on TV, minus the guard with one rubber glove and cavity searches. It seemed efficient and fast, and before Jazz knew it, he was in a cream bricked room facing a wall of phones and plexiglass, just like the movies.

Jazz followed the guard's instructions and sat down. He placed his notepad on the table before him and reviewed the notes he'd written to keep himself on track. Russell could take any conversation and spin it off in a new direction, and Jazz needed to keep his focus. There was a lot of background clatter, but a loud buzzing sound made Jazz sit up straighter.

An armed guard escorted Russell through the door and to the seat across from Jazz.

Jazz sucked in his breath.

Russell looked impeccable.

What the actual fuck?

Hastily Jazz smoothed his hair, pissed off the hoodie had built up enough static electricity to power the prison.

They picked up the phones at the same time.

Neither spoke. They stared at each other. Finally, Jazz cleared his throat and ventured, "You're looking rather... well." He begrudgingly noted Russell's highlights and hair were nicely done.

Russell gestured airily. "Yes, well, it's amazing the things you can access in prison if you have enough money in your commissary. I can even get my hair colored."

How did Russell always manage to fall in shit and get up smelling like roses? *This* was exactly why Jazz hadn't given him an easy separation. He hadn't wanted to make it easy for him. He would regret that decision—he often did—but that choice had placed Michael in his path and changed his life. Of course, Jazz eventually would've run into Michael, right? Misty hated working at the funeral parlor, and it was Jazz's clients who seemed to all be dying of late, so chance would have crossed their paths. Lacetown wasn't so big, to imagine they'd never meet.

Yes, that totally would have happened.

Jazz needed to stop giving Russell *any* credit for having a hand in the best relationship of his life.

And if Jazz wanted things to move on to the next level with Michael—and hopefully the next and the next—Russell's influence on said relationship had to stop.

Just remember, he's killed once and has probably hired out these latest murders.

"And orange always was a good color on me," Russell added, focusing Jazz's thoughts.

Damn Russell's autumnal color palette! The bastard *did* look good in orange.

"How are they treating you?" Jazz heard himself ask. For all the practicing, shouting, arguing with, and accusing Russell out loud as he drove here, Jazz suddenly found himself at a loss. The last time they'd seen each other, Russell had tried to kill him.

And Michael.

Jazz would not forgive that.

Russell sighed. "The food is terrible, as to be expected. But I'm getting a lot of exercise and it's really helping with my mental health."

"*Mental* health?" Jazz questioned. That ship sailed the second he stole Dylan's book.

"Yes, I haven't quite been myself since the loss of Dylan. Thank you so much for checking up on me. Grief can be terrible when one is taken by shock."

Jazz scrunched up his face. Was he for reals?

"I'm not here to check up on you or your so-called mental health," Jazz began, forcing his voice to be calm per the guard's warnings not to provoke the inmates. He glanced at his notepad and pushed forward. "I'm here to discuss our divorce and your role in—"

Russell waved his hand. "That's what lawyers are for, Jasper dear. Did you know, I've begun writing again," he said, smiling. "I'm thinking of revisiting Brock Hammer. Wouldn't it be a hoot if he's wrongfully accused and placed behind bars? I've always wanted to write a prison escape."

"I think you'd find some plot holes in that story. Like the fact that Brock Hammer isn't a hero, never has been."

"What are you speaking of, Jasper?" Russell asked with believable incredulity.

"You *killed* Dylan. And you tried to kill me and Michael and the sheriff. Not to mention Norbert and Dylan's uncle."

Russell shook his head. "That's what my lawyer has told me you all keep saying. But I simply don't remember anything. After Dylan's death, I couldn't tell the difference between the real world and my fictional world. Everything people tell me about that period of time sounds like snippets from my novels."

Holy shit, Michael had been right to look in the books for clues to the case. He'd told Jazz that Russell was claiming insanity, amnesia. Russell intended to use his own books as his alibi, and claim he must've acted out his stories while insane with grief.

Had *this* been the son of a bitch's backup plan if he got caught? Had he planned his crime so precisely that he'd even created a perfect defense on the ground of insanity?

The intense weight of Russell's evil mind washed through Jazz's every pore, flushing out of his system like one of Misty's yoga moves pushing away all the bad energy.

Jazz had been berating himself over his shit taste in men, but how was he in charge of other people's crazy?

If Russell had plotted with *this* much detail, it was no stretch he might be secretly paying off a murderer to clean up after him, all while acting confused and innocent.

"Withingham!" The guard by the door pointed to the clock. "Five minutes more. Your interview is being set up now."

Jazz reeled back in his chair. "Interview?"

Russell preened a bit, the fucker. "Oh, didn't I mention it? I agreed to an interview with a local news channel."

"Can you do that when you're awaiting trial?"

"Oh, Jasper, my dear innocent boy." Russell leaned closer to the glass and lowered his voice. "In here, I can do *anything*."

The word was like a whisper of icy wind down Jazz's back and he shuddered involuntarily.

Then Russell sat back with a satisfied smirk and said in a more normal tone, "How's dear Norbie? Hmm? Do you see him at all?"

Jazz blinked as he tried to keep up with the many twists and turns in their conversation. He'd come here to accuse Russell of being an accomplice to murder, but.... "Norbert? Um...."

Russell watched him, expression completely relaxed and open. Could he really not know?

"Don't tell me you've been tormenting him," Russell said with a pout. "He really was never a match for your sharp tongue."

"Russell, Norbert is dead."

The surprised expression looked genuine enough, but Jazz had to wonder. If Russell intended to plead insanity in Dylan's murder, wouldn't he be able to pull off a good innocent act after ordering murders from prison?

"Oh dear," Russell finally said. He brushed his perfectly coiffed hair into place, his hand shaking. "Norbert's dead? H-how? What happened? Did he...?"

The worry, the concern in Russell's eyes gave Jazz pause. Did he worry that Norbert might harm himself?

Struggling to come to terms with Russell's expressions and their possible meanings, Jazz cleared his throat. "He was murdered."

"Oh my." Russell's gaze drifted off to the side and his expression went slack. "Oh, at least he didn't hurt himself. I've worried about him.... But it does come as a terrible shock, I must say."

Russell worried about someone other than himself was almost more disturbing than carefully feigned amnesia.

"Does it?" Jazz narrowed his eyes. "Does it really?"

"Surely you don't think I had anything to do with it!" Russell gestured to the walls around them. "I could think of a list of things I'd rather do should I get out from this place."

"You have a lot of contacts on the outside," Jazz countered, refusing to look away lest he miss some clue Russell couldn't conceal. "You could have paid someone to do the job."

"Oh, Jasper." Russell shook his head, that condescending expression so easy, so casual Jazz didn't know how to interpret it. "Such a tragically skewed impression you have of me," he went on. "It's no wonder we just couldn't make our marriage work." Russell pushed back his chair and stood, still holding the handset. "I do hope you'll sign the divorce papers so we can both move on with our lives. It is a pity about poor, dear Norbie." Russell smiled and it did nothing to warm Jazz up. On the contrary, it sent another shiver down his back. "Goodbye, Jasper. I'll drop you a letter when I find out what day they're going to air my interview. Give my best to your new beau."

Russell replaced the handset and walked off without a backward glance. Jazz sat there for a long moment, the handset pressed to his ear as he stared at the wall on the other side of the glass. After his thoughts had settled some, he hung up the handset and gathered his notepad full of useless talking points he'd never used.

Well, shit.

"This way, Mr. Dilworth," the guard said.

In a daze, Jazz followed the guard, signed a timesheet, and eventually stepped out into the sunshine. He breathed in the fresh air, grateful to be out of the confines of the prison. Unlike Russell, Jazz was a free man, but he wasn't quite sure what to make of their conversation. Russell hadn't even asked *how* Norbert had been killed, whether he had been shot, stabbed, or strangled. Did that make him culpable? Or had prison just brought all of Russell's self-centeredness to the fore? He'd been distracted, as if in another world, like he used to get when he was deep in the throes of writing. Was it real, or all an act?

Jazz truly had no answer.

For a long time, he sat in his parked car, staring up at the prison. He still had no idea if Russell was guilty of these latest murders. He'd been hoping to figure that out with this visit, and he'd intended to accuse Russell to his face, but the fucker had twisted the conversation around so much Jazz had lost his path. And now he wasn't so sure. Maybe Michael was right, and Ally really was the killer.

As if by instinct, his attention turned to his glove box. He withdrew his phone and found a single message from Michael.

Smiling, he mutely dialed the number again.

"Jazz," Michael whispered frantically, answering on the second ring. "Hold on one second."

There was a shuffling sound, and then Michael spoke in a normal volume. "I'm here. What's wrong? Are you okay?"

Jazz chuckled at Michael's frantic questions. "I'm fine."

"You're sure? You called me seven times and didn't leave a single message."

His tone was almost scolding, and Jazz winced. "Sorry, sweetie. I wanted a pep talk, but settled on listening to your voice on your message."

"I'm so sorry."

Jazz sighed. "No need to apologize. It's all over now."

"How did it go?"

"Not sure. Maybe the drive will help it all make sense."

The phone went silent.

"Sweetie, you still there?"

"Um, yes, I'm here." Michael cleared his throat. "So you're on your way home, then?"

There was an oddly formal note in his voice. "Yeah, soon as I get the car started. Do you wanna come over to my place tonight and watch the fireworks from my loft? Think you'll be finished up in time?"

"Oh, yes, sure," he said. "I could be there shortly after nine. Will that work?"

"That would be perfect." He scrunched up his face. "You sound off. Everything okay on your end?"

"Yeah, yeah," Michael said unconvincingly. "Just a long, weird day. And I'm worried about you. I miss you."

That last part was said with a note that left Jazz wondering if Michael had more to say. When he didn't, Jazz said, "I miss you too. Think you can spend the night?"

Michael sighed. "I hope so."

Again Jazz made a face. "You sure everything is okay?"

"I should be the one asking you that," Michael countered.

"Well, I'm not sure how to answer that. But I'll be okay as soon as I see you again."

AFTER HE'D FINALLY talked with Jazz, Michael felt like the vise tightening his chest had loosened. Jazz was okay, and he was on his way home. Their rendezvous couldn't come fast enough.

But first, there was something Michael had to resolve.

He located Ezra in the kitchen, cleaning the counters. The final funeral of the day would be happening soon, and this was the first chance Michael had found Ezra alone.

"Here you are," Michael said.

Ezra stiffened, but did not turn around to look at him, intent on scrubbing the counter.

After shutting the door, Michael wiped his sweaty palms on his pants, dreading this conversation. But it needed to be done. They would be working together for another ten months as Ezra finished out his apprenticeship. The sooner he addressed the kiss, the better it would be for both of them. But getting started was always the hardest part.

"Ezra, could you look at me, please?" Michael kept his tone calm and low.

After a final polishing wipe, Ezra placed the towel down and slowly faced Michael. "Am I fired?"

"What?" Michael frowned and shook his head. "No, of course not. Why would you think—okay, I know why you would think that, but I'm not going to fire you. You're a very good apprentice."

"Oh. Okay." Ezra's shoulders relaxed, but he dropped his gaze. "I'm sorry, Michael. I shouldn't have... I wasn't thinking, and I.... You've been so distracted these last few days, and you looked so upset, and I just wanted... I thought maybe that you guys broke up... and I...." Ezra finished with a heavy sigh and his shoulders slumped as if he didn't have the strength to hold them up.

"Ezra, I'm not angry with you, but I want to be very clear. You did cross a line that needs to be addressed." Michael ducked his head to catch Ezra's eyes. "Are you listening to me?"

"Yes." Ezra lifted his gaze and fixed his wide, slightly teary, eyes on him.

"You are not fired, nor am I going to mention this in my write-up at the end of your apprenticeship. While I am fond of you, I'm in a committed, exclusive relationship. I don't want you to feel like our professional association and friendship will develop into something more intimate. But that does not reflect on you as a person or your work. Do you understand what I'm saying?"

Ezra gave him a fast nod, his eyes even wider as he stared at Michael.

"Are you okay with everything I've just told you?" Michael asked.

"I am, Michael," Ezra said, cheeks turning pink. "And I apologize once again for crossing that line. I hope we can put this mistake behind us."

Michael hoped his smile looked reassuring. "I do too. Now, it's been a long weekend, but there is one last funeral today. Let's try to make sure the family is well taken care of."

"Certainly." Ezra ducked past Michael and opened the door to hurry off down the hall.

With the difficult conversation out of the way, Michael's tension eased up a bit more and his thoughts turned back to Jazz and the evening ahead. While he wasn't looking forward to telling Jazz what had happened, he was mostly concerned how Jazz might be feeling after seeing Russell. Michael wanted the evening to be relaxing, easy on Jazz, despite the drama of late. Maybe he should bring dinner, or go by the grocery store and grab some margarita mix.

Then again, maybe all they needed was some long overdue physical reconnection.

CHAPTER TWENTY-FOUR

What a weird day, Jazz thought as he killed the engine. He'd taken a long route home, allowing himself time for contemplation, but he didn't feel like he'd solved anything. He looked forward to seeing Michael later tonight and hugging him really hard. That simple physical contact would go a long way toward anchoring Jazz's troubled mind.

The visit with Russell clung to him like a bad smell. Russell's deviousness at playing insane, claiming amnesia, left Jazz edgy and agitated. While his surprise about Norbert's murder had seemed genuine, Jazz knew it could possibly be another act. Even though he was disappointed that he hadn't been able to figure out if Russell was in on these latest murders, Jazz did feel as if he'd managed to push Russell even further into his past.

Without Michael there to talk through things, however, Jazz itched for something to relieve some of the physical tension and mental stress. But what? He wasn't really the type to work out, and he didn't know enough yoga moves to do a session on his own.

The gun range. The idea popped into his head, and he smiled.

That would help him not only kill some time until he could see Michael again, but also pretend he was shooting Russell, the murderous liar and plagiarist. With that decided, Jazz grabbed his gun case from the closet in his bedroom and then drove his Miata to Bullseye Target Range on the other side of Lacetown.

A couple of hours later, Jazz left the shooting range in a better mood than before. He'd had a good time laughing and chatting with some of the regulars at the range, all but forgetting everything that had transpired over the weekend. With a good buffer of time before Michael was supposed to be at his apartment, he drove to Gruff's Grub. The shooting had gone a long way toward clearing Russell from his mind, and a thick, juicy burger at Gruff's would get him even closer to being done with the nasty bitch.

Time with Michael later would be the final ingredient for a complete exorcism.

With his sister still off visiting their other sibling, Gruff was running the place on his own, so he didn't spend a lot of time talking with Jazz. After the adrenaline rush and conversation at the gun range, though, Jazz was content to sip his iced tea and devour his burger and fries on his own.

No sign of Misty's whackadoo cousins in the diner, either, for which he was grateful.

Misty wouldn't buy it, but Jazz thought his visit to the gun range might have been better for his state of mind than the yoga.

As he slurped up the last of his tea, he read over the text Misty had sent him while he'd been on the road. She'd gone to the salon and found it sparkling clean. Jazz's chair had been taken into evidence by the police, so he'd have to use the station next to hers, which he was fine with, since his space had some bad mojo associated with it.

He chuckled when he read the part where she said she'd burned enough sage to clear bad energy from the entire town.

Jazz sent her a text: *Let's hope the sage helps. Mind if I go in tonight and set up the new station?*

No problem, she sent back. *How did it go with the visit?*

That was way too much to try to explain in a text, so he wrote back, *Call me?*

Can't, I'm having dinner with the girls

No preacher? Lucky you

LOL, you're bad! No he and Oslo are off doing some male bonding

Jazz sniffed. What the hell could Herschel's idea of male bonding be? *Ok, have fun. TTYL*

He left some cash on the table, including a generous tip, and waved to Gruff on his way out the door. He drove back to his apartment as the sun dropped toward the waves of Lake Michigan, and he parked his car in the back corner as usual. Pocketing his phone, he gathered his nylon bag, which housed his pistol and ammo, before getting out of the Miata with a groan.

Gruff's food was good, but heavy. He locked the car and headed toward the salon.

If he was being honest with himself—which he was trying to do—he also wanted some closure about the whole Norbert thing.

He still had no idea why anyone would kill the guy and leave him in Misty's place and in his chair.

It felt like a warning.

But after seeing Russell, he doubted the message was from his ex.

So if it hadn't been a message from his ex, then from whom? Ally might have had a beef with him after he'd saved Norbie's bacon, but enough to try to implicate him in the murder? And what was she doing with the odd Airbnb guy from next door? Too many questions and not enough answers.

Just like life, baby.

His bag was heavy, and he switched it to his left hand so he could unlock the salon. The motion-sensing light above the door buzzed into life as he approached.

He held his breath as he turned the key, anxious about walking in there again. But if he was gonna freak out, best to do it without clients around, right?

Jazz slipped inside and locked the door behind him. The salon was dark and the pungent aroma of sage lingered in the air. As he reached for the light switch, the murmur of voices drew him up short.

His heart leaped in his chest.

Not again....

What the fuck should he do? Had someone broken in? Was someone leaving another body? Were the cops still here collecting evidence? No, they wouldn't leave the lights off. He should call the cops, but it was dark and whoever had broken in would surely see the cop's red-and-blue lights and make a break for it right toward him.

The break room. If he could get in there, he could make a quiet call.

Dammit, he'd never oiled those hinges! Shit! His tendency to procrastination was going to be the death of him for sure. His heart raced and helpless panic threatened his hard-fought-for serenity.

The weight of the bag in his hand seemed to speak to him.

I'm not helpless....

Moving carefully, so as to not make a sound, Jazz set it on the floor and ever so quietly opened the zipper. His .45 was tucked into a secure compartment. When Jazz released the snap holding it into place, he held his breath.

Out in the salon, the low rhythmic voice never wavered.

Jazz was surprised by how calm and collected his hands were as he deftly removed the unloaded pistol and a full magazine. After spending time at the range, the weapon felt comfortable, confident in his hand. He slipped the magazine in, but didn't clip it in place.

He crept forward, eyes adjusting to the dark, gun toward the ground and palm underneath the magazine, holding it in place.

Streetlamps outside the front window illuminated two silhouettes in the main salon, one tall and imposing, standing before another figure on its knees.

For a flash Jazz thought one of his coworkers might be giving her boyfriend a BJ, but then he heard the voice.

"...forgive my son for his impure actions, Lord. He knows not what he does. Let this serve as a reminder—"

"What the fuck!" Jazz snarled as he slapped his magazine in place and flipped on the safety. Time seemed to speed up, and his brain caught up to his pulse when he realized what he was seeing. "How the hell did you get in here, Herschel?"

"Jazz!"

Jazz shook his head as the figure on its knees spoke.

"Oslo? What the hell are you two in here for?" He was about to set his gun down and flip on the lights, but then Herschel's harsh command halted him in his tracks.

"You should not be here, sinner," Herschel declared. "We are doing the Lord's work. Unless you intend to repent of your sinning ways, like my son is doing, leave us at once!"

Jazz let out a bark of laughter. "I ain't going anywhere. Does Misty know you're here?"

"Of course she does," Herschel scoffed.

Jazz narrowed his gaze, and his hand tightened on his pistol grip. Hadn't Misty said that Oslo and Herschel were "male bonding"? Why would they need to do that here, and in the dark? He hesitated to flip his gun's safety off, even though every hair on his scalp prickled in warning.

And then his earlier thought of a blow job in progress went through his mind. He felt a sickening feeling in the pit of his stomach. Michael had been right to worry about poor Oslo.

"Yeah," Jazz said, reaching with his free hand for his phone. "Something's not adding up. I'll just give Misty a call."

Jazz's hand never reached his pocket.

MICHAEL PULLED INTO the parking lot of the Holland Harbor Lofts, anxious to see Jazz. The day had been hectic, but all the services had run smoothly. While Steve cleaned the rental hearse to return tomorrow, Michael had sent Ezra to deliver the unwanted floral arrangements to the Bluffs. Like a well-oiled machine, Kitty and Michael had put the funeral parlor back to rights, and Michael was actually done earlier than he'd expected. He couldn't see if Jazz's scooter was in the lot, but his car was there. It was almost 9:00 p.m., giving them plenty of time to relax before the fireworks started.

Independence Day was later in the week, but the Lacetown City Council had scheduled the fireworks for Monday night to capitalize on the festival crowd—and avoid competition with Bridlestop, who always set their fireworks for July Fourth, and who always had a better show.

The crowds had been too thick for him to hit the store, so they would have to make do with whatever refreshments and snacks Jazz had on hand. Michael opened the building's exterior door with the four-digit code he'd easily memorized and made his way up the stairs. He knocked on Jazz's door, but there was no response. Maybe Jazz had braved the crowded streets and taken Beulah out to the store. Delighted Jazz had given him a key to his apartment, he slid it into the lock, feeling incredibly honored.

Jazz trusted him, and that meant so much to Michael. Not just with his personal items and all the things he held dear inside his apartment, but with their decision to forego the use of condoms too. Michael knew this level of trust on Jazz's part was a major step in their relationship, especially considering the awful betrayals Russell had piled on during their marriage.

Such a deep relationship was new to both of them.

Hopefully Jazz wouldn't see the incident with Ezra as a betrayal.

Dammit, why did he do that? And why didn't I see it coming?

Michael barely had the key in the lock when the door to the neighboring apartment flew open. The tall man they'd followed from Misty's block party stepped out into the hallway.

"What are you doing here?" Joe demanded as if startled to see Michael standing at Jazz's door.

Not liking the man's tone, Michael drew up to his full height, grateful he was at least bulkier than the taller man, and hopefully a little bit intimidating.

"I could ask you the same," Michael queried. "And why are you so evasive about the reason you're in town?"

Joe let out a weary sigh. "If you must know, I follow the festival circuit."

Michael eyed his bright orange hawaiian shirt covered in parrots. "You strike me more as a Jimmy Buffett fan than a folk fan."

Joe flashed a grin, which made him look more attractive. "No denying that."

"Then why is it you follow an acoustic festival?"

He took a step closer and lowered his voice. "I'm doing some investigative work."

Michael cocked his head. "Your voice sounds really familiar. Why is that?"

"Do you like podcasts?" Joe asked.

Understanding hit Michael at that moment, and he gasped. "You're Blake Hanson from *Frigid Forensics*!"

Joe smiled. "You know it?"

"I listen every week!" Michael laughed. "It's my favorite podcast. I even tweet with you. I'm Captain Coroner."

"You're the Captain?" Joe clapped his hands, and his eyes twinkled. "I can't believe it!"

"What a small world," Michael said. "But why are you calling yourself Joe Stinson?"

"That's my real name. Blake Hanson is an alias. I do that so I can travel around and not be noticed when I register for hotels or conferences or festivals."

"Smart idea," Michael said. "Any chance you could give me a spoiler about the widow who ran away to Vietnam? Do they catch her?"

Joe grinned. "You'll have to tune in Thursday."

Michael smiled back, then cocked his head to the side. "So is the show why you're here in Lacetown? Are you here doing a podcast on Dylan Roberts's murder?"

"That might happen if I find something the police missed. But that story's been beaten to death, no pun intended. I mean, Withingham was caught red-handed and he's already behind bars," Joe said with a shrug. "I'm actually here tracking a serial killer case."

"Serial killer?" An uneasy thrill shot down Michael's spine. "Here in Lacetown?"

A loud cracking sound downstairs made them jump.

Bang, bang!

"Are those fireworks?" Joe asked.

Bang!

"Those are gunshots!" Michael exclaimed. "Call 9-1-1!"

CHAPTER TWENTY-FIVE

Herschel was a big man, but he was fast for his size.

As Jazz reached for his phone to call Misty, Herschel lunged at him. The sight of the big man barreling down on him was so frightening, Jazz couldn't think of how he should react. Before he could grab his phone or raise his gun, Herschel tackled him.

The air left Jazz's lungs as he hit the floor. His ass took the brunt of his fall, which sent a spark of pain up his spine. His teeth clicked together, just missing the tip of his tongue.

Thankfully he kept hold of his gun and a measure of his wits. He flipped off the safety with his thumb.

Herschel moved quickly, sliding off Jazz and around behind him.

He lifted Jazz's shoulders off the floor. Right as Jazz started to wonder if this had all been a huge misunderstanding and Herschel intended to help him to his feet, something looped around his throat. It pulled tight, stopping his breath and digging into his skin. It kicked off a wave of panic that rolled through him.

He's trying to strangle me like....

Herschel was the killer.

Herschel had killed Bill Denton and Norbert.

And now Jazz would be next.

But why?

Jazz lifted his hand and tried to turn his gun toward Herschel. He pulled the trigger once, twice, and a third time. Herschel jumped, but his grip didn't loosen.

On his side, with Herschel all but atop him, Jazz struggled and tried to get his fingers beneath the ligature, but it was too damn tight. He stomped his feet against the floor and clawed at Herschel's forearms as he gasped for air. Wildly he fought one-armed, refusing to release his gun, though the arm that held it was all but pinned beneath him. He got off another shot, but it went wild.

God, I hope someone hears the gunfire....

A shadowy shape paced in the salon, and Jazz thought for a moment it might be Michael, come to save him. But then the figure strode through the glow of a streetlamp.

Oslo! The boy had his hands fisted in his hair, his face scrunched up in anguish.

"Stop!" Oslo screamed. "This is bad!"

"Silence, boy! This is what cleansing sin looks like!" Herschel shouted, yanking back on Jazz and forcing a gagging sound out of him. "I brought you to this place where I've cleansed the Earth to help you see that sin has no place here."

"No, stop! It has to stop!"

"Never, son. Not until the Lord's work is done!"

Herschel's grip loosened only slightly as he rambled to Oslo.

But it was enough for Jazz. He twisted in place, rolling partially onto his back and feeling the cord around his neck rip across his skin, burning the flesh. Herschel's grip loosened even more with Jazz's movements, and Jazz sucked in a thin breath. It helped, but he needed more. He managed to get his bottom arm free, twisted his gun across his body, and pressed the barrel into Herschel's gut.

He pulled the trigger without hesitation.

The gun recoiled hard against Jazz's hand, the loud rapport swallowing Herschel's cry of anguish and surprise.

The weight on Jazz's body disappeared, and the cord loosened, draping around his shoulders.

Gasping for air, Jazz scrambled away from the man, coughing wetly, desperate for oxygen. His head spun, and he blinked back the lights swirling in his vision. His ears were ringing as he tried to get his bearings.

What the...? What just happened...?

He sucked in another trembling breath as the ringing in his ears receded. Suddenly he became aware of his surroundings, the sound of his ragged breathing, the pain in his neck.

No, this wasn't a dream.

I'm in the salon.... Herschel tried to kill me....

Shit! Herschel!

Frantic, Jazz threw the thin cord away from him. Drawing in deep lungfuls of air, he used his feet to push himself across the floor. He had to put distance between them. Images of Russell scrambling after him naked and wet spurred Jazz on with frantic urgency.

Nearby, someone moaned in pain.

Someone else was wracked with deep, gut-clenching sobs.

But where was Michael? Shouldn't Michael be here?

Jazz crawled a little farther along the floor, and no one pursued him. Breathless, he turned around when he reached the wall. He rested his back against it. His throat burned and his chest ached, but he was thinking more clearly now.

Herschel lay to Jazz's left, doubled up in pain near the back hall as blood pooled on the floor tiles. The guys at the range would be proud of Jazz for that hit.

He let out a strangled-sounding bark of inappropriate laughter.

Okay, so maybe I'm not thinking clearly.

But Herschel was down, and he wasn't coming for Jazz, so Jazz took a minute to take inventory of the situation and himself. He felt his neck, and it hurt, but there was no blood. And he could breathe and think again.

Herschel was the killer.

Norbert's murder had not been a threat sent from Russell in prison. It had been a punishment dealt out by Misty's cousin's psycho husband.

To Jazz's right, Oslo knelt sobbing with his head hanging down and his hands covering his face.

What the actual fuck did I walk in on?

The back door opened, and three figures burst through, nearly stepping on Herschel. Jazz lifted his hand to point his gun at the new intruders, but then realized he wasn't holding it. Where had he dropped his gun?

"Jazz!"

The sound of Michael's voice was like the finest breath of fresh air on a summer night, and Jazz squinted as someone switched on the lights.

Jazz managed a weak smile. "Mich—" The word was cut off in a coughing fit that came out of nowhere. His throat burned and his neck hurt, but then Michael was there, kneeling beside him and touching Jazz's face. Just the smell of him and the sound of his voice made Jazz feel safe.

"Jesus, you're hurt," Michael said. "Let me see. This may hurt."

Jazz winced as Michael carefully tipped his head back. "How bad is it, Doc?" His voice was hoarse, and the sound of it made him chuckle, in spite of everything that had happened. He wanted to tell Michael that he sounded like Brenda Vaccaro, but that felt like too many words to try and say. And he didn't think Michael would know who she was anyway.

"The skin's bruised," Michael said. "Broken in spots. But it doesn't look like any deep tissue or muscle damage." He gently moved Jazz's head around, then smiled as their eyes met.

Jazz managed a smile. "Am I your first breathing patient?"

Tears welled up in Michael's eyes, and he placed a warm palm against Jazz's cheek. "You're my first, my last, my everything."

Jazz felt tears threatening as well. He'd just been through a lot, but he didn't think Michael was referring to a patient examination any longer. His heart pounded, and a warm feeling spread through him. Before he could respond, however, a woman spoke from close by.

"Hey, guys?" she said. "This dude's been shot. He's bleeding pretty badly."

"Call 9-1-1," Michael said calmly, though he didn't leave Jazz's side. "Tell them we have a gunshot wound and someone who's been a victim of an attempted strangulation."

Over Michael's shoulder, Jazz saw Ally Roberts kneeling by Herschel. Looking back at Michael, Jazz frowned and asked, "Ally?"

"She let us in," Michael said with a wan smile.

Jazz pushed himself up a bit more, and Michael helped him. "She let you in? How?"

"I was up at your apartment, talking to Joe—"

"Joe?" None of this was making sense to Jazz. Maybe he'd lost some brain cells while being strangled.

His face serene and patient, Michael brushed some mussed hair off his face, the touch incredibly tender and soothing despite the nearby moans of pain and Oslo's quiet sobs.

For a breath, a single heartbeat, however, Jazz only had eyes for Michael.

"You remember Joe? The guy renting the apartment next door to you?" Michael prompted, pointing at a familiar man in another gaudy hawaiian shirt.

Jazz nodded. "Why are you here?"

"As it turns out," Michael explained, "Joe is in Lacetown on an investigation. He's Blake Hanson from my favorite podcast, *Frigid Forensics*."

"You like that too?" Ally asked, her face bright with an excitement that seemed wildly out of place after Jazz had almost been murdered.

Grinning, Michael looked at her over his shoulder. "It's my latest obsession."

None of this is important right now! Jazz let their voices fade away as he pushed onto his hands and knees, searching frantically around on the floor. "Forget all that. Where's my gun? Help me find it, Michael!"

"Your gun?" Michael sat back on his haunches and looked around. "I don't see it."

"Oh, shit," Joe muttered.

Flinching, Jazz turned his attention to the guy staying in his neighbor's place—Blake or Joe from some podcast apparently.

Joe had his cell phone out, but he was staring past them with wide eyes. He raised a placating hand and his voice wavered as he said, "Be cool, man."

Jazz carefully turned his head.

No longer crying but wearing an angry scowl, Oslo had gotten to his feet. He gripped Jazz's gun in both hands and had it aimed at them.

"Don't move," Oslo warned, his scowl deepening into something maniacal.

Michael rose up to his knees and lifted his hands overhead on reflex. "Oslo...," he began hesitantly. "We're not the enemy. Please, put down the gun."

Blinking a few times, Jazz shifted until he had the whole scene before him, and he slowly realized what was going on. He placed a hand on Michael's raised arm and tipped his head toward Herschel.

"I think we're good, sweetie," he said, his voice hoarse.

Michael's gaze darted quickly away from Oslo, and he sucked in a quiet "Oh!" the instant he saw what Jazz had seen.

Hands shaking, Oslo held the gun trained on Herschel, who had crawled a little closer to them. The preacher clutched a pair of scissors in one hand, the glint in his eyes dark and full of hate, his gaze locked on Jazz and Michael.

How the hell did he get ahold of a pair of shears without them noticing?

"No more killing!" Oslo shouted, face screwed up in anguish and fury.

Herschel glared as Michael crawled toward him, Michael's attention carefully divided between the two suspects. Herschel's jaw was set in stone, and he didn't fight when Michael took the scissors from him. Nearby, Ally edged up to Oslo and slowly reached out until she got her hand on the gun.

"Let me have that, okay?" Ally said.

"Is it done?" Oslo asked, his voice a whisper. "Is he going away?"

"He's going far away," Joe announced confidently. "And for a very long time."

Looking broken and weary, Oslo let Ally take the gun from his hand. Then he fell heavily into one of the salon chairs, weeping.

Michael focused his attention on Oslo, his face concerned.

"Ally." Jazz spoke firmly, more in control than he felt, and held out his hand. "Give me my gun."

She studied him, and Jazz felt his heart skip. *Shit, what if...?*

Before the thought could cross one side of his brain to the other, Ally flipped the gun around in her hand and held it out to Jazz, butt first.

"Sinners, all of you!"

Everyone flinched at Herschel's shout, his anger swallowed up by a gurgling cough.

"What?" Michael and Ally both said at once.

"The Lord has seen fit for me to suffer the fate of his son," Herschel said, voice shaking with pain as he glared at Jazz and Michael. "Sinners have no place on this Earth. I shall remake this place in his vision."

After checking that he still had ammo and a bullet ready to go, Jazz expertly aimed it at Herschel. "First of all, you nutjob gasbag, Jesus never said a word about homosexuality. Secondly, you fucking *murdered* people. Last time I checked, that breaks one of the Ten Commandments. Funny how being gay isn't even mentioned on those tablets."

"He murdered a lot of people," Joe added.

"So many," Oslo said quietly.

"Did you call 9-1-1?" Michael asked.

"Oh, shit, sorry," Joe said, then grinned as he tapped in the numbers. "I'm going to be famous. Fucking famous! Fuck you, Mrs. Ernsthausen!" Then he flipped off the ceiling.

"Who's that?" Ally asked.

"My fifth grade computer teacher," he said. "Gave me a D in computer and said I'd never be anything. Shows what she knew. I'm going to be on *Ellen* and *Good Morning America*. That'll show her wrinkled ass."

"Hey, here's that guy's Bible." Ally picked up the book.

"Don't touch that!" Herschel shouted.

A chorus of "shut up" went through the salon.

Ally studied the Bible. "Maybe he's made a list of names or something in the margins. Dylan thought that would be a good clue for a murder mystery."

A sad expression crossed her face at the mention of her cousin, and Jazz's heart went out to her. Ally shook her head slightly as if shaking off her grief, and she opened the Bible that Herschel had dropped when he rushed Jazz. She flipped through it, checking the pages, then looked disappointed. "No list. Nothing's been marked either."

"Wait a minute," Michael said and got to his feet. "Don't touch another page. Let me see it." He turned to Jazz. "Gloves?"

Jazz pointed at Misty's nearby station. "Top drawer."

He opened the drawer and plucked two latex gloves from a box, then collected the Bible. Jazz turned away to watch Herschel closely, keeping his gun trained on him.

The preacher clutched his bleeding abdomen and glared hatefully at Jazz. If Jazz's voice wasn't raw, he would have added another "fuck you."

Jazz watched Michael studying the Bible. "What do you see, sweetie?"

"The long bookmark is gone...," Michael said.

The dreamy quality of his voice made Jazz smile. His sexy mortician was onto a clue.

Michael turned to him. "What did Herschel attack you with?"

Jazz gingerly touched the wound on his neck and flinched. "I'm not sure. Some kind of thin rope."

"Find it," Michael instructed, taking charge and pointing around the salon. "Everyone look for a thin rope. But don't touch it."

"None of you can stop the cleansing that is coming."

"Didn't we tell you to shut up?" Jazz waved the gun at him. Herschel glared, coughing blood and clutching his side.

Joe was talking to the 9-1-1 operator, asking for police and paramedics, but Ally pointed toward the break room doorway.

"There! Is that it?"

Michael hurried over and picked up the cord by one end. "I think so. Yes, this is the bookmark I saw Herschel with while they performed. And like I suspected, it's not one cord, but a collection of very fine strings. They're very thin and braided together...."

He stopped and looked at Oslo, then back at Jazz, eyes widening.

"The strings."

"Strings?" Jazz said, then realized what Michael was saying, and his eyes widened as well. "The strings from Oslo's bow! We saw him collecting them at the festival! And he was braiding them together at Misty's house!"

"Exactly," Michael said, his eyes bright with discovery.

Oslo's sobbing intensified, and he managed to say, "He made me braid the strings I broke and give them to him. He told me tonight he's been using them to kill people and that I needed to learn how to do it too. He took all of my braids and made his bookmark! I didn't know he was using them for murder! I didn't know!"

"You strangled people with the braids of bowstring Oslo made, and afterward combined them to use as a bookmark in your Bible?" Michael seemed both confused and disgusted as he asked Herschel, "Why?"

Behind them, Joe was talking to 9-1-1. "I totally caught the Banjo Killer!" Then he lowered the phone and looked at Jazz and Michael. "That's a good name, right?"

"Yeah, actually it's pretty good," Jazz conceded with a nod.

"You need to get the sheriff down to the salon," Joe said into the phone. "We're holding them by gunpoint... um.... Well? One of them is shot... yeah, you should probably send an ambulance."

"Give me the phone," Michael said, snatching it out of his hands. "This is Michael Fleishman, the Harbor County coroner. It seems there's been a break-in at Misty's Makeover Palace. Yes, a firearm was discharged." Michael answered the questions methodically as Herschel groaned and seethed.

"Okay, thank you. I'll put you on speaker and set the phone down." He touched a button on the phone's display and set it on a cabinet. "They'll be here momentarily, but we need to keep the line open." He gave the room a studying sweep as he set the braided strings and Bible on a nearby station.

"You'll pay for this, you homosexuals," Herschel said through clenched teeth.

"You shitting me?" Jazz questioned, his temper rising. "*That's* what this was? A hate crime? You just killed two random gay men, then left them at our places? Why? To frame us?"

Herschel's eyes narrowed, watery and mean. "Nothing in the Lord's world is random, sinner."

Though the man bled, none of their group had stepped forward to help. Jazz had no intention to do so—*bleed out for all I care, asshole*—but it should have been no surprise that Michael collected some towels stacked near the sink and approached Herschel.

"Save your strength and confession for the authorities," Michael began, holding out the towels. "Here, let's get some pressure on—"

"Leave me be!" Herschel cried with surprising gusto. "Do not touch me!"

Michael stopped, his lips frozen in a tight line, as if struggling with professionalism, human kindness, and revulsion for the man before him. He impressed the hell out of Jazz when he placed the towels within reach and said, "You'll need to apply pressure until the paramedics get here."

Herschel eyed him shrewdly, coughed some blood, then snatched the towels up and pressed them to his side. Blood immediately blossomed on the fabric. "You can pretend to be kind and compassionate, but I know what you really are."

"I'm not pretending," Michael said, standing tall and giving the man a pitying look. He walked toward Jazz and knelt at his side. Their eyes met and Jazz let out a breath of air, relieved once more. "You still okay?" Michael asked, effectively ignoring Herschel.

"Yeah, I'm good, sweetie." Jazz reached up and brushed his hand across Michael's brow. "You're such a good man."

Herschel went into another spasm of coughing. "My son will *not* become one of you. I won't allow him to be tainted by your agenda!"

"Oh snap, it's the gay agenda," Jazz said, rolling his eyes.

Behind Michael, Ally laughed.

"Jazz, I'm going to unlock the door for the authorities." Michael pointed at Ally. "Keep an eye on Herschel." He walked to the front of the salon, and Jazz watched him go with a smile on his face. Michael was taking charge now, and Jazz felt so grateful for the man he loved.

"I can see blue-and-red lights flashing," Michael said. "They're close."

Ally approached Michael. "What were you saying about strings?"

Stepping back to the counter where he laid it, Michael picked up the long, twisted braid of violin strings again. "This is what he used to attack Jazz." Face creased with concern, Michael glanced at Jazz, then quickly cleared his throat. Maintaining his composure, he indicated the dark fibers woven through it. "I don't think Herschel had planned on killing anyone tonight, so he didn't have a freshly braided cord with him. All he had when Jazz walked in on them was his bookmark. Thankfully it is thicker and didn't break the skin like it did on his... p-previous victims." His voice wavered before he continued. "These dark spots are most likely bloodstains, souvenirs, if you will. And the DNA evidence that will link him to every other murder Joe's been tracking."

"What other murders?" Jazz asked. His butt started to get numb, and he tried pushing to his feet. Michael rushed over to assist, gently guiding Jazz to an empty salon chair.

"Easy, hon," Michael insisted. "Don't hurt yourself."

"I'm okay." Well, he would be. Jazz kept the gun fixed on Herschel as he sat down.

"The Banjo Killer, I can't believe it," Joe said, and patted his pockets. He looked around, then walked toward Michael. "Can I have my phone back?"

"We still have the line open for the emergency dispatcher," Michael said and gestured to where he'd set it down. "Once the authorities arrive you can end the call and use your phone."

"This is going to be my most downloaded podcast," Joe said as he strode across the room and picked up his phone. "I don't think I'm going to sleep for a week, I'm so excited."

"I can't wait to listen to it," Michael said.

"Me too!" Ally said.

Joe turned, his face lighting up. "You have to be special guests!"

Michael and Ally exchanged excited looks before turning back to Joe and saying together, "Okay!"

"Seriously?" Jazz said, frowning at his boyfriend and Ally. "Could we all stop fangirling for a minute?" They appeared appropriately chagrined, so Jazz addressed Joe. "You've been following Herschel? Why? Has he killed before?"

"Oh yeah," Joe said with a frantic nod. "I've been following the clues for over a year. Once I started putting all of this together, I really got into it. He's been pretty slick, but I picked up on the similarities. All strangled, their hands cleaned with bleach, and propped up in seemingly random places. He's left a lot of bodies behind him. A lot."

"Well, in that case, I really don't feel bad for shooting an old man," Jazz said and sighed happily. He felt remarkably calm despite everything he had been through, and he wondered where this oddly relaxed feeling came from.

Then it hit him.

It was over.

Jazz smiled at Michael. "You know what this means, sweetie? None of this had anything to do with Russell. It's just a crazy old religious nutjob. Isn't that *great*?"

Michael returned his smile. "It is good." Then he frowned. "And more than a little disturbing. Maybe you should put your gun away before Musgrave gets here."

"I'll wait," Jazz said, then glared at Herschel. "I don't trust him."

Two sheriff's deputy cruisers pulled up in front of the salon, tires squealing as they slammed on their brakes in the middle of the street. Michael gave Jazz's shoulder a squeeze, then hurried to meet the deputies at the door.

Musgrave burst into the salon, gun drawn, Tanner right behind him.

"Sheriff's Department! Nobody move!"

Michael leaped out of their way and threw his hands up. "Don't shoot! It's all over."

Musgrave's beady eyes took in the room in one sweep, landing on Jazz and narrowing when he noticed the gun. "Dilworth, lower your firearm!

Finger off the trigger and put the gun down. On your knees. Hands behind your head. Keep 'em where I can see 'em."

Jazz flipped the gun to his thumb, fingers splayed and spread his arms wide. He slid out of the chair and slowly knelt on the ground, lowering the hand holding the gun. He carefully set the weapon on the floor before placing his hands behind his head and interlocking his fingers.

Michael stepped up beside Musgrave, his expression furious. "Jazz is the victim! You're treating him like a common criminal!"

"No worries, sweetie," Jazz quipped, feeling remarkably relaxed, given the situation. "Seems like standard procedure when you're the one who discharged a weapon."

"Back off, Fleishman," Musgrave growled. "Now somebody tell me what the devil is going on in here."

CHAPTER TWENTY-SIX

"I came in the back door to get ready for the day tomorrow," Jazz explained. "I found Oslo and Herschel in here without permission. Herschel attacked me and I shot him."

"He's the Banjo Killer!" Joe exclaimed.

"None of us play the banjo, you sinning fool!" Herschel shouted, voice quivering with pain.

Musgrave squinted at Herschel lying on the floor. "That's Misty's cousin's husband."

"Yes, it is," Jazz said, exchanging a glance with Michael. "He tried to strangle me, and I shot him. Can I lower my arms now?"

"Yeah, fine," Musgrave grumbled, then addressed his deputy. "Tanner, see if that man needs your help before the ambulance arrives. But for God's sake, holster your weapon and secure it before you approach him." He stepped closer to Michael, and Jazz heard the sheriff say in a quiet voice, "Don't need another gun pulled from law enforcement during an arrest."

As Jazz returned to the styling chair, he had to agree with the sheriff on that one. Back when Musgrave had been about to handcuff Russell, the fucker had snatched the sheriff's gun right out of his holster and nearly killed them all. Nice to see the good sheriff was able to learn from his mistakes.

"Sheriff, do you have evidence bags?" Michael asked. Still wearing gloves, he picked up the weird braid of violin bow strings.

Jazz felt squeamish looking at it.

Musgrave held out his hand toward Tanner, and wordlessly the deputy produced several bags from his pocket. Michael placed Herschel's Bible and the suspect braid stained with blood inside the bag.

"What the hell is all that?" Musgrave demanded.

"Possible evidence and the weapon *he* choked Jazz with," Michael replied, shooting a cool look at Herschel. The fucker glared right back at him.

The paramedics arrived then and wheeled a stretcher through the salon.

"Over here," Tanner said. He stood guard a short distance away, looking green around the gills at the sight of Herschel's blood.

As they got to work, Michael spoke up. "Jazz has been hurt too."

"I'm fine." Jazz waved it off, but a third paramedic from a second ambulance came up to him.

"You don't appear so fine," the young woman said, smiling kindly. "Lemme just check you out, 'kay?"

Jazz intended to protest—far more interested in what the hell was going on—but a stern look from Michael had him conceding to care. "If you insist, sweetie," he said, and Michael's sternness changed to relief. He placed the evidence bag on the station beside Jazz, stripped off the gloves, and crouched at Jazz's side to take his hand.

"I do insist, but the name is Cortney, not sweetie," the paramedic teased.

Jazz chuckled— *damn, my neck does hurt*—and he gripped Michael's hand tight. Their eyes met, a million things unsaid, and a thousand more spoken with that glance.

Jazz was seconds away from a mushy love confession he didn't want to be having here and now, when Musgrave interrupted the moment.

"Why the hell did you call him the Banjo Killer?" Musgrave surveyed the scene with his usual glower, scowling at Ally before addressing Joe. "And who the hell are you in all this?"

"I coined that name," Joe said proudly, too excited to cower under Musgrave's irritation. "The Banjo Killer. I produce a podcast called *Frigid Forensics*, where I dig into cold cases. I've been tracking clues about a possible serial killer for almost a year now."

Musgrave actually paled. "Serial killer?"

The paramedics tending to Herschel shared furtive looks, and even Cortney paled before she squeezed the blood pressure cuff on Jazz's arm.

Joe was undaunted, the gleam in his eye so like Michael's when he stumbled upon a clue, it made Jazz smile.

"There have been a number of unsolved murders coinciding with musical festivals all over the country," Joe explained. "All the victims were strangled and propped up in weird places. And each victim was involved in something biblically immoral, one might say. Gay, adulterous, gamblers. You get the idea."

Musgrave glared at Herschel. "I do."

"Since it was usually an acoustic musical festival, I named my killer the Banjo Killer," Joe went on proudly.

"There is no banjo!" Herschel screamed, startling Tanner so much he scooted several feet away from him. "They were my son's violin bow strings, you idiot!"

"I'm not your son!" Oslo's voice was loud and filled with so much pain, Jazz's eyes teared up. Misty's cousins must have lived through hell under Herschel's command.

"They deserved it, all of them!" Herschel raved as the paramedics struggled to get him onto the gurney. "I was cleansing the Earth of sinners! I washed their hands of their sins so they could find the Lord's grace!"

"Is *that* why you bleached their hands?" Joe asked. "I thought it was to remove possible DNA evidence."

"Maybe both?" Michael offered.

Musgrave approached Herschel where he thrashed on the stretcher.

"I am legally obligated to ensure you know your rights." As the sheriff Mirandized him, Herschel muttered something that sounded like the Lord's Prayer.

"Did you know Bill Denton?" Michael asked afterward, his intense gaze locked on Herschel. "And Norbert? And why situate them at our places of employment?"

Herschel raised his head, eyes wild and burning and teeth grinding together against the pain. "I followed my boy into the woods, and thought he was admiring the Lord's celestial magnificence. But instead I caught him watching dirty acts, being done in the dark, out of shame. Filthy sinners in a field of immorality."

Oslo was openly sobbing now. "I told you I didn't see anything. I told you! You didn't have to hurt anyone!"

"See anything?" Jazz questioned, catching Michael's eye at the same time Cortney dabbed something on Jazz's neck. He hissed. "Ow!"

"Sorry, just gotta get this cleaned and sterilized. Skin's not cut, but it's rubbed a little raw in places."

Herschel was a less cooperative patient. He struggled against the paramedics, still ranting. "Those sodomites exposed my innocent son to their sins of *porneia*."

"What the hell does that mean?" Musgrave demanded. Then he caught Tanner's eye and pointed at Oslo sobbing. "Calm him down."

Tanner seemed grateful to be away from the blood and moved to Oslo's side, speaking softly.

"Porneia, also translated as prostitution, fornication," Michael supplied as he studied Herschel. Then his sad gaze drifted to Oslo. "He probably saw Bill and Norbert hooking up."

"At the HPP," Musgrave said. "Where Farthington met Denton."

"Via Grind Him," Jazz said, his chuckle breaking off in a raspy cough.

"I didn't see anything, I swear!" Oslo cried. "I never saw what they were doing!"

"Shh, shh," Tanner cooed. He wet a towel at the nearby sink, wrung it out, and approached Oslo. "Here's a cool towel—"

"No! Get that bleach away from me!" Oslo cried, and darted to the other side of the salon. "It burns. I didn't do anything wrong. I don't need to be cleansed."

"Jesus hopped up Christ, Tanner," Musgrave exclaimed. "Get him under control."

Tanner tossed the wet towel aside and raised his hands as he slowly approached Oslo. "It's okay. You're safe. I'm not going to do anything to you, okay?" He got close enough to place a gentle hand on Oslo's shoulder. "You didn't do anything wrong. It's all gonna be okay, buddy."

"He sinned, you foolish boy," Herschel snarled at Tanner. "He cannot lie to me. He needs to wipe his hands clean of sin!"

"I don't know what that means," Tanner said, scowling at Herschel. "But I know this boy is a good sight scared."

"He made me wipe my hands clean," Oslo said in a quiet voice.

"With bleach?" Tanner whispered.

Oslo nodded, big eyes hopeful and trusting, staring up at Tanner.

"Yes!" Herschel said. "Wipe your filthy hands clean of sin, boy. I know all your sinful thoughts. I know all about...." His words broke off in a coughing hack of blood, but Jazz got the drift.

Creepy ol' Herschel had probably caught Oslo masturbating at some point and made him use those bleach-laced wipes to clean his hands. Jazz remembered Oslo using them at Misty's house. Was that a thing he made the boy do often? Could it be how he cleaned his victim's hands too? And the night Bill Denton was murdered, Herschel must have caught Oslo watching Norbert and Bill in *flagrante delicto*, then what? Killed the two of them? No, Norbert had been at the festival the next day. So Herschel had most likely followed Bill and killed him, then caught Norbert alone after he'd been questioned by Musgrave Friday night. All because Herschel was trying to teach his gay stepson what happens to "sinners."

What the fuck?

Michael had been right to worry about poor Oslo in a house with that hatemonger.

"Sir, you need to calm down," one of the paramedics told Herschel.

"Yeah, take a pill," Tanner scolded, obviously taking his job as Oslo's protector seriously as he glared at Herschel.

Musgrave crossed his arms as he loomed above Herschel. "So you saw Denton and Farthington at the HPP together? Then what? Decided to seek some sort of vengeance?"

"Yes, I did," Herschel said, a spark of evil in his eyes. "I sent Oslo home, to deal with later. Then when the sinners finished, I followed one of them and sent him on to be judged."

"Oh, he waited for them to finish at least," Jazz muttered. "Is that polite or creepy?"

"Both," Cortney and Michael said at the same time.

Herschel seemed to relish telling everyone about his "righteous acts," but it just made Jazz feel sick.

"And then?" Musgrave prompted.

"Decided to have some fun and see what kind of blame I could spread. The other abomination I followed after he finished talking to you, Sheriff, and I dragged him in here and sent him on to his judgment." Herschel licked his lips and his smile widened, growing even colder as he looked right at Jazz. "Oh, how he struggled. But I finished my work and left him here as a gift for you, *sodomite*."

"The name's Jazz, and sodomy is only a fun pastime of mine. And I usually only accept gifts from clients, but thanks," Jazz snarked.

Michael buried a snicker, and Musgrave seemed on the verge of a chuckle. Or maybe it was gas. Hard to tell with Musgrave.

Herschel began to bluster, as if working himself up for another hate-filled sermon.

"I think it's time for some morphine," one of the paramedics said, and plunged a needle into Herschel's arm. Herschel's expression softened almost immediately and his head went back.

Nighty night, fuckface.

"Sounded like a confession to two murders to me," Musgrave announced. He gestured to the paramedics. "Get him out of here."

"Yes, sir," the one paramedic said.

"Tanner," Musgrave snapped, and the deputy jumped. "Go with the suspect and make sure he's secured the entire time. Ride in the back with them and see to it the suspect is cuffed to the gurney. Do not leave his side."

"Even during the surgery?" Tanner went paler still.

"No, not in surgery," Musgrave said with a heavy sigh. "But stay close until I get there and we can decide how to manage him."

"Okay, yeah, sure."

Jazz watched as Tanner spoke quietly to Oslo, waited for the boy to nod, and then, with an expression of distaste, followed the stretcher out the door. Under the influence of the morphine, Herschel was now quiet, staring up at the ceiling with glassy eyes.

"You should see a doctor," Cortney told Jazz. "To see if you have internal damage."

"That sounds fun," Jazz said and rolled his eyes in Michael's direction.

"I'll drive him to the hospital myself," Musgrave said to the woman.

"When I'm done being questioned, I'm sure," Jazz muttered, and then he started coughing again. Michael was right there, caressing his back.

"Lemme get you some water," Michael said. "I'm assuming there is some in the break room?"

Jazz nodded, loving how Michael cared for him. Misty had been right. He had a wonderful, handsome boyfriend, and he didn't have to do things alone anymore.

Michael returned a moment later, and Jazz accepted the bottle of water. The coolness of it soothed his sore throat. Before he could thank Michael, the sound of a drawer opening behind Jazz startled him.

He turned to see Ally trying to act innocent as she kept her hands behind her back.

Jazz's senses went on alert, and he pushed to his feet. He stepped past Cortney and Michael, saying in a demanding tone of voice, "What are you holding?"

Musgrave moved in front of Jazz and aimed his weapon at Ally.

"Show me your hands. Slowly."

Ally very slowly brought her hands out from behind her back. A long length of blonde hair hung over the palm of one hand.

"It's nothing," Ally said.

"Is that...?" Jazz noticed her frightened and embarrassed expression. "Oh." Even more became clear, and he nodded as he smiled. "Ohhhh."

"What is that?" Musgrave asked and sneered at Jazz. "Is that *hair*?"

"Yes, it is."

"What the hell are you doing with that hair?" Musgrave demanded. "And why the fuck are you even here? We've been looking all over for you for questioning."

Jazz frowned at Michael. "That's a good question, actually. Why is she here?"

"She was, um... she let us into the salon," Michael said, gaze jumping from Jazz to Musgrave to Ally and back again.

"Yeah," Joe said, stepping forward. "If she hadn't let us in, he might've been killed."

When Joe pointed at him, Jazz swallowed hard. Really, why were people trying to kill him all the time?

"Be that as it may," Musgrave said. He kept his gaze on Ally, but he'd holstered his weapon at least—though he kept a hand on the butt, ready to draw if needed. "How did you get inside? You don't have a key." He half turned to Jazz. "Does she?"

"I wouldn't think so, but—" Jazz started, but Ally cut him off.

"I was working on picking the lock when I heard the gunshots from inside. I was scared and about to run away, but then Michael and Joe came running up and told me to open the door, so I did it."

Before Musgrave could ask another question, Misty rushed in through the front door. She wore a bright floral print sundress with a light sweater over her shoulders. Her hair was down around her shoulders, and her skin glowed a lovely bronze from the sun she'd gotten at the cookout the day before.

Jazz saw Musgrave's gaze drop to the swell of Misty's breasts, bounce up to her face and hair, then back down to her chest. *No bra... oh boy.*

"What the hell is going on here?" Misty demanded.

"That's what I'm trying to figure out," Musgrave replied.

"Was that Herschel being loaded into the ambulance outside?" Misty asked, then looked at each of them, her gaze finally stopping on Jazz. "Oh my God! Your throat! Who did that?"

"Could you just stand down for a damn hot minute," Musgrave said. "I'm trying to figure all of this out."

Misty snapped her mouth shut, but the expression on her face pretty much told Jazz she was going to give the sheriff an earful once they were alone.

Ugh, he really didn't want to consider what else might happen when they were alone.

"Oslo?" Misty noticed the boy for the first time. "Are you okay? What happened?"

"He hurt them," Oslo muttered, his face crumpling at the sight of Misty's concern. "But it's over now."

"Over?" Misty rushed to Oslo and threw an arm around the boy's shoulders as he sat and stared at the floor. "Hilton, what happened?"

To Jazz's shock, Musgrave didn't give Misty any more attitude. Rather, he waved airily in Jazz's direction. "You heard the lady, Dilworth. Catch her up."

As Jazz repeated how he'd discovered Herschel and Oslo in the salon, and the events that followed, Misty's eyes grew wider and wider with each revelation. When he'd finished, Misty inspected the braided length inside the evidence bag Musgrave held.

"Those are strings from a bow?" she asked.

"Correct," Michael said. "A violin bow. Namely Oslo's."

"Then why the fuck are you calling him the Banjo Killer?" Musgrave snapped at Joe.

"I figured he used banjo strings to strangle his victims," Joe said. "After all, he's been part of a folk festival."

Musgrave waved a hand. "Fine. Whatever." He looked back at Jazz. "Why do so many people try to kill you, Dilworth?"

"I was just asking myself the same thing. Must be they're jealous of my charming personality and succulent ass," Jazz said. Michael made a choking sound, and Jazz shot him a wink.

"Yeah, must be," Musgrave said dryly.

"Hilton, I'd like to take Oslo home," Misty said.

"I'd really like to allow that, but I need to get a statement from him," Musgrave said, only able to meet Misty's gaze for a second or two at a time before looking away again.

Jazz sighed. "Let her take him back to her house, and you can talk to him there once you finish at the hospital."

"You're not running this show, Dilworth," Musgrave said.

"No, but my throat hurts, and I'd like to finish telling you what happened before my voice gives out."

He didn't think he was anywhere close to losing his voice, but Jazz's heart went out to poor Oslo. The kid had been through a lot ever since Herschel had married his mother.

"Fine." Musgrave nodded to Misty. "But dammit, make sure he stays put. I don't want him running off."

Misty mouthed "thank you" to Jazz before leading Oslo out the door as the Tompkins twins walked in.

"Keep an eye on those two." Musgrave directed his deputies to watch Joe and Ally, who still held the tied clump of hair, and then he turned to Jazz. "Let's wrap this up. You were being strangled. Then what?"

"I managed to roll onto my stomach, and I pushed my gun into his gut and shot him. After that, I got the fuck away from him, and then Michael was there with these two."

"All right, Fleishman, you're up," Musgrave said. "Why were you here?"

"I stopped by Jazz's apartment and had just let myself in when Joe came out of the apartment next door," Michael said. "We talked a bit, and I realized he's the host of my favorite podcast—"

"What the fuck is a podcast?" Musgrave asked with a snarl.

Grace Tompkins stepped up. "It's like a radio show you download to your phone, Sheriff."

Musgrave released a long, drawn-out sigh and shook his head. "Technology exhausts me. Fine, your favorite podcasting guy was there. Then what?"

"We heard gunshots, and I thought they came from inside the salon, so we ran to the back door." Michael gestured to Ally. "We found Ally standing by the door, with a lock-picking kit."

"So you caught her breaking and entering," Musgrave said with a satisfied smirk. "That should keep her off the streets for a while."

Jazz pretty much heard, "and out of my daughter's life," without Musgrave saying a word.

Musgrave's beady eyes shot to Ally next. "Why were you breaking into Misty's salon?"

"I only wanted to get this," Ally said quietly and held up the blonde ponytail.

"Hair?" Musgrave practically shouted. "You were breaking in here for some goddamn hair? Why the fuck would you do that?"

"Sheriff," Jazz said, and when Musgrave turned his withering gaze on him, Jazz lowered his voice. "That is Rae's hair that I cut off."

Musgrave's face went slack. He stared blankly at Jazz a moment, and then his face steadily turned red as his anger level increased. Very slowly, he turned back to Ally. "That's my daughter's hair?"

Ally squirmed, her gaze darting from Musgrave to Jazz to the deputies and back again. "Y-yes. I wanted to make hair art out of it. I didn't want her to cut it. I tried to talk her out of it. I thought I'd convinced her, but after she got home for the summer, she must have changed her mind."

"What the fuck is hair art?" Joe wanted to know.

"It's a Victorian custom. You weave scenes and make bows out of hair of loved ones. Mostly after they die, but...." Ally slid the hair through her fingers and looked lovingly down at it. "I really loved her hair."

Jazz watched Musgrave's anger soften and then vanish, the transition making him appear older and very tired.

"Yeah, I did too," the sheriff said. He might have heard how emotional that sounded and followed it up with a throat-clearing cough. "But it doesn't mean you can just break into a place of business to steal someone's hair to make some weird art thingy."

"Yeah, I know," Ally said as she stroked the hair again.

"Fine. All right, so the hairdresser shot the preacher, and then we've got the podcaster, the hair thief, and the mortician coming in through the back door. What happened next?"

Jazz listened as Michael explained everything in his succinct way. The soothing sound of Michael's voice helped Jazz feel better. Musgrave took it all in without interrupting, which Jazz found particularly interesting. Musgrave usually loved to interrupt.

"And how do you two know each other?" Musgrave pointed at Ally and Joe.

"I contacted him to investigate Dylan's murder. I was hoping he could help expose Norbert Farthington as an accomplice, find clues with the help of all the listeners on his podcast."

"We agreed to meet and discuss a possible interview this weekend because we were both following the music circuit," Joe added. "Me because of the Banjo Killer—I mean Violin Killer? Jeesh, that really doesn't sound as cool, does it? Maybe the Music Man?" He looked at Jazz.

"Already taken."

Joe nodded. "Yeah, I'll have to think about it. Bowstring Killer, maybe?"

"It has a ring," Jazz conceded.

Before Musgrave could explode, Joe quickly went on, "Anyway, Ally was here to perform, and I was following the serial killer. I never thought Herschel would go after a suspect from a different story I was working on. From what I've been able to piece together, Herschel has probably murdered at least eighteen people. Quite possibly more."

Jazz's stomach knotted. What the actual fuck was wrong with that guy?

"All right, I've heard enough for now," Musgrave said. He pointed at Ally and Joe. "Do not move. I'm not finished with you. Dilworth, let's get you to the hospital. Fleishman, I'm assuming you'll want to ride along."

"You assume correctly, Hilton," Michael said, and gave him a smile as he reached out to squeeze Jazz's hand.

"Go out and wait by my car," Musgrave said. "I'll be there in a minute."

Jazz let Michael lead him by the hand out the front door of the salon. Behind them, Jazz heard Musgrave giving the Tompkins twins instructions on securing the crime scene and calling for more officers to take Ally and Joe to the station to give their statements. Joe was more than willing to provide the department with all of the evidence he'd collected, so long as he got credit for breaking the story and first dibs on giving the killer his nickname.

Jazz thought about wishing the guy good luck, because Musgrave had taken full credit for arresting and catching Russell, even though Michael and Jazz had really done it, but Jazz was done—with Russell, cops, Herschel, all of it. He just wanted a big hug from his boyfriend.

Outside the summer air was still warm and sultry. People lingered nearby, lured away from the upcoming fireworks to watch—yet again—as cops swarmed the salon. Red-and-blue lights flashed across curious faces, and thankfully two more deputies arrived and kept the people back.

When they reached the sheriff's cruiser, Jazz rested his butt against the side and turned to face Michael. "You saved me."

"You saved yourself," Michael replied. "I showed up a little late."

"I was pretty scared for a minute there," Jazz said and was surprised to find himself fighting back tears. "I didn't think I'd get to see you again."

"Oh, Jazz." Michael stepped closer, wedging himself between Jazz's legs and resting a hand against Jazz's cheek.

Jazz quickly wrapped his arms around Michael's waist. He rested his cheek on that strong, safe chest.

"I can't believe I could have lost you," Michael murmured, hands shaking.

"You and me both. But mostly I was scared I wouldn't get to tell you things I needed to," he whispered. "Important things."

Holding him close, Michael dipped his head and gave Jazz a soft, quick kiss on his brow. "Like what? Tell me now."

Jazz raised his head, caressing Michael's back. He took a breath and slowly released it. Russell was out of his life. All of this craziness had nothing to do with him. Jazz was finally free of everything that had been haunting him since Dylan's death. He felt an incredible weight lift off his shoulders, and his breaths came easier. With Michael's arms around him, despite everything they'd been through, or maybe because of it, Jazz knew then that Michael was the best thing to ever happen to him.

He met Michael's curious gaze.

He took another breath and let it out.

"I love you, Michael."

Michael's eyes widened in time with his smile. He leaned in for a long, deep kiss as a sudden boom from overhead startled them both. Fireworks lit up the entire sky, and from Lacetown Park they could hear the crowd ooo-ing and ahhh-ing over the display.

"I love you too, Jazz," Michael said, raising his voice to be heard over the boom of another firework. He stroked Jazz's cheek softly. "So very, very much."

They kissed again beneath the beautiful fireworks, and Jazz had never felt so happy.

CHAPTER TWENTY-SEVEN

The passion, terror, and love that had pounded through Michael's body when he saw Jazz hurt were the most intense emotions he'd ever felt in his entire life.

At least until Jazz told him he loved him.

And that was something worth fighting for.

Two days had passed since Jazz was released from the hospital. Michael could still feel the delicious tingle of that kiss after their shared passionate declarations of love under the fireworks, all in the aftermath of another almost murder. Michael had insisted Jazz come home with him, though it might have been presumptuous to call his house Jazz's "home." Jazz had willingly agreed, and Michael had been caring for him since.

Misty closed the salon until at least Thursday, and no one seemed terribly upset. Dorothy and the two children were staying with Misty, and Musgrave had called Child Protective Services to help get those poor teenagers back on track.

After several rounds of questioning, Musgrave determined Dorothy and Beatrice had no knowledge of Herschel's murderous side. Herschel had secretly made a copy of Misty's salon key, and he'd been telling his stepson of his righteous cleansing mission and trying to get him to join his cause when Jazz walked in on them. Apparently, for years before they visited Lacetown, Herschel had forced Oslo to make braids of his broken bow strings, which unbeknownst to poor Oslo, Herschel had then used to strangle those he considered sinners. Afterward, in true serial-killer fashion, Herschel had kept each souvenir of murder close by braiding the strings into the longer cord which he used as a bookmark. That DNA evidence linked him to six unsolved murders so far. The residue and fibers Trevino discovered on Norbert's wound were rosin and horsehair, and the bleach on the victim's nails was a chemical match to the wipes Herschel apparently made his whole family wash their hands with, like some sort of disturbed ritual.

A sick fuck, as Jazz had aptly labeled him.

The other sicko in their life was supposed to have a televised interview next Sunday, and they'd both decided not to watch. Russell might not have sent someone to kill them, but his heavy presence affected their relationship, and they'd decided to eliminate his influence as much as possible. And that included Michael no longer rereading the books for clues.

Helping the prosecution wasn't as important as their relationship.

Though dreams teased Michael with visions of Jazz being hurt—many including Russell—having Jazz in his home made Michael feel a little better. Hopefully in time, they would be able to move on and stop reliving the nightmare.

"Here you go," Michael announced as he entered the living room, carrying a tray of hot tea, Jazz's prescription, and a pastry from Robichaux Bakery.

"Oh, sweetie, I could have come and got that." Jazz put down the TV remote and looked up at him, those cognac-colored eyes open and earnest. "I really don't like how I keep being hurt and necessitating you take care of me, but... does it make me selfish that I love it when you take care of me?"

When Jazz's voice cracked, Michael murmured, "I love taking care of you."

"Then I shall let you take care of me. After all, I'd do anything to make you happy." Jazz clicked off the TV as Michael set the tray down and sat beside him on the couch.

At once, they wrapped themselves into each other's arms, holding on tight.

"Damn," Michael whispered. He shuddered at what he could have lost that night. "I'm so glad you're okay and that bastard didn't really hurt you."

Jazz's grip on Michael tightened, almost painfully so. "I don't know what I would do without you."

Those words were a balm to Michael's soul, and he drew back to gently brush the long tendrils of hair from Jazz's brow and cheek, tucking the hair behind one ear and then the other. He kissed Jazz on the forehead. "C'mon, time for your antibiotics."

Jazz gave him a quirk of his perfect brows, but allowed Michael to open the bottle and hand him the pill. Jazz might have joked about Michael seeing to his needs, but he seemed to understand how desperately Michael needed to do so.

After Jazz obediently took his pill with the tea, he said, "How is it you get the water the perfect temperature to drink? Not too hot and not too cold?"

"It's a secret."

Jazz set the teacup back on the tray. Michael kissed him on the cheek and brushed another imaginary stray hair off his brow. They exchanged a tender look, then Jazz reached out and placed his hand palm up on Michael's thigh. Michael smiled and clasped it. Jazz used his free hand to pick up the croissant and take a bite. The pills usually upset his stomach, and something starchy helped.

"Any word from Misty today?" Michael asked.

Jazz grinned. "Oh, yes. Apparently everyone's favorite sheriff paid a visit to Misty's house to talk to the kids and Dorothy one more time... and then he invited Ms. Misty out for dinner."

"Oh my," Michael said with a smirk. "The scandal of it all."

Jazz shook his head slightly. "I kind of get the attraction and kind of don't. Mostly don't, because of how much of an ass Musgrave's been to us."

"Maybe Misty can help tame his wild beast."

"Is that a dirty euphemism, Mr. Fleishman?" Jazz asked.

"That's up to you to decide."

"Your turn, any word from Joe or Ally?"

"I did receive a text from Joe last night after you went to bed," Michael replied. "Ally's been helping him with research to try and link up even more cold cases to Herschel's murderous cleansing. They suspect he might possibly have killed Dorothy's husband too."

Jazz gingerly touched the red mark on his throat. "So awful."

Michael leaned down and gently kissed the injury. The doctors had said it would heal but Jazz might have a light scar around his throat, to which Jazz had shrugged and remarked, *"I've always wanted to look like a badass."* But in quiet moments like this, Jazz let his guard down enough for Michael to see the toll the attack had truly taken on him.

Perhaps lured by the smell of food, Mr. Pickles joined them, jumping onto the back of the couch. He blinked impudently, then pawed Jazz's shoulder and made a few curious meows.

Jazz looked up at Mr. Pickles with a genuine smile on his face.

"I've taught you bad habits, haven't I? I don't think Daddy wants you begging."

Michael smiled when Mr. Pickles arched into Jazz's touch, welcoming him as if he were part of their little family.

That's what it felt like to Michael as well. Jazz was his family. He just hoped that damnable kiss from Ezra wouldn't end that feeling.

They'd seemed to have an unspoken agreement not to talk about anything too serious since the attack. Michael hadn't known how to talk about the kiss with Ezra and hadn't wanted to do anything to upset Jazz's recovery. And Jazz hadn't brought up his visit to see Russell, and Michael had decided to leave that slimy rock unturned for now.

But that damnable kiss kept Michael from sleeping soundly. He really didn't want to bring it up now, but the thought of keeping secrets from Jazz made him feel awful. He hadn't told Jazz about rereading Russell's books and that alone had made him feel guilty, especially when he'd seen the disappointment in Jazz's eyes. He had to be honest about this too. If the incident with Herschel taught Michael anything, it was that life was short and nothing was more important to him than Jazz Dilworth.

With a sigh, he sat back heavily on the couch.

Jazz looked up from feeding Mr. Pickles part of his croissant, his soft smile fading into concern. "What's wrong?"

"I could've lost you," Michael said, voice and lips trembling. It was no surprise when warm tears spilled from his eyes, even now.

Jazz was there at once, pulling him in tight. "But you didn't lose me. You saved me just like you saved Mr. Pickles when he was taken." Jazz gazed up at Michael's face, caressing his jawline. "You're our hero."

Michael buried his face in Jazz's neck, inhaling his familiar scent. He'd come so close to losing Jazz, it was too terrible to even think about. Borrowing a page out of Jazz's playbook, Michael forced a chuckle and wiped his face dry. "As much as I like hearing that, I'd really like to lay off the heroics for a while."

Jazz sighed and pulled back. "I know. And I'm sorry about that."

He cocked his head in confusion. "For what?"

"All this drama that we've both been avoiding talking about. And me mooching off your good nature because I can't stand the thought of being alone right now. I don't know how you can put up with me."

"First of all, you aren't mooching. I invited you here to specifically take care of you. And secondly, putting up with you is very easy," Michael said with a smile.

Jazz quirked his brows. "Even though I keep putting us in danger?"

Michael gaped in surprise. "How can you say that? You're not responsible for the unhinged psychopaths who've been coming into our town lately."

"That's perfectly logical to say, and one side of my brain actually believes it. But the other side?" He shook his head, hugging himself tightly.

"You have to admit, I've brought a lot of toxic vibes into your life."

"No, you haven't."

Jazz gave him an intense expression. "Have you forgotten everybody's favorite plagiarizing pervert I'm still legally married to?"

"Married to *for now*," Michael corrected.

"Yeah, for now."

Silence hung between them for a moment, and eventually Michael asked a question that had been plaguing him. "How *did* the visit go?"

Jazz sighed and shifted to face Michael, stroking Mr. Pickles's back. "Jesus, that seems like a lifetime ago. And pretty unimportant in the light of almost dying at the hands of some homophobe fuckstain."

Snark has been initiated. Translation? Jazz is far more upset than he's pretending to be.

Michael placed his hand on the small of Jazz's back and rubbed him in soft circles. "Okay, no playing Mr. Sarcastic and pretending you're not shaken."

Jazz let out a sniff. "You know me far too well, Mr. Fleishman."

"I do."

"Then you know I'm shaken as shit about all this," Jazz admitted, his voice catching. "I could have died. Again."

Michael's heart stopped for a flash and he sucked in a breath. "But you didn't," he insisted quickly, resting his chin on Jazz's shoulder. "You didn't."

Jazz was quick to wrap his arms around Michael's waist. "My visit with Russell, his bullshit amnesia game, none of it's important."

Michael sat up straight, eyes wide. "He is playing that game?"

"Confirmed," Jazz said with a nod. "So you reading through his books again will help. But, you know, I'm done with Russell. Whatever the hell he put in those divorce papers, I'm just gonna sign it and let it be over. I don't even care. I want this finished so I can be with you one hundred percent."

Michael refrained from saying Jazz should have a lawyer make sure that everything was fair. Now was not the time for his usual Debbie Downer remarks.

Instead he hugged Jazz tighter and whispered, "I like the sound of one hundred percent."

"Me too. You deserve that." Jazz rubbed his back as they hugged. "I was so frikking worried about Russell coming after us, letting him fuck with my head, that I almost ruined our honeymoon phase."

"Honeymoon phase?"

"Yeah." Jazz lifted his head to look at Michael. "Our honeymoon phase. Everything's been so great between us. Like scary good, ya know?"

Chewing his lower lip, Michael nodded. "Yeah, I know. But you haven't ruined anything."

"That's a shocker, considering all this toxic bullshit I've brought into your life. Hell, if I hadn't gone off on Norbert, or made you go to Gruff's, then Herschel—"

Michael cut Jazz off by squeezing his lips together. "No, don't even go there. The only thing you've brought to my life is a happiness that I never thought possible. Every day I wake up, and I have to pinch myself that someone like you has decided to notice me. To love me." His voice trembled on those last words, and he swallowed hard, forcing a watery smile. "And I'd like to think of this 'toxic bullshit,' as you call it, as unforeseen adversities. Working through them just makes us stronger."

Jazz gave him a wobbly smile. "How did I get so lucky to find a guy like you?"

"You lost a bet?"

"Ha-ha, hardly." Jazz studied him for a moment.

And then he kissed Michael, soft at first, then more insistent. Hard, demanding. Michael's body responded at once, but before Jazz could take it further, to where they both wanted and needed, Michael pulled back, gasping for air.

Jazz would not be denied, and clutched the back of Michael's neck, tugging. "It's been a long couple of days, sweetie. I need you...."

"Wait," Michael managed.

Jazz scrunched up his face.

Heart aching, Michael pulled out of Jazz's embrace and stood. He needed to tell Jazz about the kiss with Ezra, and at that moment he felt as if he was too tainted and dirty to touch the man he loved. He'd actually avoided initiating anything sexual since the assault, insisting that Jazz follow the doctor's orders and not do anything strenuous that might induce heavy breathing. Jazz had thought it more of a suggestion than an order, but Michael had been firm.

And guilty.

"Sweetie?" Jazz prompted.

"I have to tell you something else that... happened that day."

"You look pale. What's wrong?"

"I was so worried about you wanting to go see Russell on your own that all of my staff noticed something was wrong," Michael began, his stomach in knots. "And Ezra asked me if I was okay, but I wasn't really paying attention to him because I was thinking and worrying about you. You called all those times but didn't leave a message, and I was very concerned." Michael wrung his hands, unable to meet Jazz's eye for long, but a quick glance at Jazz revealed his troubled expression.

"I'm sorry, sweetie. I didn't intend to worry you," Jazz said.

Michael managed a distracted nod. *Just spit it out!*

"A-and then...," Michael managed. "Um, he leaned in. And I didn't realize what he'd intended to do until he... he kissed me."

Jazz's eyes grew so wide the whites all around his cognac irises were visible. "You kissed Ezra?"

"No, no! I didn't kiss *him*. He kissed *me*."

"For how long did he kiss you?" Jazz asked, brows raised and tone firm. "One or two seconds? Or like five to six minutes? And did you get turned-on?"

"No! I was in no way turned-on, not even a little. And it wasn't even a second or two," Michael insisted.

When Jazz's eyes narrowed, Michael could feel everything unraveling. He couldn't stop the shudder that went through his body and the hot wash of shame that followed.

The first time Michael found a *real* boyfriend who he'd fallen madly in love with, and he'd ruined it before it had even really gotten started by not seeing Ezra's attraction sooner and putting a stop to it before things got out of hand.

"How did this come about?" Jazz asked.

"I wasn't paying attention to what he was saying or how he was acting, I swear." Michael took a breath. "He said my name, and I looked at him. Then all of a sudden his mouth was on mine. I guess my lips might have puckered back very briefly, like a reflex action, but I shoved him away really quick. I didn't knock him over or anything, but I pushed him away and said 'Whoa, whoa, whoa! Why did you do that?' I know I hurt his feelings, but I did not want to kiss him. At all. I didn't want that at all!"

Jazz was silent, and Michael could hear his own pulse pounding in his ears.

Finally Jazz said, "One, Mississippi. Two, Mississippi."

When Michael realized what Jazz was doing, he quickly insisted, "No, not even two seconds. It wasn't that long. I swear to you."

Jazz's body seemed to soften before Michael's eyes, and his expression did as well. Standing, he nodded and shrugged at the same time. "All right. I believe you. It's okay."

Michael was a little stunned at Jazz's laissez-faire tone. "What do you mean, it's okay? I cheated on you." As he said the words, his eyes burned with unshed tears, and he blinked rapidly, trying to stop them.

Jazz's chuckle startled him. As did the gentle touch on his arm. "Michael, you didn't *cheat* on me. You were talking to a friend, and your friend took it too far and kissed you. That's not cheating."

"But...," Michael said, fumbling for some way to convince Jazz that what he'd done was horrible. That Jazz needed to be angry at him, like Michael was angry at himself. Though it was completely self-destructive, he couldn't help but say, "If you kissed someone else, I would die a thousand deaths."

Michael couldn't look Jazz in the eye, even when warm hands cupped his face.

"Oh, sweetie," Jazz said in the most conciliatory tone. "That was simultaneously the sweetest and most overdramatic thing anyone has ever said to me. *You* didn't kiss Ezra. *He* kissed you. You said that yourself. And I'm not upset. Really, honestly, I'm not. I might have to give Ezra a 'keep your grubby mitts off my man, you little home-wrecking SOB' talking-to, but I'm not upset with *you*. And for the record, I don't want to kiss anyone else. Just you, Michael. Just you."

"You're really not upset?"

"Have you ever known me to mince words? No, I'm not upset."

Overcome with relief and a desperate need to replace the tarnished feel of that kiss with the only ones he craved, Michael dove toward Jazz and kissed him for everything he was worth.

Jazz made a startled sound, but his arms quickly wrapped around Michael's neck, drawing him in tighter, kissing him deeper.

Desire shot through Michael, his love for the man in his arms overwhelming him. He pulled back and cupped Jazz's cheeks, staring at him. "I love you, Jazz," he said, feeling breathless. "I love you so much."

Jazz kissed him again and smiled as he pulled back. "I love you too."

Michael grinned. "I love hearing that."

Jazz chuckled. "Me too. I've never felt like this about anyone before. Which means, apparently, I've never been in love before."

"Really?" Michael's heart fluttered and he couldn't stop his grin.

"Really and truly," Jazz said. He looked thoughtful, then continued. "We both seem to get distracted and obsess over really small things. I was worried about infecting your life with toxicity and that Russell was lashing out from prison, and you were worrying I'd be mad that Ezra hit on you, just like you convinced yourself that I hadn't enjoyed that hot, rough sex."

Michael's cock took notice of Jazz's deepening tone when he said that last part, but he refrained from taking things any further. Yet. Instead, he said,

"I'm sorry. I overthink things as it is, and this deep of a relationship is all new to me."

"How about we both agree to keeping the internal hamster-wheel thinking to a minimum and talk about whatever we're concerned about, be it puckering creep-terns or psycho ex-husbands. Deal?"

Michael smiled. "Deal." He leaned in for a long, tongue-heavy kiss.

"Mmm," Jazz moaned. He pulled back and rolled his lips together and that flutter changed to a shudder of red hot desire. "I do believe the two days of taking things easy has been satisfied, and regular activities can resume. Any ideas on what some of those activities could be?"

"Oh, I have ideas," Michael assured him.

Jazz ran his hands up Michael's sides, making him tremble with want. "Do those ideas have anything to do with that special drawer in your bathroom?"

Michael's face flushed but not from embarrassment like he'd expected. "Why, Mr. Dilworth. Have you been snooping through my things?"

"Of course I have. I'm a very naughty boy, remember?"

"Yes, I do. And doesn't that make me rather lucky?"

"It does."

Jazz kissed Michael again, cutting off any more witty banter. As with every interaction Michael had with his man, things escalated quickly. Their shared passion was always lurking right below the surface, and the faintest touch ignited it like kindling.

Overcome, Michael devoured Jazz's mouth with desperate, grateful kisses. Jazz's hands found Michael's ass and grabbed tight, pulling him close so they could grind together. Teeth banged, shirts were yanked from pants, and moans and whimpers of ecstasy amplified.

Mr. Pickles released a loud meow of disapproval, and a shuffling sound indicated the cat had leaped from the couch and disappeared.

Their lips broke apart just enough for their eyes to meet. They both started chuckling at the same time.

"Do you know how many times we've probably traumatized poor Mr. Pickles?" Jazz asked.

Michael threw back his head and laughed louder. "Do you know how many times he's traumatized *me* by licking himself where his balls used to be? Turnaround is fair play."

At that, Jazz kissed Michael lightly on the lips, his eyes bright with happiness, and the darkness lingering within him all but gone. Michael imagined Jazz still had a lot to work through, but after their profession of love, it seemed the weight of their own guilt and worry had disappeared, and it was simply the two of them, Michael and Jazz.

Exactly how it was supposed to be.

Jazz took Michael's hand and raised it to his lips to kiss the knuckles. "C'mon, let's go do things in your bedroom that we can't let Mr. Pickles know about."

Struck with inspiration, Michael took Jazz's hand and led him into the kitchen. "I have an idea."

"As much as I love fucking in your kitchen, I think our kitty is already too disgusted with us."

Our kitty... oh, I adore the sound of that.

"No, not that... yet," Michael said as he opened the pantry drawer and grabbed the corkscrew. He handed it to Jazz, who smiled, catching on to Michael's plan.

"I like the way you think."

Michael went for the glasses, and Jazz retrieved the bottle of pinot grigio in the refrigerator and grabbed the bottle of sauvignon beside it.

Michael raised his brows when he saw the second bottle.

"What?" Jazz said. "We're going to get thirsty."

Laughing, Michael gestured for Jazz to lead the way up to the bedroom. They remained PG as they went upstairs. The Fourth of July weather turned out to be as tempestuous and unpredictable as Lake Michigan herself, and it had been a surprisingly cool evening, so Michael didn't have on the AC and the french doors were open, the screen in place, letting in the night air. They'd had coffee on Michael's second-story deck more than once, but there was one thing they had never done out there.

Make love under the stars.

Hopefully Jazz would be up for the idea.

Michael followed Jazz out onto the deck, closing the screen behind him. The flowers and vines blooming on the trellis ensured privacy, as did the large oak to the right. If Rob Wilkerson across the alley behind Michael's house went into his garage's attic, he'd be able to see them, but the risk of getting caught just added to the excitement. Jazz set the sauvignon on the table beside the lounger and then popped the cork on the pinot grigio. He filled the glasses in Michael's hands.

The Cheshire Cat Moon—as Grandpa always called it—provided plenty of light. When Jazz reached for the timer to turn on the twinkling lights, Michael said, "No, let it stay dark. I plan on making love to you under the stars."

Even in the soft glow of moonlight, Michael saw Jazz tremble with desire.

Jazz stepped closer and slipped an arm around Michael's waist. He held up his glass. "To new love and us."

The toast was so succinct, yet so utterly perfect, another tear—but this one of joy and wonder—trickled down Michael's cheek. It must have caught the light, because Jazz reached up with his hand holding his wineglass and brushed it away with the back of his fingers. "No crying. We're celebrating."

"We are?"

"Yes. It's America's birthday. We're alive. We solved another mystery with true Brock Hammer panache. We're in love." Jazz startled Michael a bit with his casual reference to Russell's books. "We also have wine, and neither of us need Viagra yet. I'd say that's plenty of reasons to celebrate, don't you?"

"Yes, I suppose when you put it like that, it is a celebration." Then Michael repeated the toast, and they clinked glasses and shared a sweet kiss before they sipped the wine.

Arm in arm, they walked over to the railing and took in the view. The sky was dark, save for the moon and stars, the occasional hiss and pop of a private firework going off to the south, and the Lacetown Light shining its beacon to their right. A blanket of rich navy velvet with diamond stars and a crescent moon hung above them while cicadas sang and the oak tree's leaves rustled. It truly was a magical moment.

They didn't talk, just sipped their wine and enjoyed the view. When they both drained their glasses, Michael turned to Jazz and said, "You get us refills, and I'll be right back."

He opened the screen and crossed his bedroom. In the hallway, he retrieved the puffy old comforter from his childhood bed from the linen closet. Then he flipped off the light. Now the only light came from nature and the soft night-light in the hallway. Their eyes would adjust to the darkness so they could see each other as they made love. Grabbing a pillow from his bed, he rejoined Jazz on the patio and shut the screen door behind him.

"What do you have there?" Jazz was pouring wine into their glasses.

"So we can be comfy," he explained.

"While we make love under the stars?"

"Exactly."

Michael folded the comforter to fit the length of the cedar lounger.

He hoped it would be comfortable enough on Jazz's knees—depending on which of them ended up on top, that is.

Grinning, Michael made a mental note to go online and order a dense cushion for the lounger so they could do this again. At least he'd bought the streamlined lounger without armrests so they would have plenty of mobility. He lowered the top half of the chair so it was flat, and put the pillow in place. His groin stirred and his dick inched down his leg at the prospect of having Jazz all to himself outside.

After he made their cozy bed, he turned to look at Jazz. The mark on his neck made Michael's heart ache.

Thank God he hadn't lost him. It had been close, too close. But Herschel would go to prison and never hurt anyone again.

How many people has he murdered?

No, Michael wouldn't let himself get distracted with such dark thoughts. He'd leave the mystery solving to the police and Joe this time. There were more important things for Michael to take care of right now. Like making love to the man who'd made his every wish come true.

Michael had gained even more than he ever dreamed possible.

Jazz loved him.

"Jazz?"

"Yes?"

"No one's ever told me they loved me before," Michael whispered. "I just thought you should know that."

"Oh, sweetie," Jazz said in the gentlest tone. "I hope you like hearing it, because I plan on telling you all the time."

Arms as wide as the grin on his face, Michael gestured to the lounger.

Jazz placed both of their glasses on the table next to it, then sat down, opening his legs. Michael quickly sat in the space he created. But as soon as their bodies were in close proximity, their wine refills were forgotten as hands and lips explored.

Michael gently pressed Jazz onto his back, then took his time kissing every inch of Jazz's exposed neck and then up along his jaw. Jazz explored each contour of Michael's back and arms with his fingertips. When Michael pushed Jazz's T-shirt up his torso to tongue-bathe first one nipple and then the other, Jazz trembled beneath him.

"How naked do you wanna get out here?" Jazz whispered. "You have neighbors."

"I don't care," he all but growled as he worked his tongue and kisses downward to his navel. "You're not getting off this lounger until I've kissed every inch of your beautiful body and we're both covered in cum."

Jazz laughed, his stomach fluttering against Michael's chest from the action. "Well, if you don't care about giving the neighbors a show, neither do I. Especially when you make declarations like that."

"Not a declaration," Michael assured him. Resting his chin on Jazz's rounded stomach, Michael gazed up at him. "It's a promise."

Jazz smiled and cupped the back of his head. He traced the fingertips of his other hand along Michael's jaw. His eyes were wide and glistening in the moonlight. Michael locked gazes with Jazz, and his lip quivered a little because he still had trouble believing this was all really happening.

"I love you so much, Jazz, that it... it scares me."

"You don't ever have to be afraid with me," Jazz promised.

Those whispers of doubts faded away, and Michael threw himself into the moment. He devoted himself to kissing and exploring Jazz's naked torso, nibbling and teasing his nipples. Then he drove his tongue into Jazz's belly button until Jazz panted and writhed beneath him. Michael was still fully dressed, Jazz only in jeans, but their cocks both strained for freedom.

"Fuck, I need you naked, baby," Jazz whispered, both hands rubbing Michael's shoulders. "Please...."

That helpless begging was like a jolt of blood and steel through Michael's already hard cock. He sat back, but didn't go far while they quickly shed their clothing and Michael set his glasses aside near the wine. Once fully exposed, Michael straddled Jazz's lap, his sudden need to be filled with his lover's cock overwhelming him. Jazz sat up and they met in a tender kiss. With their height difference, Michael's chin could all but rest on top of Jazz's head, so he had to dip down to kiss that decadent mouth. They kissed for a long time, hands exploring torsos, hard cocks gently rubbing. Jazz reached down and took hold of their cocks as they kept kissing. They were both seeping enough precum that the glide of his hand was absolutely wonderful.

"I need you in me," Michael leaned down and whispered in Jazz's ear, nibbling on the lobe and licking the shell.

"You need to get the lube," Jazz panted in reply.

Michael had both feet on the patio, straddling the chair and Jazz.

He cupped Jazz's face with a smile. "What did I tell you? We're not getting out of this lounger until there's cum everywhere."

Jazz chuckled and lay back on the pillow and comforter Michael had spread out for them. "I don't wanna hurt you."

"Then never leave me." He couldn't believe he said that, or how desperately he meant it.

"Deal."

Grinning, Michael inched away and knelt between Jazz's thighs. He took hold of Jazz's cock and let a runner of spit pool down first one side and then the other. He did that several times before looking up at Jazz. "Let's go old-school."

Michael was quick to straddle Jazz once more, standing over him this time. Jazz put a hand on either thigh and gazed up at Michael with so much love and desire it stole Michael's breath. When he started to squat down, he reached behind him to take hold of Jazz's spit-coated cock and aim it at his asshole.

It hurt at first and the skin pulled, but Michael didn't care. The pain felt good because it meant Jazz was still here with him. That he was inching inside of him.

Their gazes never broke as Michael slowly worked Jazz's dick into his ass until he was lowered all the way. When they were fully united, Jazz ran his hands up Michael's thighs, then sat up to pull him into a gentle embrace. Panting, Michael put his chin on top of Jazz's head and they held each other. Michael stroked Jazz's back gently, then reached up to release his hair.

Jazz let out a soft chuckle at their personal joke of Michael's obsession with his hair. Michael's cock was pressed tight between their bodies, and the rumble of Jazz's chuckle teased the skin.

When his hair was freed, Michael took a deep inhale of the intoxicating scent of his hair products, mingled with the scent of their arousal and everything else that was uniquely Jazz. Michael kissed his forehead, then drew back so he could look into Jazz's eyes. "You feel amazing inside me."

"I agree." Jazz wore a lopsided grin. "But you're kind of driving me crazy by not moving."

Michael let out a breathless chuckle and gazed down at Jazz's wanton expression. "Like this?"

Using his feet firmly planted on the deck to his advantage, Michael lifted his torso a few inches, gliding up Jazz's cock. He'd intended it to be a slow seductive stroke, but when both of them released hungry whimpers for more, Michael sank back down and Jazz fumbled between their bodies to grip Michael's aching prick. He gave it a firm stroke, his mouth agape and eyes wide, as if stunned by the intensity of their connection. They stared into each other's eyes, and Michael clung to Jazz and trembled as he moved up and down with more momentum. Jazz matched his speed with strokes on Michael's cock, and they did not look away from each other.

Michael gripped Jazz's shoulders and fucked himself harder. Jazz jerked him with a matched passion, his other hand pressed firmly to the small of Michael's back. Then his fingers slipped lower to where Michael was impaled on his cock. He put his thumb and forefinger on either side of Michael's hole and held them snug, increasing the pressure on his own cock while heightening Michael's pleasure by rubbing him there. Every part of Michael's body came alive with ecstasy, from the fire of Jazz's naked cock deep inside him, to the insistent pressure of those fingers on his ring, and the rough glide of Jazz's other hand on his dick.

"Oh, Jazz," Michael groaned. "So *gooooood*."

"Ride it, baby. Take what you need." They went like that for a few moments, slow, deep, and intense. Eventually Jazz raised his knees and put both hands on Michael's hips and began thrusting up, meeting Michael's need with wonderful hard jabs.

"Oh!" Michael cried when Jazz nailed his prostate harder. His balls pulled up snug against his body and his insides churned for release as he fucked himself on Jazz's dick and Jazz fucked him deep in return.

Though he was so close, he didn't want it to end yet.

Tonight was a milestone for them and Michael needed this moment to last as long as possible, but when Jazz gripped his cock again, one hand all but bruising his hip and his thighs pushing on Michael's ass, he didn't know if he would be able to hold back. Every torturous stroke Jazz delivered on his cock made him gasp and tremble. He clung to Jazz's shoulders, riding out the pleasure.

When Michael dropped back down and Jazz slammed up, Michael suppressed a cry, still vaguely aware that they were outside and a random passerby could hear them if they got too rowdy—as they usually did.

Hips rocking now, Michael dipped his head and kissed Jazz passionately, swallowing his gasps as they both moved faster, finding that perfect rhythm. Groaning into the kiss, Jazz grabbed both Michael's hips again and dug in, his body jerking up to meet Michael in that place of passion they both needed to reach.

Any intention of dragging it out was abandoned as their bodies took over. Struggling, thrusting, grasping, and kissing, all of their limbs moving furiously toward completion.

Jazz buried his face against Michael's chest, his head tucked under his chin. Michael gripped him tight around the shoulders, and they bounced and fucked, Michael riding Jazz's cock with a renewed fury. The wooden lounger creaked beneath them and the breeze rustled in the trees. There was another crackling pop sound as a random firework ignited.

But the fireworks between Michael and Jazz were more immediate, intense and electric. Michael couldn't hold back any longer. The friction of their writhing bodies with his dick pinned between them sent him over the edge. With a strangled cry, he burst between them, gasping as a million tiny lights exploded within. He felt it when Jazz's momentum sped up, shifting rhythm too as he found his need and emptied his hot load deep inside Michael's ass.

Sweat slicked their bodies as Michael thrust through his orgasm, slowing down as it faded, but relishing the way his cum-covered cock mashed between their torsos. Gasping for breath, they clung to each other. Michael wasn't sure which one of them trembled the most.

Michael shifted to cup the back of Jazz's head, fingers coiling in his hair. He held on tightly, dipping his head so he could gently kiss Jazz on the forehead.

Jazz's hot breaths huffed against Michael's sweaty chest. They held still, reveling in bliss.

"I love you, Michael. I really, really do," Jazz whispered in a voice so tiny Michael let out a faint strangled sound he was sure he'd never made before.

He drew back slightly and his hand shifted to cup Jazz's cheek. Their eyes met and Michael kissed him, soul-deep and for everything he was worth. Only when his body was starved for oxygen did Michael withdraw from that kiss to gaze at his whole world, his heart. His everything.

"I love you too, Jazz."

STAY TUNED FOR MORE adventures with Michael and Jazz... and of course Mr. Pickles!

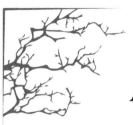

Acknowledgments

C over art concept by Bree Archer ~ breearcher.com
Updated cover art by Ron Perry Graphic Design ~ rperrydesign.com

Hank Edwards

Hank Edwards (he/him) has been writing gay fiction for more than twenty years. He has published over forty novels and novellas and dozens of short stories. His writing crosses many sub-genres, including contemporary romance, rom-com, paranormal, suspense, mystery, wacky comedy, and erotica. He has written a number of series such as the funny and spooky Critter Catchers, Old West historical horror of Venom Valley, suspenseful FBI and civilian Up to Trouble, and the erotic and funny Fluffers, Inc. Under the pen name R. G. Thomas, he has written a young adult urban fantasy gay romance series called The Town of Superstition. He was born and still lives in a northwest suburb of the Motor City, Detroit, Michigan.

For more information:
Website: hankedwardsbooks dot com
Email: hankedwardsbooks at gmail
Facebook Group: Hank's Hangout

HANK'S ALSO WRITTEN the following books, available at your favorite online book seller:

Critter Catchers Series:
Terror by Moonlight
Chasing the Chupacabra
Swamped by Fear
The Devil of Pinesville
Screams of the Season
Horror at Hideaway Cove

Dread of Night
Critter Catchers: Level Up Series:
Grave Danger
Williamsville Inn Gay Romance:
Snowflakes and Song Lyrics
The Cupid Crawl
Fake Date Flip-Flop
Star-Spangled Showdown
Lacetown Murder Mysteries:
(co-written with Deanna Wadsworth)
Murder Most Lovely
Murder Most Deserving
Venom Valley Series:
Cowboys & Vampires
Stakes & Spurs
Blood & Stone
Up to Trouble Series:
Holed Up
Shacked Up
Roughed Up
Choked Up
Fluffers, Inc. Series:
Fluffers, Inc.
A Carnal Cruise
Vancouver Nights
Standalone Gay Romance:
Buried Secrets
Destiny's Bastard
Hired Muscle
Plus Ones
Repossession is 9/10ths of the Law
Holiday Gay Romance:
A Gift for Greg (A Story Orgy Single)
Mistletoe at Midnight (A Story Orgy Single)
The Christmas Accomplice

<u>Story Orgy Singles Gay Romance:</u>
A Gift for Greg
By the Book
Cross Country Foreplay
Mistletoe at Midnight
The Cheapskate: Bad Boyfriends
With This Ring
<u>Gay Erotic Short Story Collections:</u>
A Very Dirty Dozen
Another Very Dirty Dozen
<u>Salacious Singles Gay Erotic Short Stories:</u>
Bear Market
Convoy
Double Down
Exchange Rate
Finding North
Hotel Dick
Kindred Spirits
Sacked
Stroking Midnight
Vanity Loves Company
Wet Lands

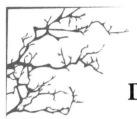

Deanna Wadsworth

D eanna Wadsworth might be a bestselling erotica author, but she leads a pretty vanilla life in Ohio with her wonderful husband and a couple adorable cocker spaniels. She has been spinning tales and penning stories since childhood, and her first erotic novella was published in 2010. When she isn't writing books or brainstorming with friends, you can find her making people gorgeous in a beauty salon. She loves music and dancing, and can often be seen hanging out on the sandbar in the muddy Maumee River or chilling with her hubby and a cocktail in their basement bar. In between all that fun, Deanna cherishes the quiet times when she can let her wildly active imagination have the full run of her mind. Her fascination with people and the innerworkings of their relationships have always inspired her to write romance with spice and love without boundaries.

For more information about Deanna
Facebook Group: Dishing with Deanna
Website: DeannaWadsworth dot com
Email: deanna at deannawadsworth dot com
You can also read her young adult alter ego: K.D. Worth

DEANNA'S CURRENT TITLES available
Stand-alone gay romances
Naughty Cupid
Wrecked
Easy Ryder
Pride of the Caribbean getaways
The Boyfriend Cruise ~ getaway one

Vacation Tails ~ getaway two
Dream Vacation ~ getaway three
Coming summer 2022
Paradise Bound ~ getaway four
Western Passions
His Ranch Hand
Lacetown Murder Mysteries
(co-written with Hank Edwards)
Murder Most Lovely
Murder Most Deserving
Men of Gilead
The Rhubarb Patch
La Famiglia
Welcome Home, Soldier
MM Sci-Fi Romance Series
Rookie
Patriot
Comrade

DEANNA'S BACKLIST TITLES currently unavailable are being revamped with brand new scenes, while others will be published in their original forms.

Stay tuned for the return of the following titles in 2022:

Destiny Ink Series

Welcome to Destiny Ink, where a swipe of a pen changes the lives of mortals forever. The proprietors of this organization, a trio of sister Fates. These agents behind the scenes have been manipulating outcomes, dampening fallout and repairing broken hearts since living, breathing, emoting beings first began wandering the earth thinking on their own. So, the next time something good, bad, insightful or banal happens in your life, remember it's not 'how life is,' it's *Destiny*.

Bear It All

Lightning Source UK Ltd.
Milton Keynes UK
UKHW010755130622
404345UK00001B/33